The Vagabonds of Dublin

The Vagabonds of Dublin

Patrick Martens

Praise for *The Vagabonds of Dublin*

Paperback ISBN: 978-0-578-67892-4

It is commonplace to dedicate books and songs and things
to the living,
however
this ol' song goes out to my best friend,
my J.,
my sister,
who never let me down,
never gave up on me,
and always insisted we have a good time.

CHAPTER ONE
The Burden of Choice

Tucked within the clefts and folds of Dublin's shopping district, in a dark and narrow lane commonly forgotten somewhere between Grafton and Dawson streets, stood an old, arthritic building. The Chivalric Nobleman de La Mancha Bookshop populated the ground floor and one above while the top two stories remained empty, due possibly to the building's immediate vicinity to nothing. The bookshop had been bequeathed to John Doyle fourteen years prior by his beloved Grandad, the shop's founder, who'd spent sixty years buying and selling and caring for second-hand books as though they were orphaned children placed in his care. John's life had found meaning when he inherited the shop, for he'd matured within its walls and felt very much at home amid the paper and must and dust. Like Grampy Doyle, John's least favorite aspect of bookselling was selling the books; he would much rather have kept every one.

To John, the shop was home. A small room behind the shelves on the ground floor was where he slept, while most of his waking hours were spent among the books. He adored the shop's underlying mood of serenity and nature; the colors of the books, the maple finish in the furniture, the rustic scent of parchment, like leaves in rain, all combined to give everyone who entered a sense of homecoming.

Every morning at nine o'clock John opened his doors to business and traditionally spent his first hours cataloguing recent acquisitions. Each new book would be wiped clean, tears in the jackets carefully repaired, dogeared pages mended and pressed. With these chores complete, John would wait for a break between customers and wander the aisles to admire his stock, stopping randomly to pull a book from its habitation and inspect the jacket and boards, the condition of its binding, the color of its pages. He would open a novel to any random page, carefully minding not to overexert the spine, and allow himself to be warmed by words until the bell over the front door announced company and summoned him from his love.

On this cool morning in April, before the sun had penetrated the veil of shadow shrouding the street, the bell announced Mr. Tinky O'Shea vigorously. At least once each week, John's oldest friend diverted his walk to work with a visit to the Chivalric Nobleman. Tinky found great amusement in making his entrance known, so relishing the sound of loose panes rattling in the door coupled with the coloratura soprano of the overhead bell that he would open and close the door repeatedly, noisily fanning it to and fro as though dispelling a foul odor. Tinky and John had known each other since childhood, had grown up together in the same schools, had experienced the joys of childhood and the horrors of puberty together while living in neighboring flats. Tinky shared John's adoration of books and was by far his best customer.

After the fourth rattle and jangle, John returned Proust to the shelf and went to greet his friend. Tinky was remarkably slight and when they grinned and hugged and slapped masculinity into each other's arms, John was careful not to slap too hard for fear of knocking the man over. "I've breads an' jam fer yer mornin' tae, Johnny boy," Tinky announced in his unusually high pitch, "given me by the lovely Widow Mullan at Bewley's. Forced 'em into me hand, she did, with a spark in her eye an' a swell in her magnificent bosom!"

"Bless yer soul, man!" John's gentle features softened further from his smile. "An' bless yer allergy to wheat. Tell Rosie not a crumb was wasted." He accepted the wrapped pastries and said with a wink, "I'll keep me eyes out fer any love notes baked inside."

Tinky thrust his narrow chest out proudly. "To be tirty-five an' still enjoyin' the freedoms o' bachelorhood as we do, 'tis like an open invitation to every maid in town!"

John rolled his eyes. "Cool yer trousers, loverboy." He reached for a load of new acquisitions he'd set aside for his friend. John knew Tinky's taste in fiction well and always kept an eye out for titles that might sate his curiosity.

"Have ye seen him this week?" Tinky inquired, thumbing through the new stock.

The question followed in Tinky's wake with each visit. "None yet this week," John said. "Ye'll be the first to know, as always, if Herman finds his way to La Mancha."

Tinky inspected the gilded edge on a leather-bound collection by Poe. "Melville's not passed through in some time. I wonder if public interest is wanin'." He placed Poe back on the pile. "Some rich ol' codger must have a *Billy Budd* or a *Piazza Tales* fer me. A fine first edition just lyin' about while her owner dies peacefully o' women an' drink." His eyes swelled with imagination. "Wouldn't that be somethin', a first edition o' Melville! Why, I'd cherish it as though it were me own beat an' breath."

John took Tinky's arm in his. "We'll find it, you an' I. An' never fear a decline in his popularity, I can barely keep Herman on me shelf fer more than a few days' time. The students eat him up, second only to Dylan Thomas."

Tinky retained one book from the pile and returned the rest to John's desk. "Edgar Allen, I've got. However, I'll tank ye to put Mister Yeats here on me account. I trust 'tis all in good order?"

John hesitated only briefly. "Sure, sure, boy-o! I'll put 'er on the bill."

"Fine, then. I'll ask ye now to wish me a good day. I'm late fer work, an' this after receivin' blustery words from Jacko just last week 'bout the hours I keep." He took John's elbow in hand and squeezed it intimately, drawing confidentially closer. "Although the ol' rot can't get *too* blustery. I have in me cap certain information regarding him and a certain politician's daughter which certainly could be embarrassin' if it found its way to a certain *public's knowledge*." He smiled conspiratorially and kissed John's hand. "Until week's end, Master Doyle!"

John waved him out. "Farewell, Master O'Shea!" The door rattled, the bell jangled, and the shop was quiet once more.

John crossed to the till and opened his ledger, taking pencil in hand to add Yeats to the swelling list of Tinky's debt. He looked over the dates and titles and numbers and was reminded that he'd memorized them long ago.

He warmed his tea on the hot plate in back — attentively remembering to unplug the cord afterward, lest his loves be incinerated by careless accident — and focused his attention on the Widow Mullan's breads and jam. Before the bells of St. Bartholomew's announced half nine with their robust chimes, his belly was full. The rest of the day was spent in the company of Alighieri and Dumas as John Doyle read and patiently waited for calling patrons to summon his eyes from their pleasure.

*   *   *   *

Clouds sailed in from the western seaboard during the night, blanketing the city by daybreak. Farm cocks sensed the impending downpour and muted their morning calls. Stables housing carriage horses showed little movement as their tenants remained sheltered. Their masters gladly returned to the bosom of bed, knowing that no tourist would be willing to brave the rain for a ride through Phoenix Park. All was quiet throughout the city, as though the clouds had drawn the comforter up under each chilled nose and granted Dublin the gift of an extra hour's rest.

John's diary listed only one item for the day, an appointment to visit an estate sale being held several miles away in Dun Laoghaire. It was John's duty to make sure the car was well-fueled and oiled, for the aged and battered coach demanded constant care and a simple six-mile trip was enough to ruin her. He had no intention of finding himself stranded with crippled transportation in foreign territory while the heavens flushed, so he planned an additional thirty minutes to warm the engine and make sure it was operating tolerably.

Streams of water had been gushing over the sewer grates for almost an hour by the time John gathered the courage to run out to where the car lay parked on Molesworth Street. It was another three-quarters of an hour before he started the ignition and headed south, for he'd stepped from the shop directly into the rushing rapids and found himself wearing a pair of sopping, sodden socks and none to replace them with, as they were all off at the launderers. He retreated inside to hang his dripping stockings over the hot plate (*"unplug unplug unplug!"* he thought) until they'd achieved a slightly tolerable dampness, then grabbed his coat and squished out. By a quarter after eight, he was merging onto the motorway and arrived on the estate grounds slightly before his scheduled nine o'clock meeting.

The sale had come about after months of debate within the Hogan clan, whose matriarch had passed on during the bitter winter and, in doing so, ignited an equally bitter battle amongst her five children and one gardener. With help from a fleet of attorneys, they'd finally sorted out their respective inheritances — but not their respective differences — and announced that an assortment of furniture, lighting, art, books, and home decorations would be sold via silent auction, by appointment only. As a large portion of John Doyle's stock was acquired at estate auctions, he was diligent in being the first to inspect the goods.

He was met at the mansion's door by Charles Exter-Jones, auction broker for Tisdale's of England. Exter-Jones was dressed handsomely in an immaculately-pressed Saville Row worsted wool suit that smelled of crisp pound notes. He ushered John into the hall.

"Please, come in out of that weather!" Exter-Jones invited. He gathered John's coat and cap and hung them on a rack to dry, then gave a surreptitious glance to a notecard cupped in his hand. "Mister Doyle, I presume?" he asked in his posh London accent through expensive yet flawed teeth. "I do hope you haven't been inconvenienced much by the rain." He gestured to the sky. "This murkiness may be my own fault. It seems to have followed me over from London!" Exter-Jones laughed nervously at his own humor, then added solemnly, "That's a joke. I'm just kidding." John grinned and accepted a fresh hand towel, which he used to dry his face and hands. Exter-Jones continued, "I certainly hope this doesn't lead to some sort of reputation as a conjurer of weather. I can't say my career would advance very far if I earned the title of Rain King!" He again laughed awkwardly before his smile vanished and the fear returned. "That's a joke as well. I was just kidding. Please, follow me."

Informal chat led them down a hall to a spacious library, a room lined with empty shelves over a sprawling floor of green Connemara marble. Eight impeccable rows of storage boxes lay, ten to a row, each box arranged in sharp symmetry to those around it, as though the distance separating them had been measured to the millimeter. The sheer perfection of the sight caused John to better understand Charles Exter-Jones.

His host adopted an earnest tone, stepping in from the doorway yet intentionally keeping his distance from the boxes. "There are two thousand and fourteen books in the Hogan collection. I took the liberty of placing the more accessible titles in the front row, as well as any I felt might rouse a collector's attention. All the best is up front, though the entire collection is quite stunning, take my word." A wry smile cocked his lips and he said proudly, "My occupation has provided an informal education regarding valuable books and I can honestly say this is one of the most stunning collections I've seen. Simply stunning! If you're not careful, I'll bid it out from under you!" He looked at John intensely, searching for a reaction, before clarifying, "That was a joke. I was just kidding."

John stepped forward and peered inside a box in the second row. "Ye shan't mind if I take time to look 'em over?" he asked.

"All of them?" Exter-Jones seemed to be caught off-guard. "Well, yes, if you must. Just make certain to, umm...." He looked over the sterling display of his arrangement sadly, as if to bid it farewell. "Right," he said, conceding. "Have at them! I'll leave you in peace to do so. Give a shout when satisfied." At the door, he turned and feigned a smile. "As is common in sales of this nature, the collection is auctioned as a whole and not in part. All or nothing!" With a final glare back to the boxes, he turned and left, slamming the door behind him.

"*Sorry!*"

John focused his attention on the books and his expertise allowed him to work quickly. He scanned the topmost contents of each box with a judicious eye, pausing intermittently to examine any book that piqued his interest. The collection was standard upper class fare, expensive art and architecture compilations as well as first printings of popular novels, mostly unread, some inscribed by their authors. A number of leather-bound volumes filled the lot, too, anthologies published by insignificant clubs that were advertised as investments yet rarely returned more than a refund. John paid them little mind.

His once-over was soon complete and he began the more significant work. Returning to the first box in the first row, he sat on the floor and proceeded to dig. When presented with a potential trove like this, John fancied himself a prospector, for in order to find diamonds one must burrow deep into the mountain. Besides, he'd met Charles Exter-Joneses many times under varying guises and they always laid claim to expertise in matters they barely understood.

An hour later, having caught Charles Exter-Jones glowering at him through the garden window twice and with only three boxes of the collection left to probe, John found his peace interrupted when Exter-Jones ushered another gentleman in. The man was tall and burly, baby-faced yet likely in his late-thirties, with softly-cut features and hair curled and darkened by rain.

Exter-Jones let loose a stifled whine and scowled disapprovingly at the sight of his fractured masterpiece, box lids askew, his symmetry destroyed. "Ah, Mr. Doyle, still working diligently, I see. May I present Mr. Corrigan from Enniskerry."

John laboriously rose to his feet and accepted Corrigan's handshake. "How d'do?" John offered. "Come to see the books, have ye?"

Corrigan nodded. "Although I'm not a merchant like yerself. Personal collector, I am."

John disguised his confusion with a nod while Exter-Jones fidgeted with the door handle. He, too, was wondering what interest someone not in the business of books had in an auction of this size. He smiled curtly and said, "I'll leave you both to examine at your will." Before exiting, he added, "Mr. Corrigan. Ah. You do understand the library is being auctioned as one complete lot rather than ... *fragmentally*?" He finished the question with a well-practiced cock of the brow.

"Aye, that I do," Corrigan assured.

"Fine, then," Exter-Jones said, adding, "and please pardon the disarray of the display. Normally it would appear much more organized." He looked to John and, hearing no laugh and seeing no smile, exclaimed, "That's a joke! I was just kidding." With that, he slammed the door behind him.

"*Sorry!*"

John returned to the final three boxes and continued scouring through. Corrigan remained on his feet, leisurely peering into each box, hands nestled in pockets. He periodically stopped to flip through a trade edition. When John moved on to the next box, Corrigan broke the silence by saying, "Found anythin' o' worth?"

John was startled by the brazen question and concealed his incredulity with a smile. "Not much," he replied honestly.

Corrigan strolled past the boxes, casually scanning the titles. "I hope ye'll pay me no mind. I shan't consider meself competition. I'm only searchin' fer a handful o' titles, an' those so rare 'tis doubtful I'll find 'em here." He resumed his walk down the second row.

"Do this often?" John asked.

"Whenever I spy an advert," said Corrigan.

John paused his dig. "Pardon me askin', Mr. Corrigan," he said genuinely, "but doesn't this method o' shoppin' tend to be a bit costly? I mean, if it's only a few particulars ye're lookin' fer, why browse such a vast lot?"

Corrigan chuckled. "I get yer point. But ye see, Mr. Doyle, I've been cursed with *inheritance*. Do ye know what it is to have inheritance?" John shook his head. "'Tis *awful*," Corrigan continued, "just *teddible*! To make it worse, I have a very poor work ethic. I've developed a great passion fer lethargy an' vice." He laughed softly to himself at his own candor. "I am, however, a terrific reader. 'Tis how I pass the time. An' I find that when I'm not settled down with a novel, I'm in pursuit o' what I call *The Divine*. Classics. First editions. All the books I adore. Pristine copies, first printings, endorsed by the pen o' their authors when attainable. Call it me pursuit of excellence."

John nodded his understanding. "No need to explain further, Mr. Corrigan. I share yer lust fer the things. Can't explain *why* I get goosepimply when I'm around first editions, I just do. An' I would absolutely do the same thing had I the money." He picked himself up from the floor, his study complete. "But tell me, now. Which novels are ye after? Perhaps I can help."

Corrigan scoffed. "Saints alive, man, I would bore ye with a list o' titles. I will say 'tis the classics that hold me interest, mostly literature from the nineteenth-century. Tolstoy, Dickens. Melville. Oscar Wilde an' Poe have a particular way o' chillin' me spine. Joyce, too." Here he rolled his eyes at his own perceived self-adulation. "Ah, enough o' me ramblin'. Ye follow."

"I do indeed," John said approvingly. "More than most." He approached Corrigan, limping slightly from the numbness in his legs, and drew conversationally near. "Truth be told, I've always held in high regard anyone who shares me affection fer the printed page, so allow me to say how grand it is to meet ye."

Corrigan accepted his hand warmly. "Mr. Doyle—"

"John."

"John," he said, "I've had many conversations with men who share yer occupation an' I'll admit ye're the first to not turn me sour. So many o' the upscale booksellers, I tell ye, 'tis all gluttony o' profit an' a bit o' lechery, yet it seems ye've none o' that. So 'tis a true pleasure to meet ye." He again pumped the hand of his newfound friend. "And do call me Brian."

"Tanks, Brian. Although I'm leagues from bein' an *upscale* bookseller, I'll accept the compliment."

Brian and John spoke a good deal longer until Charles Exter-Jones returned to introduce another potential bidder into the fray. The downpour outside had settled to a mild patter and John excused himself with a promise to meet Brian again and an insignificant bid to Exter-Jones on the library. The sun appeared as he exited the estate but again withdrew behind a dark curtain of ominous treachery by the time his lumbering four-cylinder made it back to the motorway. It was on the return trip to Dublin, not a full mile from the estate at Dun Laoghaire and with the rain pelting the roof with greater force than before, that a broken fan belt caused the engine to overheat and abruptly abandon its mission.

*   *   *   *

By the time John walked to the nearest town and found shelter in a small café, he was as wet as the day of his birth. The young lass behind the counter followed his every step with her reproachful gaze until her eyes sat with him at a corner table. John twisted and tugged free from his coat and looked down to see a shallow river following him to his seat. The girl brought a cup of tea and a dry dishtowel. "Rag's on the house," she said, her tone as lathered in sarcasm as John was in water. John failed to conceal his embarrassment and blushed wetly. He then noticed he was the sole patron in the room.

The café was comfortable and homey, cottage-style with a surging fire in the stone fireplace and handmade crafts offered for sale around its hearth. The owner, a middle-aged man made round by day-old pastries and bald by the stress of three matrimonial disasters, heaved and hoed as he carried a burdensome cardboard box up from the cellar and dropped it heavily among four matching cartons. The girl working the counter turned her tired face in his direction.

"D'ye have to make such fuss in yer breathin' an' groanin'?" she complained.

He braced his back and bent rearward to stretch out the pain. "Girlie, have ye not counters to clean or some other business to distract ye from yer *wicked tongue*?" This last part was shouted in exasperation, as though he'd received her criticism far too many times for far too many years.

He noticed John in the corner and stiffened. "Oh, pardon me, sir." He jerked his thumb toward the girl. "This daughter o' mine loves to provide commentary. Never mind her disrespect." He turned to her and gave a disapproving look which only made her giggle, causing his anger to swell. Grabbing a mop from behind a closet door, he thrust it in her hands. "Sop up that mess!" he demanded, motioning to the rivulet along the floor.

When he saw where the water led, the man was again embarrassed. Turning his crimson face to John, he said, "Pardon me again, I didn't mean to imply 'twas you made the mess...." He bit his tongue and made a motion as though swatting flies around his head, then retreated into the kitchen, returning a moment later with a brimming shot glass in hand. He delivered it to John, explaining, "Take this to warm yerself. If the county knew I was serving whiskey to customers, they'd have me license faster than I can spit." Here he shut one eye in a prolonged, conspiratorial wink. "But I happen to know the county inspector was draggin' his boots through every pub in Arklow with his old brigade last night, so, as 'tis early yet, enjoy this medicine with me compliments."

John welcomed the drink and gulped it down. "Many tanks," he said, then glanced at the boxes. "Rearrangin', are ye?"

"Oh, just makin' the most of a dreary day by cleanin' out the cellar. This rot's been takin' up space an' puttin' an odor in the air fer years." He walked back to the steps. "Only two more cartons!" he called as he disappeared down the stairwell.

The owner's daughter worked the water into the hardwood boards with her mop, occasionally lifting her eyes to glare at him. John smiled shamefully.

He sat and sipped his tea, warming by the fireside, wisps of steam wafting gently from his clothes. His sullen gaze explored the room, slowly taking in every detail if only to avoid making contact with her, before fixing on the cluster of torn and stained boxes by the cellar door. One of them, a hefty container at least three feet square, appeared to be full of books. He instinctively sat up to get a better look, but settled back again when the heavy man groaned his way up the stairs and tossed another carton on the pile, wiping sweat from his brow with his sleeve.

"Rubbish, is it?" John inquired with a purposely carefree tone.

The man was caught off guard by the question and spun toward John. "Ongh?" he blurted loudly.

"Put it out with the refuse, will ye?" John asked again, lifting his head to the boxes.

The balding man breathed heavily. "Sure, sure! 'Tis all bound fer the tip!" He bent and braced his arms against his knees, panting.

John stood and approached the boxes, trying to get a better look. "Say, would ye mind if I took this one here? I'm a bit of a bookworm an' would fancy a gander."

The owner stood erect and waved his hand passively. "Fine by me. Ye'll save me the grief o' gettin' it to the car." He turned to retrieve the final load from the cellar.

"Tanks much!" John called to deaf ears. The clamor of falling rain had quieted and the view outside was no longer blurred by motion. He returned to the table and dropped his heaviest coins on its surface, then wrapped himself in his dripping overcoat. Hefting the box, he shuffled to the door uneasily, as he was carrying an additional fifty pounds in both books and water.

He stopped and asked the owner's daughter, "Know where I might find an auto mechanic?"

She refused to look at him, her vindictive stare locked on the new brook his clothes had leaked from table to door. She merely pointed across the street to a filling station.

"Tanks," John said abashedly. "An' sorry!"

*   *   *   *

Dusk was settling when John arrived back at the Chivalric Nobleman de La Mancha, the business day lost to a combination of atmospheric discourtesy and irregular transport.   Finding his car on the highway and replacing the fan belt had taken hours and when his lumbering body sloped through the threshold of home he found a pulsing and relentless ache flowing through his head.   Undressing took twice as long as usual and, rather than hang the garments up to dry, he carelessly tossed them in the bathtub and clambered into bed. A profoundly deep sleep took hold of him before the last of the evening light receded below the horizon.

Eight hours later his internal clock stirred, peeling his mind softly from its dream.   While shaving, he remembered the carton of books he'd left in the car and soon he was dressed and out in the morning air to fetch it.   The box seemed heavier than before and he carried it blunderingly back to the shop, where he heaved it onto the front counter and began sifting through.

The volume that first sparked his interest in the café was there on top, a ragged copy of *This Side of Paradise*. The copyright page informed him it was a later printing of the first British edition.   It was in fair condition at best, yet a find nonetheless. He set it aside and continued his inspection.

Most of the books crowning the pile were in poor condition, some of them downright haggard. Moisture had caused ample foxing to the fore-edges and many smelled of mildew. A few dust jackets were considerably torn and hung loosely while others had disintegrated entirely. They were books browned with age and, although mostly popular novels of their time, made valueless and occasionally unreadable by the elements.

As he dug deeper, however, John found that the condition of the books improved. He began sorting them on the counter according to their appearance. In one pile lay books ranging from poor to fair states, in another he organized volumes in good health to very good, and a third pile was reserved for those of fine appearance or better. Although the latter pile remained an empty block of countertop, the good pile eventually outgrew that of the poor. John's heart became increasingly energized with each title he extracted. What joy to discover such worth in the refuse of others!

When at last he reached in to pull the final books from their haven, he noticed lying at the base of the carton three squares wrapped in waxed paper, bound together with string.

John paused. His imagination rocketed to faraway places and he became giddy before his own sensibility forced him back to reality. Cautiously, deliberately, he reached in and removed the bundles, tossing the tattered box aside to increase his workspace.

With the focus and care of a surgeon, he drew the string to loosen its knot and removed the first package. The ends of the paper were cemented down, creating a steadfast binding, and he tenderly pulled the seals free and unwrapped the parcel. Cocooned within was an elderly yet immaculate copy of Robert Louis Stevenson's *Treasure Island*.

John Doyle ceased to breathe. His lids failed to blink and rumor passed that his heart skipped several beats while he sat with *Treasure* in his trembling hands. Eventually he exhaled deeply and slumped the pressure from his spine, although the sense of rapture remained. It was as though he was young Jim Hawkins standing before a chest unearthed.

Knowledge of particular details regarding the first state of Stevenson's iconic novel swarmed from his deepest memory and he cracked the binding slightly, *ever so gently*, barely enough to expose the title page. It read, "Cassell & Company, Limited" and, below that, the year, "1883." Excitedly yet gently, *ever so gently*, he turned the pages until he found what he was looking for, the old seafarer's song topping the second page of text. In subsequent printings, the phrase "Dead Man's Chest" had been capitalized. The first printing, however, did not. And there it lay, before his electrified eyes:

Fifteen men on the dead man's chest—

John closed the cover. A long minute passed before his senses were restored. He returned the Stevenson to its wrapping, then focused his attention on the second of the packages (*There are more!*, he thought deliriously). As he began to strip the book of its waxed paper, he paused to calm his jittery hands. It would do him no good to drop or damage the mystery within from his own dimwittedness — best to slow the pace now and protect whatever gem lie in wait.

The gem, as fate would present, was *Poems* by Emily Dickinson, the 1890 publication of the first series, many decades old yet preserved in exquisite condition. The child within John kicked up his heels and whoops of joy reverberated against the underside of his skin as John's eyes goggled in disbelief. His bare fingers caressed the spine's edge and proved it to be entirely real. Responsibility snapped into working order once again and demanded that he don a pair of cotton gloves to prevent the oils in his naked hands from further soiling the sacraments.

The third and final parcel was thick and unwieldy. John's hands strained under its weight as he clumsily peeled away the paper swathing it. When at last free, the book fell inelegantly from his grasp and landed heavily on the counter, shooting a thin plume of dust in the air. John was momentarily distracted by a feeble sneeze and when he opened his eyes, he found lying before him a very simple book, a book thick in pages and bound with green cloth.

The Great White Whale sat sublimely within his reach and returned his silent stare.

It was Master Melville come to pay a visit to La Mancha.

It was *Moby Dick*.

"John Doyle," said the shopkeeper softly to himself, "thar be whales here!"

How fate had brought these masterworks to him, John could not guess. He failed to wrap his brain around the idea, for he knew that he of all people appreciated them more than most. Notions of destiny and chance and theology and serendipity swarmed his mind and made him dizzy. Although he sat with his crupper centered squarely on the stool, he nearly tumbled off it.

A flurry of questions ambushed him, but he dared not handle the books to find answers for fear of having the pages disintegrate cruelly in his hands; John had never been one to tempt the devils of fortune. He was certain the books were originals, first printings, for he'd seen them before—never in person, but in photos and listings from rare book dealers, certainly—and knew all three to be true first states of the first editions. He recognized their unique properties as a carpenter recognizes the grain in his wood.

The remaining hours of the morning were spent cleaning and cataloging the collected trove from the box, yet John found himself distracted, pausing time and again to stare at or touch the three pinnacles of his discovery. He was enamored, like a young man under the spell of his first love, and could not bear to leave them unsupervised, even when his natural plumbing began to demand relief. When the pressure on his bladder could no longer be dismissed, he wrapped the books in a triad layer of fresh paper and locked them in a small safe under the till, then rushed, squirming, to manage his other business.

While utilizing the loo in back, John heard the sound of his tinkling water blend with the repeated tinkling of the entrance bell that merrily announced the presence of Tinky O'Shea. He washed his hands and went to greet his friend, but not before pausing at the door, a new angst creeping over him, a realization of the dilemma he was likely soon to encounter. He wiped the dread from his face with a forced smile and proceeded into the shop.

"Tinky O'Shea, a comforting sight fer me lonesome eyes!" he lied, arms outstretched. Tinky whirled to face him from the single shelf of Erotic Lit like a child caught, then relaxed and approached John to take his paw and smother it with a hearty and dual-handed embrace.

"A fine afternoon to ye, Johnny boy! Thought I'd venture over durin' me lunch hour." Tinky leaned against the raised desk. "I got to tinkin', do ye still fancy that darlin' Sharon Smyth from up the block? Ye've not spoken o' her in some time. Tell me ye've not abandoned the pursuit o' her virtue!" He lowered his tone. "What's left of it, at least."

John waved off the talk of women. "Ye know I can't be spendin' the few punts I make here on supplements like romance. 'Tis an expensive hobby an' me budget can't spare more than a trifle fer an annual visit to Mrs. Talbot at the county faire."

"Ah, the beloved Clara Talbot! The dear celebrated seventy-five years o' plantin' kisses from her booth just last summer. Still as popular as ever, she is. But, aye, there's truth in yer words. Lasses are a costly way to pass the time, whether she's yer wife or yer waitress."

John felt he should reiterate his current financial state, if only to bolster any arguments forthcoming. "Ye know, I've resorted to sellin' certain precious elements o' me body to help pay the bills. I'll not give details, but in a few years' time, if ye happen upon a few runts runnin' 'round town that bear a strikin' resemblance, I hope ye'll not be startled."

Tinky laughed and was drawn to the piles of new stock on the counter, as curious a cat as ever there was. He balanced his reading glasses over his nose and said, "What ye got here?"

John's apprehension grew. "Oh, a few titters 'n tatters to further expand me achin' walls. Have at 'em an' take what ye like."

Tinky rummaged through, his inquisitiveness blossoming to fascination. "Say, there's some mighty fine material here." The stack in his hands grew in number. "Where did ye find such a garden?"

"Outskirts o' town, in a small café. Owner was throwin' 'em out an' I bartered 'em into me care."

"Bartered what?"

"A mere sprinkle o' charm an' a word o' tanks is all. Amazin' what people are willin' to discard as rubbish, wouldn't ye say?"

"Aye, indeed."

A quiet lull followed, during which Tinky unleashed the question from its scabbard. "Have ye seen him this week?"

The answering silence prompted Tinky to look up from his inspection. He peered over the bridge of his glasses at John in wait. No need repeating the question; John was familiar with it and Tinky knew he'd spoken clearly.

John's anxiety raced. The moment had come much sooner than he'd anticipated. Unfortunately, he only knew how to respond with truth. "Have a look here." He crossed around the desk and bent at his safe to retrieve the lode.

Before revealing his stash, John tossed his friend a fresh pair of cotton gloves. "Slide these on first," he encouraged. With Tinky's interest sufficiently piqued, John then displayed the books in the order he'd first found them in: first Stevenson, then Dickinson. He intentionally held Melville back until Tinky's vision was restored and his heart settled to a flutter.

When at last the gallant *Pequod* sailed into Tinky's grasp, he beheld it and at first failed to comprehend. A slow dawn crept over him, numbing his senses, and after a moment a single tear crept from his eye and fell heavily toward the book quivering in his hands.

With the instinct of a mother pulling her child close in the presence of danger, John lashed out and <pock!> caught the tear in his gloved palm before it could damage the book. The sudden movement woke Tinky from his trance and he wiped the remaining tears away with his shoulders. "Tanks," he spoke softly.

Tinky was ashamed to speak of business while holding such a sacred object, yet he failed to confine his emotion. "John—" he began. His eyes focused on the floor, studying the grooves between the boards as he cautiously chose his words. "The value...the value o' coin an' printed pound are made insignificant by this here book. But whatever trade ye seek, whatever I have, whatever cost ye put on this most priceless o' treasures, I'll pay it an' never once the rest o' me days tink twice of it."

The evil that John prophesied had come sooner than he'd imagined. It simply could not be, he knew, and he shook his head in discouragement, despondent by the betrayal and dishonor he was forced into now. "Tinky—" was all he managed to say.

His dearest friend felt the drag of humiliation pulling at them both and became energized to counter it. "John, hear me out—" Tinky spat his words in rapid succession for fear that one hiccup would give cause for interruption. "—I've dreamt o' this since I was a lad in knee breeches, ye know that...I've spent more time with Melville than I have with me own *father*...no man living or dead has had greater influence on me than Herman an' no single book has fed me soul nor given greater sustenance than this one here...ye're a learned man, Johnny, a man o' literature, ye know what I'm talkin' about!...ye must, ye *must* let me have it!" He was crazed with emotion and his tears came easily. "If ye yerself can't keep it, then bequeath it to me! Family, I am! Ye can't prostitute yer soul fer shekels an' pence, man! D'ye hear? This is not a matter o' money, John, but of honor...friendship...*integrity!*"

John reached out and tried to knead sanity back into his mate. "Let's not do this, kiddo, we can't allow emotions to get the best of us, either of us. Listen now, the facts are plain. My accounts are dry — ye know I'm scrapin' rock's bottom — an' ye've nothin' to give. I know this fer a fact. Ye already owe me—" He looked over to consult his debtor's ledger.

Tinky pulled from John's grip and backed away, fury possessing his eyes. "I do *not* know this man blatherin' about finance an' favors. This man has no familiarity. This man has no friend." His trance broke suddenly and he looked away. A moment passed before he continued. "But yer mind seems to be set in the matter. Prob'ly was before I ever laid foot inside. I'll leave ye, then, with yer book an' yer friendship, an' say 'farewell.'" He trod stiffly out, leaving John alienated with only a single fit from the overhead bell.

It was, John thought, the most lonesome sound he'd ever heard.

With boulders in his heart, John picked up the telephone and dialed the residence of Mr. Brian Corrigan.

*   *   *   *

The price was settled over lunch the next day for not only *Moby Dick*, but *Treasure Island* as well ("Dickinson reminds me o' me first wife," said Corrigan. "Far too depressin'."). After an invigorating yet brief period of negotiation, John Doyle was temporarily relieved of his financial woes.

As the clouds had been brushed away like cotton bolls by a rejuvenated breeze, the sun sparkling once again over Dublin Town, the men thought it an agreeable idea to travel on foot first to the Bank of Ireland, then back to the bookshop, where John delivered the treasures into the proud ownership of Mr. Corrigan. John was remorseful at having to part with Melville's masterpiece, naturally, yet he was eager to be rid of the stresses it had carried into his home.

As the men exchanged post-sale pleasantries, John was distracted by a curious idea. It dominated his thoughts during the conversation and made him distant as he twirled it through his head. By the way his gaze continually drifted to a shelf labeled "Postmodern Soviet Philosophy," Corrigan assumed he was boring his host and promptly wrapped up his dialogue. As he headed for the door, John stopped him.

"Brian, wait. Forgive me if I seem distracted, I've had so much churnin' through me mind since I found these books. I'd, uh…I'd actually fancy a favor from ye."

"What's that, cap'n?"

"If ever ye find need to be rid of 'em, especially the Melville, fer whatever reason, I wonder if ye'd do me the courtesy of offerin' 'em back to me first. Fer fair profit, o' course. I know 'tis not very mercantile o' me, but I consider meself a lover o' books more than a seller an' I'd rather enjoy seein' these again one day."

Corrigan nodded his understanding. "Certainly. Ye'll see 'em again, never fear. An' know ye're always welcome to come scrutinize me own library. But I'll be seein' ye soon, anyhow — I haven't yet had the pleasure o' wanderin' the aisles here. I'd do it now, but me concentration is limited as long as I carry these." He raised the package John had diligently made to house the two nautical marvels.

John opened the door for him and Brian turned before exiting. "It'll give me great pleasure to prove what a friend I can be," he said. "I look forward to it. Until next time, good sir!"

CHAPTER TWO
The Fiery Plague of Possession

The vagabonds of Dublin are a curious lot. Predominantly, they are not the sort of people to have found their rock-bottom status in society caused by a nasty habit like vice, which often describes the homeless you might find residing the streets of, say, Amsterdam, nor is their situation a result of faults in their personality or judgment, as best describes the derelicts of, for instance, Paris. Whereas greed, lust, pride, fear, jealousy, sloth, and gluttony are all popular causes of vagrancy in America, they seldom apply to those "living rough" on the streets of Dublin.

On the contrary, the homeless citizens of Dublin are, in large, a good-natured, jovial, and upstanding group of people. They care for and nurture those in need. They gather and eat together, drink together, and bother to know one another. They endeavor to preserve and defend the culture and virtue of the city, *their* city, and help maintain the optimism, humor, and humanity that thrive throughout Ireland. Unlike the destitute of other cultures, these good men and women find themselves without shelter due not to sins of flesh or conscience, but due merely to misfortune and circumstance.

The exception to this is Mac Malone.

A fleet of words shine out and beg to describe Mac Malone, the kind of words that are often used to describe feculent farm animals or bitterly divorced spouses or criminals who viciously poke fun at their own mothers. They are not pleasant words, nor are they spoken in the presence of children or people we respect. Any virtuous mind will best maintain its virginal luster by being sheltered from the adjectives commonly applied to this man, therefore it is necessary to present Mac honestly, without refinery, and allow one's own judgment to find words to best illustrate his character.

On a foggy and unusually silent night, under a moon whose luminescence could not penetrate the atmospheric duvet bundled around it, Mac Malone stood on the Father Mathew Bridge over the River Liffey, emptying his bladder onto a drowning man. To his credit, Mac didn't know there was a person flailing directly under his stream, nor was he aware that this man was struggling to stay afloat by frantically scraping his fingers along the bridge side, searching for something steady to grasp. All Mac knew was that the sounds traditionally associated with tinkling into the Liffey were not audible tonight; in their stead were noises of intermittent splashing plus the deep, hollow resonance of water as it gently soaks wet canvas and/or human flesh. In addition to this was what sounded like a pair of lustful frogs buggering the wits out of each other.

The frogs were, in fact, the quietly pleading protestations of Mr. Shea Heaney as he struggled to maintain a breathable position above water. The matter of *how* Mr. Heaney found himself in the river, fully clothed, completely sober, having never had a swimming lesson, is such a complex and tangential story that even Mr. Heaney was bewildered by his predicament. Suffice it to say he was in quite a pickle.

Still, he did not lack a survival instinct, and as such was able to take in enough air between submersions to give a bleat powerful enough to be heard by his assailant. Mac looked down to see the steady stream flowing out of him arc and strike a quietly floundering stranger squarely on the forehead. Startled and confounded, Mac jumped back and ceased his urination with a tightening of muscles. A moment of disbelief passed before he could look into the river again to confirm the vision. He stared as the man below bobbed under and over the waterline, gasping each time his mouth surfaced.

Finally, Mr. Heaney was able to stay afloat long enough to speak. "Help!" he choked.

Mac wasn't accustomed to being spoken to by strangers, but when he looked around he saw no other sign of life. He responded, "You there! The one in the river! Is it me ye're addressin'?"

Heaney's awkward gesticulations were ceased momentarily by his stunned incredulity. When he found enough momentum to speak again, he repeated his cry as before. "Help!"

"What's with the flappin' o' yer arms there?" Mac asked. "Attemptin' to fly in that water, are ye?"

Heaney managed to grab a finger hold in the cracks of the bridge stone and held to it with the last of his strength. He coughed water from his lungs and looked beseechingly at his potential rescuer. "I'm attemptin' to keep a firm grasp on *livin'*!" His eyes were swollen with terror. "Will ye help me?"

"Help ye to do what?"

"Help me up to the safety o' dry land, man!"

"Ye want me to help ye get out o' there, then?"

"Please!"

There stood between the men roughly twelve feet of sheer stone and Mac put his hands on his hips and said reproachfully, "Well how do ye want me to go about doin' *that*?"

"I don't know!" Shea Heaney hawed as he thought of how best to be saved. "Find a rope, sir, an' throw it to me!"

Mac rolled his eyes and shouted, "Heavenly Christ! Ye want me to go runnin' fer rope when I finished me supper mere moments ago? Why, I'd be brought to me knees with cramps an' pain tearin' through me belly! Besides," he called, "although this body is fine an' strong an' fit, 'tis sufferin' somethin' awful due to undercooked sardines an' I'd never be able to gather enough strength simply to accommodate *you*." He rubbed the belly that spilled over his belt like an octopus cinched with twine and scratched at his massive buttocks.

A moment passed, during which Mr. Heaney shot an uncomfortable silence in Mac's direction. Finally, he said, "Then run — or walk, if ye must — to find a cop!"

The overwhelming gall of the man losing his grasp on the column below was enough to rile Mac's fury. "Blasphemous dog! 'Tis a fact that several precincts of our local Garda have reason to wreak havoc on me fundamental rights o' freedom. How would that make me look, if I grabbed a copper in order to help *you* an' the swine wound up locking *me* away fer a few alleged indiscretions from me past? Eh? A prominent man such as I has no place behind the impenetrable walls of a station house!" Mac blew his nose into the torn sleeve of his overcoat and spat on the ground. "In fact, it would not surprise me in the least to discover that ye yerself are workin' in tandem with the coppers an' that you bein' down there with yer arms an' legs a-flailin' is all part of an operation real covert-like to bring me in!"

Mac spat again and added, "Curses to ye, ye stoolie!"

Shea Heaney lost his grip and slid back into the perilous waters. After a protracted moment of thrashing about, he was again able to find a curl in the stone to cling to.

"Please, good sir!" he wept as his mind searched for a plan, "At the very least...yes! Yes, there'll be a life ring nearby! They plant 'em round the quay fer safety! Find one an' toss it down — hurry, man, I implore ye!" Then, to himself, "God in Heaven, can there be no soul other than this wretch walkin' the streets tonight?"

Mac turned, his eyes settling on the nearest life ring. A band of rowdy juveniles had nicked one and shoved it in a rubbish bin and it was now covered with garbage piled high, a mountain of filth and sludge and toxins and obscenity. Mac took several steps toward the iron basket, wary and unsure, stepping lightly so as not to disturb whatever beasts lay within, and a trifling breeze caught a ball of crumpled paper and blew it off the top of the pile and Mac turned and bolted back to the lip of the bridge to shake his filth-encrusted finger at the stranger below.

"Send me to the Gates o' Hell, ye would! Want me to venture into the soul o' dirt an' depravity just to help ye out from yer swim, eh? Who knows what creatures seethe inside, just waitin' to ambush any chump come to rassle out a silly lifesaver! An' to demand that I foul me own fine clothing on top of it all!" He raised two offending fingers at the man below and an elbow soiled with grime poked through a frayed hole worn through his sleeve.

The silence surrounding them was broken by approaching footsteps and Mac's attention was pilfered by two forms in the distance. He recognized one of the shapes to be that of his darling true, Miss Sweet Emily Moore. She was strolling beside what appeared to be a well-built man. Mac saw the silhouette of the man and guessed that he was young and handsome and charming and sexually potent and the very pit of Mac's body instantly churned and burned. His mind snapped to rapt attention and promptly forgot about Mr. Shea Heaney bobbing precariously in the river below.

*   *   *   *

Several minutes earlier, Sweet Emily Moore was out walking her nightly beat when she was joined by old Constable Cooney, who was walking his. They did this on most evenings in order to maintain familiarity and to while away the evening lulls. Mostly, though, they did this to adhere to the popular adage, "know thy enemy." Although Sweet Emily Moore and Copper Cooney, as he was known, were on friendly and familiar terms and certainly meant no harm to one another, their respective professions historically tangled in conflict and dispute, as had their ancestry. A long line of law-enforcing Cooneys had been squabbling with a long line of streetwalking Moores about ethics and law and basic human nature, yet, despite generations of hooting and hollering and carrying on, the sons and grandsons and great-grandsons of Cooneys were still able to sit down at the end of a day with the daughters and granddaughters and great-granddaughters of Moores and laugh about their differences over a pint.

As it was still early in the week, Copper Cooney was bored, with little to focus his professional attention on. Scrappers, thieves, beaters, looters, gamblers, peepers, and vandals traditionally didn't become riled enough to act on their indiscretions until later in the week. Lasciviousness was the one crime that enjoyed no rest, a fact which kept Sweet Emily Moore's appointment book full throughout the week and provided her with little respite to ease her stings and sores. The greatest furloughs she was likely to find came between The Quick and The Belated, which afforded her time now to enjoy the company of Copper Cooney, a man who, at the sprightly age of sixty-two, was the eldest and therefore most experienced of the beat walkers.

The Constable was now imparting snippets of wisdom to Sweet Emily Moore. "If I only teach ye one thing in life, lass, let it be this," he routinely repeated this phrase before delivering each lesson. "Do not allow yer passions to overtake yer sensibilities. Follow yer heart, not yer urges. Thousands have passed through the irons o' me jail an' precious few arrived who were not motivated by their own wanton desires." He gave her a sanctimonious, sideways glance through his bifocals and smiled proudly.

Sweet Emily Moore blew her nose onto the street. "Bollix!" she cried. "What'ya want me to do, die o' *boredom*?" She grabbed his bum playfully and squeezed. A startled cry three octaves higher than Cooney's usual tone pierced the quiet and left him flustered and blushing. "Ah, woman!" he whispered shrilly as he smoothed his trousers. "Control that ungodly hand an' behave! Here comes me pup!"

A young man had emerged from the fog and was walking briskly toward them. Built with square shoulders and a chiseled jaw, the man wore a peacoat wrapped snugly around his frame, defining a density of muscle not to be trifled with.

"A pleasant evenin', Officer-In-Trainin' Bonner!" Copper Cooney took the young man's hand and tried to prove his virility by crushing it, but Bonner failed to notice.

"Officer Cooney!" said Bonner hurriedly. "I've just passed a row outside Dooley's, four blocks over. Follow me!" He headed off, leading the way, until he noticed he marched alone. Cooney remained with Sweet Emily Moore, chuckling and sucking his teeth and looking fatherly.

"*Where* are ye goin'?" asked Cooney sardonically.

Trainee Bonner suddenly lost the confidence in his voice. "To break up the fight," he said. Then, with the tone of a scolded child, he added cautiously, "An'. To. Enforce. The law?"

Copper Cooney stepped forward and draped his arm over Bonner's shoulders. "Enforce the law, eh? Ah, young Bonner! If I only teach ye one thing in life, let it be this: we Irishmen are a hard-workin' people. We are an easy-goin' people, yet we are very set in our ways. At the end of a difficult day, we fancy joinin' our mates an' havin' a good time. Don't ye agree? An' sometimes as we are havin' a good time, we are called upon by some numb-arse to defend our ideals, or perhaps the ideals of a loved one. Do ye follow me? Words get heated, curses are thrown, an' before ye know it, the fists come a-flyin'. Even I have fallen into a few scuffles, mostly in me youth, o' course." Here he dropped his head and gave his sanctimonious look over the top of his glasses. "Does that make me a criminal? Hmmm? Ye might say that scrappin' is in the blood of us all. Heredity, it is. You an' me, we're proud, we're passionate, we'll fight fer what we hold to be true, as will our neighbors. So tell me, who are we to stifle our brethren simply fer bein' honest to themselves? Who are we to break up that tussle an', in doin' so, deny our very own o' their *heritage*?"

Bonner was silent. Cooney's steadfast gaze pierced the young man's eyes and held them, driving his point home. Cooney then raised his arm in a welcoming gesture and said merrily, "Sweet Emily Moore! May I introduce ye to the next addition to our streetwalking beat, Probationer Garda Peter Bonner!"

Sweet Emily Moore greeted Bonner the way she greeted all men upon first meeting: she took his hand in hers and ran her fingers seductively over his palm, cocking her head down and looking up to him with dewy and lustful eyes. Her mouth parted, allowing her tongue to traipse slowly along the base of her teeth. In a practiced tone sounding both vulnerable and sensual, she said, enunciating each syllable, "I come to meet ye with great pleasure, Constable." She lingered over each letter of the last word, never taking her eyes from his.

A ball of chewing gum fell from Bonner's mouth. Sweet Emily Moore giggled like a schoolgirl. Copper Cooney rolled his eyes.

"Break yer trance, boy!" said Cooney. "Sweet Emily Moore is a favorite among Dubs. Let it be yer duty to see she knows no harm."

Sweet Emily Moore abandoned her charade and scratched her crotch, saying gruffly, "So! Bonner. What made ye become a copper? Did yer mother beat ye as a child?"

Her sudden switch from seductress to vulgarian offset Bonner. "Eh? Oh. Not at all, ma'am. I enlisted to enforce the law an' help maintain the upright morals an' standards adhered to by the citizens o' Dublin." He delivered the line as though reading text from a book.

"Followin' in yer father's footsteps like ol' Cooney here?"

Cooney slapped Bonner's back and said, "Quite the opposite, actually. The young gentleman comes from a long line o' pastors o' the Protestant faith—"

"A hundred an' twelve," Bonner interjected.

"A hundred an' twelve pastors in his family! Dating back, what was it?"

"Eight generations."

"Eight generations! No, the constable has broken with tradition to introduce a new line o' work to the family. Chosen quite well, if ye ask me." Cooney affectionately took Bonner's arm in his. "An' tonight he continues his trainin' in my company. They told him to learn from the best an' this evenin' he'll do just that. 'Tis my duty to make sure he's fit an' ready to don the prestigious uniform of An Garda Siochana, hopefully sometime next week."

Sweet Emily Moore was still unsatisfied. "Copper Cooney, ye're actin' proud about someone ye know nothin' about." She turned her attention back to Bonner. "Ye haven't told us yet *why* ye've become a beat cop."

"I have joined the Garda," Bonner recited, "in order to work with the community to protect an' serve."

"Protect an' serve *what*?" Sweet Emily Moore persisted.

"The *people*, ye pesky monkey!" Again it was Copper Cooney answering, weary of her inquisition. "Now, if ye'll pardon me, I must find a quiet spot to shake the dew from me lily. Back in a moment!" He tipped his hat for the lady and crept off to find a dark corner, but not before turning to impart advice on Bonner.

"If I only teach ye one thing in life, young Bonner, let it be this," he called. "Hold yer own against the persistence o' this one!"

*   *   *   *

Bonner walked with Sweet Emily Moore but soon wished he were elsewhere, for she was a persistent pesky monkey indeed, pushing him aggressively for answers to her questions. She probed about his childhood, schooling, his family and friends. He answered diligently, choosing his words carefully, and remained ever honest. Sweet Emily Moore listened intently and was soon able to draw a definitive conclusion about Bonner: he was bollix. A prude. A wet blanket. A morally righteous copper with an over-inflated sense of integrity and an inability to recognize the complexities of life. In short, he was an immediate threat to her livelihood.

On they strolled, slowly approaching the Father Matthew Bridge, where Mac Malone was dealing with a rude disruption in his evening urination. Shea Heaney was proving to be quite the affront to Mac's very being and Mac welcomed the distraction of Sweet Emily Moore and her unknown paramour emerging from the shadows, even though the sight of them gave him the strangest cramping feeling in his belly, worse than any sensation he'd endured before, worse even than the flatulence he'd suffered two days earlier caused by the lactose in two gallons of sharp cheddar iced cream assaulting his intolerant constitution.

The fires of jealousy had never bothered Mac before; he'd never possessed anything to be jealous about. Yet, upon seeing the couple together, both his body and mind were overcome by a swarm of sensations: the initial tingling in his nethers led to a shock that numbed his thinking mind, leading to a tickling of the skull behind the nasal cavity that threatened to drain his tear ducts, which then morphed into the flaming fist digging trenches through his belly. Quite unexpectedly, and for the very first time, Mac was made to kneel before the demon of Dryden's jaundice of the soul, Shakespeare's green-eyed monster, or the common man's fiery plague of possession; he was, at that moment, introduced to the venial sin of jealousy.

How curious that Mac, fully aware of Sweet Emily Moore's standing in society and professional obligations, would feel so protective — and possessive — of her now. He could tolerate her associations with other men, her shameless flirtations, her holding of hands other than his. He would have rolled his sleeves to box any man, woman, or child who insulted her integrity, but never a man who merely craved a few moments in her company. Yet seeing her illumined by the warm glow of the city streetlamps, walking in the presence of a man she *deserved* — young, handsome, seemingly upright and strong — caused Mac to suffer the reeling sensations now assaulting his innards. It was this passion which demanded he draw the young knave far away from the object of his affection.

Mac's stocky legs carried him stiffly yet swiftly toward Sweet Emily Moore's suitor. He ran at them in a serpentine pattern, sprinting east, then west, then jogging in circles before progressing forward, hoping to disorient and discombobulate his prey. Crisp night air filled his lungs and he expelled a shrill and piercing war cry, a high C-sharp, powerful enough to rattle the large display window of Mrs. Liddy's Pie Shoppe some thirty feet away and cause Sweet Emily Moore and Bonner to stop and notice his primordial charge.

Drained from screaming and flailing his arms about, Mac paused to grab his knees and pant fresh oxygen into his system. Looking up again, he saw his Sweet Emily Moore standing with her beau, both staring at him with expressionless faces. The sight of them together fueled the fire in his belly and he stood erect to howl another chilling war cry. This time he eighty-sixed the serpentine and ran straight at the buggers.

Within seconds he was upon them and stopped just short of wrapping his hands around the young man's throat. Instead, Mac stared daggers into the fellow's eyes, standing with legs apart and loins thrust forward and arms spread broadly in a bombardment of masculinity, and sang another chorus of screeching horrors at Bonner. In his excitement, he failed to notice that he'd forgotten to sheathe his member after having his piddle in the river and that his exposed sex now pointed directly at the pair.

"AYEEAYEEAAAYEEEAYEEAYYYAI!" Mac cried.

Bonner stepped forward, shielding Sweet Emily Moore with his girth. "Sir, I wonder if ye'd mind—"

"AAAYEEEOYAAAEYYOOWAHYYYAAAAA!!!" Mac repeated.

"Michael Malone!" This time it was Sweet Emily Moore who spoke. "Quit yer wailin' an' stuff that pepper back in yer trousers! Have ye no respect fer a lady?"

Mac abruptly silenced his screech, looked south, and was warmed by blood blushing his cheeks. He turned and stashed the tackle back in his grimy corduroys, then, having a breath of cool air and regaining momentum, faced them again and began goading Bonner.

"Oy! You thar, Mister Musclebum! Yeah, you, ye thickie! Ye know what ye are? Eh? Ye're just a common *goon* is what ye are! A lungin', knuckle-scrapin' *primate!*"

"Sir, I request that ye continue on yer way—"

"A beastly, beauty-lackin' *thug*, ye are! Ye got a brain made o' cornmeal an' a face made o' *mush!*"

"Mac, ye devil, what's got into ye tonight?" Sweet Emily Moore was indignant. "Ye should know that Mister Bonner here is soon to be—"

"Yer mother," Mac interrupted, staring squarely at Bonner, "is numb enough in mind to tink that worsted wool is simply inferior flannel!"

Bonner gazed at Mac uncomprehendingly.

"Yer mother," Mac continued, "lacks beauty to such a degree that even John Merrick can't stand to look at her!"

"Sir, settle down, now, an' move on, please."

"Yer mother," now he was on a roll, "is so astoundingly overweight, she must squat over Bantry Bay every time she has to use the privy!"

"Look, sir, this is becoming quite—"

"*AAAAAARRRRRRHHHHH!*" Discouraged by Bonner's inability to be fazed and give chase, Mac attempted another approach, desperate to find a way of coaxing the strapping lad away from the affections of Sweet Emily Moore. Nearby stood a rubbish bin, not as brimming as the one on the Father Matthew Bridge, but full enough to hold possible tools of inducement. Mac rushed over and began rooting through.

Soon he had in his hand a robust, rotting bologna, three feet long and reeking of decay. Mac swung to face Bonner, brandishing the sausage like a machete, and, growling like a bear protecting his young, whirled the meat over his head three times before smashing it down against the pavement as though cracking a whip. Rather than making a blunt and threatening sound to chill Bonner's bones as intended, the bologna disintegrated into a mess of rind and fat and grease and Mac was left with only a fistful of sausage. Pocketing that for later consumption, he twirled back to the bin and burrowed deeper.

Bonner turned to Sweet Emily Moore. "Ye know this man?"

"Aye. He's very sweet, but I suppose ye could say he has a history."

"A history o' what?"

"Of everythin', really."

Suddenly Mac was upon them, brandishing an advert promoting McElligott's Den of Burlesque as though brandishing a deadly blade. Spittle glazed his lips and he wore the crazed look of a rat plagued with rabies. The flyer was printed on thick stock and Mac lashed out and scraped Bonner's forearm with it, leaving a white trail of torn, dead skin.

"*HAAAAAYYYYAAAAAAHHH!*" cried Mac.

Bonner looked at the scrape. "Oy, now—"

Again Mac thrust his weapon toward Bonner's arm, but this time Bonner parried and knocked his assailant's hand easily away. "Sir, yer contempt is tryin' me patience, to be certain."

A third attempt with the card left Bonner's forearm engraved with a nasty, stinging cut that began to bleed.

"*That's it!*" Bonner lunged at him, but Mac was already off, headed for the protective maze of the Usher's Quay car park, the nubbins that were his legs fueled by a dynamic shot of adrenaline. Bonner gave chase, slowing briefly after slipping on the remnants of the smashed bologna, leaving Sweet Emily Moore in peace to probe for her nightly income and to contemplate the proud smile she'd noticed gracing Mac's lips as he ran.

*   *   *   *

Ahead of Sweet Emily Moore lay Scratchy Sullivan's pharmacy, closed and boarded since Scratchy's untimely demise five months earlier. The planks sealing the entrance were decorated with colorful graffiti, mostly political statements, but one in particular, the brightest and most flavorful of the bunch, was a brief declaration by the artist about his feelings for Sweet Emily Moore. Surely, it was not uncommon for her to come across her own name in large and gaudy letters adorning public locations; vandals and graffiti artists utilized Sweet Emily Moore's name more than any other, for many a concrete wall or billboard or toilet stall had been graced with poems like *Johnny Loves Sweet Emily Moore* or *Sweet Emily Moore's kisses are sweeter than your mum's*. Although she generally found truth in the notion that there is no such thing as bad publicity, the object of so many budding artist's affections still carried with her a thick stick of white chalk to help camouflage any phrases that lacked basic courtesy, like this one.

She held the chalk loosely in her fist and began to draw. Although she had no formal training in the function or aesthetics of visual arts, her natural talent allowed her to work quickly and soon she stepped back from her creation to examine it. Not a single smudge of paint from the offending lampoon was left exposed under her scintillating work. In fact, in just two weeks' time a construction foreman assigned to renovate Scratchy's pharmacy would fall so deeply entranced with Sweet Emily Moore's illustration that he would carry the boards home and smile profoundly to his wife as he mounted them on the wall of his living room for all to admire.

Satisfied, Sweet Emily Moore pocketed the chalk and turned her attention to Copper Cooney, who approached with a young lady in tow.

"Ahoy, lass!" called Cooney. "Found ye, I did! What's become o' young Bonner, then? Did ye frighten him into the seminary?" He chuckled and snorted and motioned to his companion. "The lass has been inquirin' to yer whereabouts, so I thought I'd accompany her to ye. I believe ye know Miss Donal?"

"Hiya, Katy." Sweet Emily Moore raised her chin to acknowledge the young lady. "How's tricks?"

"Oh, I haven't turned any just yet. Ye was gonna help me out with that, remember?"

Copper Cooney and Sweet Emily Moore exchanged glances. "I see," said Cooney, motioning his thumb toward Katy. "Is she—?"

Sweet Emily Moore's eyes rolled up and she shrugged, implying both indifference and ignorance in the matter.

Cooney tucked in his chin and looked down his glasses at Katy. "My dear Ms. Donal, it is my opinion that in this life, one may do whatever it is that melts one's own butter, however, if I only teach ye one thing in life, let it be this—"

Here Sweet Emily Moore coughed loudly and said, "Cooney! *Ixnay* on the *essonlay*, would'ja? Let me take care o' this one, if ye please." She grabbed Katy's arm and drew her into a protective embrace.

Wounded by having his lesson halted so abruptly, Copper Cooney decided to let the matter pass. "Well. Then. If ye'll pardon me, I should investigate the matter o' those splashin' sounds I heard by Merchant's Quay a while back." He tipped his hat and said, "Evenin', ladies!" then was off.

As soon as the fog had swallowed the departing Constable, Sweet Emily Moore unhooked from Katy's arm and looked her over. The lady was very young, perhaps nineteen, with a face as round and as fair and as beautiful as the most treasured pearl. Muscles behind her brows lifted them permanently, giving her a perpetual look of surprise. Her dress was a size too small and out of fashion, most likely her best even though she'd outgrown it, and vivid cosmetics caked her lashes, cheeks, and lips, lending the appearance of one trying to impress. She carried herself stiffly, her body tense, arms folded protectively over her torso, and she looked now at Sweet Emily Moore as a timid schoolgirl would at a stern schoolmarm.

"Look at ye!" said Sweet Emily Moore as she patted Katy's cheeks with both hands. "Yer first night on the job an' ye've covered all that nat'ral beauty with fancy paints!" She withdrew a frayed handkerchief and spat in it, then rubbed at the makeup until it was significantly muted. "First lesson: ye've no need fer it, not until ye reach twenty-three."

Katy bowed her head and spoke to the ground. "Yes'm."

"Second lesson: cease callin' me ma'am. Me Grand-mum was a ma'am, but not I. I'm Sweet Emily Moore, nothin' less, nothin' more."

Still Katy bowed her head. "Yes'm."

"Jaysus, do ye not hear? No more o' that, now. An' look at me when we're discussin'! Third lesson: eye contact. Nothin'll get ye work better than makin' eyes." She grabbed Katy's chin and raised it until she could see her eyes. "There now. Ye've got lovely browns that should be pointed at people rather than at the dirt on yer shoes."

Katy began to speak, but Sweet Emily Moore silenced her. "No more *yes'ms*, remember!"

This made Katy smile. "Yes'm," she said playfully.

"Alright, enough o' that, now. Yer turn at speak. Tell me yer story."

"Me story?"

They began to stroll along Bridge Street Upper toward Cornmarket. "Everyone's got a story to tell," said Sweet Emily Moore. "So what led ye to seek me out last night an' ask fer advice on workin' the streets, then? No lass who does that comes without a story to tell."

"Me story, eh? Alrighty then." Katy Donal was comforted by Sweet Emily Moore's grounded, no-nonsense nature and felt an immediate connection that helped loosen her guard. She gave her age as eighteen and told of the many generations of Donal women who'd married Protestant pastors. She'd grown up in her father's church and her small family had enjoyed a tight bond until the day tragedy beset them a year prior. Her mother, father, sister, two aunts and two uncles, three cousins, and one senile yet strong octogenarian grandfather had all been killed when a whale-watching tour they'd taken around Dublin Bay was swallowed first by a squall, then by a whale. The only thing that kept Katy from a wet and blubbery grave was a splinter that embedded in her foot and prevented her from walking to the docks.

That single, horrific event wiped out her entire family and Katy suffered a severe depression, spending what little inheritance she received on menial items and sometimes giving loads of it away to the destitute. Now she herself was destitute and, two nights earlier, had spent the last of her finances becoming sufficiently inebriated for the first time in her young life. After a pint and a half of lager, she found herself crawling the floor of Oliver St. John Gogarty's pub, thoroughly pickled and besieged by the feet of tourists stamping in time to traditional live Irish music, and decided in the despair of the moment that she would have to turn tricks for a living.

Sweet Emily Moore had listened attentively and now paused to scratch her pubis. "So ye never had an abusive father or an uncle who molested ye or nothin'?"

Katy's eyes grew wide. "Oh, no! Never anythin' like that!"

"Exactly how many gentlemen have ye been with?"

"How d'ye mean?"

Oh, brother. "What I mean is how many men have ye been intimate with in yer eighteen years?"

Katy's doe-like eyes wandered while she thought. "Three?"

"Ye sound uncertain. Are ye askin' three or tellin' three?"

"Well there were two fellers I let touch me knee, one at the cinema, the other at the park, an' another boy I knew from twelfth year kissed me once behind the little girls' room at the gymnasium. So, yeah, three."

Sweet Emily Moore threw her arms out and brought them to rest on her head. "Baby God an' his poppa Jaysus! So's ye're a virgin, then?"

"Yeah?" said Katy, not very assuredly.

Sweet Emily Moore's incredulous tone softened and her lips turned to form a maternal smile. "Ye've said enough, darlin'. Now I've got to quit bein' distracted an' find some work, so ye stand over here an' observe how I do it." They'd reached High Street and found it slightly more dense with pedestrians and traffic, so Sweet Emily Moore planted Katy in the doorway of Caitlin O'Hanegan's Confectionery, then proceeded across the street to make herself known to her public.

Katy witnessed that within one minute of Sweet Emily Moore's arrival on the adjacent corner, she had an inquirer. The man was short and heavyset, his pronounced shape hidden under a disheveled overcoat yet giving the overall impression of a tortoise standing on hind legs. He appeared to be in quite a lustful state, for he was panting deeply and shimmering with sweat and a plume of steam rose visibly from the top of his bald head when he removed his cap. After a brief exchange between the two, Katy was surprised to see Sweet Emily Moore slap the man's face with an open hand and heard the resounding echo of flesh against flesh even here across the street. Katy made a mental note of the abuse, which she assumed was standard practice in the profession, and continued to watch.

Sweet Emily Moore kept her voice low and her fury muted to avoid alarming Katy across the street, then repeated her gibe. "Ye *heathen!*"

Mac Malone cradled his sore cheek. "How was I suppos'ta know he was a copper?"

"Copper-in-trainin', ye thickwit! But never mind that, what if he'd been a client o' mine? Where would that put me with you chasin' me supper off, eh? Ye could run me out o' business doin' a thing like that!" She smacked his mouth three times, <*pock!*> <*pock!*> <*pock!*>.

Under the confectionary awning, Katy Donal made another mental note. *Mouth-pocking...check.*

Dejected, Mac rubbed his swelling lips. "I could not stand to watch him walk with ye, it made me veins burn an' me belly seize up like nothin' I ever felt before! It makes no difference whether he was a copper or the Lord High God of All Gods, I'd no desire to see him gettin' any closer to ye!"

Sweet Emily Moore's fury subsided and she softened visibly. "Michael Malone, are ye tellin' me ye was *jealous*?"

Embarrassed, Mac said nothing, but threw his hands up to protect his head all the same.

She pulled him to her breast and engulfed him in an embrace. "Oh, yer sweet heart. Bless ye for that. I'm charmed, I am." She kissed the buttery hair that lined the base of his baldness, then smiled and stood back and gruffly boxed his ears with both fists. "But never try it again!"

She added, "He was likely to 'ave *killed* ye!"

Mac said, "I just tink the world o' ye, is all! Why, ye've got talent seepin' from yer pores! I know no other who can twist an' tongue the stem from a simple cherry into a knot as ye can, all without usin' a hand! An' yer gymnastic abilities, why, who else can down a pint — from the tap! — while bendin' over backward-like with feet planted firmly on the tile? None but me own Sweet Emily Moore!" He nestled his nose into the fragrant flesh of her neck and breathed an exhausted sigh. "Now how do we rid ourselves o' the dirty eggsucker?"

"Why on earth would ye want to be rid o' Bonner?"

"Because if I ever see him walkin' sweetly an' nobly an' handsomely with ye again, I'm likely to do somethin' *crazy.*"

Sweet Emily Moore stood back and tried to make sense of the enigma standing before her, but found it an impossible task. Planting her fists on her hips, she got tough. "I'm with ye in wantin' to be rid of him. The last thing a lady needs is an upright Johnny to come in an' muck up her business. Young Bonner's the type who feels it his duty to enforce the law *an'* his own brand o' morals, as though he's the hero o' some action serial down the cinema. Lucky fer us the boy's a simpleton — righteous men often are. He should be easy enough to overcome."

"How do we go about it?"

"I'll tell ye tomorrow, but it involves the lady 'cross the street there."

Tears welled around the parapets of Mac's lids and threatened to burst over. He took her hand and said earnestly, "I love ye, Sweet Emily Moore."

WHACK! Her palm met his forehead sharply and his head thrust backward from the force. "Cool yer coals, ye heathen!" she cried.

Across the street, Katy Donal had learned quite a bit in regard to body language and the art of making a deal. Roaming the footpath toward her was a balding man in middle-age, face unshaved, mouth desperate for even a bucktooth or fang. He came uncomfortably near and stared at her bosom.

"Lookin' fer a date?" he inquired.

Katy took a deep breath, closed her eyes, and said a quick prayer. Then she put on her most seductive smile, said, "Sure!," and knocked him out cold with a swift punch to the face.

*   *   *   *

It took several days of plotting and finagling and goading, but by Thursday both Katy Donal and Peter Bonner had agreed with Sweet Emily Moore to meet over lunch. Katy had little objection to a blind date based on how Bonner had been described to her: upstanding, proud, strong, chiseled and handsome, having earned high regard from the Protestant community. Bonner, on the other hand, was apprehensive. He had reservations based on his moral dislike of the matchmaker, Sweet Emily Moore, and was also numb to the idea of courting ladies while being so immersed in establishing his career. Katy had been described as beautiful, funny, aloof, and a quick learner, but it was Sweet Emily Moore's strategic mention that Ms. Donal's mum had been married to a pastor that began to sway Bonner's mind in the matter. Three days of aggressive encouragement from Sweet Emily Moore resulted in Bonner's agreement (or, more accurately, a leaden sigh and an exasperated shout of "Yes, yes, woman, now leave me be!"), and a date was set for Saturday afternoon.

The Bumbershoot Café on South Great Georges Street provided the ideal atmosphere for an introductory luncheon. The pair could sit outside and enjoy the fresh air in the beautiful brick courtyard. At least that's how Sweet Emily Moore sold the couple on the idea. What she really wanted was for them to sit outside so she and Mac could watch from afar. It had been Mac's idea — he insisted that Katy and Bonner be exposed to spying in order to make sure their meeting went swimmingly. Mac was intent on seeing the courtship through to holy matrimony; only then, he felt, would the fires of jealousy incinerating his soul be cooled and the threat of Peter Bonner be eradicated.

Saturday was pleasantly warm and Mac arrived with Sweet Emily Moore twenty minutes before the date was scheduled. They found the perfect peeping spot in front of the Adagio musical instrument shop directly across the street from the café. The Adagio was closed on weekends and the dark interior allowed for a clear view in the reflection of its display window, which permitted Mac and Sweet Emily Moore to keep their backs to the Bumbershoot, lest they be spotted snooping.   Within minutes, they observed Peter Bonner arriving and watched as he chose a table in a quiet corner of the patio, away from the other tables. His nervous restlessness was apparent, for he filled the time before Katy arrived with his attention on the table itself. He grasped the lip of the table and pushed; when it wobbled slightly, he crouched at its base to investigate.

It was while he was soiling the knees of his gabardines that Katy Donal arrived. She, too, appeared stiff and nearly collided with a waiter carrying a dessert tray. She looked around for the man who'd been described to her but saw no one, failing to see the fellow under the table buried in the corner. When she turned and began walking out, both Sweet Emily Moore and Mac began shouting at the window of the Adagio.

"*Nonononononononononono!*" they cried.

"*GO BACK!*" hollered Mac.

In the glass, they saw Katy stop and look around. Mac and Sweet Emily Moore huddled together and tried to become smaller, hoping their backs were not recognizable. They watched Katy return to the patio, where she saw Bonner on his feet, brushing dirt and pavement from his britches. He looked up and they stared at each other for a moment before speaking. Bonner thrust his hand out and Katy shook it, then he motioned for her to sit.

"Step one complete," said Sweet Emily Moore.

"I hope they order somethin' delectable," said Mac. "I fancy gettin' me hands on the remnants when they depart."

Two hours later, after a shared appetizer, salads, sandwiches, a square of cake with two forks, tea, and seven rounds of lemonade, the young pair still gave no sign of leaving. They were talking and laughing, leaning in to each other and appearing quite comfortable. On the other side of the road, Sweet Emily Moore continued to stare into the shop window, fending off advances from unknown men and a few regulars, while Mac stood sleeping beside her. Eventually, he gave a snore so resounding, it woke him with a start and he defensively broke wind at both ends.

Sweet Emily Moore smiled at what she saw in the window. "It appears we might be lookin' at the future Pastor an' Mrs. Peter Bonner. Good luck to us all."

Mac looked at her proudly and felt his love for her return. He palmed the arch of her buttock and squeezed playfully.

On the patio of the Bumbershoot Café, all eyes turned in the direction of the horrible wail coming from the man across the street. Peter Bonner and Katy Donal, interrupted from a lovely conversation about soup, looked up to see the man hobbling in circles as he rubbed his shin. The shape of the man's unusual form was familiar to Bonner and he shielded the sun from his eyes to better glimpse the fellow's contorted and tear-stained face.

"That poor man!" said Katy as she turned her attention back to Bonner. "So...what are yer feelings on gazpacho?"

Bonner continued to squint at the howling man and soon perked up in his seat. "The dirty dog—!"

"Wha?" Katy asked plainly.

Bonner was out of his chair and running toward the exit, leaving Katy to wonder if he'd been overcome by a burning case of the skitters. In a moment, however, he was back, leaning over her hurriedly and planting a light kiss on her cheek. He pulled back and they both blushed.

"I shall return!" he assured. With that, he was off to chase after the crying man who started to hobble away into the growing crowd of pedestrians, all out to enjoy a beautiful Dublin afternoon along South Great Georges Street.

CHAPTER THREE
Neither Business Nor Pleasure

Spring was reacquainting itself with Dublin. Heavy clouds ceased meddling and allowed the sun to take center stage once again. With the warmth returned, John Doyle felt a youthful giddiness energizing him to action and he suddenly yearned to clean the stifling winter from the pores of his shop. He began by dusting and spraying and scrubbing his bedroom and living area, all during lulls in business. He would see one customer out, then strip to his undershirt and clean before the bell over the door chimed and thrust him back to bookselling. With the living quarters properly polished, he turned his attention to the shop itself, soaping and scouring the floor, then digging out the stepladder to sweep out the cobwebs hanging high. Spiders, like bacteria and viruses, *loathe* spring.

A bundle of other chores beckoned John as well. The Chivalric Nobleman's facade desperately needed a new coat of paint. The tiles on the roof were beginning to slip and fall, causing a few minor yet potentially disastrous leaks (the two elements most harmful to books were, of course, *fire* and *water*). Adding to it all was an invasion of rodents — John had woken one morning to find three of the vermin feasting on a paperback of Evelyn Waugh's *Scoop*, their jaws gnawing animatedly at arguably the funniest part of the book. *Everyone's a critic*, he thought, and he knew the time had come to hire an exterminator. Unfortunately, painters and repairmen and pest controllers cost money, a commodity John had always gazed at from afar but had not yet become cozy with.

Of all the tasks before him, however, the most important was to contact his friend, Tinky O'Shea. Ever since the great white whale came between them, John had been haunted by guilt and struck with a profound loneliness. His business sense, what little of it there was, conflicted with his senses of honor and friendship and he actually allowed it to keep him awake some nights. Although he'd earned enough with the sale of *Moby Dick* and *Treasure Island* to shorten the distance between him and an acceptable credit score, he felt the income had not been enough to warrant the severing of a relationship. *Never do business with friends* was an adage he now understood intimately. Daily, the Angel of Fraternity went hand-to-hand with the Devil of Commerce over the battlefield of his shoulders and never once did a victor prevail.

He telephoned Tinky every day, but the man was not picking up his 'phone. John even walked the two-and-a-half miles to the O'Shea residence after closing up one evening, braving a raucous crowd out to celebrate the start of a week-end, but found no answer to his repeated knocking. He cracked the seal of his peace offering and sipped his way back to the Chivalric Nobleman, joining the rest of the birds in their caws thanking the Gods for the gift of a Friday evening, before passing out early enough to miss the very best parts of it.

Still another matter was his need to visit with the owner of a small café on the way to Dun Laoghaire, the man who'd gifted him the treasure of a tattered box of books, and compensate him for possessions he surely failed to know he had. This was one of several traits that differentiated John's character from those of the Regular Joe; whereas many a man would have appeased his own conscience with evidence that 1) the books had been given with no expected recompense and 2) what the fellow didn't know surely wouldn't hurt him, John Doyle insisted on returning a share of the sale to the man in good faith. Down at the pub, no one claiming John to be a good businessman would go unchallenged, just as no one insulting his honesty or integrity would complete the statement unscathed.

On Saturday the shop was busy, due strictly to weather. With spring comes a desire to be outside, to reconnect with nature, to feel youthful, to picnic in the park and lay under the sun with a good book grasped in one hand and the fingers of a lover grasping the other. Thirty-six paying customers came through, more than the entire week previous, before the sun and all her youthful vigor were masked by cooling vapors blowing in from the west. Steely skies and impending rainfall chased the townspeople home and the bookshop was relieved of its civic duties for the rest of the afternoon.

By three on the clock, John was convinced his mercantile responsibilities had ceased for the day, so he pulled out the broom and again returned the floor to a presentable state. While he swept, his memory filed through familiar names and faces, searching for an ideal candidate to help him around the shop. The reality of slow business hardly warranted adding an employee to the payroll, despite the fact that there was no payroll, but the active imagination of a constant reader like John made him think that every time he closed the shop early to run an errand or tend to personal matters, he was shutting the door on a multitude of customers who came by while he was out. Two years ago, he'd mounted a box by the entrance with a pad and pencil inside and a note to missed clientele to please write their name and any particulars they were shopping for, but to date the only notes he'd retrieved were ones scrawled in chicken scratch by randy juveniles. One note had simply read, "*vagina.*"

Perhaps it was best, he mused, to hire the son or daughter of a friend. This was the type of job that required youth: a poor wage, a random schedule, and no knowledge of books or business necessary. *Hell*, thought John, *that rather applies to me as well.* The only true requirement was trustworthiness. He could think of few available candidates for the job, so he thrust the idea into his subconscious to contemplate another time.

The following morning, a Sunday, the sun reappeared and John decided to delay opening the shop until noon in order to visit a certain café outside of town. Following the tradition of Sunday mornings, he enjoyed a slow start and strategically hit the road at ten o'clock while most of the town was either rubbing sleep from their eyes or attending mass. Twenty-four minutes later, he parked in front of the café, stepping out into a vast and muddy puddle left over from the rain. Finding no way around it, he bounded through the pool and entered the café, slowing on the footpath long enough to read the name painted over the window: *The Rosie Grace Café*.

Inside, John found a tranquil scene. Two of the eight tables were occupied by patrons attired in their Sunday-go-to-meeting best, post-sermon brunchers come to scarf egg and bacon sandwiches while considering the lessons of the morning's sermon. The owner's daughter leaned on the counter and greeted him with sour eyes that followed his every step to the couch sitting before the fireplace, now cold and dark due to nature's warm embrace. Although John sat with his back to her, he felt the ice of her glower chilling the base of his skull. For several minutes he sat looking at the trinkets adorning the hearth until the young lady's failure to appear with tea as she had before caused him to finally turn and seek her out, finding her still planted behind the counter and, as imagined, gazing her unequivocal hatred straight into him. He averted his eyes to the floor and saw the cause of her expression: a trail of muddy water ran the length of the room, landing directly at his own feet. His head sank and he rose and approached the counter. The only words he could speak were,

"I'll get it."

She broke her damning stare and came around the counter to thrust a mop in his hands, then went back to the register and focused her languid eyes on a worn paperback of

Lady Chatterley's Lover. John was massaging mud into the tentacles of the mop when the owner appeared, looking fresh, the hair circling his bald dome still wet from bath and combed behind the ears. The man's thumbs rested in his belt as he surveyed the room. There he found John bent over the mop, hard at work. His neck snapped from John to his daughter and back again and the grog of morning evaporated, replaced by both appall and bewilderment. He ran to John and kindly pried the handle from his grasp.

"Sir, if ye please, I'll finish that up." His face swelled with embarrassment and he turned to his daughter. "Rosie!"

Rosie slapped her book down and snatched the mop from him with silent sass, then began swabbing the floor with deliberate disregard. The man took John's arm and led him graciously to the couch and made him sit. "Ye're the book man, yah?" he asked.

"The book man, aye," said John, amused by the title. "Pleased to see ye again."

"What can I bring?"

"Tae would be grand."

The man was back with a steeping pot in moments and laid it with a cup on the low table at John's knees. "When ye left here last time, I didn't tink ye'd make it with that lumberin' crate in yer arms. Find anythin' o' worth to ye in that ol' box o' beaters?"

John tried to sound nonchalant. "Oh, a few...a few things in there weren't too bad." He motioned to the empty seat beside him. "Will ye join me?"

As business was slow, the man obliged and sat, introducing himself as Sean Brannon. Their conversation revealed that Sean lived in a flat upstairs, having been left by his third wife several years earlier. "She accused both me piss an' me vinegar o' dryin' up an' she walked out on me, out that very door," explained Sean, pointing to the café entrance. "I would'a chased her down, but I just didn't have it in me. Perhaps she was right. Anyhow. She lives up the road now with a musician who walks the land in constant quest of a job. The irony is *epic*."

After she left, he continued operating the restaurant with Rosie, his daughter, working the counter and his younger daughter, Grace, serving as cook. "Rosie has the personality that Gracie lacks, so I keep her up front. 'Tis best if Gracie stays away from customers…she's a feisty one!"

Then, switching gears, Sean said, "Say, would ye care fer a cigar? I know 'tis early yet, but I've had a hankerin' since last night — I'd be happy if ye joined me."

John wasn't in much of a mood for one, but he accepted in the spirit of camaraderie. Sean stole away and returned with two freshly-clipped Dominicans in his pocket and two brimming teacups in his hands. Although John lacked enthusiasm for an eleven o'clock smoke, it was a very fine tobacco. He drew on it twice and let the smoke roll around his tongue before blowing it toward the ceiling. It caused his throat to dry and he took a sip from the teacup.

The contents of the cup made him sputter and cough and he nearly blew it out his nose. Sean grinned widely. "Me apologies, John, I should'a warned ye what was in there. There's not a cigar in the world that's right without a glass o' whiskey to support it."

John coughed the shock from his system and raised his cup. They toasted each other's health and both swallowed a hearty pull. It was a fine whiskey and complemented the tobacco.

The cigars lasted the better part of an hour and both John and Sean felt the natural inhibitions that accompany adulthood slowly recede. Their conversation covered a wide spectrum of subjects; they began by speaking of Sean's wives and the perplexities of marriage. At one point, Sean offered his biased opinion on the matter.

"What with three separate alimony payments, I consider m'self an authority on the subject, so elect me Taoiseach so I may decree the followin'." He puffed his chest out and lifted his chin and said loudly, as though making a proclamation, "In the interest of all people an' their unalienable right to equality an' to preserve the everlastin' divinity o' love an' happiness, I hereby *ban marriage*." He poked his cigar at John. "An' me words deserve to be heard, fer no one knows marriage better or worse than I!"

They were having a jolly time together and the discussion took many erratic turns. Eventually two more saucers landed, each cradling a refill from Sean's liquor cabinet, and the conversation turned randomly to John and his love of reading. John explained that not only was it his hobby, but his business as well. "Ah," said Sean. "So that box ye found here, did ye want that fer pleasure or profit?"

John took a moment to examine his answer from all sides before delivering it. "A bit o' both."

Sean's whiskey-wet eyes considered him a moment before continuing. "Is that yer passion, then? Sellin' books?"

"I suppose so." John thought about it and added, "'Tis less the sellin' an' more about the books themselves, the tangible mass o' words an' thoughts on paper, ye see? Like every other Jack an' his mum I wanted to write a book, a novel. Buy a cottage on a lake somewhere an' hunker down an' just get it done an' make some sort o' livin' doin' it."

"Ever publish anythin'? Short stories? Poems?"

John took another gulp and rested the cup on his belly. "Nay, nothin'. I never even got 'round to writin' anythin' outside o' sixth year at secondary. Still, I won a few awards at school." He looked at his shoes. "'Twas a ton o' fun. When I was doin' it. How 'bout you? Is this beautiful café yer pride an' passion?"

"Ye might say that, though I didn't open her up 'til I was forty." He, too, looked at his shoes. "Me dream as a lad was to fly aeroplanes." He chuckled at the thought and sneezed as some men will whose sinus is tickled by sentiment.

"Did ye?" John sat up, his interest piqued.

"What? *Fly*? No, but I did serve as chief clerk in a barrister's office fer nineteen years!" Sean's amusement grew from a chuckle to a hearty laugh, as though he'd uttered the most profoundly humorous words since the Lord Mayor lost a wager and publicly professed his love to the Daniel O'Connell statue.

The laughter was infectious and John found himself grinning widely. "What kept ye?"

Sean's case of the giggles began to subside. "Life? Time? Family? What is it that makes any man give up his dream? Our firstborn came an' I went fer a stable job. Never really thought about it, it just happened. Next thing ye know, a few decades pass an' there I was, still treading through shallow water." He paused to open his throat to more whiskey. "I turned forty an' figured 'twas time to get me arse in gear. I walked out o' the office an' put everythin' I had into this beauty." His hand waved over the room and he looked around proudly. "Eight years later an' still goin."

John raised his cup. "Eight years an' still goin'!"

Sean touched his cup to John's and they drank together, swallowing the last of what the china held. John gave a gander around the room and saw the other tables now sat empty. "What time does the luncheon crowd come in?"

Sean checked his pocket watch. "Slow day. 'Tis half twelve now."

John gave a start. "God a'mighty! I must be on me way. I never meant to abandon the shop fer such a time." He rose and pulled several large bills from his pocket. "Before I go, I must tell ye I was able to sell a few o' the books in the box ye gave me, two in particular, an' I should have no problem sellin' one other. 'Tis only right we share in the profits since they were yers to begin with." He offered the bills to Sean.

Whatever doubts Sean had about John ceased to be with that offering. He didn't even look at the money when he said, "No, no. I gave 'em over, which means they're yers to do with what ye will."

"I appreciate that, Sean. But please take it, if only because we both know 'tis right." His words were backed by a sobriety of conscience and Sean knew it was futile to argue, so he accepted the bills, still not bothering to count or even look at them.

They left each other with firm handshakes, John promising to visit again in short time, and when he arrived at the bookshop it was just past one o'clock. On his way in, he checked the box by the door but found it empty of notes. Still, he imagined a great number of customers had arrived to find locked doors decorated with his hand-scrawled sign promising to "be back by 11:00." He was reminded of his need to hire a surrogate for when he was out.

John passed the rest of the day writing letters and telephoning friends, pausing now and then to tend to a smattering of customers. One call was to his newfound mate, Brian Corrigan, to invite him for drinks later in the week. The conversation flowed to the subject of their favorite villains in literature and the call lasted just shy of an hour. When John cradled the receiver, his mind was dancing and he sat to write one of the most creative and humorous correspondences he'd ever composed. He addressed it to a pen pal, a college crush who'd passed him over for a football midfielder so many years ago yet still shared an endearing affection with him. John missed her and wanted to boast his creative edge and his ego was very much satisfied by the time he sealed the envelope and put his charming letter in with the outgoing post.

Much later that evening, after a lackadaisical hour spent halfheartedly reading, he was struck with a brooding case of blue lonesome. Loneliness, like her sisters, grief and melancholy, is purely a product of boredom and arrives while the mind lays idle. She often comes as a dinner guest might — usually in the evening and rarely bothering to stay until morning. Tonight, the simple task of taking out the rubbish sparked in John a memory of a woman he once loved, although, in retrospect, he had not truly loved *her*, merely his own mind's *notion* of her. The lonesome memory then became a longing for the woman who came after her, the cauterizing agent who'd appeared when his wound was deepest, a woman he'd never felt love for, and he had an impulse to call her and speak with her and lay in bed with her. The truth of that fair lady's current situation prevented him from doing so and John assumed that neither she nor her husband would appreciate a call at this hour, so he instead cuddled up with the honesty of a hearty glass of good scotch and this time left out the two squares of ice he usually threw in to weaken its stamina. He played the B-side of his favorite record three times over and sang along with a gorgeous and soulful voice that few had ever heard. By the time his head swam into the bosom of his pillow, he'd lost his care for companionship and was able to sleep unencumbered by the burden of dreams.

$$*\qquad *\qquad *\qquad *$$

Ah, fate! Such a fun and funny notion, a wonderful entertainment created by the mind to help explain certain mysteries that appear from time to time. Those who embrace it tend also to rely on hope and karma to crutch their misconceptions or misperceptions of the unknowable. Although these concepts help maintain a sense of normalcy when all around is mad, they are all simply mythical substitutes for the scientific fact that *timing* is *everything*.

And so it was that timing thrust John Doyle into a life-changing encounter during another slow day at the shop. It was midday and John sat at the till, re-reading Steinbeck's *Cup of Gold* while lunching on a ham and melted cheese sandwich with a side of carrots. When he reached for his tea to help dislodge a bit of carrot stuck behind his deepest molar, he heard a faint whistle and the front door flew open and shut, throwing the bell overhead into a flurry of jingles as a form ran past him and into the back. The blow of the whistle grew in intensity and seconds later another form ran past outside, a black and blue blur that may have been the uniform of a cop. It certainly sounded like a cop, with the Doppler effect bending the tone of the mouth whistle as it distanced. John stood and placed his napkin over the sandwich and followed the fleeing form's path deep into the bowels of his shop.

He found the man with his back to the wall in aisle thirty-two, Architectural Photography. A baggy mackintosh ripped down the seam on the left side hid the man's shape and he wore an oversized pair of women's zebra-striped sunglasses with one lens missing. His lungs huffed and wheezed and John saw that his one exposed eye had the frantic look of a trapped tomcat.

"May I help ye find somethin'?" John asked.

The man was perplexed. His head swiveled, looking this way and that. He was surrounded by books. "What are these? Where am I?"

John found himself speaking to the fellow as he had to his great uncle when the ninety-seven-year-old suffered from dementia. "Ye're in me shop, the Chivalric Nobleman de La Mancha Bookshop," he said, slowly and clearly.

"Ungh?" said the man.

"What did ye tink it was?"

"I thought it was abandoned."

John didn't know how to respond to that.

The man listened for a moment, his good ear tilted to the ceiling, brows moving rapidly with concentration. John listened with him. Neither heard a thing but the breathing of the other. The man tilted his ear another direction, then another. He listened carefully to every corner of his surroundings. When at last he was convinced the silence was genuine, the tension binding his body relaxed and he looked at the shelf before him.

"I fail to see what I'm lookin' fer. Good-day." He squeezed past John and looked left, then right. The labyrinth created by narrow aisles and tall, mahogany shelves confused his sense of direction, but he made a commitment based on his catlike talent to perceive his bearings and turned right.

Wrong.

John poked his head around the corner and said, "Are you Mac Malone?"

Upon hearing his name, Mac showed his heels and ran.

John returned to the front and continued his business with Steinbeck and a ham toastie. Over the course of the next forty minutes or so, he heard intermittent footsteps that ran and stopped and walked and stopped and shuffled and stopped, seemingly emanating from every corner of the shop. At one point a member of his regular clientele stepped in, a lovely student from Trinity College who bought her textbooks here as well as various fictions to fit her fancy. She disappeared down the Fiction W-X aisle and the frantic footsteps surged now from overhead on the second floor. The girl appeared minutes later with a handful of Edith Wharton and asked John to ring them up. As they made friendly chit-chat, the heavy steps above paused before a terrible pounding exploded from directly overhead and shook the bulbs in the ceiling lights. It was as though someone were jumping up and down with great force, caused perhaps by incalculable frustration. They then heard a sound that could best be described as the helpless wail of a man who had reached the very precipice of his own sanity.

"What *is* that?" she asked as she brushed ceiling fan dust from her bangs.

John shrugged his eyebrows and used the receipt to bookmark a worthwhile passage in one of the novels, as he was known to do. "I tink I'll soon find out," he said as he handed the books over with her change and the young lady took her leave with a pleasant farewell that brought cheer to John's day.

It was a solid fifteen minutes more before Mac finally appeared, wearing an expression of shock and defeat. His body slumped from exhaustion and moved like a geriatric snail in wet glue. Both lenses were now missing from his sunglasses. Sweat dripped slowly from the hem of his overcoat and left a trail behind him as his feet scraped the floor and staggered their way to the freedom of the front door.

"As I was sayin' before," John said as Mac reached the door, "are ye Mac Malone? Mac Malone from St. Joseph's?"

Mac stopped, his hand on the door pull. "Never heard of 'im."

John continued, "There's quite a resemblance. Granted, I've not seen the lad since this face o' mine was plagued with pimples, but. Anyhow. Perhaps I'm mistaken."

Mac still did not make his exit, just stood framed by the door, his fingers resting on its handle.

John went on. "This Malone gent was a year or two ahead o' me at St. Joseph's, but we knew each other from the neighborhood an' ran about in the same circles. We were chums fer awhile, got into some trouble together here an' there. He had a unique character to say the least but was a good lad at heart." John grinned at the memory. "Fer a while he had a dog, I tink he called it Snarky or some such. 'Twas the ugliest poodle ye ever laid eyes on."

"Narkissos," Mac said.

"Beg pardon?" said John.

"The poodle's name," Mac turned, "was Narkissos. An' he wasn't ugly, neither. He was a good, kind pup whose appearances would put yers to shame."

"That he was, a good, kind pup!" John came around the counter, grinning. "Do ye remember when we painted the ol' boy blue?"

"I do recall him turnin' blue once, but I'll not remember you bein' present." Mac eyed John suspiciously through his lensless glasses.

"Mac, I'm John. John Doyle. I sat next to ye in Mister O'Sullivan's class after they made ye take the year over again. Back then I had a part in me hair an' a bridge o' freckles over me nose."

Mac stared strangely at John, his memory unstirred.

John continued, "You an' I were the only students O'Sullivan *didn't* make write those book reports over again. If ye recall, we each had to stand in front o' the class an' give a presentation 'bout a book we'd read. Mine was *Notes From Underground* an' yers was, uh, *Jekyll an' Hyde*, if memory serves." Mac's look of befuddlement stood unmoved and John went on. "All the rest o' the reports were so bad, everyone had to start fresh an' write 'em from scratch. But not us. Dostoevsky an' Stevenson pulled us through with high marks!"

Mac made a noise that sounded oddly like an *oink!* and said, "Never read it. I saw the filum an' did me report on that."

"But ye remember?"

"Aye, o' course, 'tis the only time that playin' hooky at the cinema paid off. But I'll not be rememberin' *you*."

"Fine, that's fine. I'm sure it'll come to ye. We spent quite a lot o' time together back then."

"Fine, then. Must be going!" Mac pulled the door open and ran out.

A curious case, that one, John thought, and he took his place at the till. Not a tenth of a minute went by before the bell jingled orgasmically with the rapid opening and closing of the door and a figure fell to its knees and crawled furiously past the aisles of Irish Authors and into aisle six, Psychological Studies. Outside, another blue, whistling blur sped noisily by.

Rather than chase after Mac, John stayed put this time. He called out, "There was a time we had to gather funds fer the class trip to Dingle, d'ye remember? We were eleven, perhaps twelve. They gave us cans to collect money in, enough to cover a weekend excursion. Ye were havin' a bugger of a time makin' the goal. When I finally had a full can, I brought it to school an', wouldn't ye know it, someone made off with it. I always figured it was that bastard Bobby Molloy, but who knows?"

"He was a right bastard!" came a voice from aisle six.

John continued. "We had a substitute teacher, that curmudgeon Smythe. He didn't know any of our characters too well an' sent me to see the Headmaster, sayin' I's the one to steal it. Oh, it got nasty with threats o' Garda an' expulsion. Never mind the coppers, if me mum had found out, I'd have been a corpse with no fair trial. I was convinced I was done fer. But a day or two later a canister full o' bills showed up under Smythe's chair with me own name on it an' everythin' was alright. Only you didn't get to go on the trip due to yer own can gone missin'."

Mac appeared from aisle six, still groveling on his knees and palms. The shop appeared to show no sign of officials enforcing law, but he stayed put nonetheless. "Who the hell wants to go to Dingle, anyhow?"

John walked over and extended his hand, helping Mac awkwardly to his feet, and asked, "How would ye fancy a job?"

"Never!" Mac spat defiantly. "I neither want nor need the tax man to come a-chasin' over somethin' as silly an' senseless as a *job*. Besides, it would knock me unemployment benefit payments completely off kilter!"

"It wouldn't be a full-time job, far from it. I need someone to be available to watch this here shop whenever I run out, maybe twice each week. Ye'd just have to stand by the till there an' ring up any sale that comes through an' make sure the place doesn't burn down. Easy as eatin' cake. What'ye say?"

The answer was growled and spit through Mac's sneer. "It'll be a cold day in Hell when I take a taxable job with no steady schedule nor medical nor dental!"

John thought for a moment. "I can pay cash."

"*FINE!*" roared Mac and he spat in his palm and John spat in his and they shook on it.

A dainty jangle announced another visitor and both men looked to see the young lady from Trinity who'd recently come through. She took a few steps into the shop and offered her palm. Unlike the palms of the men, hers was dry and on it lay a single heavy coin.

"Hello," she said. "Ye gave me too much change."

John's heart folded in on itself, inspired that a woman as lovely and as honest as she existed. He took the coin and smiled devotedly. "Grand, just grand. Ye have a good soul."

She blushed at the compliment and turned to the door. "I'll see ye again fer more Edith Wharton. Cheers!" And she was gone.

From the time the lass entered, Mac had been unable to break his stare from her exquisite form. He was still ogling at the space where she'd stood when John noticed his paralysis.

"Careful, Mac," he warned. "Nothin' good ever came from lust. Ye'd best get her out o' yer mind."

"Although," he added, "I share yer sentiment."

Mac's trance was broken by John's playful slap on the shoulder and he began regaining his senses. "Back in a moment, stick right here," said John, who jogged down the aisle of Fiction S (Cont.) and scanned the spines until he found his target. He returned and placed a large-print, illustrated edition of *The Strange Case of Dr. Jekyll and Mr. Hyde* in Mac's hands.

"A gift," he said.

Mac scowled. "I'll not be readin' yer loathsome book, it hurts me head."

John laughed and said, "That's why ye hold the version with words *an'* pictures. Anyhow, now ye can read what the filum's about." His hand embraced Mac's shoulder and they walked together to the door.

"Drop in from time to time an' I'll let ye know when I need yer services. I'll have appointments planned in advance so's to give proper leeway. An' Mac," he said as Mac stepped through the threshold, "where'd that money come from?"

Mac, accused, sounded concerned and defensive and flustered and unbalanced when he said, "Wha money???"

"The money in the can. The Dingle trip money."

The concern vanished from Mac's expression and he looked at John and cocked an eyebrow behind his white and black oversized zebra-striped frames. He turned and opened *Jekyll and Hyde* to a random page, holding it close to obscure his face, and moved cautiously, attentively, prowlingly down the lane.

CHAPTER FOUR
Settling the Score With a Desire of Yore

Ah, lust!

It's nothing but trouble with a happy finish.

From the time when a man first feels that familiar amorous tickle buried deep within his most unscratchable nethers, all other matters are abruptly forgotten and the rhythm of the second hand begins slowing until the time between a *tick* and a *tock* seems to teeter on eternity. Any unwilling target of his affection would be well-advised to take the high ground, to hide away in the nearest fortified compound until the chemicals causing ill effect on the brain of their admirer settled and waned. No animal exhibits more animalistic behavior than a man in lust and no idea shall be considered, no achievement accomplished, and no sense made until that man reaches his moment of deliverance and turns his attention back to the telly.

This evening, such a man afflicted was Mac Malone. Since his eyes first beheld the goddess in the doorway of the Chivalric Nobleman de La Mancha, an overpowering heat had crozzled his loins to such a degree that madness loomed over what little rationality he possessed. During the course of the evening, his desire swelled like a sustained note swirling from a Hammond organ's Leslie speaker, pulsing and grinding and sending waves of electricity to stimulate even the most remote roots of his nervous system. No creature was safe on the streets of Dublin tonight; the only force protecting the general population from a dynamic buggering was Mac's own deeply buried sense of decency.

Any ears within the vicinity of the Iveagh Gardens certainly heard the moans emanating from behind the garden walls. Although coyotes are not indigenous to Ireland, Mrs. Dee Murphy of Hatch Street Upper was convinced the city had been overrun by packs of them and she insisted her husband prime the shotgun. Mr. Alan Sheridan, a janitor working the evening shift at University College Dublin, was certain the moans he heard reverberated from within the breast of a banshee. And the Widow O'Shaughnessy of Stable Lane sat frozen before her television, a fork of corned beef hovering just outside her gaping mouth, convinced it was her dead bastard of a husband come home to taunt her.

None of these neighbors could surmise that the wretched groans came from a living human, yet it was Mac who sloped and slued and soughed his way aimlessly through the hidden gardens like a zombie in search of fresh flesh. At one point he tripped over the head of old Dribble O'Doole, who slept soundly in a fetal position in the open space of the archery grounds. Mac picked himself up and resumed his ululating ramble as Dribble, undisturbed, dreamt of rowdy mules bucking their way through the garden.

Mac soon found himself on a gravel trail that cut through the center of the park and his ears caught the calming and comforting sound of falling water from somewhere ahead. "Ye Gods!" he shouted to the skies, for what he heard was the perfect tool he needed to numb his urges.

He ran toward the sound, as anxious as a pubescent boy who's just stumbled across an advert for ladies' undergarments, and was soon met by a comforting sight: a small pond, out of which grew a sheer, curving wall of glistening rock. A steady cascade of water fell over its crown to float and whirl and waltz through the air before splashing over the stony foundation below. Without hesitation, Mac jumped into the pond and carefully climbed the slick rocks jutting from the base of the formation. He balanced on the ledge directly under the streaming water and stood within the waterfall to enjoy the greatest cold shower the city had to offer. Mist rising around him gave the appearance of steam as it might mushroom over a seared skillet placed in cool dishwater. The chill forced his frenzied lust to recede deep into his gut and become merely a bothersome feather titillating the dusty recesses of his own amorous cravings.

For twenty minutes, he remained under the pour and soaked his soul. When at last he felt sated, he stepped out from under the falls into the coolness of the night and exclaimed his relief with a loud sigh. His traction-less soles failed to grip the lubricious rock, however, and he slipped down the mossy precipice and bellyflopped into the pond. As he crawled out of the water onto dry land, the gravel of the path made indents that stung his pruned, wet flesh before he was able to stand and feel safe and whole once more.

Having been led blindly by the wolf in wolf's clothing that is the male libido, a profound fatigue overcame him and he ventured back to the archery field and lay dripping near his friend Dribble O'Doole. The earth beneath Mac was soon a shallow pool of mud sucking his body under like quicksand and he rolled over to escape it. He found the soothing warmth of Dribble's body and mirrored the man's fetal form, his knees settling perfectly in the crook of bent legs, his nose nestling into the heat under Dribble's ear. He threw an arm over Dribble's dozing torso for further comfort. As sleep carried him off, Mac's lips pursed and kissed his friend's lobe sweetly, leading Dribble to enjoy the rest of his slumber dreaming of large, buxom mermaids sucking and nibbling and savoring the salty confection of his whiskered neck.

*   *   *   *

Mac is a perpetual dreamer. He routinely rolls and kicks and tumbles his way through each nap as his mind imagines fantastic worlds and visions. If only he woke each morning inspired to jot down or draw the ideas created by his subconscious, he could easily establish a career as a creative force powerful enough to give the likes of Salvador Dalí, Jean Cocteau, and William Faulkner a run for their money.

As he lay drying in the Iveagh Gardens, napping while recovering from a debilitating case of hot pants, his mind swam through a stream of recent memories to create a smorgasbord of wonders fit to intrigue — or perhaps baffle — any student of Freudian psychology. Tonight he dreamed of a house built on the underside of the ocean floor. In it, he lay on a couch of coral and his pet octopus crawled to him and lay eight fuzzy chew toys on his belly, then sat back eagerly on its hind tentacles and waited to fetch. Mac flung the balls away and the octopus caught them all and ate them along with its own arms.

A woman walked into the room, dressed neck-to-ankle in a burlap potato sack. She hummed *Thus Spoke Zarathustra* and her titanic bosoms sounded like timpani as she beat them like drums. Mrs. Quirke had been Mac's schoolteacher when he was a lad of thirteen and she appeared now as she had then: gaping nostrils, one more cavernous than the other, with a single thick eyebrow and a hare-lip exposing a gap between her front teeth that allowed her to whistle deafeningly at sporting events. She never had been much of a looker, but the figure hidden beneath the potato sack was worthy of being the most sought-after body double in all of Hollywood. Or so Mac thought. Mrs. Quirke was always covered in thick fabrics and what lay underneath was seed for the imagination.

He was immediately aroused by her presence. From the moment he first walked into her classroom so many years ago, his urges for her had been strong. The nine months he'd spent in her company were pure agony and he'd done everything he could to get near her. During exams he would go to her desk and lean in to whisper a question just so he could sniff the red curls in her hair, gracing his nose with the odor of patchouli and a hint of bleu cheese. His criminal tendencies were born in her wake and he'd pinched a pencil eraser here, a box of wax pastels there, all with the intent of being caught and made to stay after school with her while he wrote *The hand of a thief will cause me much grief* on the chalkboard one hundred times over. He'd begun a series of naughty flirtations with other girls in class just to see if it drove Mrs. Quirke mad with jealousy. Alas, it did not. Still, every weekday after spending six-and-a-half excruciating hours in the shadow of her sex, he would hasten home to lock the toilet door behind him and spend no more than seven minutes of quality time with himself.

Mrs. Quirke looked at him now in his dream world, her familiar angry eye burning him with masochistic shame. "Ye're late, Mister Malone," she said sternly, and into his hand she thrust a nub of black chalk. "Get to work!"

Mac rose and walked stiffly to the wall and scribbled the phrase *Having lewd thoughts is why I got caught.* Under that, he wrote *I will act most demure and have no thought impure,* then *I confess I have lusted and that's why I got busted.* Soon the wall was covered in rhyming prose. Mrs. Quirke loomed over Mac as he worked and he inhaled the familiar scent of her bargain shampoo and it stirred within him an uprising that threatened a coup over his celibacy.

"Again!" she ordered, but Mac twirled to face her, crouching down on his bending knees.

"I cannot!" he cried. "I must…uh…sit an' rest me crampin' hand!" Keeping his posture bent, he duck-walked to the couch and threw himself on it, huddled in a fetal position.

"Mister Malone, ye try me patience! Back to work or I'll sic the 'puss on ye!" Her octopus appeared from under the harpsichord and wagged its regenerated tentacles hungrily, then sat at the instrument and played *I've Got You Under My Skin*.

Mac was filled with embarrassment and terror. "There'll be no standin' presently fer me, Mrs. Quirke! I promise to do yer bidding in due time, but as long as ye hover over with nostrils flarin' an' sweat makin' that sack cling to yer mighty bosom, I cannot rise from this here position!" He pulled his legs further in and hugged them to his chest.

Mrs. Quirke leaned in and placed her hand on his knee. She drew her head so close to Mac's that her pungent breath warmed his lips and he could hear the air whistling through the gap in her teeth. "Stand up, Mister Malone, an' explain to the class why ye won't stand up," she ordered sultrily.

In typical dreamlike fashion, the house vanished suddenly and Mac found himself seated at his desk in Mrs. Quirke's classroom at St. Joseph's National School. The entire student body was packed in the room, staring at him, hundreds of boys and girls clustered together, waiting to hear his reason for not standing. Mrs. Quirke walked to the front and took hold of a wooden pointer and *THWACKED!* it against her desk. A fearful silence possessed the room.

"Mister Malone," she said calmly. "Why do ye disobey me directions? Up ye go to the blackboard! Write it one hundred thousand times. *NOW.*"

Mac slowly slid from his seat and stood. The room burst into sudden and ferocious laughter and all hands pointed to him. He crept to the chalkboard and was horrified to see his parents, staring and laughing and pointing with the others. He took a stick of chalk from Mrs. Quirke's hand and wrote *I ignore your direction to hide my*

"*BBBRAAAAAAGGGHHECCCHHHH!*"

Consciousness came over Mac like a mallet to the groin. Dawn was just breaking over Dublin and Dribble O'Doole hopped up and down over him, screaming bloody murder. Mac's ears were ringing from Dribble's shriek, but the whine soon subsided and he caught his compatriot in mid-rant:

"An' they says, 'why don'cha sleep here with us tonight, Dribble?' 'I've no desire to impose on ye,' says I, so's I finds this beautiful spot to rest all by me lonesome an' what do I wake to? I wake to find Mac Malone ridin' m'leg like a dog plantin' pups!" Dribble aimed a fist at Mac. "Touch me like that again an' I'll knock yer face clean off yer skull, I will!" Mac prepared to see the old man keel over from a burst vessel, he was so worked up.

"Wha'd I do, Dribble?" He picked crust from his eye and flicked it over the lawn.

"Ye been smackin' yer lips on me arm all night, ye have! An' ye was just tryin' to make fire with me leg! Leave me be, Mac — go wrap yer thrustin' pelvis 'round a female instead o' ol' Dribble O'Doole!" With that, he stomped off, muttering curses all the way to the door in the garden wall.

Mac lay back and promptly forgot about Dribble O'Doole. He was anxious to revive his dream and be back in the company of Mrs. Quirke and perhaps drive the storyline to a more pleasing finale. As he recessed back into slumber and saw her appealing figure once more, the single cloud hovering over Iveagh Gardens let loose and Mac unwillingly received his second cold shower of the night.

*　　　　*　　　　*　　　　*

The textbook example of a man is one who is strong; strong of virtue, of mind, of body, one who has a firm clutch on his emotions and is able to maintain prowess in the shadow of defeat. A man is meant to be immune to everyday perils; he shall fearlessly provide for those he loves, he shall overcome his own demons in order to carry on regardless, and he shall meet death by laughing in its face with his final breath. Since the dawn of the Homo sapiens, strength of body and mind have been man's paramount responsibilities and yet, despite his muscles and prowess and virility, *nothing* is more weak, vulnerable, or pathetic than a man in love.

It was a weak, vulnerable, and pathetic man who scrambled out from the Iveagh Gardens that morning. The yearnings plaguing Mac's masculinity were bearing heavily on him, for they created a dichotomy of conflicting emotions. While his body desired Mrs. Quirke, his mind was lathered in guilt over his love for Sweet Emily Moore.

He had no idea his love for her was so pure until it was challenged by a desire for another. The few times he'd uttered the words professing his feeling to Sweet Emily Moore, he thought they came less out of sincerity and more out of convenience or circumstance. In all his life, Mac had never been in love before, yet he found a strange sensation when he actually spoke the words "I love you" to Sweet Emily Moore. He felt invigorated, motivated, sublimated and spry. It was, by far, the greatest feeling he'd known. If only his lady love reciprocated the sentiment, Mac thought he could be the happiest lad that ever was.

Sadly, she did not. Sweet Emily Moore had never gone out of her way to do something nice for Mac, nor had she ever spoken endearing words to him. The acts that Mac witnessed other loving couples practicing in the streets had never once been exercised on him by Sweet Emily Moore; she'd never taken him to the cinema to play pattyfingers or strolled the shops on Grafton Street to buy him jewelry or rubbed his back while serving him lunch. The way she knocked him about, it was as though she didn't like him at all.

Mac had not felt such conflict since the time he'd wandered upon two fresh beer kegs lying unguarded in a Temple Bar laneway, one a porter, the other a stout. The threat of a returning barkeep allowed him time to pinch just one and he was forced to choose between the two just as he was now forced to choose between a life of monogamy with

Sweet Emily Moore or a life of sin with Mrs. Quirke. (The fact that neither of these could ever be an actual, viable reality never crossed his mind.) Mac was thoroughly despondent. For perhaps the first time in his life, he had no idea what to do.

The one person who had a chance of directing his misguided soul was Lousy the Soothsayer. Lousy was a sage of the streets, a confidante to many and a general giver of advice and wisdom. She was a fortuneteller, a practitioner of voodoo, and a speaker for the dead. She doubled as a fine bookmaker and could talk you out of one wager and into another based on the alignment of the earth with the seventh moon of Jupiter and do it so convincingly that you wouldn't think twice when your first choice won the Grand National and left you with nothing.

Lousy's name was unfortunate, but had forced her to wrangle her wits at an early age. Her parents had youth working against them and were enmeshed in a period of philosophical awakening and a study of the Tao Te Ching when they conceived her. Human tradition dictates that with the passing of each new moon, a pair of hapless parents must curse the life of their child with a ludicrous name, and so it was that Lao Tse O'Hara entered the world, doomed by her own blood. In the schoolyard, of course, it didn't take long for *Lao Tse* to become *Lousy*, a name she was almost happier to put up with, and the cruel mockery of her fellow students forced her to adapt. Her colorful personality formed as a product of her defenses, and every time a group of children jeered and sniggered and pooh-poohed her name, Lousy would sit them down and read the palms of their hands, which placed them, enthralled, directly into hers. Vengeance would come under the guise of fortune, when Lousy bestowed a variety of predictions involving destitution, poverty, calamity, loss, and sickness on each of her adversaries, and it was not uncommon for a child to run screaming to hug the leg of the nearest adult, panic-stricken by the report of what was to come.

Mac knew he would find Lousy the Soothsayer soapboxing somewhere around the General Post Office, so he kicked his soles back and ran. He arrived to find her standing on a crate of bottled minerals at the base of Nelson's Pillar, between the crammed north- and southbound traffic on O'Connell Street Upper, just in front of the bustling GPO. She was dressed colorfully, as always, in a long, loose sari of red and orange and yellow, and the flowing hair that had only been cut once in her lifetime sat perched on her skull, wrapped in a Nefertiti head wrap of green and white and black. Her words rang out over the street and prevailed over the rattling diesels of passing traffic; years of orating in public had given her a robust and commanding voice which she utilized to address a sprinkle of dilly-dalliers and tourists come to mount or climb Lord Nelson.

"I stand before you a lover of all people," her voice projected while maintaining its soothing quality, "a thinker, an observer, a fighter, a participant. I think to benefit all, I observe to absorb, I fight for peace, I participate for posterity. May you consume what I speak now and allow it to echo through your souls, through the deepest recesses of your mind and the chambers of your heart." Here Lousy raised her hand high and bowed her head. "She who ventures in search of accomplishment shall do so with vigor in her heart, or not at all. While riding the crest of life's wave, keep it in your mind to breathe, look, and remember. If you come upon children singing, discard your load so you may join their chorus."

She lowered her arm and drew from her sleeve a handful of small bones belonging to the butch rooster who used to shrewdly wake her neighborhood each morning. With one swift motion, she scattered them on the ground. From her other sleeve she produced a small flask and drank from it, then lit a match and spit half the liquid evenly through the flame, creating a brilliant fireball that engulfed the bones before vanishing in a black vapor. What remained in Lousy's mouth, she swallowed.

The crate creaked as she stepped down to peer at the bones. "A great war shall be fought between many factions," she said, reading the talismans. "Enemies who once were friends shall manifest, just as friends who once were enemies shall align. Of these enemies, a single man shall hold power over a great many. And the people shall follow, and kill, and be killed."

A man in coveralls, smoking a cigarette, scoffed. "But that's already 'appened!" he shouted.

Lousy the Soothsayer stood upright and faced the man, smiling. "We learn nothing from history, nor from our mistakes. The bones have shown it shall happen again. Hiya, Mac!"

Mac stood enthralled by her performance and failed to notice her greeting until he saw her waving and smiling gaily at him. He took that as his cue to step forward past the onlookers and join her in a more intimate fashion. He pulled her to the iron fence surrounding the pillar, away from the hubbub of street activity.

"What does all that jabber *mean*, Lousy?" He spoke in a hushed tone to disguise their conversation from passersby. "I been listenin' to ye fer years an' never once did anythin' sproutin' from that mouth o' yers make a lick o' sense!"

A demeanor of tranquility was so strong with Lousy that it came perilously close to rubbing off on Mac. "The words I speaketh shall have meaning only when she who listens alloweth herself to listen with open ears as well as an open heart." Mac thought her smile was saintly as she spoke. "The words are there. One day your heart will open to receive them. Give me your hand." She took Mac's hand in hers, flipping his palm over to examine. Her smile faded as she concentrated carefully on every line, crease, and imperfection. "Tragedy. Pain. Suffering. It will all find its way to you."

Mac's eyes bulged with incredulity. "Why do ye *tell* me these things, Lousy! I'm not here fer that! If ye must do it, can't ye say somethin' like 'ye'll find a quid in the gutter by lunchtime' or some such? Good *Christ!*"

Lousy the Soothsayer cradled Mac's palm in both her hands and held it against her breast. The smile with power to end wars returned. "Never fear, Mac," she said, her words coddling his unease. "For every action, there must be an equal and opposite reaction. This is certain. Every negative shall be met with beauty, and the beauty shall prosper."

"Fine!" shouted Mac, befuddled. "Thou hast spoken, bla-diddy-bla-bla-bla. What I'm here about has nothin' to do with me. 'Tis a friend's problem, ye see, so's I'm definitely *not* askin' fer advice on the matter. D'ye understand?"

Her smile continued to warm the earth. "Yes, I see, Mac."

"Good. I wouldn't want ye tinkin' I wasn't able to figure things out fer me own self, so there." He inhaled thoughtfully before presenting his dilemma. "What would ye do, Lousy, if ye found yerself suddenly feelin' the binds o' love fer a woman while yer body continued to lust fer other women?"

When Lousy had dropped her comforting hands, Mac had kept his paw planted firmly on her breast, and she now removed it and patted it maternally. "A woman who looketh on a man lustfully hath committed adultery with him already in her heart." She shrugged and crunched her lips against her teeth as if to say, "sorry!"

"Blast it all, woman! Do ye have no encouragin' words fer me at all? Must I be damned so thoroughly?" Mac caught himself. "I mean, must *me friend* be damned so thoroughly?"

"Nay, child. Hear me now. A pure heart belongs only to an honest man."

Mac walked in a circle and flapped his arms in frustration. "Could ye abandon the fancy speak an' fer once talk plain Irish?!"

Lousy stopped Mac by cradling his head in the cup of her hands. "You must seek out each of these lambs. Gather the keeper of your heart together with the possessor of your desire and confront them."

"Ye mean I've got to get 'em both together an' discuss the matter civilized-like?"

"Together as one."

Mac's head rolled to the heavens in exasperation. "Does that mean, 'yes?' Look here, perhaps ye could write it all down on paper so's I can try to make head or tail of it later...."

"Only then shall she of crippled faith discover the path to righteousness."

"Say, who's this 'she' ye keep referrin' to? Ye're scramblin' me brain with all this boo-jwaa talk!"

"She. He. Ye." Lousy pointed both fingers to Mac's chest.

"*AAAAAAAAHHHHHHHTAHELLWITYE!*" he burst, stomping loudly away. A moment later he returned, his hand rummaging down his pants. He withdrew a shriveled five-pound note, still dripping from his waterfall soak, and thrust it into Lousy's mitt. "Leopardstown, second race. Five on Chunky Spunky to win, if ye please."

Lousy the Soothsayer stuffed the bill in her sleeve and winked at Mac. As he ran off, she smiled graciously and waved. "See 'ya around, Mac!"

*　　　　*　　　　*　　　　*

It had turned into a day ripe with spring, a storybook day when writers step outside with pen in hand and make love with words, songwriters sit in the park and seduce with music, and poets hide in their bedrooms and weep alone. There was plenty of hustling and bustling and being merry, people doing anything just to be out of doors, where they could congregate with neighbors and catch up on events from the past winter. Bicyclists outnumbered drivers and young mothers took to the streets to push prams through the neighborhood and gloat over their infants. Children danced, the sick were cured, couples fell in love all over again, and tourists stood on the perimeter to photograph it all.

Mac had a difficult time finding Sweet Emily Moore in the crowd. At this time of day, she could have been working any number of streets. Keeping an eye on the lady was a difficult task, for she was transient in nature and followed her whim rather than stick to a set daily schedule. Still, her popularity meant she never had to venture far from home, so Mac navigated his way to her own turf and carved a path through the pedestrian traffic, keeping his nose to the ground in search of her shoes. Sweet Emily Moore spent a good amount of her working day walking and was known for taking good care of her trotters. She frequently wore crisp white tennis shoes tied tight, replacing them with a new pair as soon as they showed any sign of scuff or wear. She'd developed such a reputation for this quirk that many Dubs began calling a new pair of runners "Sweets." A joke among the lads was that she spent a lot more time off her feet than on them and what was the use in new shoes anyway, but that was really no one's affair but Sweet Emily Moore's.

It was one o'clock, nearly a full three hours since his search began, by the time the sun glinted off her new shoes and into Mac's eyes. He found her on Parnell Street, just off the beaten path but still beaten enough to give her a steady clientele. Mac was so focused and running so quickly that he passed her and ran a further eighth of a mile before he registered the shoes and doubled back. When he caught up with her, he was an exhausted mess and sounded as though he were hacking through an asthma attack.

"Mac! Fancy meetin' you here." Sweet Emily Moore seemed genuinely pleased to see him. "Ye're not cannon-ballin' from the cops again, are ye?"

A flurry of hacks and rasps and gasps came out of Mac, but he waved his finger in the negative.

"Oy. Are ye in a lonesome way, then? Come to share me company?"

Still croaking. He raised his palm flat to the ground and swiveled his wrist from side to side.

"Ah. I'm on the right track." She patted his back aggressively, as though a good burping would help his condition. "There, now, settle yerself," she said. "That's a good lad."

A final tempest of hideous coughs erupted from him until he retched and spat an impressive nugget of thick hair onto the footpath. They both stared in wonder at the hairball before Mac wiped his mouth and turned to face her.

"I love ye," he said matter-of-factly, feeling once again the tingle. This time, he was ready for her reaction and ducked low to avoid her passing fist. He stood back up.

"HOVEVER—!" he barked, throwing his index fingers in front of his face to signal a time out, "I know ye yerself are still comin' to terms with what we got an' I respek that, just as I respek ye takin' the time to let it come over ye real gradual instead o' sudden-like. That's fine with me, lass, I can wait. The problem is, see—" here he paused to consider his words before blurting them, "—I've got a hankerin' lately, as though someone's been a-tuggin' at me innertubes. I suppose ye could say 'tis the male version o' havin' female trouble. Do ye get me?" His eye squinched in hopes that he was making sense.

"Not in the least, ye filthy hooligan! If ye got somethin' to say, spit it out!" She looked down at the puck of hair he'd just spat out. "No, don't. Take a breath to calm yer britches an' tell me what's on that deranged mind o' yers."

A moment passed while Mac gathered courage. Finally, he blurted, "I've cheated on ye."

Sweet Emily Moore stared at him in disbelief, not believing her ears. Her face broke into a mask of seeming agony and she raised her head to the clouds and howled long and hard. Minutes drifted by while her body shuddered with seizures, tears flowing in rivulets down cheeks turning scarlet red. Finally she began to calm and threw her arms around Mac to lean her exhausted weight on him. It was the most satisfying laughter she'd ever had.

"Oh! Oh, Mac, ye dog!" She buried her cramping face in his shoulder and blew her nose in his sleeve. "Ye're makin' me sides hurt! I canna'...I canna' *breathe*...!"

Mac grasped her firmly by the shoulders and gazed sternly at her. "I promise no physicality has occurred between I an' her exceptin' in me dreams. 'Tis just that Lousy the Soothsayer says that since I lusted after her, I already done her good an' proper carnal-like in me heart. Lousy says I must tell ye, so's that's what I'm doin'. I got a burnin' fer Mrs. Quirke as certain as the rash on me bottom, but it'll not be changin' the way I feel about ye, m'love."

"But, Mac," said Sweet Emily Moore as she leisurely walloped his scrag, "ye had that same burnin' in yer belly last week an' look where it got ye! Snagged by Officer-In-Trainin' Bonner with three days in the clink!"

"'Tis different, I tell ye!" said Mac as he leisurely rubbed his sore neck. "The fires'll not be scorchin' me *belly* this time, they're lickin' a bit farther south. I feel as though me manhood's been charred an' toasted!"

"Well, that's fine, then. What do ye want me to do about it? Before ye answer, remember 'tis a lady ye're speakin' to."

"Come with me!" Mac grabbed her hand and turned to run but was pulled back by the anchor of her unrelenting body. She eyed him suspiciously.

"Come with me, *please*," he corrected. "I need ye to meet this woman so's we can all have it out together. As one. That's what Lousy says we gots to do."

Sweet Emily Moore knew there would be no arguing the matter; when Mac was set on something, he stubbornly saw it through. Besides, she knew it would help him and she was inclined toward taking a break to enjoy at least part of this lovely day and he had, after all, given her the gift of a painful and hearty laugh. She said, "I'm no dummy, Mac. I'll get farther humorin' yer peculiarities than I will fightin' 'em. Where we goin'?"

Mac estimated the time and said, "We should arrive just in time, providin' she still holds tenure there." With that, he grabbed Sweet Emily Moore's hand and towed her toward St. Joseph's National School.

*   *   *   *

They stood on the perimeter of the school's main entrance and watched as the last of the stragglers filed out. The boys wore the same uniform Mac had worn when he'd attended: gray slacks, white shirt with navy striped clip-on, a neat navy blazer over it all, everything a maturing boy needs to be stripped of his identity. The girls dressed in the feminine rendition of the boys' costume, yet they appeared much more comfortable than the lads. The last of these students disbanded and a quiet settled over the school as it does over a battlefield after the final weapon has discharged.

Sweet Emily Moore made small talk to kill time. "So, Mac, what'ye been doin' since they let ye out o' the lockup?"

Mac was proud to answer and raised his chin vainly. "I have...*a job*!"

Sweet Emily Moore's laughter exploded from her nostrils and covered Mac's cheek wetly. "Michael Malone, really! Next ye'll be tellin' me they drew yer number in the Sweeps an' made ye a millionaire!" She wiped her lip with her palm as her laughter subsided.

"Anyhow. Shan't be long now," Mac said dismissively. "Provided she's still here, o' course."

He knew Mrs. Quirke was indeed still there when he witnessed her husband arrive and walk into the building. Just as routinely as he had twenty-four years ago, Mr. Quirke still showed up each afternoon to walk his spouse home. The man looked older, yet he seemed somehow larger, which is to say meatier, thicker, stronger. So many years of walking to and from the school five days a week in addition to whatever great weight he was lifting to put such muscle on his arms seemed to be doing the trick. Mr. Quirke, aged roughly sixty-five, somehow resembled Charles Atlas aged twenty-six. Mac recessed into the shade of a towering sessile oak and thought the first of his second thoughts.

Ten minutes passed before she finally emerged from the mouth of the building. Mrs. Quirke seemed to appear in slow motion, the wind blowing through her loose, turquoise hair, a rim of sunlight circling round the back of her head as it would to Grace Kelly in a Hitchcock picture. Had there been a camera present, it would have dollied in slowly to Mac's awed expression and Nelson Riddle's strings would have hit the most sentimental of notes, guaranteed.

Mac saw that she was still as homely as ever, if a bit older, a mite grayer, a wee saggier, and a tad humpier in places. Her body was covered neck-to-ankle with a baggy dress of floral-patterned polyester, yet he imagined the body lying within was just as shapely as it had been when he was a smitten lad of thirteen. The hunch rising slightly over her left shoulder worked with the rest of her specter to reignite the stirrings within Mac and he was suddenly forced to flood his thoughts with visions of nuns and bedpans and cheese mould to prevent his passion from growing. He glanced again at the water wings of muscle circling Mr. Quirke's biceps and

82

receded nonchalantly behind Sweet Emily Moore for protection.

"Now's yer time, Mac," said Sweet Emily Moore with a snigger. "'Tis all come down to this here moment. Go get 'er!"

Mac peered out from under Sweet Emily Moore's armpit and saw that the Quirkes had turned the corner out of the school and were heading away, far, far away into the realm of the out-of-sight and out-of-mind. Mac knew he could not allow this. He closed his eyes to gather the courage needed and breathed a heavy sigh and emerged from the shadow of Sweet Emily Moore to feel the sun swathing his face like a newborn.

"*OY!*" he cried. "*HOLD UP THAR!*" He forced his legs to run toward them and ignored every pulse within his brain to stop and turn and tremble behind his own cowardice.

Mr. and Mrs. Quirke looked back and saw the ogre running at them, saw the untamed violation in his eye, the determination in his step, the camber jutting atop his trident. Mrs. Quirke stepped instinctively behind her husband, clenching his luxuriant arms in her clutch, and held her breath. Mr. Quirke inhaled and thrust out his chest and seemed to swell to a size twice that of his everyday appearance.

Mac stopped just shy of toppling them over and threw his arms behind him like a soaring hawk, leaving himself exposed and unprotected. "Mrs. Quirke! Ye stand before me a luscious, sultry, desirable beauty, albeit covered by the shield o' yer husband's massivity, but I present meself an' demand we shutter our shameful shenanigans! Put an end to this enticin' entanglement! Lock away our lustful lovemakin'! Let us go our separate ways an' henceforth intermix our fluids with one an' only one! Me true love stands with me—" Mac pointed behind him to Sweet Emily More standing quite a distance away, "—an' holds ready to protect me if need be!" Mac dramatically thrust his outstretched arms toward Mrs. Quirke three times as though casting a spell. "I hereby exile ye from me wakin' dreams to behold ye no more!" When he was done, he collapsed on the cold concrete and spasmed as though demons were being exorcised from his body.

Mr. and Mrs. Quirke looked at the body writhing before them, then at each other. "D'ye know this man?" asked Mr. Quirke. Mrs. Quirke shook her head vehemently in the negative.

Mr. Quirke tenderly helped Mac to his feet. He shook Mac's jowls delicately until Mac returned from his altered state and opened his eyes. He cradled Mac until Mac's energy returned and he was able to stand on his own. He then plowed his fist into Mac's midsection and lifted him a full two feet off the ground. Mac crumpled to writhe once more.

Mr. Quirke took his wife by the arm to lead her away, but she resisted. She went to Mac and bent gingerly over his pathetic form and examined his features closely, then looked up to her husband. "I do know this man," she said.

She took Mac's arm in one hand and his shoulder in the other and helped him to his feet. Mac sputtered and coughed and spit another hairball onto the lawn. Mrs. Quirke looked at him with her familiar expression of patience and understanding.

"Yer name is Michael Malone, is it not?" she asked. Mac nodded like a guilty schoolboy caught in a shameful act. "I thought it might be," said Mrs. Quirke, and she smiled her lovely teacher's smile, the one she wore to calm overexcited children, before sending her knuckles flying into his mouth to dislodge his upper right cuspid. He fell writhing to the ground yet again and she stood over him and said, "Ye always were a troubled child."

Mr. Quirke gathered his wife in his arms and led her away. Mac lay on the lawn and looked up at the glorious sun and felt good despite the pain. He wiggled the loosened canine with his tongue and tasted the blood as it trickled from his mouth.

Sweet Emily Moore appeared over him to block out the sun. "Feel better?" she asked. Mac nodded greedily. "C'mon, then, up ye go!"

She helped him to his feet and wrapped her arm around his shoulders to keep him upright. Mac smelled the sweet freshness of her breath and gazed up at her adoringly. "I swears by the spring an' the trees an' the all-seein' eye o' the sun, I love ye," he professed.

This time it was his upper left cuspid that was knocked loose by a flying fist, only now his attacker was courteous enough to sit with him and hold him as he flailed about like an elderly tortoise in the final throes of an unremarkable death. "Here endeth the lesson," she said, shaking her head. She sang to him an ancient lullaby remembered from her childhood and sat to contemplate the mystery that lay placidly, bleeding yet satiated, like an infant in her arms.

CHAPTER FIVE
Reacquaintance

BBBBBBRRRRRRRAAANNNNNGGGGGGGG!!!

The incessant sound of mechanical obscenity sliced through John Doyle's ears and rebounded against every hard surface of his head like a rubberized cannonball, catapulting him from his dream into the disappointing reality of a Tuesday morning. His mind felt like it was drenched in Novocain. Grogginess of this magnitude would render him useless for most of the day, he knew, and he wanted suddenly to be feline, to roll on his back with legs in the air and slip back into the snug parcel of sleep, responsibility be damned.

The clock ceased barking like the Hounds of Hell only after being flung viciously against the wall. Several minutes were lost before John's sense of responsibility urged him to accept his predicament and rise. When he did, he was so muddled by the lobotomy of a premature awakening that he thoughtlessly tossed an unused roll of toilet tissue into the bowl after his morning piddle. Upon realizing the utter lack of sense in this, he fished the roll out with the handle of a plunger and was humiliated in his own company for the rest of the morning.

He began the day as always, by making porridge on the hot plate (*unplug! unplug! unplug!*) and eating at the front desk while his grog evaporated. When his breakfast and morning toilet were finished, he donned a pair of cotton gloves and went to the magnificent mahogany cabinet with glass doors that stood near the till station. A small key freed the casements and John opened them wide to let the books within breathe and to inhale the piquant sweetness of the Chivalric Nobleman's rare books collection.

The case stood nearly full and each volume inside represented the finest of what he offered for sale. Most of the books were old and suffered from various negligible ailments, but together they made an impressive collection. Lying within was the edition of Dickinson's *Poems* he'd found, along with the Three Mountains Press edition of *In Our Time*, Hemingway's second collection of stories. A first printing of Fitzgerald's book of tales called *All the Sad Young Men* was displayed, truly in remarkable condition, as well as a third issue of Jerome K. Jerome's hysterical *Three Men In a Boat* from 1889 and a first printing of its sister, *Three Men On the Bummel*, from 1900. A grin lifted John's cheeks as he recalled the tandem bicycle trip between the husband and wife in *Bummel*, a master stroke of comedic writing. He sat on the floor and pulled random books out to handle and smell and skim and adore. It was one of his very favorite things to do and made him feel as though he were holding court over an intimate circle of friends.

He was eventually forced by the hour to rise and return the cabinet to a secured state. On his way to open the door to business, he stepped on the loose floorboard that always spoke to him, creaking out its pleasure, pain, or indifference, depending on the mood of the shop. John's Grandfather had explained many years ago that the loose board was the voice of the Chivalric Nobleman de La Mancha, that the building had the power of communication and would answer any question if only provoked at that one weak point in the floor. John stepped on it again deliberately and the shop uttered a high squeak.

"A pleasant mornin' to ye as well, me friend," John offered. "May yers be blessed with the brightness o' the day, fer mine has begun clouded by debilitatin' drowsiness."

Steeling himself to meet the day, he raised the blinds and was surprised to find a man waiting outside, looking casually over the building's façade. He opened the door to let the fellow in.

"Top o' the mornin' to ye," John greeted, as brightly as he could in his weary state.

The man entered and gave the shop a once-over. He was dressed well in a wool herringbone jacket and vest with cuffed gabardines. His emerald tie was held in place by an ivory clasp and he wore the most perfectly-groomed beard John had ever noticed. The man carried with him a new leather satchel with polished brass latches.

"Good day to ye, Mister Doyle," he said, tipping his cap. "Name's Devlin, Peter Devlin. We met once briefly 'round this time last year."

"Aye," said John, shaking his hand. "Mister Devlin from Belfast, if I recall. Come in, may I make ye a cup o' tae?"

Devlin came further into the room and looked at the books and shelves and walls and ceiling. Although his gaze rarely focused on John, his conversation seemed undistracted. "No, no, tanks. I won't keep ye." He looked at the fixtures and the crown moulding.

John asked directly, "Are ye here fer books or business, Mister Devlin?"

Devlin ceased his examination of the room and turned his eyes to John. "Business, I'm afraid. Can't say I'm much of a reader, although a good mystery will lull me to sleep some nights. No, what brings me in is this here buildin'. Looks as though it's in need of work, wouldn't ye say?"

"Perhaps. But aren't we all?"

Devlin brought his chin down and smiled humbly. "True, man, true. Since we last met, have ye given any further thought to, ah, makin' the place available fer purchase?"

"About as much thought as I gave it a year ago."

"I see," said Devlin. "Well, much can change in a year, so I wanted to meet with ye again to see if yer thoughts differ at all."

"Can't say they do, beggin' yer pardon, Mister Devlin." A brief pause followed while Devlin continued to smile at John. "No...." said John to fill the space. "But how 'bout you? I see several o' the local buildin's are under new ownership. Is that you? Are we neighbors?"

"Oh, no, no, not at all," Devlin said with a chuckle. "My business is brokerage, is all. However, I am pleased to say I oversaw most of the transactions fer the surroundin' businesses. 'Tis been a busy year fer me in this area, yessir."

"Because I see they all lie unoccupied. Mine seems to be the only business on the lane anymore."

"Quite, it seems that way, hmm? Which is why I wonder if ye'd be willin' to consider a sale, now that ye've had time to flesh out the idea. Such a quiet street, hidden from the flurry on Grafton, it can't be conducive to thriving sales, now, can it?" He sounded officious and John began to loathe him for it. "Mister Doyle, my offer still stands firmly. If ye recall, 'tis a very liberal offer, considerin' the location and condition of this buildin'. Very liberal indeed." Devlin offered a calling card from his vest pocket. "Please take my card an' ring me at yer convenience so we might talk it through. I'm available night an' day."

John accepted the card and pinched its corner apprehensively. "If ye'll pardon me, Mister Devlin, I can tell ye me answer stands." He looked around at the old cast iron till, the countertop, the rickety and aged stool behind it all. "Thing is, this here isn't as much me business as it is, well.... The Chivalric Nobleman de La Mancha, this buildin', as ye call it, has been in me family fer—" his mind quickly ran through the math "—right 'round eighty years. I mean, 'tis where I live. I grew up here, 'tis all I've ever really known. 'Tis me friend, me home. Quite frankly, ye can't put a price

on a home an' ye certainly can't put a price on family. So...."
He offered the card back to Mr. Devlin.

His visitor put up his hands in polite refusal. "Hold on to that, if ye will. No harm can come of it." John buried the card in his pocket and Devlin continued, "Yers is a mighty firm stand to take in this economy, but I respect it. I'll wish ye a fine mornin', Mister Doyle, an' hope to make yer acquaintance again in good time." He tipped his cap and made leave, but only after turning to examine the exterior of the shop once more before heading up the lane.

Devlin's visit upset John, not because he felt intimidated, but because he knew he would consider the offer. The number mentioned during their initial meeting — already a loose figure surely open for negotiation — was generous and he'd certainly thought about it then. Money had never been of much interest to John; he knew it was merely a tool that most people utilize to cater to their own conceit. Still, no man was ever born without some degree of vanity, and John understood the necessities of finance. His only security other than the shop was a small investment account he'd opened as a young man, currently comparable in value to a five-year-old luxury sedan, stripped, in reasonable condition. Between the dividends from that portfolio and the small income provided by the shop, he was able to meet his simple conditions for living, but just. He could not help but roll numbers around his imagination, thinking of what might be, and he suddenly hated himself for being so human.

He was concerned also because he knew Devlin would return. Two appearances in a year could not be misinterpreted as tenacious by any means, but today's second nudge meant the real estate barons, Devlin's clients, were still interested. They were after the entire block, presumably to transform it into something massive and obnoxious and profitable, perhaps even to demolish the existing structures and start anew. Now that most of the block was sold, John knew he would meet Devlin again, and soon.

He headed to the back to fetch a glass of water. On his way, he stepped on the loose board and the Chivalric Nobleman groaned at him. "I know, darlin'," John said solemnly. "I hear ye."

*   *   *   *

The previous day, Mac Malone had poked his head in to inquire whether John needed him to begin his caretaking duties anytime soon. John was anxious to get him accustomed to the shop and show him how it worked, so he planned an excursion for Tuesday afternoon and told Mac to come back then. By the time Mac arrived, he was ten minutes late and only slightly gassy. John had expected worse.

The first order of business was to make Mac more presentable. John had prepared a few articles of his own clothing and laid them out over an armchair in back. He sent Mac to try them on and suggested a scrub in the washroom to start.

Nearly twenty minutes passed before Mac emerged and, when he did, he was the picture of absurdity. John's collared shirt was the best-fitting piece and even that looked ludicrous. John was a full head taller than Mac, mostly in the torso, and his shirt was much too long, which worked to their advantage since Mac's belly was significant and required the additional cloth to cover it. Still, the buttons along his chest were straining to stay anchored and two of them couldn't be fastened at all, leaving a gaping window to the thick down circling his belly. The necktie John had chosen was clamped around Mac's throat like a stretched rubber band and knotted as one might tie a shoelace, fastened so tightly that the flesh under his already bulbous chin bulged, his face appearing blue from strangulation. On top of it all, Mac's naked legs sprouted from under the hem of his shirt like two fat cactuses and came to rest in his own shabby loafers. He held a pair of John's khakis loosely in one hand.

"I cann'a get the trousers on past me knees," he choked.

John trotted to him and tried to free him of the necktie garrote. The knot had been tied with such force that it refused to budge. He went to the counter and came back with a pair of scissors and sheared it free.

Mac's face turned from blue to red as he coughed. "I never did see the use in formal wear," he said.

John rolled the sleeves up on Mac's shirt and ushered him toward the bedroom. "Go put yer own pants back on, an' while ye're there, give a look through the closet. Ye'll find a cardigan hangin'. Bring it out."

Mac returned ere long looking slightly less cattywampus than before. His hair was combed wetly back over his ears and he looked much more comfortable from the waist down in his own ragged pants. The pants wouldn't matter since he'd be sitting behind the counter anyway. John took the cardigan and helped him into it.

"A sweater in springtime? I'll cook!" grumbled Mac.

John fastened the lower buttons and stepped back to evaluate. The cardigan covered the gape in Mac's shirt and made him look dapper to boot. "Ye can push the sleeves up like that," he said as he did it. "That'll help, at least. Ye look much more professional."

Mac was obviously uncomfortable in this new getup but gnashed his teeth and accepted it nonetheless. John led him to the till and walked him through its mechanics. Despite the simplicity of the adding machine, John had to repeat his tutorial three times over before Mac finally nodded his head in understanding. "If anyone wants to trade their second-hand books fer store credit, which is most of 'em," John explained, "tell 'em the buyer is out an'll be back tomorrow. Now. Why not give it a shot? Sell me somethin'."

"I got nothin' to sell!" exclaimed Mac.

"No, I mean pretend I'm buyin' a book. This one here. Ye open the front cover an' there'll be a price marked in pencil. See, right there. Punch that number into the machine an' hit the Total key like I showed ye. Okay. Now suppose I give ye a pound. What do ye give me back in change?"

Mac punched the numbers into the till and hit "Total." "Ye get nine pounds, twenty in return!" he said proudly.

"No, no, something's gone awry. Here, let me show ye again." And he went through it three more times until Mac seemed to catch on. When one of the two customers perusing the shop approached the desk to check out, John felt confident enough to let Mac handle the transaction. With minor coaxing and support, Mac was able to handle each step well enough and gave the right amount of change. As the customer walked out, John whispered to Mac, "Always leave 'em with a word o' farewell."

Mac waved at the exiting customer. "*Scram!*" he shouted. The woman gave him a baffled look, but returned his wave just the same as she left.

John addressed his friend patiently. "Okay. Very good. Ye seem to have the hang o' the till an' got through yer first transaction just fine." He paused. "Aside from 'scram,' what else might ye say to a departin' customer?"

*   *   *   *

Satisfied that Mac could handle business on a slow day, John decided to take his leave of the shop. He had an appointment to meet Brian Corrigan at O'Toole's Pub shortly. Not only was O'Toole's nearby, giving John peace of mind to know he was close to Mac, it was also a pub frequented by his old friend, Tinky O'Shea. John very much wanted to see him again.

It took a moment for his eyes to adjust when he first stepped into the pub. It was a dark room with a long, oak bar by the entrance, a row of snugs hidden behind a thin wall to the right. The bar itself was nicked generously by decades of wear and a magnificent mirror advertising a local whiskey hung between shelves overladen with liquor bottles. The place was congested with men sitting hunched on stools, elbows fastened to the countertop, the elders carrying slightly humped backs as though they'd been leaning over the bar all their lives. Not a hair in the pub was in place, for caps came off at the door and no hand bothered to correct the mess. Men touched the shoulders of their mates as they conversed and there was much slapping of backs and rolling of cigarettes and downing of drinks going on. In any Dublin pub, the entire room will be family within three hours (or five pints, whichever comes first), and it appeared as though most of this room was well beyond that mark already.

William, the man tending bar, saw John and threw him a warm salutation, as did several patrons. John waved and said loudly, "Is it too early fer a pint?" A roar of laughter erupted and hands reached out to touch John's arm in approval. "One Guinness in yer own time, William!" John said, and motioned that he'd be back in a snug.

Once settled at a table in the closest snug, John watched in the reflection of a large mirror as William went through the steps of pouring a Guinness. He tilted the glass and let the heavy liquid fall in halfway, then rested it under the tap to settle. In another minute he continued the pour, bringing the thick, caramel-colored head to rest flush with the lip of the glass. John watched patiently as it settled once more, his trance ultimately broken by a man who crossed through and took a seat at the bar with his back to the snugs. The fellow began speaking brassily to the men around him and, although John could not see his face, the voice was unusually high and clamorous and he knew it belonged to Tinky O'Shea.

"William, the loo needs to be imploded an' rebuilt!" Tinky was lubricated with lager and his words carried over the gibber-jabber of the crowd easily. "There must be a hundred million pints that's passed through livers into that there bowl. Hell, 'tis a national treasure, the O'Toole loo! Ye should charge us fer the pure pleasure of *usin'* it an' *smellin'* it!" The men around Tinky laughed and raised their glasses and drank to his idea.

Another voice, sonorous and booming, cut through the din of the crowd from the opposite end of the bar. "You thar, the twiggish runt who's been sprayin' us with bark an' malarkey fer the past hour! Can ye shut yer trap kindly so's the rest of us can hear voices other than *yers*?"

Quiet settled over the room as the challenge echoed. Tinky did not respond and the voice erupted again. "Ye seem to enjoy attention, why shut up now? Or can't ye stand up fer yerself?"

He couldn't see his face, but John knew Tinky was receding inside himself. He did not handle scrutiny well and was never able to defend himself properly in fights. Even Tinky's friends lay quiet.

Tinky's challenger was obviously in the mood for a broil and wouldn't relent. "Perhaps ye can show me the toilet ye keep flappin' yer lips over an' I can stuff yer head in it, how 'bout that? Ye tink that'd teach ye to keep yer mouth tight?"

At this point, the bodies filling the bar seemed to fidget from the electricity coursing through the air. It was coming to a head, and quickly. John stood and walked to the front.

All eyes focused between Tinky at one end of the bar and a big brute of a man at the other. The man towered over six feet, had a crooked nose from a lifetime of brawling, and was wrapped tightly in a thickness of muscle that fueled his effrontery. As it was still a confrontation between just the two men, no one had bothered to step in just yet, so John approached the beast and stood on tiptoe to whisper in his ear.

"The man ye're speakin' to is a friend o' mine," he said quietly. "I admit he's a bit vexin' at times, especially with a few pints in him, but he's a damn fine fellow with a heart o' gold. Ye should know that."

Goliath stared down at David and shouted, "I should know, too, that ye're an *arsehole!*"

John smiled and turned and walked toward Tinky, who'd seen him and was eyeing him cautiously. The brute called after him, called out to everyone, "In fact, this whole bleedin' *place* is filled with arseholes!"

Oh, what glorious words! What a sumptuous phrase to unleash before a ravenous crowd! That one simple sentence was the spark to ignite the room. Glasses were slammed and jackets were doffed and sleeves were rolled and caps were thrown. The grins of a roomful of men had to be stifled in order to preserve the appearance of grit, yet they all felt the same current flowing through their veins like the strange, sensory connection that often bonds identical twins.

"Take it outside, lads!" shouted William sternly, but before he could finish the final syllable, the first fist flew. No one recalls who threw it or who was near to receive it, but it didn't matter. In an instant, the place was one vast mob of thrashing arms and legs and heads and teeth, all moving as one toward the door, through it, and onto the street. When the front door smacked shut and the mob was brawling safely outdoors, William put down the glass he'd been polishing and peeked over the lip of the bar to survey the damage. A handful of men were left, mostly those too old to tussle, and only two broken glasses littered the floor, along with a single tooth. Pleased, William collected his broom and pan and came around to sweep up the shards.

John seated himself next to Tinky, who'd stayed as well, and placed his elbows on the bar to mirror his friend's.

They both stared ahead at the bottles behind the bar. "Who's mindin' the shop?" asked Tinky, soberly.

"A friend, just fer a short time," said John. "How've ye been carryin' yerself these past weeks?"

Tinky looked at the head on his beer and said, "Oh, fine, fine. All the same." He took a swig, then, "You?"

"All's well." John looked around the place. It was quiet other than the muffled racket coming from outside and an occasional bang or thud that rebounded against the door. "Sure. Everthin's grand." He ordered a draught from William and finally turned to face Tinky. "I'm mighty glad to see ye."

"Glad to see ye as well." Tinky said it without a trace of sentiment and continued to stare ahead at the bottles. "Tell me, have ye seen him this week?"

The old, familiar question. Master Melville come back to haunt him. It broke John's heart to hear and he stuttered before answering, but Tinky beat him to it. "Johnny boy, ye'll not be answerin' that." He finally looked at John and winked. "I'm just pullin' yer leg."

John settled and forced a smile. "Ye always had a devil in yer wit, Tinky. Let's drink to old pals." He raised his glass and Tinky raised his and both men looked at the other as one should when making a toast in earnest.

Tinky said, "What'd ye whisper to the goon?"

"The Neanderthal? Nothin' to upset him. I just stepped forward to be somethin' of a character witness."

"Well, ye started a helluva rouser. Sounds as though they's havin' quite a time."

As if on cue, the front door blew open and one of the brawlers staggered in, collar torn, a trickle of blood rolling from his nostril over the contours of his lip. Through the door closing behind him, John could see a flurry of bodies engaged in a gladiatorial dance. The man smacked the bar with his palm and shouted, "William! Have ye a rag to sop up some o' this blood?"

William dug deep under the washbasin and threw the man his most disposable dishrag, soiled with filth and muck. He also handed the man a fresh stout from a line of beers he'd been pre-pouring. The man's eyes doubled in size and he sloppily downed the pint in four easy gulps. "Ye sure are good to me, William! On the tab, if ye please!" he said, wiping his mouth with the rag as he headed out.

"As always, ye stingy spanner!" William called playfully after him.

John reached in his pocket and placed a small paperback on the bar. Tinky picked it up and looked it over. "What's this?"

"*Whirligigs*. A good one from O. Henry. I recall ye sayin' in the recent past that ye've yet to read him. This here's a fine place to start."

Tinky held the book away from his longsighted eyes and read the cover. "I tank ye, however I got nothin' to pay ye with at the moment…."

John brushed his hand over the bar. "Nay, this here's a gift. O. Henry's one o' the finest writers to come out o' the United States. If ye fancy him, I'll find ye some more."

"Grand!" Tinky thumbed through the pages, then raised the book to his nose and inhaled deeply. "Oh, this here's a fine specimen. Smell that. Must'a been one fine-lookin' lass who made 'er smell so fragrant. Blessed be the books, man, fer they tell a story inside *an'* out."

Once again the door creaked and the sound of the rumble outside grew louder. Both men glanced over to get a peek and John recognized Brian Corrigan in the doorway. A pair of scufflers rebounded against the doorjamb and collapsed against Brian, who shoved them roughly into the pub. Realizing they were back inside, the fellows helped each other up and limped to the bar. William handed each a glass from the waiting line and both men chugged them clean before returning outside, waving their thanks.

"Brian!" John called, and Brian made his way over. The men shook hands like old friends.

"Pardon me showin' up late," said Brian, "but gettin' past that row took some finaglin'. Me Achilles took a thrashin' from some tosser's boot heel!"

John turned to Tinky and said, "Tinky, may I present Brian Corrigan, a fellow lover o' printed page. Brian, this here's Tinky O'Shea, one o' me oldest mates." The gentlemen greeted each other by pumping hands and Brian sat down with them. He said, "John, have ye found a buyer yet fer the Dickinson poems?"

"'Fraid not," said John. "'Tis one o' those things, worth a lot on paper, but the number o' people actually willin' to buy it at this moment are few. I've listed an advert in a monthly collector's magazine, so perhaps I'll be gettin' a call. We'll see."

Tinky spoke up. "Do y'ever consider takin' the valuable ones to auction?"

John shook his head. "Nay, unless I've got somethin' truly remarkable. Auction houses add a twenty percent premium to each lot, 'tis hard to come away with anythin' significant. The best customers are the private collectors, the ones willin' to deal with ye directly." He looked between the two men. "Come to tink of it, I'm sittin' with me two best customers right now. Here's to ye both!" They threw their heads back and each downed a healthy guzzle.

The men conversed for a while, speaking mostly of books but getting to know each other as well. Soon the bar began to fill with the bruisers and rousers coming in from the fight, a rambunctious gaggle of battered, bleeding, grinning men. Together, they made a congregate, jovial mess, punch-drunk and drink-drunk, slapping each other's backs and faces warmly, buying drinks for each other and toasting the good health of one and all. Their communal roar caused John and his friends to seek shelter in one of the more intimate snugs in back, where it was only mildly quieter but much less perilous.

In time, their chat turned from books to more philosophical subjects, as is often the case when alcohol relaxes the brain. "Me mum," John mused, "rest her dear soul, always used to ask if I was happy. I never knew what to tell her. The unanswerable question, right?" He palmed a fistful of peanuts from a dish and tossed one in his mouth. "How would ye's answer that one?"

"Christ," Tinky said. "I never know how to respond to that."

Brian followed John's lead and scooped a few peanuts. "I dunno. I'd say I'm a happy man. Why brood? Why worry? There's no use in any o' that. Why not be happy?"

John nodded. "I always thought it came down to wants versus haves. We always want what we've not got, wouldn't ye agree?"

"Sure!" said Tinky.

"I suppose so," said Brian.

"So what leads to happiness? Brian, what do ye tink?"

Brian shook his head. "Ye're askin' the wrong man. I can't tell ye how, but I would say I'm happy."

Tinky looked to John and said, "Yer theory on wants an' haves is credible. What if happiness comes with havin' what ye want?"

John said, "Perhaps the only truly happy man is he who can say 'I have what I want' as well as 'I want what I have.' Maybe *that's* the gauge, hmmm?"

Brian shrugged. "Oh...I, ahhh...I believe 'tis really a lot simpler even than that. I mean, either ye are or ye're not. I'll not be tinkin' there's levels o' happiness or anythin' o' that sort. An' havin' an' wantin'...every man wants *somethin'*, wouldn't ye agree?"

"Hmmm...." said John. He wasn't making his point well. "All I'm sure of is what I want at this moment, an' that's to get this naggin' pressure off me bladder." He stood. "Gennamen, I shall return!" He excused himself to brave both the crowd and the toilet.

Tinky kept the conversation going. "Tell me, Brian, how did ye come to know our good man John?"

"Met 'im recently at an estate auction," Brian explained. "'Tis hard not to admire the man from the get-go."

"Aye," said Tinky. "Well said."

"I bought from him an extraordinary first run o' *Moby Dick*. Ever seen one o' those?"

Tinky was silent for a moment as he eyed Brian. "I have. Once."

"'Tis a beautiful beast of a book, that one. One o' the prizes o' me collection."

Tinky said, "Must'a paid a handsome price fer such treasure."

Brian chuckled. "Not as much as ye'd tink. A dealer in New York has already offered me a good deal more." He looked over his shoulder. "Ye can't tell John, though. I'll not be havin' the man cursin' himself fer what might'a been."

"Right," said Tinky. Although it was just one word, it was formed of ice.

"How 'bout you?" Brian asked. "How d'ye know him?"

"Grew up with him, I did. We've been chums since damn near Day One." Tinky's eye contact never faltered, nor did his voice ever soften. "I an' he have been through a lot, but there's nothin' I would'na do fer him."

"That's grand," said Brian. "Here he is now."

John returned but remained standing. "'Tis ages since I'd been in there, but I'm reminded of the truth in yer words, Tinky, when ye described the water closet earlier. A worse misery is unlikely to be found on this here Earth. Now, I'm afraid I need to be makin' me way back to the shop before closin' time. Got a new hand watchin' the place an' I'm not sure how I feel about him just yet."

Brian and Tinky rose and rustled through their pockets for bills. "Let's settle up the tab, then," said Brian.

John put up his hand. "That's all taken care of."

Tinky and Brian exchanged glances. "Oh...," said Brian. "That's very kind o' ye."

Tinky nodded. "Very kind indeed."

They pushed and tore and snaked their way to the door through the mob surrounding the bar. By now the battered whole of them were roaring through a verse of *Star of the County Down*, each man showering spittle by the many plosives in the lyric *"from Bantry Bay an' the Derry Quay an' from Galway to Dublintown."* The escaping trio were nearly out the door when the meaty brute who'd challenged Tinky pulled alongside and grabbed him roughly, patting Tinky's cheek gingerly. "What a lad!" he cried. "What a good lad ye are! An' with a true, good friend at yer side!" He slapped John's shoulder, nearly toppling him over. "Wish I had a friend as good an' true as he!" They popped through the exit and John looked back at the gorilla waving from the doorway and was certain he saw dewy sentiment glistening in the man's eye.

*   *   *   *

The men parted in the street and a short walk had John back to the Chivalric Nobleman by half four. He opened the door to the welcoming chime of the bell and, to his surprise, found Mac sound asleep on the front counter. Not merely *sitting* asleep at the counter, but *lying* atop the platform, arms and legs splayed over the sides like a corpse that's just fallen from the heavens and landed awkwardly by the till of a second-hand bookshop. A resounding thunder escaped the depths of his nasal cavity, a snore so piercing it vibrated the bell over John's head.

In addition, a jar of peanut butter lay broken in the middle of the floor and a pack of six stray dogs stood slurping the paste from the floorboards and from the roofs of their mouths. No other soul appeared to be inside.

John clapped his hands loudly, disturbing the dogs from their feast. He shooed them out one by one, going back several times to catch a few of the mongrels who wandered back in. When they were all safely out, he left them licking their chops at the window, wet noses smearing the glass. One hound began howling and soon the others joined in chorus.

John was then faced with the daunting task of waking Mac. He shook him gently and spoke his name, then shook him harder and spoke his name louder. He clapped his hands, then clapped his hands harder. Mac never so much as twitched. Finally, John took from the Reference shelf a slipcased edition of *The Shorter Oxford English Dictionary, Third Edition* and brought all two thousand, four hundred and ninety-four pages barreling down onto the counter by Mac's head. It sounded like he'd fired a bazooka.

Mac squawked and his lids opened slowly. "Hrrrrmmmm," he said.

"C'mon, Mac! Rise an' meet the day!" John shouted. Mac rolled his back to John and crashed to the floor.

"Hrrrrmmmm," he repeated from four feet below.

Eventually, John was able to hoist Mac up and get him moving. While Mac changed back into his own clothes, John set about cleaning up the peanut butter, which mystified him because he didn't recall owning a jar of peanut butter. Mac appeared from the back dressed as his old self and ruffled the hair over his temples loose from its naturally oiled hold.

"Did ye ring up any sales?" John inquired.

"Two," Mac replied, scratching his thigh and yawning. "Small stuff."

John opened his wallet and removed several bills and handed them to Mac. "Tanks fer comin' in, Mac. If we do this again, though, I'll have to talk with ye about nappin' on the job. An' bringin' dogs into the place."

Mac's eyes were foggy. "Dogs?"

"Never mind." John saw Mac to the door and was relieved to find the dogs had dispersed. "G'night, Mac. Hope to see ye again soon."

On his way out, Mac asked, "How'd I do?"

John laughed quietly to himself and sighed. "Let me put it this way — ye've got room fer improvement."

Mac seemed strangely satisfied by this response. He thrust his chest out proudly and left his first day on the job at the Chivalric Nobleman de La Mancha as a man in tune with the music of his own inner harmony.

CHAPTER SIX
King Michael's Feast

Mac took great pride in spreading word of his new job amongst his fellow street dwellers. Despite the fact that he'd only been employed there for roughly two hours, he spoke as though he were the President and CEO of the Chivalric Nobleman de La Mancha Bookshop. He referred to the shop as the Chives and Nutty Munchies Bar and Grille and seemed to be under the impression that it was a restaurant; he lacked any sort of grasp of what John did there. None of his friends had ever heard of the Chives and Nutty Munchies, which lent credence to their unified assumption that Mac was once again boasting about something beyond the realm of truth. Still, the majority of people he told acted like they were happy for him and he received many congratulations to his face while many eyeballs rolled behind his back. The few who challenged him to provide proof of this job were met by a diatribe so scathingly counteroffensive and seemingly rehearsed that none felt obligated to ever second-guess the honesty of Mac Malone again while in his company.

Encouraged by the attention he'd received over the job, Mac made it a point to poke his head in the shop every morning to inquire whether John needed help that day. As yet the answer had always been a polite "no," however John always invited him in for tea and a chat. On the third straight morning of poking his head in, Mac found John at the front speaking with another man. John waved Mac in and introduced him to Tinky O'Shea.

"What a coincidence," said John. "Tinky an' I were just speakin' o' ye. We were all in school together 'round the same time, but Tinky doesn't seem to know ye."

Mac studied Tinky closely. "I've never met this man. Unless ye're Danny Denny. Sure, sure, that's you. Ol' Danny. 'Course, ye're much shorter now."

John said, "Ah, sorry, Tinky's name isn't Danny, 'tis—"

"Ye opened that bollix café years back," Mac interrupted. "Had the worst rump steak I ever pulled from a rubbish bin—"

He was silenced by John's gentle hand on his shoulder. "Mac," said John, "allow me to *re-introduce* ye to me friend, Tinky O'Shea. Any resemblance to Danny Denny is entirely coincidental."

The men nodded in greeting and stood awkwardly quiet as John excused himself to make tea. The water was heated already and he wasn't gone but a moment, thankfully. Tinky and Mac were still standing silently when he returned, examining the space above each other's heads as people do while riding in elevators with strangers. John presented them each with a teacup.

"Mac, I've been wonderin'," said John, "where is it ye live exactly?"

"Over the Olympia," Mac said.

"Over by the theatre?" John asked.

"Over it, yah."

Tinky finally spoke up. "Are ye north or south o' Dame Street? There was a time I lived in a flat by the castle."

"The Olympia's on Dame. I live on it."

"What, ye mean ye live *on top* of it?"

"Aye, under the *larger* o' the two exhaust vents," Mac gloated. "Moved in last year after they kicked me out o' me basement flat in the National Library."

"Why'd they kick ye out?" asked John.

"They found out I was livin' there."

John smiled, then spoke with compassion softening his voice. "I could give ye a place here, Mac. I've got two floors unoccupied, ye'd have as much space as needed, free o' charge. All ye'd have to do is mind the shop now an' again. What's say?"

Mac's reaction was not what John had expected. "An' live like a transient? Never! I couldn't possibly."

Tinky could not grasp the sense in this and said, incredulously, "Do ye not fancy a shelter over yer head? What'ye do when it rains? Or snows? This dear man has just offered ye a *home*!"

Mac could not grasp the sense in this and said, incredulously, "I've got a home already!"

"Ye've got a *hovel* maybe, but a home? Hardly!" Tinky was getting visibly upset.

Mac became more gruff and took a step toward Tinky. "I'd lay good money 'tis a sight better than what *ye've* got!"

John clutched Tinky's arm and squeezed gingerly as he addressed Mac. "We did not mean to suggest ye have no home. Livin' rough is obviously a perspective that eludes us. Just know I've got shelter here if ever in need."

Mac thought for a moment. When he did speak, it was quick and loud as though he were overcome suddenly by a very good idea. "I'll show ye, both o' ye! We'll meet here tonight an' ye can follow me to the feast."

"The feast," Tinky repeated, failing to understand.

"Supper!" Mac shouted. "Tonight we dine at my place. Nine o'clock *sharp*!"

*   *   *   *

When the clock struck ten and there was still no sign of Mac, Tinky was ready to head home. They'd been waiting together since half eight and Tinky still wasn't sold on the idea of what awaited them, especially at so late an hour. John talked him into staying just fifteen minutes more, explaining Mac's ineptitude for punctuality. Tinky reluctantly agreed, somewhat intrigued by what they might find, and ten minutes later Mac trudged in.

The first thing Mac did was to look John over with a disapproving shake of his head. "Aye, no. This won't do." He snapped his fingers and said, "Join me at the closet!" He ran to John's bedroom and both men followed.

Mac pulled the closet doors and rummaged through, paying no mind to the shirts hanging in the center, instead going straight for the seldom-used extremities. He filed rapidly through each garment, muttering all the way. "No. No. No. Hell no. Nay, no, nay, no, nay." As nothing in the closet satisfied him, he turned to John. "Where's the rest of it?"

John pointed to a dresser in the corner and Mac went straight for the bottom drawer. Inside, he found perfection, two piles of worn shirts and grubby pants. He pulled the shirts out and shook them free of their folds, discarding them on the floor until he found one to his liking, a flannel button-down, faded and moth-bitten. He tossed it to John.

"That shirt's twenty years old!" John protested.

"Perfec!" said Mac. "On it goes. An' these." He threw over a pair of denim jeans, ripped wide at the knees and vibrantly decorated with splatters of paint.

While John adjourned inside the washroom to change, Tinky stood expectantly. "What about I?"

Mac looked him over with his most judicial eye. "Ye look fine, ye'll fit right in."

John returned momentarily and spun around in his new old clothes. "What'ye tink?"

Mac held his chin and gave him a critical once-over. The shirt was definitely out of fashion and a bit ill-fitting to boot. Mac pumped his head in approval. "It'll do. The shoe is a nice touch. I fancy how the sole flaps when ye walk." John hadn't been aware of this and craned his neck to get a look as Mac plowed past them toward the front door.

"Follow me, then!"

The boys had to hasten their steps to keep up. Mac led them hurriedly out of the shop and down the lane to Grafton Street and turned right, taking them along the quiet promenade and darkened storefronts, on past the perimeter of Trinity College and across College Green to hang left at the Bank of Ireland. Just past the bank, Mac veered right and disappeared between two rows of maple trees whose burgeoning limbs sealed the cobblestone lane underneath from all sources of light. John and Tinky hesitated before entering the blackness, straining their eyes to see what lay within. They saw nothing, but Mac's voice echoed all around them.

"In here!"

John took the first slow steps into the murkiness as Tinky clutched his arm and stumbled blindly behind. Though their nostrils were soured by the stench of urine, their ears were soothed by a constant undertone, like many pigeons cooing. As their irises dilated, they began to make out a light at the end of the lane.

"Where in God's hell *are* ye?" Mac's words found them, but he remained unseen. The men continued toward the glow and managed to make their way to the last of the shady trees. Here, at the end of the footpath, they stopped and gawked at the breathtaking scene before them.

"*OY!*"

Mac appeared suddenly behind them and Tinky, startled, squawked like he'd just been goosed. "What'd ye fellas do, stop fer a game o' tiddlywinks?"

Mac noticed their awe-struck faces and allowed them time to absorb the sight. "Here 'tis," he said. "Behold — the weekly feast!"

The trio stood at the edge of Foster Place, a cul-de-sac of bright marbled architecture that appeared to glow in the moonlight. The structures surrounding the square gave it an enclosed feeling, as though it were a set built inside a soundstage at Pinewood Studios. Several rusted burn barrels lay scattered about, each emitting a warm orange candescence that licked the air and splashed the towering walls. The cooing pigeons they'd heard turned out to be just that, bolstered by the murmurs of many conversing voices. There were perhaps eighty shabbily-attired men and women standing, sitting, leaning, and lying in groups across the square, making conversation as though at a cocktail party in the posh Sandymount district. One group under the Bank of Ireland arch erupted in a tremendous fit of laughter and everyone else paused their patter to watch the gaiety. Another group was gathered around a fire drum, harmonizing on a rollicking, a cappella rendition of *The Newry Highwayman*. Still another group clapped a beat and roared their approval while an old man danced in the center of their circle, his single tooth sparkling in the firelight through a sizable grin. The overall picture was enchanting and everyone appeared to be having a hell of a time.

John and Tinky were entranced. John leaned in to Mac and asked, "Do ye know them all?"

"Ever one of 'em, man, woman, an' child. Although I doubt there's any children here." He gazed over the scene and spread his arms before them. "These people love me, they do. If we was to hold open, democratic-like elections, why, they'd pick me Grand High Priest of 'em all." He raised his arms higher and brought his voice to its fullest and shouted into the crowd, "*MY PEOPLE! I HAVE RETURNED!*"

The music stopped, the laughter ceased, and the voices hushed as all eyes turned to Mac and stared.

"Hi, Mac," a small voice said from somewhere. The eyes turned away and the acts of merrymaking resumed.

"Right!" Mac growled, and he led them into the crowd. As they made their way through, John and Tinky found many welcoming smiles. Strangers stepped forward to greet them and introduce themselves; everyone wanted to know about them and learn their names. It took ten minutes to walk to a stack of crates in back, where Mac sat and motioned for his guests to do the same.

"Tell us about 'em," John spurred, still amazed at the sight.

Mac pointed to a middle-aged woman pushing a wheelbarrow through the group. Lying sprawled inside was a middle-aged man, singing drunkenly and off-key, his arms waving through the air to mark time. He was so swacked, soused, and sozzled, they could practically see a mirage of heat waving over him.

"That thar is Old Mother Fodder. Delightful woman, she is, provided ye fancy the strong, silent, muscular type o' female. Spends her day pushin' her husband thar, Old Father Fodder. She pushes him to the pub in the mornin' an' when he comes out at night, he's as pickled as a pepper an' she pushes him home. I swears on me boots he talks every wakin' hour 'bout what a kind an' good an' lovin' woman he's got. The only time he shuts up is when he's passed out!"

A very short man with red hair and the sort of round face common to Irishmen approached and stood smiling before them, his hand outstretched to shake each of their mitts. "Guten Abend, meine Freunde!" he said in perfect German. "Willkommen zum Fest!"

The three men smiled in return and shook his hand as Mac explained, "Fellers, meet Archie Farchy, born an' raised right here in Dublin. Never been outside the city, not even as close as Wicklow. A few years ago, the poor lad was crossin' the street an' along comes a taxi an' *WHAM!*" He smacked his hands together to illustrate the violence. "He was un-conscious fer about a minute an' when he came to spoke nothin' but German."

Tinky stared at Archie and said, "But surely he must've learned the language in school. Or fer his trade or somethin'?"

Archie shook his head sadly. "Nein, nein. Nicht ein Wort."

Mac went on. "He can understand Irish just as always, but the only language that makes it past his lips is Kraut Monkey."

Archie pursed his lips and frowned at Mac over the epithet. "Du Schwein!"

"Well," said John to Archie, "I trust ye're still able to get yer point across."

"Ja," said Archie, "es ist aber wirklich nicht leicht." He slapped Mac on the shoulder and waved before walking off. "Wir sehen uns jungs!"

"Yawp, see ye 'round, Archie," Mac replied.

Tinky sat up as though just struck with an idea. "But Mac," he said, "ye keep calling it a feast. Where's the food?"

"Should be comin' any minute now," said Mac. "Five people is chosen to rummage fer the grub — they gather what they can an' bring it back an' we all eat here. Thing is, we gots to wait until the local eateries is done servin' an' throw out the remnants. So it takes a while."

Tinky looked mortified. "We're to eat food picked out o' *rubbish bins*?"

"Only bins o' the finest establishments, mind ye," Mac replied valiantly.

"How often do ye yerself get chosen to rummage?" asked John.

"Me?" Mac scoffed. "I got a crummy back. Made sure everyone knows it so's they'll not pick me."

"An' they still let's ye eat every week?" wondered Tinky.

"O' course! I'm *adored* here, ye silly man! Me *people*, remember? An' ye want me to move in under a roof right an' proper an' leave this? Never!"

Tinky began to protest, but John grasped his arm and stopped him. "The man is set in his ways," he whispered.

A distinguished-looking gentleman with thinning white hair wearing a frayed country club blazer sat beside Tinky. He pulled a harmonica from his pocket and began to play a ditty, looking at them with eyes sparkling, seemingly for encouragement.

Mac leaned over John and Tinky to address the gentleman. "Ye see, Georgie," he said, annoyed, "the thing 'bout people who play the harmonica is that *nobody* fancies a harmonica player, since precious few harmonica players can actually *play* the harmonica!"

Georgie stopped and pocketed the instrument. He smiled and shook Tinky's hand, then extended his hand to John and said, "I offered my hand in friendship and the young man welcomed it in his. 'Pleased to know ye,' says I. 'The name's Georgie O'Brien an' I'll hope ye let me know if there's anythin' I can do to make ye feel more at home.'"

John accepted Georgie's handshake while trying to decipher his gibberish. "I'm John."

"He said," Georgie interjected.

John looked to Mac for help, but Mac offered nothing. John returned his eyes to Georgie. "Pleased to meet ye."

Georgie's eyes sparkled again through the cracked glasses on his nose. "My eyes smiled at John and I turned my attention to the preparation of an adequate meal for our guests. 'Fare thee well,' says I as I made my exit. 'Give us a shout any time!' I then stood and disappeared into the crowd." And he did.

John watched him go, baffled. Mac leaned in and explained, "Ol' Georgie was a professor at Trinity before the marbles rolled out his head. The man's been writin' his memoir fer right 'round thirty years now. Eventually, he quit writin' it an' just started speakin' it. Saves him a lot o' time, apparently."

Tinky and John could only nod together in wonder. "Ah!" said Mac. "Supper's here!"

From out of the tree-lined darkness, a woman pushing a wheelbarrow emerged. It was not Old Mother Fodder pushing her husband, either, but rather appeared to be Lousy the Soothsayer carting a full load of what could best be described as *slop*. She maneuvered the wheelbarrow carefully to avoid spillage, for the mound was piled as high as it could be without tumbling over the sides. Georgie O'Brien guided her to an immense tarp that lay over the cobblestones and they proceeded to delicately dump the food onto it. A man emerged from the shadows, also pushing a wheelbarrow piled high, and joined them at the tarp.

"Fascinatin'!" John said. "How long have they been out collectin'?"

"Oh, right near two hours, I expec'," Mac answered. "It'll be a while longer 'til the others make it back with their loads. I wish the scoundrels would hurry their arses, I'm famished! But the forefathers — damn their spirits! — established that no one eats 'til the entire feast has arrived." He spat on the street as if it were the hallowed ground entombing his inconsiderate forefathers.

"'Allo! 'Allo, one an' all!" A tall man in a long overcoat stood in the center of the square and projected his authoritative baritone over the crowd. "Listen up, if ye please!"

Mac whispered, "Thar's our town crier. Announcements comin' up."

All conversations either stopped or settled while attention turned to the man. "Good evenin' to all!" called the Crier. "An' welcome to this glorious night's gatherin'. The air is clean an' cool an' the full moon shines over like our almighty protector! 'Tis indeed a grand time to be livin' as one with nature!" A supportive cheer went round and he continued. "We have a lovely settin' here at Foster Place, where ye'll be sure to enjoy a feast o' flavors quite unknown to anyone outside our community. If only the PM an' his council knew the kind o' succulent banquet we make fer ourselves here, why, they'd be joinin' us with cup an' plate every week!" A round of applause resounded and everyone whooped their agreement. "We'd be the talk o' the town an' pretty soon would have to start makin' *reservations*!" A round of laughter and jovial *BOOOO*s erupted and spurred a minor pause for comment. When it settled, the Crier again held court, this time with a somber voice. "I bear with me sad news tonight, brothers an' sisters. As some o' ye know, our friend Padraig Fagan passed away last Wednesday. He was a good man and'll be sorely missed. Many o' ye's were here to enjoy Padraig's final meal with him an' I'm sure he left us a happy man. We'll consume tonight's feast in his honor an' later on, when we crack the kegs, we'll certainly raise a toast to his fine spirit." A round of *aye*s and *here-here*s and *good ol' Padraig!*s coursed through the crowd. "But on a pleasant note," shouted the Crier, "we have in our comp'ny tonight two guests! I've seen many o' ye greetin' 'em, but I wonder if we could call upon 'em to introduce themselves proper!" He motioned to John and Tinky and all eyes settled on them. An encouraging round of applause spread and the Crier waved for them to join him in the center.

Mac leaned in to the pair. "All guests go through this. Just tell 'em yer name."

John rose and Tinky followed. Mac whispered after them, as an afterthought. "An' ye'll be called upon to entertain as well."

"*What?*" Tinky whisper-shouted in horror, but it was too late to turn back, they were already on their way through the clapping masses, headed for the tall man at the center of everyone's attention. The Crier threw his arms over their shoulders and hugged the pair to him. His voice was piercing at such close range and both John and Tinky had to turn their heads away when he spoke. "Won't ye please tell us yer names, gentlemen?"

John spoke first. "I'm John Doyle. Tanks much fer lettin' us join ye." He gave a small, embarrassed wave and polite applause greeted him.

Tinky stood crookedly, visibly nervous, and stared with eyes wide at the masses staring back at him. John nodded to him and whispered, "Tell 'em yer name, laddie!"

"Tinky O'Shea!" Tinky O'Shea blurted, his cheeks blushing madly as a round of courtesy applause welcomed him. He stepped over to John and stood with him for security.

"John an' Tinky," the Crier addressed them with his booming orator's voice so all could hear. "As every member of our community has a task to perform at the weekly feast, we ask that any guest who joins us be responsible fer entertainment! So give us all ye got, men, an' let the show begin!" The crowd encouraged them with applause and the tall man retreated to the sidelines, leaving John and Tinky standing exposed before eighty strangers. If they'd appeared uneasy when first called up, they now looked absolutely, undoubtedly, *quite* not easy.

Several seconds passed as the crowd looked upon them expectantly while John and Tinky looked back at them nervously. John's mind raced as he thought of what to do. From the crowd came shouts of encouragement.

"Tell us a joke!" they cried.

"Sing us a song!" they shouted.

"Take off yer clothes!" one woman invited, and they all laughed.

John looked to Tinky and found him frozen, the poor man's terror-stricken eyes pleading with him for help.

A particularly tall and gruff and boulder-like man with a thick beard and a sailor's cap stepped forward and shouted, "C'mon, you! No one eats without providin' *somethin'*!"

"Now, now, Mister McKay!" called the Crier in his speech-giver's voice. "Let's not intimidate! Remember, they are our guests!"

"Yeah, shut up, Murky!" came an anonymous shout from the crowd.

Murky McKay flushed with anger and pushed his sleeves up. "Who's that? Who said that? Show yer cowardly face!"

"Please, Murky," said the Crier. "Let it go. Let's all have us a fine time tonight, eh?" He turned to John and Tinky. "Every man has a talent. What's yers? Tinky?"

Tinky's mouth opened, but nothing came out. He appeared to be in the midst of a debilitating case of stage fright. John racked his brain for something, anything, and suddenly his memory swarmed with recollections of afternoons they'd shared on the playground.

"Tinky!" he called. "Remember back in school, the limericks?"

Tinky stared at his friend as though he'd just stepped from an alien spacecraft. Then a glimmer of recognition sparked in his eye and he began nodding slowly. "Sure. Sure. The limericks. Sure. The limericks?" he said with un-certainty.

"The limericks!" John encouraged.

Now the memory was fully with Tinky and his eyes flushed with life once again. "Sure! Let's have at it, Johnny!"

John turned to the crowd. "Master Tinky O'Shea here shall lead us all in a challenge! He'll recite to us a limerick to be made up right now, on this very spot, an' he welcomes all challengers to join in. Nothin' pre-written, now! 'Tis all got to be done impromptu an' spur-o'-the-moment. So get yer tinkin' caps on an' have at it! Mister McKay," he called to the boulder-like man, "Murky. Will ye play judge fer us?"

Murky stepped forward, grinning devilishly, and said, "Oh, this'll be a right good beatin'! Let's give it a go! Look thar, the final barrow's just been wheeled in, so give yer brains a lash o' the crop an' hurry it up! Me belly's quakin' with hunger!"

The Crier said, "It'll just be a few minutes more while the preparers tidy up the feast an' make it presentable. Should be time enough fer the challenge."

From the stacked crates in back, Mac's grumbling voice carried for all to hear. "Can we kindly *GET ON WIT' IT*! I'm dyin' o' starvation while ye drag yer loafers gettin' me supper fancied up, somethin' *no one* cares about! We're not gonna *look* at it, we're gonna *devour* it, so slop it on a plate an' let's *have at it* before I die o' malnourishment!" He stomped noisily through the crowd to the tarp, now piled high with scraps of meat and fish and vegetables and half-eaten cakes and melted iced cream, and planted himself before it, the first man in a queue of one.

John looked to Tinky, who nodded back. He was ready. "First up shall be Tinky O'Shea!" John called. "Take it away, O'Shea!"

Tinky stood with his chest thrust and his legs spread as he'd seen so many public speakers do. He reviewed his limerick once more in his mind, then delivered it with the confidence of a member of government addressing parliament.

"There once was a pig on a roast
He cried as his toes turned to toast
He spit out his apple
With chains, he did grapple
Got his pig's feet unhooked
With his belly half-cooked
He wiggled the spit over
Ran all the way to Dover
An' retired to a cottage on the coast!"

Oh, the approval! The thunder of hands clapping, the detonation of wild cheers, the cannon of voices as they chanted his name! It was entirely overwhelming and Tinky was made to stand in their adoration and receive it all with nothing but a silly grin on his head. John slapped him on the back and cheered loudest of all.

Eventually the hubbub faded and all eyes turned to their fair judge. Murky McKay stepped forward, scratching his massive beard, his face betraying nothing. The crowd dangled over a cliff of expectation and waited in silence for judgement.

His verdict cracked through the square like a gunshot. "Too long!" he cried, and the crowd booed and jeered him in disappointment. Tinky failed to be discouraged, however, for he'd received his celebrity and still bathed in its glow.

John asked the crowd, "Who else has one? Come forth an' deliver!"

Archie Farchy stepped into the center circle and began,

"Es war einmal ein Mann aus Berlin...."

Immediately, Murky ran forward and threw a meaty palm over Archie's mouth to stop him. "Too *German!*" he shouted. "Next!"

A thin young woman carrying a funereal pall over her pale face replaced Archie in the center. Her eyes were sunken and half-moons of dark shadow hung under her lids. She recited,

> *"A lad walked the streets with his mate*
> *They'd been drinking in pubs until late*
> *Two girls in a car*
> *Just come from the bar*
> *Swerving the same street*
> *Where the lads were on feet*
> *Caused all four to meet with their fate."*

The applause wasn't as boisterous as it had been with Tinky, but it was encouraging and courteous nonetheless.

Murky barked, "Too depressin'! *Much* too depressin'!" and called for another. A man of about fifty took the stage, bowed, and said,

> *"There once lived a beast in a lake*
> *Whose tooth was besieged with an ache*
> *Found a doctor o' dental*
> *Who went outright mental*
> *Upon finding the beast there*
> *In his dentistry chair*
> An' still *the beast cannot eat cake!"*

The crowd enjoyed that one alright, but Murky passed his opinion bluntly. "Too *lame!*" he bellowed. "'Tis been a load o' crap so far! Someone give us a good 'un!"

John himself had thought of one and he waved his hand politely until called upon by Murky. He took a deep breath and spoke,

> *"A man saw his hairline receding*
> *His doctor advised a good bleeding*
> *A leech sucked on his crown*
> *As the man walked through town*
> *His friends laughed themselves hoarse*
> *But the man stayed his course*
> *Since a hairpiece would surely be cheating!"*

Oh, how they loved it! The gratification was instant as the people praised him with applause and slaps on the back. John smiled sheepishly, embarrassed by their enthusiasm, as everyone's attention turned to Murky.

"Damn near perfec', but still lackin' in somethin'!" he announced. "Do we have one more? Can anyone step forward an' attempt to outdo this man?"

Into the circle marched Sweet Emily Moore, reeking of confidence, and when the crowd saw her take the stage, they went nuts. Absolutely, shrill-shriekingly bonkers. They whooped and hollered and danced and sang her name. After soaking in their adoration for nearly a full minute, Sweet Emily Moore raised an arm with the grace of a ballerina and the entire gallery hushed. She delivered her limerick then, enunciating like a pro, making each word count, twirling her dress and pantomiming a scene and generally making a show of it.

> *"A man came home slightly belated*
> *By his wife, he was cursed and was hated*
> *So he took up her dress*
> *Made the linens a mess*
> *'Til his wife passed out, thoroughly sated!"*

The man on the moon was rudely awoken that night by fanfare so uproarious, he probably thought an everlasting world peace had been declared by the citizens of Earth. If the greeting Sweet Emily Moore had received was heavenly, then the response to her limerick was cosmic...otherworldly... *transmundane*. They stomped and screeched, clapped and caterwauled, tallyho-ed and testified. The windows hanging over the square rattled from the hullabaloo until one cracked pane shattered and showered some of the cheering crowd in glass.

The feast in Foster Place this evening was a scene of resplendence.

A long time passed before the clamor settled, and it was John who ultimately suggested they all eat before the food got cold. "Never ye mind, sir!" said the Crier jovially. "'Twas cold hours ago!" Still, hunger was afflicting most of those present and it was generally decided that it was time to sup. Before they could form a line for the buffet, however, an ear-bashing scream shot through the crowd and silenced everyone. The collective attention turned to the source of the scream and saw a woman quietly weeping in the arms of her husband and, behind them, the tarp holding the feast and the grisly scene that lay over it. The shock of the sight was intense; many gasped in horror, some began to weep along with the woman. Old Mother Fodder, strong as she was, fainted dead away and fell on top of her husband, who lay passed out in his wheelbarrow.

Lying on the crest of what was once a mountain of food, a grand banquet, a hearty meal to nourish eighty hungry mouths, lay Mac Malone, his belly swelled to twice its normal size, his flesh and clothing covered in a multitude of creams, juices, sauces, seasonings, and garnishes. His arms splayed out and his legs crossed over what was left of the great pile, giving him the appearance of the sacrificial son of God. Some thought he was dead until he started rocking and rolling from side to side in small movements as a pig might in its own filth. Many recognized his state as being what is often referred to as a *food coma*. The vision suggested that, by some mysterious miracle of gastrointestinal compacting, Mac had consumed a majority of the meal himself, and further proof came in the form of hideous and ghastly odors that honked and bleated and bugled from his body's portals. A massive swarm of flies buzzed around his listless shape, happy to believe they'd discovered the meat of a fresh carcass. Mac raised a hand to numbly swat at them.

How quickly a gathering of festive, cheerful citizens can produce an angry mob! How easily they turn! The mass pushed in on the scene, their fury growing as the initial shock of the image began to fade, their faces turning shades of crimson that appeared unhealthy, to say the least.

"Hang 'im!" they cried.

"Burn 'im!" they shouted.

"Draw an' quarter 'im!" they insisted.

Murky McKay stood the ground between Mac and the mob and threw his arms up, shouting, "Nay! Too good fer this loathsome man an' his loathsome act! He must be made to suffer! I say we make him fight...*A DUEL!*"

"To the death!" shouted Shackled Jack O'Hara.

"No, dear friends!" This time it was the Crier who spoke. "We must not lose our heads in this time o' tragedy! Mac Malone *will* fight a duel...I nominate Mister McKay to serve as his opponent...but not to the death...rather, to *the humiliation*!"

A roar of approval exploded over the square and the man in the moon rolled over and placed a pillow over his head.

A group of four strong men stepped lightly over the tarp, careful not to slip on the mess, and hefted Mac from his prostrate position. His head dangled lethargically and spittle fell in an unbreakable line from his mouth to his pant leg. His hindquarters combusted and the men carrying him were nearly defeated by it.

John and Tinky observed helplessly as Mac was brought before the gathering and held up to face their rage. The Crier approached him and, with his magnificent crier's voice, said, "Mac Malone! What have ye to say fer yerself?"

Mac looked up drowsily and said, "About wha?"

A partially-eaten lamb's liver drenched in onion and thyme gravy sailed through the air from within the crowd and slapped Mac squarely on the cheek.

The Crier shouted angrily, "About eatin' our supper an' then rollin' 'round in it like pigswill!"

Mac belched and wiped gravy from his eye. "It never happened!" he said defensively as a glob of hollandaise dripped from the brim of his cap and ran over his nose. He then leaned over and threw up on Murky McKay's shoes.

The Crier turned to the crowd and called, "Who here believes Mac Malone to be not guilty o' this crime?"

Sweet Emily Moore shouted, "I do!"

John, too, raised his voice in support. "Aye!" He tapped Tinky on the shoulder.

"Yeah, alright, me," said Tinky.

The Crier gave it a moment before he asked, "An' who here believes the man to be guilty?"

"*AYE!*" The call of seventy-seven-odd voices made a loud and terrible chorus that sealed Mac's fate.

"Very well!" said the Crier. "Let us prepare, then, fer the duel!"

At once, everyone scattered and took up a chore. Several people ran to the burn barrels and dragged them down the length of Foster Place, dropping one every ten paces to illuminate the entire lane. Several more began clearing the lane of debris. A man and woman bolted off toward College Green, clearly on a mission. The others formed two lines down the sides of the street as though forming a gauntlet; it appeared they'd all been through this ritual before.

John and Tinky stood back and watched in worried wonder. They saw Mac dozing on the tarp and were comforted to know that he, apparently, was not concerned. His snores cut through the air like a lumber grinder.

In ten minutes' time, the preparations were complete and all members of the audience stood lining the lane. The man and woman who had run off returned, each carrying the load of a battered child's tricycle. A long, wooden case was clamped under the woman's arm as well. They were met in the center of the lane by the Crier and Murky McKay. The tricycles were set down and the woman handed the wooden case to the Crier, who called out to the four sentries standing guard over Mac.

"Bring the condemned!"

The strong men lifted Mac with great difficulty and stumbled him over to the Crier, who slapped his face gently to wake him. He then held the wooden case over his head for all to see.

"Witness! The swatters!" The Crier opened the case dramatically and revealed a swatch of satin holding what appeared to be two flyswatters. The crowd *aaaaah*ed and were entranced as the swatters glinted in the moonlight. The Crier presented the case to Murky, who chose the weapon nearest him, and to Mac, who withdrew the other. They both simultaneously grasped the ends of the powder blue swatters and pulled. The handles of the flyswatters were affixed to television antennas and each handle telescoped to a length of four feet, creating a weapon similar to a blunt sword. Murky lashed his through the air, a vicious sneer decorating his lips, and the sharp whistle it made as it cut through the atmosphere caused the crowd to cower and tremble. Not to be outdone, Mac displayed his strength by whipping his swatter through the air with all his might, only he misjudged its trajectory and the plastic mesh connected solidly with the Crier's left cheek, cursing all ears with a blunt *SWACK!* that sent a cringe rolling through the throng.

Despite the pain prickling his face and fouling his mood, the Crier carried on. "The rules! Each man will be issued a tricycle, which he will maneuver to assume a standard joustin' position at the ends o' this here lane. He will then utilize his swatter to inflict humiliation on the other! Any swatter that retracts shall *not* be allowed to extend again! So if yer antenna collapses, gents, there'll be *no* pullin' it back out, got it?" Both men nodded their understanding. "Mount up, men, an' assume yer positions!"

Excitement electrified the air as Mac and Murky each mounted a tricycle and awkwardly pedaled to their positions at opposite ends of the lane. Mac had a rough go of it at first, trying to steer the tiny wheels over the stony lane while juggling his swatter. He hadn't traveled five feet before his trike wobbled over and sent him crashing to the ground. He did his best to disguise the pain, knowing that all eyes were on him, and was able to remount and continue toward his starting position, his tibia afire with a throbbing bite. As he pedaled, the turbulence of solid metal wheels careening over uneven cobblestones caused his muscles to contract and relax like a rubber band in the paws of a kitten and he was unable to hold back the fearsome gases that demanded freedom; with each shudder and bounce of the cycle, a hearty burst of foul wind blew from his seat. He sounded like an idling motorbike as he teetered his way down the aisle.

When the duelists were aligned at their starting positions, they faced each other with roughly sixty feet between them. The spectators watched with bated breath as the Crier took his place between them and called out, "Mac Malone! Have ye anythin' to say before the humiliation commences?"

Mac stood awkwardly, trying to free himself of the contraption he straddled, but the tricycle's tiny handlebars caught on his expansive hips and the entire three-wheeler rose with him and swung like dead weight from his groin. Speaking was made difficult by his overactive digestive system, but he managed to shout between hiccoughs, "I maintain <hic!> me innocence an' I <belch!> tink ye're all a bunch o' <urp!> mental cripples!" In one swift and well-practiced motion, he dropped his trousers and bent over, presenting the crowd with a full and pale moon even more impressive than the one hanging overhead, then hoisted his pants and sat back down to prepare for launch.

The Crier took from his pocket a white handkerchief and raised it over his head. Not a lid blinked as it wavered in his hand, fluttering in a mild evening breeze. Murky stared straight at Mac and Mac stared right back. The Crier brought the handkerchief down with a lash of his arm and the tricycle pedals began to churn.

The crowd's response was instantaneous. They clapped and shouted encouragement for their favorite and jeered and shouted curses at their foe. The *squeaksqueak-squeak!* of rusted wheels penetrating everyone's enjoyment like claws on a blackboard and the orchestra of tubas blaring from Mac's body as he pedaled furiously all made for a cornucopia of sounds and emotions that riled the citizens to frenzy. The distance between Mac and Murky was slowly constricting as the *squeaksqueaksqueak!* of each trike drew nearer to the other and threatened to combine and become one piercing blade of aural excruciation. Now only twenty feet separated the men and the cheers became louder. Fifteen feet and the riders tightened their grips on the swatters. Ten feet and the *squeaksqueaksqueak!* was unnerving...eight and the dominant hands left the handlebars to arc the swatters back into striking position...seven and the steering hands fought the quaking motion of the vigorously vibrating machines and struggled to keep them on target...six and the legs pumped madly in tiny circles, propelling them forward as palms perspired and brows furrowed and muscles clenched...five and they were nearly within reach and the *squeaksqueaksqueak!* and the cheers and sneers and whistles and gristle caused every thinking mind to melt and (*the insanity of it all!*) the swatters lay poised in the air like cobras waiting to strike and *squeaksqueaksqueak!* the tricycles drove dangerously toward each other head-on and threatened collision and *squeaksqueaksqueak!* Murky opened his throat to let loose a powerful masculine roar and *squeaksqueaksqueak!* Mac bared his yellow teeth like a warmongering barbarian and now it was four feet and they were within striking distance and *squeaksqueaksqueak!* the swatters let loose like swinging catapults and streamed through the ether and sang the shrillest of war cries as they sailed toward their targets and now the trikes were certainly going to collide and disaster was imminent and the swatters came and the people clenched and the hearts stopped as the swatters descended and

THWWWWWWWWWWWWAAAAAAAAAAAAAAAAAACK!!!

It was Mac's swatter that found its target first, smacking Murky flat in the face and sending him veering harmlessly away. A disappointed groan detonated from the audience while three lonesome voices rejoiced and yelled approval for their friend. Mac coasted several feet further, surprised at his own luck, and simmered in the heat of his own self-congratulation. This momentary lapse of attention was his downfall, however, for Murky recovered quickly. By the time Mac registered the *squeaksqueaksqueak!* coming up behind, Murky was upon him, swinging and slapping and swatting at Mac's head and torso with precise, controlled movements. Mac pulled his steering column down full starboard and pedaled madly to escape the brutal barrage, but Murky gave chase and cycled closely behind. There they were, two grown men on children's tricycles, pedaling clumsily in a tight circle, Mac's yin to Murky's yang, chasing each other round and round until Mac's right foot slipped from the tiny pedal and shot forward and caught between solid ground and the spinning crankset, abruptly stopping his motion and sending his right knee crashing into the cobblestones as his right testicle was crushed between his thigh and the tricycle seat. The *CRACK!* of his knee and his castrato-like wail were heard by all and many gallons of air were sucked through many teeth as the people reacted.

"AAAAAAAAAAAAAAAGGGHHH!" Mac screamed. "I broke me coccyx!"

Behind him in the crowd, Tinky whispered to John, "He's done fer!"

And still the disaster continued. Murky pulled up alongside and mercilessly brought his swatter down, again and again, assaulting every exposed inch of Mac's flesh until it was speckled with reddening hash marks and bruising darkly. Mac stood to get away, but the trike stuck in his legs as it had before and tripped him over into a burning barrel of fire and both man and metal fell to the ground and soon both were aflame. Mac tugged and shrugged at his burning coat, rolling about like a roly-poly weeble-wobble, and the noxious gasses that still roared from his rump ignited and shot bolts of flame at those who tried to get close to help. He managed to tear the coat off and fling it away and run a few paces backward to find his bearings.

Now that he was free of the toasting coat, Mac saw Murky approaching with his swatter in striking position. Mac brandished his own weapon like a samurai and realized the antenna had retracted during his fall and now was just one foot in length, useful only for close combat. *Damn the cursing Gods!*, he bellowed internally as he readied to defend himself.

When Murky was within swinging distance, he stood tall and proceeded to lay in on Mac relentlessly. Mac swung his swatter blindly with his right hand while his left covered his head, but it was futile; Murky had the superior weapon and the superior strength. He chased Mac in a figure eight, flicking and flacking and thwacking merrily as if it were a game. A game! Mac had a thing or two to teach that sodding, gaming bastard if ever he escaped Foster Place in one piece!

Between Mac's digestion and his strenuous physical activity, he was soon doubled over by a crippling stomach cramp and flaming heartburn. Murky stood over him and playfully swatted until Mac crouched in the center of the lane, unable to defend himself, a ball of humiliated rejection. For the first time all evening, the crowd stood quiet and somber, as though witnessing an execution. When he thought Mac had suffered enough, the Crier mercifully called a halt to the duel and raised Murky's arm over his head to declare him the victor. The crowd clapped respectfully.

"Let us not forget the lesson learned this night," the Crier called, "but let us also find it in our hearts to forgive our friend Mac Malone fer his sin!"

Mac rose from his huddled mass and presented two familiar fingers to the square. "Profanity an' curses to the lot o' ye!" he shouted. "I'm innocent, I tell ye! An' I'd've prevailed over that lumberin' orangutan if ye hadn't poisoned them cream pies to slow me down!" He thrust his index finger into the air and proclaimed, "*J'accuse!*"

But his words fell on deaf ears, for the crowd was dispersing and getting back to task. The burn barrels were dragged back, the swatters locked away in their case to be used another day, the tricycles bent back into shape and returned to their secret storeroom. A squad was sent to collect more scraps to eat as conversations resumed.

A comforting arm wrapped around Mac's shoulders and he looked up to find John holding him sympathetically. Mac was embarrassed and his pride raised its defenses. "What, are ye gonna recite a limerick to make me feel better?" he asked begrudgingly. "I'm *innocent*."

"Ye're *flawed*, Mac, may the Gods love ye fer it."

"Insult to injury!" Mac scoffed.

"Ye're a glutton, to be sure, an' one o' the most selfish men I know." John smiled.

"Yer mother's a *hag*!" Mac spat. He paused, then asked, "So ye tink I'm guilty?"

"Oh, Mac, I *know* ye're guilty!"

"Then why stick up fer me back there rather than condemn me to humiliation like the rest o' the cretins?"

"How do ye know a true friend, eh?"

Mac looked as though he'd just been asked directions to Pluto.

John said, "In public, a friend'll stand beside ye no matter what, even if ye're wrong. In private, he'll point out yer greatest flaws an' encourage ye to conquer 'em. These are the duties of a good friend."

A rumbling penetrated their ears and they looked up to see a line of men and women trotting toward them, each rolling an oak barrel. There must have been near fifty kegs in all and they thundered past like a freight train. The man leading the procession called out excitedly for all to hear, "The swill is here! Gather 'round! Swill 'as arrived!"

A great commotion followed, during which a chisel and mallet appeared and went to work pounding holes in the bottom of each barrel. The tramps lined up before each one and all means of receptacle appeared. Cups, mugs, glasses, saucers, bowls, ladles, and cupped hands all waited to receive their share of the beer swill that poured out. Additional bottles of 166-proof grain alcohol were produced to enhance both the flavor and the potency of the dregs. With the arrival of the keg brigade, the festive atmosphere returned and the laughing and singing and dancing continued even more boisterously than before. Soon, too, another contingent returned with more scraps of food, but few hands ventured to collect a supper, as it might upset the effectiveness of the alcohol.

As John stood with Mac observing the ritual, Murky McKay approached and thrust a hubcap of swill into Mac's hands. "Ye make a fine duelin' partner, Malone," he said as he slapped Mac's shoulder and nearly knocked him over. "We'll have to give it another go-round sometime."

Mac held his tongue and drank. He looked up and saw John trying to communicate silently by repeatedly opening his eyes wide and nodding in Murky's direction. "Fer God's sake, man, what is it?" Mac blurted.

John leaned in and whispered in Mac's ear. "*HAR!*" said Mac, but John nudged him with his elbow and stared at him persuasively. Finally, Mac turned to Murky and mumbled a single incomprehensible word.

"What's that?" Murky asked.

Mac shouted angrily, "I said *tanks*, ye bloated baboon!"

Murky McKay raised his head to the moon and howled in laughter. "Ye're welcome, ye gorgin' porker! Now get yer arse over to join the party an' have a good time, or I'll wallop ye again an' this time show no mercy!"

"*FINE!*" Mac left them and stomped loudly to the revelry and was engulfed by a cluster of merry and forgiving friends.

Tinky joined John and handed him one of the two soup cans he held. John sniffed the concoction inside and was nearly knocked to his knees by the fumes. "'Tis really not bad," said Tinky, examining his own can. "Like the gin ol' Scarge Delaney brewed in his bathtub. She burns like a jilted bride goin' down, but has a cool, delicate finish. Give 'er a try!"

John brought the can to his lips but, before he drank, reached in to dig out what appeared to be a slice of fish entrails. When he did take a sip, he had to hold his breath to keep from being overwhelmed. The last thing he remembered of his adventure on the streets that night was Tinky's bright smile and glistening eyes, as well as his words.

"She's got a kick to 'er, eh?"

CHAPTER SEVEN
A Vista of Variance

At nine o'clock the following morning, the Chivalric Nobleman de La Mancha sat still and silent, shuttered from the world outside. Inside, John Doyle lay twisted in sweat-soaked sheets, nursing the High Priest of all Holy Hangovers, a malady brought on by medieval drink consumed just hours prior at the feast. As he woke and his vision came into focus, he noticed his alarm clock on the floor by the bed, the glass splintered with a design resembling the intricate web of an obsessive-compulsive spider. No memory of its destruction remained, but John concluded that every act of violence toward it had been justified.

When he was finally able to lift his head, bolts of pain and nausea shot from his brain. *Never again*, he thought. He'd told himself this before under the same circumstances, but this time he meant it. *Never never ever....*

His feet hit the floor and he was off like a slug. The first order of business was to down three full glasses of water along with an analgesic. Water, that sweet nectar of life, returned to him a sense of being human again, which was a fine start. He scrubbed his teeth and washed his face and scurried to get the shop open for business. At 9:54, almost an hour late, he unlocked the front door and uncharacteristically hoped that business would be slow.

His first customer arrived within minutes. If John wore the mask of the opera's Phantom, then Tinky O'Shea wore the mask of Death itself. He slogged into the shop and embraced John, hanging his chin impotently over his friend's shoulder, whispering to the floor, "Never again. Never never ever...."

"Not so loud, please," said John delicately. He broke the embrace but kept his hand on Tinky's shoulder. "The drink last night. What was it?"

"Potent."

John went to the back and returned with two glasses of water. They toasted their mortality and gulped the water down. "Next time we do that, I'll see to it there'll be no work the followin' day," Tinky proclaimed.

"Next time," John said, feeling another wave of nausea pass. "Right."

Tinky wandered over to the rare book collection and peered in through the glass. "I haven't examined yer rarities in some time. Anythin' new?"

"Not a thing. A customer brought in a first edition o' *Tropic of Cancer* last week, but I found it was a pirated edition printed right here in Dublin back in '35." He filed through some papers by the till. "I saw a notice fer another estate sale next week over in Mullingar. The owner was an avid reader an' collector, used to come through the shop now 'n again. Perhaps I'll find some tantalizin' tidbits there."

The telephone rang, causing the heads of both men to shatter like bullet-riddled crystal. John ran to pick it up before a second ring destroyed them, taking a moment to inhale deeply before addressing the caller. "Bookshop," he said in a soft voice, choosing to forego his traditional recitation of the shop's proper name. "Ah, Brian. 'Tis a joy to hear yer voice."

Tinky heard the name and pricked up his ears. "Oh, I'm fine, tanks," John was saying. "Just a wee headache this mornin.'" Tinky could see he was holding the receiver several inches from his ear. "Aye, I do need to find some hair o' that wretched dog, but only when I tink I can keep it down...right!...I agree. We need to get ye in here sometime. Ye're welcome anytime...I usually shut the door 'round six o'clock...oh, that sounds lovely. I've definitely had an itch to see what ye've got...perhaps, but I believe I'll be alright by then...that's grand...aye...half five, that'll be fine...grand. I look forward to it...cheers, Brian."

He placed the phone in its cradle tenderly. Tinky put his nose against the glass of the cabinet and pretended to examine the books. "Was that Corrigan?" he asked.

"Aye," John said. "He'll be comin' to town later, so I told him to swing by. He's never seen the shop before. After that, he's invited me to his house fer dinner an' to show me his collection, which I hear is extraordinary. Ye'd probably love it as well, I should ask him if ye could tag along."

Tinky seemed reluctant. "Tanks. I'd rather not. Brian is, ah...what d'ye know 'bout him, really?"

"He's an amiable sort, seems a good fellow," John said. "I know he spends a lot on books. Came into inheritance a while back, he said, an' cures his boredom by feedin' his cravin' fer novels. I'm excited to see what he's got." John nonchalantly tidied up around the register. "Why do ye ask? There's a bit o' trepidation in yer voice."

"Well, I'm not entirely certain, really...." Here Tinky paused before continuing. "I don't trust 'im. There's somethin' about the man I can't warm up to. At the pub, he mentioned a book dealer in New York, said he was offered a substantial amount fer that copy o' *Moby Dick* ye sold him, a lot more than he paid fer it, apparently."

John was quiet for a moment. "Well," he said, "there's nothin' *wrong* with that. It just means he's got a keen eye fer value."

"It just means he's been shoppin' it around already, is what it means. Ye said he'd promised to give ye first refusal, yah?"

"The book is his. He can do with it as he pleases. An' who says the dealer didn't contact *him*? Word gets 'round 'bout a book such as that."

Tinky was unconvinced. "Still...."

"Brian seems a fine fellow. He an' I are cut from the same sort o' cloth. An' let's be truthful here, yer opinion is biased in the matter. Brian's the one who took what you wanted."

"'Tis not that, John." Tinky looked dissuaded. "Anyhow, I know nothin' about the man an' feel no need to. Go see what he's got tonight an' report back. An' if he owns anythin' else from Master Melville, feel free to put it in yer pocket an' gift it to me, eh? Brian owes me at least that after piratin' *my* ship." Then he added, "Damn his fortune!"

*   *   *   *

As promised, Brian Corrigan arrived very near to half five. When he finally entered the shop, he wore a Cheshire cat grin and a look of wonder. "'Tis hard fer me to believe ye *live* here! It'd be like livin' in a library. What heaven!"

"Aye, I suppose it is," said John, and he proceeded to give Brian a quick tour. Through the downstairs, the flat in back, upstairs, and inside the maze of shelves they went. When they wound up back at the front counter with another twenty minutes left of business, Brian excused himself to peruse the rarities cabinet and the fiction aisles while John rang up his final customers and prepared to close. At five minutes to six, Brian appeared again with a handful of novels to purchase. He even had John open the cabinet and ring up the edition of *Three Men In a Boat* and its follow-up. John granted him a respectable discount and Brian paid cash for the lot.

He opened one of the books, a seemingly unread hardback by an up-and-coming novelist. Inside the front flap lay a loose bookplate signed by its author. "Did ye know this was floatin' about inside?"

John took the square of paper and examined it, then handed it back. "So it is. Looks authentic, too. A good find, that."

"The things ye find in second-hand shops!" said Brian, rather proud of himself. "Ye always hear 'bout people comin' across undiscovered treasures in antique shops an' the like. Have ye ever found somethin' similar in here?"

"As a matter o' fact, I have. Ye own two of 'em."

"Which ones, these or the other two?"

"I found *Treasure Island* an' *Moby Dick* at the bottom of a rubbish pile."

Brian's mouth cracked open, but no sound came. In a moment, he managed to merely repeat John's words. "A rubbish pile!"

"So, aye, I do know what it's like to find value in the discard bin o' life, so to speak."

Brian laughed. "I'll say! A rubbish pile!" He stood, shaking his head and staring at the wall, while John excused himself to begin his evening round of the shop to make sure no stragglers were hiding in the maze. Within minutes he was back, spruced by a tweed jacket and ready to go. He drew the shutters and locked the door, making sure to close it gently since his head still held a residual aggravation from the previous evening's libations.

Brian had parked his sparkling, scratch-less beast of a sedan on the lane near the storefront and he stood now before it, staring at the rear passenger-side wing. "I don't believe it!" Brian shouted. "In the name o' sanity!"

"What's happened?"

"Someone's pissed on me car is all! Fer the love o' Christ, how do these things happen?" He got in and unlocked the passenger door for John. Sure enough, the odor of urine was strong. John stepped over the puddle and climbed in.

"Sorry," John said. "Those things rarely happen 'round here."

"I'm reminded o' why I live in the country an' not the city," said Brian. He looked over and winked at John. "Wait'll ye see it. Ye've got yer little slice o' Paradise here in the shop an' I've got mine. Let's have a look." He started the engine and they were off.

With traffic, it took a little over forty-five minutes to drive to Enniskerry. On the outskirts of Dublin, the terrain became green and luxurious, the concrete of the city replaced with rolling hills and sprawling fields. Traffic dissipated and they were soon surrounded by thatched cottages and grazing sheep. It was a few minutes past six o'clock, the magic hour when the sun hovers just over the skyline and drapes a majestic orange sheet over the land, and John assumed the postcard photographers were busy affixing their widest lenses in attempt to capture even a fraction of its beauty. He sat and thoroughly enjoyed the ride.

Brian suggested rolling the windows down to breathe the country air. The delicious fragrance of nature swept into the car and filled their lungs with a cool flavor that was like a sweet dessert for the soul. They passed a farm and the sound of a buzz saw blared at them, temporarily releasing them from nature's trance, and Brian quipped, "I'd rather it be an electric saw than sounds of a hundred idling diesels!" John slapped the knee of his friend in agreement and continued to admire the scenery.

"I must warn ye," Brian said over the rushing wind, "I'm currently carin' fer me uncle. He's gettin' on in years an' suffers from a bit o' dementia, poor man, so if he appears, don't be startled. I'd fancy ye meetin' him. He was quite the reader, back when he could."

"Ye're a good man fer takin' him in," John said, also projecting over the wind. "Must be a lot o' work. Have ye any help?"

"I sure do, durin' the—." Here Brian stopped speaking abruptly as wretchedness contorted his face. "Great Balls o' Fury, but that's awful!"

A horrendous odor assaulted them and John turned his head this way and that in a futile attempt to escape it. It surrounded them, seeming to emit from the floorboards, the vents, the upholstery. Brian rolled his window up and John followed suit, but it didn't help much. In fact, it didn't help at all.

"One o' the few drawbacks to livin' in the country," Brian said, still grimacing. "Spring fertilization! But, Christ A-mighty, this is worse than last year! Saints alive, that's teddible!"

John lowered his window again, desperate for a breeze to clear the air. Brian followed suit and pulled the top of his turtleneck over his nose. "Oh, ye sick, sick man!" He was looking straight at John, his voice muffled by the fabric. "If that's come out o' ye as a result o' yer drinkin' binge last night, I'll make ye walk the rest o' the way!"

John giggled. "'Tis not I, I swear it!"

"Don't soil me car!" Brian, too, was caught in a fit of giggles. "Someone's already *pissed* on 'er, fer Chrissakes!"

"I'll tell ye what ye want to know, all me darkest secrets," John pleaded. "Just make it stop!"

The boys were shaking with laughter as boys often will when discussing crude effects of the digestive system. Tears welled in Brian's eyes and laughter reddened his face. With the turtleneck wrapped around the lower half of his head, he looked like a sock puppet with severe allergies. The sight made John laugh even harder, so much that his belly began to cramp.

He said between spasms, "Get a move on, man, show me what this thing can do! Get us away from this ungodly stench!" Brian took the challenge and sped up.

By the time their giggles settled, Brian was turning onto a gravel lane that continued over a hill, beyond their line of sight. He stopped under an iron archway that bore a name, *Innisfree*, and motioned to a man in coveralls standing with three others by an old van. The man pushed his cap back and approached.

"Good evenin', Mister Corrigan!" he said politely. "We made a lot o' progress today, sir! The lawns is lookin' as green as ever an' the hedges is trimmed just to yer likin'!"

Brian's voice was chilled despite his laughter of the past minutes. "That's fine, Paddy. Were ye able to finish the job?"

"Well, no, not exactly. Me initial estimate failed to take into consideration a number o' elements on this here property an'—"

"Alright, then," Brian interrupted. "You an' the boys pack up fer today. I'll expect ye early to finish up."

"Fine, fine, Mister Corrigan," Paddy said, smiling into the window. "A pleasant evenin' to ye's!"

Brian drove on, shaking his head. "Could ye smell him from where ye're sittin'?" he asked John. "'Tis like talkin' to a whiskey bottle! I've had it with those jokers. A day-an'-a-half job has stretched to three days an' most o' the time they just hide in the truck an' get scuttered!" He shook his head disappointedly. "Never again, I tell ye."

They drove up the hill and Brian slowed at its crest to allow John a chance to soak in the wonders ahead. To the left, a long, neatly-trimmed hedgerow led to a spacious rose garden laying before the rim of a forest. To the right, a vast pond sprawled over the property. Between them stood a centuries-old castle, an air of majesty surrounding it as the sun bathed it in red. As far as castles go, it was modest, standing three stories tall, and a turret hung over one of the two towers, its crenellated lip lending the appearance that the entire structure was battle-ready. The gravel drive flowed over the hill and trickled down to a circular plot near the manor's entrance and Brian pulled up beside two other cars and parked. In all, the property made the vehicles look minuscule and John felt intimidated as he stepped out and stood in the castle's shadow.

"A-mazin'," he said, almost to himself. Brian joined him and John repeated his criticism. "Ab-solutely a-mazin."

"Ye shan't judge me based on this property, if ye please," Brian said. "I'm fourth generation to live here. A part o' me wants to move to a small cottage somewhere, but, hell —." He led the way to the front step and ushered John inside.

The interior of Innisfree Castle was just as breathtaking as the outside. The rugged stonework was left exposed; the walls and pillars running floor to ceiling were made of flagstones specifically chosen for their color and texture. Pale shades of red, green, violet, and orange blended with variants of gray and white and the stones were intentionally stacked unevenly to give the overall texture an unrefined yet pleasing appearance. Oak panels had been added to segregate rooms and a wide oak staircase near the entrance led to the second and third stories. Walls were adorned with regal tapestries and gold-framed paintings depicting scenes set in the local countryside, while Persian rugs lined the hardwood floors and eliminated echoes that might have rebounded against the many hard surfaces. Unlike most manors built by excessive wealth, Innisfree was not designed to dwarf the people living within; the ceilings were high but not exceedingly so and the rooms were not halls but, rather, comfortable living spaces. It was an ideal home and John adored it instantly.

Until Bucephalus appeared, that is. While John was still agog and taking in the sights, a tremendous, black Rottweiler came running in to welcome Brian. When he saw John, the dog halted and crouched defensively, lips curling to reveal long, jutting fangs, a basso growl gurgling from his throat. The dog's coat shined like oil and his hateful brown eyes stared menacingly into John's.

Brian took control instantly. "NO!" he shouted, wagging his finger at the dog. "Back!" He placed both hands on John's shoulders. "Friend!" The dog stopped growling but still did not break his scorching stare.

"Bucephalus, John. John, this is Bucephalus, me puppy. He's a good boy, aren't ye, Bucie?" Brian bent and aggressively scratched the dog's ears and Bucie's tongue rolled out as he savored the attention. Yet when John slowly presented his hand, palm inward, for the dog to sniff, Bucephalus bared his teeth and snapped at him.

Brian caught the dog's collar and again shouted, "NO!" He looked up at John. "Sorry, he can be aggressive. I'll put him away fer now." He pulled the collar and led the dog away. Bucephalus kept his eyes on John until they were around the corner.

"I see ye've met the dog!"

John looked up to see a lass in her mid-twenties leaning over the bannister. Her hair was red and full and loose and her blouse hung free from the stifling confines of its top three buttons, attracting John's eye. She stepped down and said, "Normally he's a sweetheart, but at times he can be a real arse."

"I assume ye're speakin' o' Brian," John said, straightening to his full height and throwing on his best smile as men do in the presence of a striking woman.

She joined him at the base of the staircase and playfully smacked his chest. "The *canine*. Watch out, if Bucie heard ye talkin' 'bout his master like that, he'd castrate ye!"

Brian returned and brightened at seeing the lady. "Evenin', Sally. I see ye've met John."

"Not really," John said as he offered his hand. "Like the dog says, I'm John."

"Who's the dog? Don't play monkeyshines with me best girl, now!"

John laughed and looked between Brian and Sally. "Are you two…?"

Brian slapped his belly. "Ha! No, nothin' like that. Sally's a nurse, in durin' the days to care fer me uncle. How was he today?"

"Fine," Sally said. "He made himself a sandwich a little while ago, so he should be good fer the night. He went wanderin' again earlier. I caught him by the rose garden an' he claimed to be headed home to Galway. The poor man!"

Brian looked to John. "That's me uncle fer ye. Never in his life has he lived in Galway." He turned back to Sally. "Is he up? I should introduce John."

Sally shook her head. "Just went down fer a nap. Ye know how that is, he could be out all night."

"Tanks fer a good day, then, Sally. I assume ye're off?"

"Aye, I'll see ye in the mornin'." She walked to the closet to retrieve her coat and Brian winked at John and called after her.

"Ye're welcome to stay fer dinner. Nothin' fancy. We'd love to have ye!"

Sally came back and went to the door. "Tanks, no, I've need to be gettin' home. But ye gents have a grand time!" Brian gave a shrug to John that said, *at least I tried*.

"Oh, Sally! The landscapers *still* haven't finished. Did ye notice 'em today? Have they been boozin' or has there been actual work goin' on?"

"They seemed to be workin'," she said, "although I did notice a few bottles 'round lunchtime. Frankly, 'tis no surprise. I'll keep me eye out tomorrow. See ye then! Good-night, John."

John smiled and watched her leave. When the door had shut, Brian said, "My, my. If I could be so lucky."

"Agreed," John agreed.

Brian clapped his hands together. "I'm afraid I've nothin' extravagant arranged fer dinner, but I could sear some steaks or salmon if it suits yer fancy."

The very mention of food upset John's rehabilitating appetite. "Ye know, I'm still tryin' to recover from that blasted hangover. I'd be perfectly happy with somethin' light an' easy."

Brian sang to the heavens. "Music to me ears! We'll do a full bachelor supper, then. Beans an' sandwiches followed by scotch an' cigars! But first, let me show ye the collection." He fluttered his eyebrows and led the way down the hall.

To describe the entire castle as modest and unassuming was, perhaps, inaccurate. *Most* of Brian's home exhibited some sort of humility (as much as a centuries-old castle sitting on seventy-seven acres can be *humble*) yet when it came to the room housing Brian's book collection, there was nothing humble or modest about it. It was, in a word, *colossal*. At twenty-five hundred square feet, it was a room as long as it was tall. The ceiling separating the first and second floors had been removed and oak wainscoting lined the walls, twenty feet high. Magnificent oak shelves filled the room and stood fifteen feet tall, each shelf stacked top to bottom with books, which numbered in the tens of thousands. Stained glass windows decorated the top of the western wall and the light of dusk drenched the room in a blaze of color.

The initial sensation to hit John was the odor. It smelled old, like a paper mill by a stream in autumn, not unlike his own shop. Only the Chivalric Nobleman, with its claustrophobic layout, had a more dense and pulpy scent; here, the mustiness was diluted by the size of the room and was sweeter, like rose petals pressed between pages. The scent of oak blended with that of the paper to lend the air an earthy tone and John inhaled and thought instinctually of motherhood, of life, of excitement and anticipation and chasing birds over the sunny greens under Saint Patrick's Cathedral as he had when he was a child. It was a scent that should have been bottled and enjoyed forever. It smelled like home.

He stepped into the room and thought he'd passed into the eighth Wonder of the World. The only collection he'd seen that was more magnificent was the impressive Old Library at Trinity College. He was literally stunned by the vision before him; when he tried to walk forward, he found that his legs wouldn't carry him. It took a nudge from Brian to get him to move. "Come in," Brian said, delighting in John's expression. "Have a look 'round!"

As if floating, John walked deeper into the room, eyes bounding over the beautiful woodwork of the shelving. On each corner of the jutting shelves lay a rounded column that eliminated the boxy feeling typical of a library and gave it a more flowing, organic appearance. He ambled down the line and stepped into a nook and felt engulfed by the towering cases. He slid a few books from their nests and examined them. Here was a first edition of Joyce's *Finnegan's Wake*, in very fine condition with a flawless dust jacket. Next to it was the first issue of *Jabberwocky* by Lewis Carroll, also in fine condition. A ladder on wheels leaned against one case and John climbed up to find an entire shelf of King James bibles, some of them more than two hundred years old. On the shelf under that he found Beckett's *Murphy*, Yeats's *The Celtic Twilight*, Steinbeck's *Tortilla Flat*, Dostoevsky's *The Gambler*, and Wolfe's *The Web and the Rock*, to name but a precious few, all of them in their first issues, all of them in striking condition. Three of those even bore authors' inscriptions. He was inside a book lover's amusement park and was so overwhelmed by the thoughts and ideas and words surrounding him that he nearly tumbled down the ladder.

Brian was at his feet, still reveling in John's reaction. "Come down a moment," he said. "I've got somethin' else to show ye."

John stepped gingerly down and followed his friend to a door at the end of the room. Brian placed his hand on John's shoulder and grinned, then opened the door to reveal another room, a mirror image of the library they stood in now, a *continuation* of this room, with as many shelves, as many books, as many stories, characters, adventures, and as many dreams as the ones currently deluging the levies of John's mind.

*   *   *   *

Just outside the first library lay an intimate parlor with a stone fireplace and two high-backed Chesterfield chairs. John and Brian slouched in them in typical bachelor fashion, a small fire burning for fragrance and atmosphere despite the tepid evening. The fellows had retired to the parlor after whipping up cold corned beef sandwiches and two bowls of potato soup along with mugs of creamy stout. Brian was enjoying a slice of celebrity as a result of John's reverence for his collection and they sat talking about the origins of the library before the conversation turned, as it always did, to books in general. Ultimately, Brian suggested a fine bottle of scotch and cigars fresh off the boat from Havana. John thought it a savory idea.

"What day do ye dread the most?" Brian asked after they'd settled back with glasses full and robustos burning.

"How d'ye mean?" John rolled the cigar between his fingers and felt it was firm with a slightly spongy give. Perfect. As for the scotch, he'd set it down on the table to consider later, having promised himself *never never ever* mere hours ago.

"I mean is there some dark day ye tink about, some day ye dread never comes? The day yer mother dies? The day yer father dies? The day the British Monarchy takes residence in Ireland?" The corners of Brian's mouth crept up in a mischievous smile. "What day do ye dread the most?"

"A very serious question, that."

"I ask it o' meself all the time but never have a meanin'ful answer. A pal down the pub asked me once an' I've been tryin' to figure it out ever since. Ye seem to have a firm grasp on life, I thought I'd ask ye."

John took a long drag and kept the smoke in his mouth a moment before expelling it. "I've witnessed that day already, the dread o' me blackest thoughts. Me Grandad was the world to me, he raised me an' gave me a tinkin' mind an' somethin' to love. He focused me, ye could say, proved to me what was important an' what was mere bollix. Do ye follow?"

Brian chuckled. "Aye, I'm with ye."

"He was like a coach, always pointin' me in the right direction, an' I was desperate to learn from him. The man had integrity. Very well respected. People who knew him loved him — there was no likin' him, it was either ye loved him or ye didn't know him at all. I'd sit at the counter o' the shop an' watch him, tryin' to absorb everythin', his knowledge of all things — tangible, assumed, spiritual — like I was his student. Ye might say I was his disciple." John grinned, then abandoned it. "He was me mother, me father, me God an' Savior. He was me world an' I lost him. It was the darkest day I've known."

John considered it further, pausing for a draw on his cigar to keep it burning, then added, "But I suppose yer question doesn't concern the past, it's what's to come. So. I'll say the day I dread the most is the day I lose track o' what I learned from him, the day I lose sight of everythin' he left me — the love, the wisdom, the integrity. That'll be it, that'll be the worst."

"I'd say that's unlikely," Brian chimed. "Ye're an honest an' good man, John, an' I doubt ye'll ever be called upon to face that day. I only wish I could have yer sense an' yer ability to see outside yerself, 'cause I'll be buggered if I know how to answer that question." He exhaled a great swirling cloud, then spat on the floor and took a healthy pull from his glass. "Tell me about yer Grandad," he said.

"Ye really want to hear about him?" John asked, flattered.

"At this point ye must! If ye don't, it'd be like tellin' a child that Superman exists an' then walkin' away without elaboratin'!"

"Very well," said John as he tapped his ash into a granite ashtray. "If ye really want to know what kind o' man Grampy Doyle was, I have the perfect story."

* * * *

Many patrons had passed through the Chivalric Nobleman de La Mancha Bookshop in its seventy-nine-year history and those familiar with *Don Quixote* assumed the shop was named after that novel. There was truth in this, with variation. The inspiration behind the shop's name came not from Cervantes's masterpiece, but, rather, from one very particular copy of that book. When Kevin Doyle, John's Grandad, first opened the shop, he decided to name it after the copy of *The Ingenious Gentleman Don Quixote of La Mancha, Part One* that had been in the possession of his family for generations. Kevin's Great-Grandfather had an earnest love for the novel and came across a first edition of the first part while traveling through Spain as a young man. He purchased the book and it had been in the family ever since, being handed down from generation to generation for nearly one hundred and fifty years by the time Kevin inherited it.

For a book printed in 1605, the Doyle copy was remarkably clean and tight. Each inheritor knew the value and importance of the book and had done their part to protect it. The volume had come to represent the legacy of the Doyle name and Kevin chose to honor it by naming his shop after it. He even displayed the book to patrons in a glass case he'd constructed by hand. Collectors ventured from near and far to see it; the book was known in the literary circuit and one gentleman had traveled from California just to have a peek. Yet a peek through a thick pane was as close as they'd come, for Kevin could not allow anyone other than a Doyle to touch the book; it was far too delicate.

The Evening Telegraph wrote about Kevin and *Don Quixote* once, in a small feature at the back of Section Two, and the publicity was good for business. People came to see the book and would typically leave with a handful of purchases. For a short period, the second-hand bookshop rivaled the sales of many first-run merchants, and during that time Kevin solidified his reputation as a knowledgeable, personable, and fair businessman and established relationships with many regular customers. The Dublin Chamber of Commerce even presented him with their Superior Independent Merchant's Award for the fourth quarter of that year.

One morning in early December, Kevin arrived from his home on Bayview Avenue to open the shop for business, just as he had six days each week for twenty-one years. When he found the lock on the front door broken, he rushed inside to have one of his worst fears realized. All that remained of the presentation case was a pile of broken glass and splintered wood. *Quixote* was gone.

Kevin was distraught. He felt, quite profoundly, that he'd betrayed himself and many generations of Doyles by not securing the book better. His faith in the virtue of his fellow man had once been so complete that for many years he refused to lock the door of the shop, until a spate of robberies on Grafton Street convinced him to bolt his door every night, albeit reluctantly. Now, with the theft of his most valued possession, his overwhelming faith in people disintegrated and he was left to question the decency of the people he so adored. He fell into a depression that not only affected himself, but his wife and daughters as well.

Less than a fortnight after the theft, a stranger appeared on his doorstep late one evening. The man was in his early twenties, balding, with the crooked nose of a boxer. He introduced himself as Declan Walsh and asked if Kevin was the owner of the Chivalric Nobleman. When Kevin replied that he was indeed, Walsh presented him with a bulk wrapped loosely in newspaper. Intrigued, Kevin opened the package. Inside he found his copy of *Don Quixote*.

Stunned, Kevin instinctively hugged the stranger and invited him in for a drink and they sat in the front room while Walsh told his story. He'd found the book lying on the kitchen table in his brother's flat. The book was visibly aged and when Walsh flipped through it and saw the title printed in Spanish over the words *Ano 1605*, he asked his brother about it. The brother became defensive and told him to mind his own affairs. Walsh suspected foul play from the start, particularly since his brother was not a reader and certainly not a reader of foreign languages, and he pressed the issue until his sibling admitted to stealing the book. He'd lost his job and needed to feed his family and didn't think something so valuable should sit uselessly behind glass, especially something as trivial as a book. Walsh hit his brother and called him a fool and found out who he'd stolen it from, which led him to Kevin's doorstep.

He begged Kevin to show mercy for his brother, explaining that the man was both dim-witted and feeble, making it difficult for him to find work and support his family. Kevin obliged, inspired by Walsh's sincerity and nobility, his faith in Man somewhat restored, and excused himself for a moment. When he returned, he presented to Walsh an envelope containing his profit from the past several days, all in cash. It was, he said, an appreciation to reward Walsh's character. The young man was overwhelmed and at first refused it politely, but Kevin insisted, delighted to have the legacy of *Quixote* returned, then sat down to get to know young Walsh.

The men sat and talked for hours and by the close of evening they were both stiff with drink. Walsh learned a great deal about Kevin Doyle that night and was inspired by his generous and endearing nature. When it was time to take his leave, Walsh followed Kevin to the door and, standing on the stoop having just said his farewell, hung his head and burst into sobs.

Walsh admitted it was he who'd stolen the book; he had no brother. He and his wife and three children were hungry and he was forced by circumstance to resort to crime. He'd read of *Don Quixote* in the *Telegraph* and decided it would be his target. The thought of thievery weighed heavily on his conscience and he wanted to steal something valuable yet meaningless. He'd never understood the importance of books and thought, of all possible items to prey, one old book was as good as anything. It was, in addition, an easy catch. Walsh took Kevin's arm and pleaded for leniency when testifying against him. Not for him, he said, but for the sake of his family.

Kevin Doyle was incensed, but he did not strike Walsh, nor did he call the police. He scolded him and said that Walsh's act was deplorable, but he did not move to seek retribution in any way. He refused even to take his reward back. Instead, he called for Walsh to report to the Chivalric Nobleman at nine o'clock the following morning to begin working off the money. Walsh was blindsided by Kevin's reaction and agreed wholeheartedly to be there first thing.

When Kevin arrived to open the shop the next day, Walsh was already waiting outside. Although there was little work for him to do, Walsh took it upon himself to find chores. He began by dusting every shelf and cleaning every corner. In taking his rag over the shelves, he read the spines and noticed that many books were out of order. Kevin kept his fiction alphabetized by author, but hadn't performed a thorough organization in years. In one week's time, every shelf of the shop was in perfect order and the entire place sparkled. Kevin was impressed.

In short time, he felt that Walsh had worked off the money and relieved him of his duty while offering to keep him on part-time until Walsh found full employment. Walsh was thrilled and thanked Kevin sincerely and even offered to work at a reduced rate. There was no need for that, Kevin said, and suggested a very fair wage, to which Walsh shook his hand in thanks.

Soon Kevin began reading to Walsh from books he thought the young man might enjoy. He had a rich voice and was a magnificent reader and every day during the slow hours of late afternoon he picked up a book and read aloud. Walsh became enthralled and adored the stories that Kevin chose and, after two months of working at the shop, Kevin began suggesting other books and allowed Walsh to take them home to read. It didn't take long for him to find an appreciation for the stories, particularly with Kevin's recommendation and guidance, and soon he was an avid reader.

For the better part of a year, Walsh worked two or three days each week at the bookshop, until one day he announced he'd been hired full-time as a stevedore at the docks. Kevin was sorry to see him go, but was encouraged to hear that he'd found work. The men continued their friendship for many years, meeting now and again at the pub to catch up and discuss what had been on their respective reading piles since the last time they met. They relayed news of their children and grumbled about their wives. They talked about Dylan Thomas and James Joyce and Walsh expressed his frustration with *Ulysses*. Kevin was happy to hear when Walsh was hired at a local printing press as a laborer and regaled in Walsh's stories as he progressed up the professional ladder. Each time they said farewell, they did so with a tight embrace.

And Walsh made sure that Kevin never once picked up the tab.

*   *   *   *

"Grampy Doyle never told me that story," John said, stretching his legs toward the dying fire. "I first heard it at his funeral. A stranger showed up an' laid a grand wreath by the casket. He was bald, with a crooked nose, somewhere in his fifties. After the service, I asked him how he knew me Grandad an' that simple question was enough to open the floodgates. Walsh told the story an' cried as though he'd lost his own father."

Brian sat engrossed, his glass empty, cigar dying in the ashtray. "Between knowin' ye an' hearin' that story, I have a very good sense o' who yer Grandad was. I wish I'd been able to sit with the man over a drink."

"I wish he were here so I could do the same," said John.

"But tell me," Brian said, leaning in. "Do ye have the book?"

John extinguished the nub of his cigar and took a second nip of scotch. "I do," he said, a proud smile stealing across his lips.

"Is it really in as good a condition as ye say?"

"It is." John couldn't wipe the grin off his face. Damn his pride!

"An' ye'll show it to me one day, right?" Brian coaxed.

"Well...."

Brian kicked his arms and legs out and writhed in his seat, laughing. "Oh, ye scoundrel! Ye must! Ye know I couldn't stand it if ye kept it from me!"

Still the grin shined. "Perhaps. One day."

"One day nothin'! One day *soon*, if ye please! Look, 'tis like it was on the playground. I showed ye mine, now show me yers!" He laughed heartily and got up to stoke the fire. "Do ye know its worth?"

"Roughly," said John, thankful that his smile was fading at last.

"And? Look, ye've suddenly gone tight-lipped. Come now, what's she worth?"

"A lot."

"Damn right, a lot! My God, ye could probably get...well, enough to be comfortable fer quite a while. Quite a while! Tell ye what, I'll give ye two thousand fer it, right here an' now."

John laughed.

"I didn't tink ye'd fall fer that one. But, really, have ye ever considered sellin'? A piece such as that under the hammer would attract great interest."

"Brian, this book has been in me family fer almost *two hundred years*."

Brian hung up the poker and sat down. "Ye tink I haven't been there? When I inherited this place, it was full o' stuff. Most of it very, very *old* stuff. But it wasn't me responsibility to care fer someone else's clutter. I kept what was important to me an' sold off the rest. If I hadn't, this here castle would be stocked to the ceilin' with possessions, an' what the hell use is that, eh? If ye can't enjoy it in the short time ye've got, then what the hell use is it? If that book makes ye happy, fulfills ye, then keep it! But if ye could be so much happier doin' what ye wanted with the money it would bring.... 'Tis what we in the business call a *no-brainer*."

John shook his head emphatically. "I could never live with meself if I did that."

Brian refilled his glass and sat back to nurse it. "'Twas a time I thought the same about all the heirlooms here. Oh, it drove me to the brink of insanity, it did! Believe me, it grows easy once ye get over the initial struggle in morality. Definitely gets better, especially with a bank full o' cash to allow me the freedom o' livin' exactly as I see fit. I'll not be tinkin' about any o' those belongin's anymore. After all, 'tis all just *stuff*." He took a drink, then chimed in again, "An' if I had children, I couldn't possibly expect 'em to keep everythin' that's important to me. If I'm dead an' gone, I'd rather me kin auction off all me worldly possessions an' make their *own* life rather than have to live *my* life in me stead!"

John looked around the parlor. "I noticed ye kept the family castle," he said.

"True. But I kept it because I *fancy* it."

"Just as I fancy *Don Quixote*."

"Look, ye can do what ye please. That's the beauty o' life, it is. But I ask, are ye a book *seller* or a book *collector*?"

John sat in the dying glow of the firelight and said nothing. He only stared at the wall and the fox hunt tableau that hung from it.

"Now, if ye'll pardon me," Brian said, rising, "I've got to hit the loo. Feels as though me bladder is about to bubble over. Back in a moment!" He headed into the first library, leaving John alone.

The fox in the painting was only a few steps ahead of the hound. Desperation lined its face while the hound seemed to smile, pleased that it was performing well for the Masters coming up behind, jacketed in regal red and riding their titan Thoroughbreds. The Masters appeared oblivious to the plight of the fox; they seemed indifferent, even bored, by the murder about to take place. John stood and stretched, then turned his back on the painting and wandered into the first library.

The room was a marvel indeed and the feeling of seeing it for the first time flooded his senses once more and raised the hair on his arms. He went to the nearest shelf and began to explore. There didn't seem to be any order to the books, they were all simply placed cover-to-cover along the shelves. John reached out to touch them, then walked along the row, running his fingers over the spines. He loved hearing the quiet crinkle of paper jackets as his fingertips caressed them. He stopped and closed his eyes and blindly pulled a book from its home. It was *A Horse's Tail*, the final novel from

Mark Twain. It had no jacket and the boards were nicked and stained and when John delicately cracked open the cover to examine the copyright page, he saw it was a second printing. But when he turned one page further, he saw the scrawl in black ink under the title.

John stared at the page a moment, then gently closed the cover and placed it back.

Behind him, a glass case stood on thin legs of pedunculate oak, several books laying within. John approached it to see which titles were worthy of being stored separately from the others and saw two familiar volumes resting atop green felt: *Moby Dick* and *Treasure Island*. Next to them was *The Adventures of Huckleberry Finn* in bright green and gold. Behind them, a true first in Russian of *Anna Karenina* beside Poe's *The Raven and Other Poems*. Behind these, a row of thin, softcover publications fanned out over each other, the illustrated cover of the topmost copy reading, *The Personal History, Adventures, Experience, and Observation of David Copperfield the Younger*. It was the true first edition in its original serial form, all nineteen issues.

Viewing just one of these books would have sent John's heart beating in double-time, but as a collective, they had the opposite effect — his beat slowed and a great calm came over him. He cradled his chin in his palm and took a breath as he gazed, entranced, over the case and the gems it held.

He walked back to the tall shelves and continued exploring, head canted to read titles, eyes poring over each spine in wonder. He was familiar with half of them, perhaps less. For every Poe or Fitzgerald there were an equal number of Smiths or Martenses.

But the words, the words! How many words were in this room alone? How many of those words formed to create ideas with the power to move minds, to influence decisions, to govern men, to inspire and instruct and record and reflect? How many people had been affected by the words present? How many bursts of laughter or gasps of surprise had been released by these words? How many tears of joy, sorrow, empathy, anger, or resolve had been shed, how many goose pimples had stiffened on how many arms, how many heartbeats had slowed or quickened due to the assortment of words gathered here? How many brains tingled or stomachs churned or dreams followed as a result of these words? How many lives had been changed by the words in this glorious cathedral? How much *life* had breathed from the very pages that held them?

John drew a long breath and exhaled. His mind was electrified with thought, as though he were suddenly thrust into a room and made to stand before God. He was exhausted by the questions and the marvel, the senses and contemplations and emotions. His head tingled and tumbled and he thought this would be the sensation he would experience were he able to fly.

Brian appeared through the door to the second library, towing behind him an elderly man in an orange shirt. "I found me uncle," he said, leading the man by the hand. "John, this here is Uncle Bercan, up from his nap, apparently."

John smiled and offered his hand to the man with the disheveled white hair. "Pleased to meet ye," he said.

Uncle Bercan stared at the hand, his cheeks rosy and dimpled, yellow and black teeth exposed behind his grin. He made no move to accept the handshake, merely looked at John with eyes sparkling and vacant and said, "I knew a man once. He told me he was a farmer!" His chin folded in and he raised his brows expectantly, as though this information were spoken with the intent to astound.

"How lovely!" John said, and Uncle Bercan was pleased.

"Did ye see the man who lives in the ceilin'?" Uncle Bercan pointed up, then motioned to Brian. "He's wearin' *yer* underpants!"

Brian exchanged a glance with John, then took his uncle by the shoulders and spoke to him directly, increasing his volume a bit to make sure he was heard. "That's wonderful, Uncle! Go back upstairs now an' turn on the telly, eh? Would ye fancy that?"

Uncle Bercan's eyes widened and he smiled brightly. "No, I don't tink I would!" he said joyfully.

"We'll be in the parlor if ye need anythin', alright? I'll be up in a while to look in on ye!" Brian walked back to the parlor and John gave an awkward wave to the old man.

"'Twas nice to meet ye!" he said.

"Have a good trip!" called Uncle Bercan. "We'll all be fine here in the library. Bring me some tulips if ye tink of it!"

In the parlor, Brian lowered his voice and said, "That's Uncle Bercan. Ye've met the legend."

"He's deep in it, eh? The dementia."

"Aye. He's been that way fer months, poor man, gettin' worse all the time. But let's have a seat, ye've hardly touched that whiskey."

They resumed their places on the Chesterfields and struck up a conversation on politics. Brian was disillusioned by the work of the new PM from the Fianna Fail and began comparing him with his predecessor from the Labour Party. John didn't follow politics too closely, but was intrigued to hear Brian's position. Twenty minutes into Brian's discourse, a great fluttering of paper was heard from the library adjacent and they heard Uncle Bercan guffawing and wheezing.

Brian stood and motioned for John to stay seated. "Sounds as though Uncle Bercan's makin' trouble again," he said, and excused himself to the library. John's gaze wandered the parlor again, his eyes purposely avoiding the foxhunt canvas, and fell on the patterns in the hearthstone. It was beautiful work and appeared as though its designer had painstakingly chosen each stone according to how well it would compliment those around it. He sat entranced by its patterns until the sound of breaking glass and heavy pounding from deep within the library woke him to trouble.

A moment later, Brian bolted through the parlor and into the hall. John stood, concerned, and looked into the first library. There was no sign of Uncle Bercan, only a tremendous mess of pages, *hundreds* of pages, littering the floor near the glass case. Floating over the sea of paper was the loose, broken binding of *Moby Dick*. He ran to the door leading to the front hall and immediately hopped back as Bucephalus appeared and charged straight for him, eyes ablaze, a thundering growl radiating from his throat.

"*Bucephalus, NO! Outside!*" Brian shouted at the Rottweiler from the end of the hall and the dog promptly changed direction and headed for the front door. Brian opened it and let the dog bolt, turning a switch on the wall that flooded the grounds with light. Rattled, John stayed put and witnessed the scene from his vantage point down the hall.

Brian ran after the dog, then hurried back and rummaged through the front closet. He emerged wielding an over/under big game shotgun and rushed outside with it. John followed him to the door and looked out, trying to discern what in Christ's name was happening.

All he saw was Brian sprinting up the drive. Bucephalus was not in sight, but he heard barking, then fierce growling in the distance. Brian hadn't gotten far on the loose gravel before he stopped and raised the shotgun and fired twice into the darkness. The explosions rang out over the property and were absorbed by the coolness in the air. The horrifying sound of Bucephalus's shouts and yelps came then and Brian charged to the rose garden and disappeared from view and John dashed out to stand helplessly in the drive.

The dog's shrieks ceased abruptly and a moment later Brian appeared, hunched over with the gun in one hand and pulling the collar of Bucephalus with the other. The dog seemed fine, although he whimpered and broke into a sneezing fit as they walked. John ran to them and took the shotgun from Brian. The dog was covered in filth and a remarkable stench rose from his fur.

"What in the high an' holy hell just happened?" he said. "Are ye alright?"

Brian brushed past and entered the house, keeping a firm grip on the dog's collar. "I've got to get him to the bath, this is awful!" Man and dog bounded up the stairs and disappeared into the toilet, leaving John standing in the foyer with a smoking shotgun in his hand and a bewildered look in his eye.

The word that John then spoke to himself is, even in our modern time, entirely unprintable.

*   *   *   *

The drive back to Dublin only took half the time it had to drive out. Both John and Brian were alert and invigorated, still reeling from what happened. Brian explained that when he'd gone to check on his uncle, he'd found two men running through the libraries, apparent burglars after his books. He chased them into the toilet through the second library, but they escaped through a window. That's when he ran to release Bucephalus and gave chase with the gun. One of the men appeared to be a Scotsman, dressed in a tartan kilt, but, unfortunately, Brian never got a good look at their faces due to bags that covered their heads.

Bucephalus's nose had led him to the rose garden, where he became entangled in a pair of soiled trousers. The yelping John heard was the dog as he attacked and rolled in the pants, becoming unbearably dirty by the filth soaking them through. Poor Bucie had squealed like a gut-shot mutt when he realized what he was wrestling. Brian fired two shells blindly after the escaping thieves, but didn't think he'd hit anything. He ran to free the dog from the pants that had twisted around his midriff, then took him inside to get him washed up.

"An' if I ever find the two who broke in," Brian said, "there's no chance I'll treat 'em with as much kindness as yer Grampy Doyle treated his burglar with. I'll rip 'em apart with these very hands!" He clenched the steering wheel tightly and kneaded it.

"I'm terribly sorry about *Moby Dick*," John said. "They seemed to know what they were after."

Brian waved his hand in the air. "'Tis no loss. I know a brilliant binder in County Cork who's done restoration work fer me in the past. He can put it all together an' bind it up like new. It looks as though the entire book is still there an' at least the original boards seem to be in one piece. Hell, maybe it'll improve its value. Cripes!" he cursed suddenly. "How do these things *happen*?"

They arrived at the shop in no time and John climbed out, thanking Brian again for the ride home. "I had a wonderful an' deeply troublin' evenin', tank ye very much," he said. "I'm sure I shan't be recoverin' anytime soon." The fellows shared a good, stress-relieving laugh.

Brian wiped his eyes. "I'd come in to take a peek at *Quixote*, but I feel I should get home quick. Still, expect a visit someday soon. I'm eager to get me hands on that!"

"Like that nurse who takes care o' yer uncle?" asked John with a twinkle.

"Perhaps not as eager as *that*," Brian said and, throwing a wave, headed off.

It was late and John prepared for bed, but his mind was far too charged to settle down for sleep. After dressing in his nightclothes, he wandered back into the shop with only the light seeping in from the bedroom to guide him. He approached the counter and halted when he stepped on the loose floorboards. They creaked a long and strident welcome. "Good evenin' to ye as well," he replied. "Have I got a story to tell! But first," he said, sitting at the loose boards and crossing his legs, "ye have a story fer me."

He dug his fingernails into the crevice between the boards and lifted. Two of the boards came up easily, revealing a hollow underneath. John pulled out a heavy package crumpled inside a paper bag, then unrolled the bag and set it aside. A wooden box sat in his hands, intricately carved with images of horses and mules and windmills, an overturned barber's basin "helmet" with a crescent moon cut from its brim decorating the center of it all. His fingers delicately rubbed the top of the woodcut as though reading Braille, then he drew from his pocket a pair of cotton gloves and slipped them over his hands. He opened the box and reached in, gingerly wrapping his fingers around what lay within, and withdrew the book, the most important book in his life, the book that quite literally *was* the Chivalric Nobleman de La Mancha. It was heavy and smelled of dry leaves and mulch with a hint of floral sweetness.

He lay the book flat in his lap and angled his body so the light from his bedroom spilled over its cover. Running his sheathed thumb along the edge of its top board, he cracked it open, minding carefully not to stress the binding, and read,

El Ingenioso
Hidalgo Don Qvi-
xote de La Mancha,
Compuefto por Miguel de Cervantes
Saavedra.

Under that, the publisher's crest with a phrase written in Latin: *Lvcem Post Tenebras Spero* — Light After Darkness — then the year, *Ano, 1605*.

John sat with the book in his hands, contemplating everything it represented and everything it was. He turned to the first page and began reading aloud to himself, translating from memory:

"In a village of La Mancha, the name of which I purposely omit, there lived not long ago one of those gentlemen who usually keep a lance upon a rack, an old target, a lean horse, and a greyhound for coursing..."

CHAPTER EIGHT
The Masque of the Read Death

When Tinky O'Shea left the Chivalric Nobleman de La Mancha Bookshop that morning, the tiny, simple chime of the bell over the door caused his suffering, swill-poisoned head to detonate in pain. A lit firecracker lodged in his ear couldn't have had a worse effect. The pain, however, was overwhelmed by turbulence rocking his brain over his severe distrust of Brian Corrigan. Tinky began his trek to work, hoping the brisk hike would clear his head and allow him to forget Corrigan and think of finer things, like women or football or friendship or Melville.

Corrigan! The weasel! The louse! The thief! John may not have been wrong when he suggested Tinky's opinion was biased. Not only did Tinky have an ingrained dislike of wealth, but Corrigan had been the one to steal away *his* book, the very book he'd been looking for all his life, the masterpiece that had influenced him since he was in knee breeches, his *Moby Dick*! The book that was rightfully his! But the elite Mister Corrigan had found his way into John's life, *weaseled* in, and flashed his charm and panache and money in John's face to triumph over a life-long friendship. Then he betrayed John by trying to sell the book to a fat American dealer (nay, *pimp!*) for profit! A profiteer! (Or so it seemed. Perhaps it was unfair to assume.) No! Nothing was unfair when it came to Brian Corrigan! *The man did not deserve the book that rightfully belonged to Tinky O'Shea!*

He was moving so quickly through the morning foot traffic that many passing pedestrians thought he was a race walker out to get his heart pumping. Tinky inhaled deeply and let it out gradually, then slowed his pace. *Calm, son,* he thought, *ease down! Yer imagination is gettin' the best o' ye!* He forced himself to notice his surroundings and relax. He sought out the beauty of the morning and his pulse began to settle. There, now. Birds flying overhead. Clear skies. Sun shining. Beautiful, buxom lasses walking rapidly past, giving him an eyeful of "The Dublin Jiggle." There was beauty all around. He began greeting everyone he passed. "Hello! Good day to ye! Top o' the mornin'!" He tipped his cap to all and was pleased with their responses. They smiled, they whistled, they said, "how d'ye do?" It really was a gorgeous morning, despite his hangover, despite his own spite, despite his loathing of that fellow Corrigan.

Corrigan! The bastard! The profanity! The blankety-blank of foulness and swearing and censorial vulgarity! He was corrupting his best friend, his John, his oldest and dearest chum! He was influencing him, distracting him, leading him away from the path of the righteous! AND he'd stolen *Moby Dick* away for mere pence, a trifle, an insignificant drop in the bucket of its worth! *His* worth! *The man must not be allowed to get away with such a crime!*

He was walking hurriedly again, this time in a decidedly different direction, a direction away from the building home to his employ. During his frenzied march, his plotting mind never ceased churning, not even when he stopped to call his employer to report he wouldn't be coming in today due to an overwhelming illness infecting both his body and soul.

*   *   *   *

Mac Malone's foot was roasting. For nine hours, it had been pressed against the largest of the exhaust vents on the roof over the Olympia Theater and the heat blowing from it was causing the rubber on the sole of his shoe to liquefy and melt. The point of contact was beginning to sizzle audibly, like a slab of steak on a seared skillet. Neither the sizzle nor the burn was enough to disturb his slumber, however, nor did it alarm the pigeon lying on his face, completely entranced as it was in a Zen-like state of relaxation caused by the soothing vibrations of Mac's sonorous snore. Not even the acrid stench of burning rubber was enough to disturb the pair.

Mac was entombed in an abyss of unconsciousness so deep that the stomps of Tinky's feet near his head failed to rouse him. Tinky had already tried words, but he couldn't shout due to his fragile and aching head. He'd spoken gently into Mac's ear and was greeted by both a rousing snore from Mac and an annoyed look from the pigeon. He'd poked, shaken, and shoved unsuccessfully. He'd clapped and slapped and punched. He'd explained to Mac that his foot was on fire. Still nothing. Finally, Tinky knelt and whispered into Mac's ear again, this time armed with a savage choice of words.

"Mac Malone, ye are one *lazy* man."

Mac sprung to his feet, dazed and disoriented, and the startled pigeon hung to his face by clenching its toes into his lips. A great, confused howl erupted from Mac's throat as the bird clung desperately to his kisser and boxed his ears with its powerful wings. Mac took a step forward and slipped on the molten rubber of his sole, as slick now as a burnt marshmallow, falling over and landing flat on his back and spewing out every ounce of air from his lungs. The indignant pigeon hopped off his face and pecked at his ear while Mac lay writhing.

"I'm *not* lazy," Mac said listlessly. "Yer mother scrubs dishes in a whorehouse!"

"Mac, I need yer help," Tinky said.

"Who's that?" Mac's eyes were closed and he spoke to the sky. "Ye'll get nothin' from me, disturbin' me nap so rudely...."

Tinky stood over him. "'Tis me, Mac, Tinky O'Shea. I was with ye last night at the feast!"

The mere mention of food was enough to send a wave of nausea through Mac's system. He belched like an elephant and was sickened by the taste. "Refrain from bringin' up that blasted supper!" he shouted. "Me body is still in a state o' rebellion over it!" He opened one eye and saw Tinky leaning over him, saw the swelling bruise on his cheek and the bleeding cut over his temple. "Was it the pigeon did that?"

"No," Tinky said, "but gettin' on top o' this here roof is no easy task. Why can't ye live on the lawns o' Phoenix Park like everyone else?"

"No view...." Slumber took hold of Mac once again.

Tinky reached out to pinch his cheek. "NO! Stay with me, ol' boy! I need yer help!"

Mac snapped out of his dream and said, "With what?"

"We need to steal back me book!"

"I don't read!" Mac said, and went back to sleep.

"'Tis no time fer that!" Tinky sat at his head and explained, "'Tis really not fer me, but fer John! Ye hear me? Fer John, I says!"

"John...," Mac said dreamily.

Hoping his words would transcend Mac's trance, Tinky explained the situation (or, more accurately, his perspective of the situation), explained about John and Brian and *Moby Dick* and the horrible polluting of John's soul that was taking place. He told how John would be venturing into the demon's lair that very night and said it was imperative they be there to do something about it.

Mac rolled over and talked in his sleep. "Whatyewantmetodo'boutit?" he slurred.

Tinky addressed his back. "We, I an' you, will take the Melville back an' give it to John. If anyone deserves a second chance with it, 'tis our John Doyle. Will ye help me? Mac!" He looked over Mac's shoulder and saw a bubble of saliva growing over Mac's open mouth, trembling in the morning breeze. He grasped the man's shoulder and shook it brusquely, disintegrating the bubble. "'Tis no time fer leisure, man! Our friend needs us! Ye've got to help!"

An idea struck him. Leaning over, he brought his voice close to Mac's ear and spoke in a sing-song. "I'll buy ye a fine supper tonight if ye come with me!"

At the mention of food, Mac's stomach tightened in knots.

"I'll treat ye to steak, chops, salmon, whatever suits yer fancy!"

Mac's body was still busy digesting and in no condition to hear about food. It raised a knife to the throat of his constitution and threatened mutiny.

"Baked potatoes overflowin' with melted cheese," Tinky enticed. "Mushy peas. Creamed spinach. French onion soup! Anythin' yer heart desires!"

Mac's belly spasmed and brought up two teaspoons of the previous night's meal. He swallowed it back down and was left with a rancid taste.

"Fer dessert, chunky banana iced cream with melted peanut butter an'...."

Mac sat up. "*FINE!*" he shouted, then leaned into the exhaust vent and threw up.

"Grand, just grand!" Tinky stood and patted Mac on the back. "I'll meet ye here at five o'clock. Ground level." He started off, then thought better and turned back. "Better make it four o'clock. Ye'll not be late, if ye please!"

Mac looked up long enough to see Tinky climb tremblingly over the lip of the roof onto the rickety fire escape ladder. A moment later he heard the sound of flesh slapping against steel, then a horrible, echoing crash of dead weight on frail metal. He put his head down, let loose a roaring burst of flatulence, and drifted into unconsciousness.

*   *   *   *

At ten minutes past five, Mac appeared on the footpath before the Olympia Theater, his head dangling like dead weight, lids drooping, mouth drooling, feet lurching and scraping the ground. A group of Japanese tourists passing by saw him and thought perhaps he'd escaped from some secret project involving the undead. One child screamed, another started crying. Their father wet his pants.

Tinky was there to meet him. "Ye're late, Mac!" he scolded. "I almost climbed up that damned perilous fire escape to get ye!"

Mac yawned and asked, "Why didn't ye use the stairs?"

"Stairs?"

"Just inside." He pointed to the lobby of the building adjacent. "Never mind 'bout that. Leave me be, I've got to be meetin' someone here soon. Whoever they is, I'll not be wantin' 'em to see me with the likes o' you."

"'Tis me ye're waitin' fer, ye numbwit! We've got to help John out, remember?"

"John. Right. We're gonna read to him, then, is that it?"

"Pick up yer feet an' let's go, we've a ride to catch!"

Tinky led the way, up Dame Street through the thick foot traffic of five o'clock, a right on South Great George's Street, then a left to cut through Wicklow Street. The next quarter mile flew past and the shopping crowd along Grafton was within sight when Tinky looked back to make sure Mac was keeping up. He saw only strangers.

"The slovenly slug!" he cursed, then retraced his steps back to his starting point, finding Mac dozing peacefully under the awning of the Olympia Theater. Pedestrians stepped over him as though he were a puddle of spilled coffee.

"Get up, ye scurvy dog!" Tinky knelt and thrust his hands under Mac's arms and aggressively hoisted him up, his strength fueled by passion, and shook him from side to side as though mopping the ground with his feet. "Wake up, Mac! We're on a mission!"

Mac woke grumblingly and Tinky pulled him by his wrist down Dame Street, up South Great George's Street and left onto Wicklow. They dove into the shopping crowd along Grafton and soon managed their way to the home and workplace of John Doyle.

When they entered the quiet lane, Tinky slowed the pace dramatically, creeping along the footpath toward the Chivalric Nobleman, eyes darting about for any sign of John or Brian. A massive motorcar was parked like a beached whale just past the shop and Tinky knew it was Corrigan's by its sheer, scratch-less perfection. He checked his watch and saw they had another twenty minutes before John closed up for the evening. Their timing was right on the mark.

Towing Mac, Tinky crossed the lane and crept forth. They were nearly in front of the bookshop when Tinky looked in and was surprised to see the front counter deserted. He took the opportunity to break into a jog, tugging Mac past the shop windows toward Brian's car. When they were halfway across, Tinky saw John appear at the counter with Brian and he raised his arm over his face to disguise his identity. He doubled his speed and yanked at the dead weight of Mac Malone, who stumbled lethargically behind.

They reached the car unnoticed and Tinky went to work. Squatting at the passenger-side door, he took from his pocket two thin, steel picks and stuck them delicately in the lock, shimmying and jimmying them like Bobby Molloy had instructed back in school. Mac stood over and swayed languidly to and fro like a frail tree in a strong wind.

"Get down!" Tinky whispered. "We can't let 'em see us!"

"Huh!" Mac was startled awake. "Are we goin' fer a ride?"

"Aye! Now hush up an' get out o' sight!"

Tinky almost had the lock open when he heard a splashing sound. He looked over to find Mac relieving his bladder on the wing of Brian's car.

"What in God's hell are ye doin'?" he whispered incredulously.

Mac looked at him drowsily. "Momma always said to do it before ye get in, 'cause Poppa don't stop."

Tinky considered it and agreed.

The lock popped and Tinky opened the door. Inside, he found an immaculate interior still carrying the odor of upholstery fresh from the factory. On the floor behind the front seat he spied a green plaid blanket and he motioned for Mac to climb in back with him.

Once inside, Tinky closed the door gently and locked it, then settled back to look at the space under the backseat. It would be tight, but there was enough room for two men to hide behind the tall front seats, provided they lie in a particular fashion. He took the blanket in hand and motioned for Mac to lay down.

"We can hide under the blanket, but we'll have to stack one on top of another. You go first, just lay on the floor there."

Mac looked at the small space, then at his own girth. "Ferget it!" he said. "I'll not be ridin' hobo in a car as fancy-like as this!"

Tinky grabbed his shoulders and tried to stress the urgency of the situation with his tone. "Mac. We cannot ride in this here car sittin' up. We're stowaways, understand? If John an' Brian discover us, we're done fer! Now will ye please, *please*, lay on the floor?"

"Fine!" Mac conceded. "But I'm on top."

Tinky scoffed. "Mac, I weigh less than eight stone. Ye'd crush me!" He looked out the rear screen, becoming increasingly frantic. "Get on the floor! They'll be comin' any minute!"

Mac folded his arms like a scorned child and looked away.

"Alright, alright!" Tinky slid to the floor and lay face upward. "Now, if this is to work, ye need to put yer head by me feet. We'll stagger ourselves, see? Lay as flat as ye can!"

It took quite some time for Mac to wrest his body between the seats and Tinky found himself both the hapless and helpless victim of his writhing form. He endured several blunt kicks to the face, an elbow in the shin, a knee to the chest and a palm in the groin before Mac was in position. By the time Mac finished squirming, Tinky was completely pinned down and struggling to breathe. To make matters worse, he found his chin nestled neatly in the crevice where Mac's legs met, his nose precariously close to Mac's upturned buttocks.

Tinky wriggled his left hand free of Mac's weight and found the blanket. He clenched a corner between his fingers and pulled, inch by inch, until it covered them completely. It was time-consuming work and forced him to twist and contort to such a degree that by the time the job was complete, he was a sweaty, panting mess.

Finally, the men lay prostrate, silent save for Tinky's heavy breathing. It was the first calm they'd had since arriving.

"Tinky," Mac said.

"Sssshhhhhh!" Tinky shushed.

"I'll not be feelin' good."

"Fear not, Mac," Tinky whispered. "'Tis all fer the good o' John."

"No. I mean I'll not be feelin' good. Me belly's still under siege from last night an' I's been sick all day."

"Well, fer Chrissake, Mac, there's nothin' I can do 'bout that. Lay still an' quit tinkin' of it. Tink of — I don't know — antacid an' French bread."

From outside, they heard someone shouting. "I don't believe it! In the name o' sanity!"

Tinky recognized Brian's deep and powerful voice. "Hush up, now, Mac! They're here!" His heart was beating like a bugler's reveille.

"Someone's pissed on me car is all!" Brian was saying. "Fer the love o' Christ, how do these things happen?" The driver's door opened and the car bounced as Brian got in. The sound of another door opening and the car bounced again.

"Sorry." This time it was John's voice. "Those things rarely happen 'round here." Mac's right leg was quickly numbing, pinched under the seat by the new weight in front. He squirmed to find a more comfortable position, but stopped when he saw Tinky's feet frantically swishing back and forth, signaling him to lay still. *Fine!*, Mac thought.

The ignition turned and they were off. The soothing vibration of the floor helped Mac and Tinky relax, despite their discomfort. The noise of the city gave way to the solitude of the country and the ride became a flowing progression rather than a series of stops and starts. *This is grand*, Tinky thought. *We're actually doin' it!* He took a slow breath of relief and let it out ever so quietly.

Thirty minutes into the ride, the peace crumbled when Brian and John rolled their windows down. Wind flooded the back of the car and the blanket concealing the men began flapping like a flag in a hurricane. The double-stitched corner rippled up and down, *smack-smack-smacking* Tinky's face and threatening his eyes.

As Tinky endured the attack, a hearty snore emitted from near his feet loud enough to send a horrified chill streaming down his spine. The jackass! He'd fallen asleep! Here they were, crushed together on the floor of a car in the most uncomfortable positions possible with a heavy woolen blanket beating them like a schoolyard bully, and Mac Malone was sawing logs direct from Dreamland! Tinky bent his wrist and locked Mac's nipple between his fingers and twisted sharply. Mac woke and twitched violently, clamping Tinky's head in the vice of his knees, and remembered to stifle his cry. They heard Brian from the front seat.

"I'd rather it be an electric saw than the sounds of a hundred idling diesels!"

Tinky breathed with relief, but Mac's clenched knees remained tight. Tinky could feel the muscles along Mac's legs contracting and relaxing in spasms. Mac began to fidget and squirm in small movements that threatened to give them away. He seemed also to be clenching his fists tightly; Tinky could feel them trembling by his waist. He could also feel a great heat emanating from Mac's body and, as his head was knocked about by Mac's jerking knees, a sudden, ominous feeling poured over him. It appeared as though Mac were girding his loins for battle. And still the blanket continued its assault.

There comes a time in everyone's life when their body rebels against them, when the controlling circuits of the mind surrender to physical necessity and let go. It is the human body's equivalent of a three-alarm fire, an emergency best observed from a safe distance, and typically results from a poisoning of the system by either chemicals, undercooked meats, or excessive consumption. At times, the introduction of foods foreign to one's typical diet can cause similar results and today Mac Malone became the unwitting victim of a combination of these catalysts. He'd eaten to such excess the night before that his body was having difficulty in the recovery stage. But it was Mac's unusual lunch that served as the primary ingredient in the explosive mixture now churning his belly. Reeling from John's accusation that he was a glutton, Mac was motivated to prove the man wrong and committed himself that very moment to something he'd never before attempted in his life: a *diet*. Inspired, he woke in the afternoon and hiked to the industrial waste bin behind St. Oliver Plunkett Junior Boys School, where he found a tremendous mound of uneaten lettuce fresh from the cafeteria.

He picked the best leaves from the pile and made himself a
small salad, complete with shredded carrots and sliced olives
and cherry tomatoes and a mixture of dressings, then sat and
forced it down his gullet.   He had no recollection of a
vegetable ever passing his lips before, but figured he would
not soon forget the experience; it was revolting, vile,
torturous, and it damn near killed him.   His throat had a
seizure in attempt to bring the first bite back up, but Mac
forced it down.   His stomach took the side of his throat and
tried to refuse it as well, performing a dance of erratic
convulsions intent on tossing the foreigner out in an act of
unfounded bigotry.   Mac held firm and closed his eyes and
concentrated on keeping the leaves down and, forty-five
minutes later, left satisfied with the three bites he'd managed.
When he returned to the Olympia and went back to sleep, the
rumblings of war were born.   His stomach awakened to the
dawn of its own Waterloo and, several hours later, when Mac
was being carried through the streets behind Tinky, he felt the
first troubling pangs of what is sometimes referred to as *the
skitters*.   And now, here on the floor of a vehicle traveling down
a charming country road during the dusk of an elegant
evening, one man looked into the darkness of his own soul
and beheld a pale horse, and his name that sat on him was
Skitters.

And Hell followed with him.

There is nothing funny about loose bowels, especially
if your head is stuck at the receiving end of them.   Like a
condemned man staring down the barrels of his own firing
squad, Tinky knew what was coming, but no amount of
mental preparation could have readied him for the onslaught
that followed.   He was like a new daddy who faints at the sight
of his firstborn's birth; although Mac was the afflicted, the one
suffering the rolling spasms, the burning, the sweating and
hyperventilation and dehydration, the exhausting contraction
of muscles and the hollow sickness in the pit of his intestinal
tract, it was Tinky who recoiled in horror.   Mac labored like a

champion to keep the dam from breaking; anyone who's ever experienced the same sort of ordeal would've cheered him on with shouts of *Yeah, laddie, that's the ticket! Ye're doin' great, just grand! 'Tis tough, I know, but hang in there!* Yet Tinky O'Shea could not find it in him to support his companion in any way. Instead, he very selfishly went out of his mind.

The first offensive came quietly yet powerfully. While Brian and John reacted in the front, blaming the spring fertilization, Tinky lay convulsing on the floor behind them as though fifty thousand watts of electricity were shooting through his meat. The heat, the stench, the mere *idea* of what was happening literally right under his nose was causing his mind to abandon all notions of sense and reality. He became lightheaded and his vision was overcome with sparkling pinpoints of light. The practical, tangible elements of the world melted into an hallucinogenic mist around him; the rich leather of the seats he was pinned between evaporated and became the wooden slats of a giant crib, the clouds visible through the rear window became a twirling mobile hovering overhead for his amusement, and the flapping blanket became a swaddle that wrapped itself around his newborn form. Intelligence dribbled from his ears like syrup, memories turned to dust, and logic performed a dynamic striptease before diving into a glass of water and disintegrating.

As for Mac, ache and sweat and fret besieged him as he lay giving birth to his demon child. The pain rolled in waves through him and continued its charge; once the first regiment was through, it was difficult to keep the rest of the detachment out. Or in, as it were. As John and Brian sat laughing about the horridness up front, Mac wept about it in back while Tinky rolled his eyes around to stare dumb-founded at his own brain.

Time slowed like the changing of seasons. It seemed like months passed before the stowaways felt the car turn and stop. They heard Brian speaking with another gentleman, but paid no mind to their dialogue. They were in motion again and heard the grinding of gravel underneath. Another century passed before the car came to rest and they heard two doors open and close, then the crunch of footsteps receding over the drive, then nothing.

A minute passed before a head appeared over the seats. It looked this way and that. It looked up and down and all around. A door opened. What was once a man crawled out. Tinky did not appear well. His glazed eyes were crimson, his complexion the color of ice. The flailing blanket had worked itself around his neck and he now unwittingly wore it like a cape. He crawled over the gravel. He scooped rocks into his fists and tried to crush them. He wept shamelessly.

A snort from within the car brought his senses rushing back and he stood, alert, wiping his eyes on his sleeve. Yes! Right! No time for groveling! He'd stared into the hindquarters of Hell and survived. There was work to be done! He crouched down and ran to the other side of the car, eyes darting, scanning, searching for any sign of movement from the castle. He filled his lungs with fresh air and held it in, then opened the car door and grabbed Mac by his arms and pulled with all his might. The sweat covering Mac's lumpy torso acted as a fine lubricant and he popped out with surprising ease, momentum sending both men toppling to the ground. Tinky found himself once again pinned under the malodorous and mammoth physique of Mac Malone and sheer terror gave him strength to roll out from under the mass and scramble to his feet.

Looking over the motionless body, Tinky was struck with a feeling of dread. Mac didn't appear to be breathing; his mouth lay open and his pale, dry tongue hung from it like cold Spam. His face was a granite mask of anguish. Tinky took a wary step toward him.

"Mac?" he asked in a hushed tone. "Ye alright?"

No response. Tinky knelt beside him and patted his cheek. "Mac? Hey-yo, Mac?"

His answer was a rasping vibration that echoed from within the deepest recesses of Mac's sinus. The snore so relieved Tinky, he nearly kissed the man's glistening cheek. Instead, he slapped it with all of his strength.

Mac rolled over, grumbling sleepily and swatting weakly at his assailant.

"Mac, ye've got to get up! We're exposed here!" Tinky was frantic, but his whispers failed to budge the slumbering rhinoceros at his feet. Seeing no way around it, he wrapped his arms around Mac's chest and hoisted. The weight was too great, however, and he had to circle around and lean against the side of Brian's car for traction. Once upright, he began dragging Mac over the driveway toward the south tower.

Three cars sat in the drive and Tinky had just made it past the second when the castle's front door opened. Tinky froze, paralyzed, heart thumping in triple time due to his position, entirely exposed with nowhere to hide and absolutely vulnerable with Mac's dead weight strapped under his arms. The young woman who emerged from the door skipped down the porch steps and headed straight for them. Strangely, she walked past without a hint of eye contact and stopped only when she arrived at the nearest car. She opened the door and paused, then turned her disgusted gaze to them.

"You boys almost finished?" she asked.

Tinky, lost in a coma of confusion, nodded in the affirmative.

"He's had enough, I'll have ye know," she said. "He's aware ye're carryin' on an' misbehavin'. Ye'd better shape up by tomorrow or he'll set the hound on ye's, an' if that happens, ye can bid a good-day to yer bollix!" She got in the car and turned the ignition over, then rolled down the window. "Look at ye! Not a lick o' shame!" She turned the car around and sped up the hill, leaving them in a mist of diesel exhaust and dust.

Tinky stared into the space she'd just possessed, eyes bulging, heart frozen mid-beat. He nearly dropped Mac in order to weep again and crush more gravel. What if Brian *was* onto their scheme? It was impossible to tell unless confronted by the man himself. Besides, they'd traveled too far — *much* too far — to be turned away by a stranger's cryptic message.

Tinky made the choice to gather his wits and continue forward. He pulled Mac around the corner to the base of the tower and lay him down out of sight from the castle entrance, then peeled the britches from Mac's legs and disgustedly carried the mess to the edge of the rose garden. He flung what was once a fine pair of hand-me-downs into the center and the ravaged pants settled within the thorny bushes, hidden from sight. Through it all, Mac continued his snooze, blissfully unaware of the cool evening air blowing into his own nudity, until he was rudely awakened by a jet of cold water from the garden hose up his backside.

"*WAAAAAAAAUUUUUUGGGGGGGGGHHHHHHH!!!*"

Mac's cry was huge and shrill and seared in agony, but Tinky had possessed the forethought to mute it by wrapping the blanket round his head. He certainly didn't enjoy waking Mac in such a fashion, but it was a necessary task before they continued their quest. Mac squirmed and screamed into his silencer until Tinky dropped the hose and unwrapped the blanket.

Mac gulped down air. "How could ye do somethin' so cruel?"

"Vengeance," whispered Tinky. "Now get up an' wrap that blanket 'round yer waist an' let's get goin'! We've work to do!"

Mac peered down and noticed his exposed jewels. With a horrified shriek, he turned his backside to Tinky and sprang to his feet. "Look away!" he cried as he folded the blanket around his midriff like a bath towel. When Mac was sure it was wrapped tightly, he turned to face Tinky again, but the blanket slipped and fell around his ankles. Mac shrieked again and hoisted it quickly to cover himself.

"Come, now," Tinky said. "Up ye go!"

"Up where?"

"Up this tower."

Mac craned his head back. Three stories up, a window lay open and waiting. Between them was twenty-five feet of sheer stone wall.

Mac looked back to Tinky. "Beg pardon?"

Tinky ran his hand over the uneven contour of the wall. "'Tis rough, see. Jagged. Plenty o' finger an' toe-holds. We climb up, we go in. Simple. Up ye go!"

Mac was reluctant. "Why will the front door not work?"

"Because John an' Corrigan might see us."

"Why can't they see us?"

"Because we're not supposed to be here."

"Why not?"

"Because we're here to steal a book."

"What book?"

"John's book."

"Why am I here?"

Tinky paused. "I been askin' meself that very question since we was in the car. In theory, ye're here to help."

"Am I gonna be made to look a fool walkin' up this here wall?"

"On the contrary, ye'll be made to look a hero. If ye can pull this off, ye'll be helpin' me an' John an' yerself."

"How meself?"

"Because ye'll feel good about what ye done here today."

Mac looked up the wall again and considered it all. "I still feel poorly."

"Sorry to hear that. But just tink, at the end o' the day, ye'll have overcome great obstacles in order to help John."

The window seemed to float a great distance over their heads. A trifling breeze fluttered its curtain. It resembled a waving hand, beckoning them on.

Mac put the toes of his right foot on the masonry and grabbed a high stone in the wall and hoisted himself up. He hung for a moment, testing the stability of the structure. It held his weight and he repeated the process. He now hung two feet over the lawn.

"That's it," Tinky encouraged. "Keep a-goin' an' never look down! I'll be right behind ye." Under his breath, he added, "God help us all."

Mac climbed another foot, then another. Four feet now. He looked up and the window seemed closer that it had been. Two more hoists. Six feet. The stones were holding.

When Mac was eight feet up, Tinky stepped to the base of the tower and curled his sweating, trembling fingers over the lip of a stone. His foot found a protruding slab and he lifted himself up thirteen inches. He remained there for a long while, mentally persuading himself to continue. It wasn't too late to turn back. No! No, he could not! He was after the book and he would have it. As he told Mac, at the end of the day he'll have overcome great obstacles in order to help John. And himself. Besides, at this point he'd be damned if he'd come all this way with his face in the cannon of Mac's illness for nothing. He yanked the leash on his fear and climbed another foot.

Up they went, scaling the wall as the sun receded behind the castle. Tinky did his best to look neither down nor up, for he had an awkward view up Mac's makeshift skirt if he raised his head. He prayed to the patron saint of rock climbers that Mac's affliction would not return, for he was positioned directly underneath and was squarely in the proverbial line of fire. He mumbled three Hail Marys to himself as a precaution and climbed on.

Mac, too, was doing well. He had no fear of heights as Tinky had and he impressed himself with his own vitality and virility. He imagined the muscles along his arms flexing and bulging through his sweat-soaked shirt and wished a photographer were present to shoot a spread for *Butch* magazine. It was tiring work, but he refused to rest until safely through that window. He was a man determined, energy and excitement pouring through him from his adrenaline reserve. He stopped to execute a massive yawn, then continued eagerly upward.

Within six minutes of starting his climb, Mac's hand touched the base of the window. He raised his head over the ledge and peered in. It was a sizable bedroom, fully furnished, with no sign of anyone inside. He pushed the window open wide and hooked his arms over the sill, feeling for a hand-hold but finding only a dainty curtain. Clutching a fistful of it, he pulled and brought the entire rod crashing down. His floundering foot found an outcropping that allowed him to lift his center of gravity over the sill and he flopped into the room, landing thunderously on the hardwood floor.

Tinky looked up, alerted to the ruckus. "Ye alright?" he shout-whispered up.

A hand waved weakly out the window and left it at that.

Tinky continued closely behind and soon was near enough to the windowsill to curl his hand around its base. He expected Mac to pull him in, but when he looked inside, Tinky found him lying comfortably in bed, unconscious. Tinky dangled from the window, launching insults and epithets in Mac's direction until the hibernating one rose and sleepwalked to the window and scraped Tinky over the edge until he lay safely on solid flooring. Mac then went back to bed.

The room was tidy and seemed unused. Tinky assumed it was a spare bedroom from the slightly musty, mothballed odor. The maid had probably left the window open to air it out.

Against one wall stood a bureau and Tinky began rifling through. Stacks of men's undergarments lay in the top drawer and he snatched two pieces out. He fashioned one pair of white underpants over his head, adjusting them so his eyes were exposed through a leg loop and his nose poked through the tackle flap, then scurried to Mac and shook him relentlessly until he woke.

Mac opened his eyes to find a man looming over, head deformed by a pair of blobby briefs, a patch of greasy hair blossoming from one hole and crazed, close-set eyes peering out from the other, and thought it was another rowdy juvenile come to pummel the homeless for sport. "Be quick about it, ye scoundrel," he mumbled, half-awake, and rolled over.

"Mac, get up! Come now, there'll be no sleepy time fer us." He pushed and pulled and poked until the drowsy spell faded and Mac begrudgingly stood. Tinky thrust the second pair of underpants at him. "Put 'em on an' let's go!"

Mac hoisted the base of his makeshift kilt out of the way and pulled the underpants up over his knees.

"Not like that, like *this*!" Tinky pointed to the glob of his own head.

Mac looked as though Tinky had just given him a problem of advanced calculus to solve.

"To disguise yerself with! If they see our faces, we's doomed."

"But...." Mac decided to let it go and threw them on his head. "Right. Off we go, then."

Tinky opened the door a crack and peered out. Finding an empty hallway, he stepped into it and motioned for Mac to join him. They made their way covertly down the hall to a staircase and headed down, taking each step slowly, quietly. With underwear covering their faces, they looked like children out to heist an imaginary coach. Tinky crouched low and moved fluidly, serpent-like, his head in constant motion while hunting for signs of life, while Mac, conversely, stood tall and plodded indifferently behind.

The men stepped down onto the second floor and heard a static-laced voice reporting news of the war from a room down the hall. Tinky increased his stealth and heightened his senses while approaching a small, decorative window set in the wall ahead. Peering through, he was met by a sight so unexpected, it sent a cluster of fireworks up his spine to explode under his scalp. He looked down onto a magnificent library, a library rich in browns and reds with gold trim, row after row of cases reaching nearly to this window, stocked top to bottom with books — my God, the books! — numbering well into the thousands. Here it was, the objective, the end of the trail, the goldmine! It was a ravishing sight and Tinky's eyes shined over it, for he knew it contained not only Melville's best, but *more*.

He squished his nose against the glass and attempted a peek of the entire room. The window was too small to allow a complete view, but he could just make out the base of a spiral staircase in one corner. He looked to his left, down the hallway and past the room where the news commentator cooed, and saw at the end a narrow door standing in the spot where the staircase would lead. That must be it, the entrance to Shangri-La! He waved Mac on and they tiptoed toward the door.

The evening news continued to waft from the unsealed room ahead. When they reached the doorframe, Tinky knelt and guardedly peered around it. Inside, a television sat before an unmade bed. What appeared to be an elderly man lay watching, his back to the door.

Tinky held his breath and scurried on all fours across the doorway to the other side. He sat up and leaned against the wall, listening intently, until he was certain he'd passed undetected. The door to the library was a mere hop away now. He turned to Mac and performed an elaborate pantomime suggesting he should do the same; get down on his knees, stay low, shuffle across the doorway, make sure not to be seen.

Mac was having difficulty interpreting Tinky's sign language. From what he could make of it, Tinky wanted him to sneak downstairs, find a toilet, and make a sandwich. When he cocked his swathed head in confusion, Tinky playacted the motions again. Finally, Mac walked over to him, crossing in front of the open door, and whispered, "Spit it out, man! I'm not deaf."

Tinky, for perhaps the fifth time that day, went out of his mind. His palm smothered the underpants against Mac's mouth and he raised a finger to his shrouded lips, silently begging Mac to remain quiet and still. He heard the squeak of mattress springs from inside the bedroom followed by plodding footsteps and his spine was instantly paralyzed by fear.

Mac belched and opened the narrow door behind them to reveal a spiral staircase leading downstairs, just as Tinky had imagined. He pulled Tinky in and shut the door and the men twirled down the slender steps and quickly found themselves at the far end of the great library.

A door on their left was ajar and Tinky grabbed Mac's arm and yanked him into the darkness within. Mac found the light switch and turned it on and saw they were inside a small loo. Tinky switched the light back off and they stood silent and still, listening for any signs of activity outside. All was quiet.

Finally, Tinky braved a peek outside. He looked up the staircase. He looked out at the library. When he was confident they were alone, he emerged from the water closet and had his first substantial survey at the splendor of the room. It was a far different view here than it had been peeking through the tiny window upstairs; here he felt dwarfed by the magnificence of the room and what it held and the hairs on his arms stood stiff to salute the most wonderful collection of books he could imagine. And the number! There were too many to even guess at the count. It was dizzying to ponder.

"Please. Please. Please." He turned to Mac. "Please tell me they're alphabetized."

He went to the nearest shelf and was thoroughly discouraged. There seemed to be no order whatsoever. Not only were the books not in alphabetical order, they weren't grouped into genres or themes, either. Each bookcase was a mishmash of random volumes and Tinky very nearly threw in the towel. He thought how wonderful it would be to be lying in his own bed with a cup of tea and his old, beaten copy of *Fanny Hill*.

It was Mac who poked his shoulder and encouraged him.

"Is John's book in here?" he asked.

"Aye. Somewheres."

"Let's find it then. I'm gettin' hungry."

Right! Absolutely! Mac's simple statement resounded profoundly through Tinky's will. If you fall off the horse, get right back on it. If life deals you lemons, make lemonade. If food poisons your system and turns you into a filthy, wretched, narcoleptic swine who staggers about lethargically and craps his pants, *make a sandwich*. Make a sandwich, snarf it down, and get on with it.

The plan was laid out: Tinky would take the high ground and Mac the low. Each row of shelving had a ladder on wheels and Tinky would ride while Mac pushed, allowing them to cover equal territory at an equal pace. Tinky mounted the ladder over the nearest aisle and Mac took his place underneath and they went to work.

It was a distressingly slow process, their eyes scanning each spine, each title. When they reached the end of the first row and had found nothing, Tinky checked his wristwatch and saw it had taken over twenty minutes just to cover one aisle. He descended the ladder and held a quick conference with Mac.

"Look," Tinky said softly, "if we're to cover all these titles swiftly, we'll have to focus on certain elements. First, look fer the color. *Moby Dick* is a faded green, so let yer eyes rule out anythin' other than faded green. Next, the title. It says *Moby Dick* an', under that, *The Whale*. Below that is the author's name, Herman Melville, all in gold font. Got it? Green an' gold, that's what we're here to find. Now. Back to work!"

Color coding was a fine idea and the next row took them half the time, yet still their target eluded them. The third row produced nothing as well. After an hour passed and they were just two aisles from the end of the room, Tinky began feeling discouraged. What if they'd been in such a hurry, their eyes had passed over it? What if Brian didn't keep that book with the others? Worse, what if he'd sold it? The realization that the book might not even be here dawned on Tinky and dampened his excitement. He began to brood and wonder and was distracted from his mission. His eyes were weary and his brain was tired. His neck was sore from reading sideways and his feet hurt from balancing on the narrow rungs of the ladder. When Mac finished scanning the bottom shelves and pushed the ladder to the next section, Tinky made him bring it back. He was falling behind and pooping out.

When at last they reached the very end, the last book on the last shelf in the last row, Tinky came down the ladder heavily and leaned against the case. It was all an exercise in futility. They had tried like the dickens and failed. *Moby Dick* was not here. His swimming mind began to wonder if the book had ever existed.

"Pssst!" It was Mac. He was standing several feet away at an open door, knob in hand, beckoning for Tinky to join him.

Tinky went to him and followed his gaze into the next room. It was a library. A very long library. Tall, too. It looked just like the one they were in now. It had as many aisles with as many shelves holding as many books. He had to look behind him to make sure it wasn't an illusion, part of some magic castle prank incorporating mirrors and pulleys and trickery. Subtle differences between the rooms told him it wasn't.

Tinky sat in the doorway and cried.

Mac sat next to him and napped.

Neither man moved for several minutes.

When at last Tinky ceased blubbering, he pinched Mac awake and lifted himself to his feet. "Come," he said, tenderly adjusting the unmentionables over Mac's head, which had slipped to the side and covered one eye. "Break's over." They took their positions at the nearest row, Tinky riding the ladder, Mac pushing, and returned to work.

A voice came from a room nearby and Tinky signaled Mac to stop. They both sharpened their ears and strained to hear. Though barely audible, it sounded like John Doyle. He talked a long while, as though telling a tale. Mac looked up and reflected Tinky's sentiment by placing his finger over his covered lips. They must go about their business in absolute silence from here on out. No whispering, no knocking about, no squeaks from the ladder. Nothing.

They made it through the first row quietly yet still empty-handed. When Tinky finished reading the spines on the topmost shelf, he started descending the ladder. Glancing down, he halted. Mac was there, looking at an old man standing directly before him. Tinky rushed as silently as he could down the ladder and joined Mac.

The man stared at them. His orange shirt was blotched with stains and his white hair sprouted every which way. He grinned at them like a tomcat who's just cornered a pair of mice. It was a chilling sight and both Tinky and Mac cowered and took a small step back.

For Tinky, it was the end. They'd been pinched. Caught. Hooked, bagged, and collared. The search was over, it was time to follow the man into the next room and present themselves to John and Brian and fess up. The jig was up and the fat lady was belting her final aria. He felt ashamed and humiliated and chagrined. He lowered his head and muttered the only words that came to mind.

"I am sorry, sir."

"That's alright," the man said through his spectacular grin. "I need to use the toilet." He spoke in a normal tone, but to Tinky and Mac it was as though he'd shouted through a bullhorn. Alas, it mattered not. The caper was over. They were going to be revealed and possibly even arrested.

Still, had he just said something about a toilet?

Mac looked at Tinky, who looked right back at him through the tapered hole in the underpants. He didn't seem to understand, either.

"Would ye help me find it, please?" It was the elder again. He was asking them a direct question.

Tinky leaned in to Mac and whispered, "What's he askin'?"

"He wants to know where the toilet is. He's askin' us to help him find the toilet."

Tinky took a second to roll this information around his brain. "Why do ye tink he's askin' us *that*?"

"Prob'ly needs to use it," Mac said. "Maybe if ye take him, he'll shut up."

Tinky nodded. "I see." He stepped toward the man and whispered into his ear, "Will ye follow me, please?" He motioned for Mac to stay put, then walked into the first library toward the loo they'd found earlier. The man followed closely behind, looking pleased.

Left in his own company with no guidance, Mac was overcome with fatigue. Without Tinky around to play look-out, however, he didn't feel comfortable napping on the ground, exposed. He looked for a quiet corner, or perhaps something to hide under. Near the open door closest to the chatting voices, there was a separate, smaller display case he could've fit under, but its legs were tall and narrow and wouldn't have provided much concealment. He peered up the ladder to the top shelf. It might just be worth a look.

Up he climbed, the ladder creaking softly under his weight. A voice, Brian's, drifted in, louder than before and closer, and said, "I've got to hit the loo. Feels as though me bladder is about to bubble over. Back in a moment!" Footsteps followed, drawing near, and Mac quickened his pace up the ladder. He stepped over the final rung onto the very top of the bookshelf, then sprawled his body flat over it, holding breathlessly still as the footsteps passed underneath and into the next library.

The steps were heading straight toward Tinky.

That was a far cry from being Mac's problem, however, so he looked around and found his bearings. The shelf he was on sat back-to-back with another and provided ample room to hide. He even had a little space to roll around in. The only drawback was the dust; a thick layer covered the shelves and now clung to his sweat.

He peered over the edge of the bookcase to find a spectacular bird's-eye view of the library. It was a pleasant perspective, fifteen feet high. The room was even more handsome and certainly more intimate than the Old Library at Trinity, the top floor of which he'd napped on many times, even as a child.

Just as Mac was about to shut his eyes for a quick snooze, John Doyle appeared in the doorway below. Mac watched him wander to a shelf and look the books over, running his hand over the spines. John plucked one out and looked it over, then returned it and continued deeper into the room. Above, Mac perched his head on his palm, snorted the dustballs from his sinus as quietly as possible, and observed.

John spied the smaller display case sitting away from the others and walked to it. He stood before it, tenderly leaning in now and then to closer examine its contents through the glass. After several minutes, he turned to face the room and Mac could see his expression. It was enough to raise the hairs on his dusty arms and make him wonder what it was that could cause a man to wear a mask of such solitude, such transcendence, appearing drunk, but not with alcohol, with *life*, as if, impossibly, he were in perfect pitch with the music of an otherwise songless world.

*   *   *   *

Tinky O'Shea had no expectations upon entering the loo with his newfound, dementia-shrouded friend. He figured it would be just another quick trip to the toilet. If it was anything like the time he'd accompanied his Grandpap to the can so many years ago, he expected to help with a few minor inconveniences. What he certainly *wasn't* expecting was a knock on the door and Brian Corrigan's deep, distinct voice cutting through from the other side.

"Uncle, ye in thar?"

Tinky reacted to the sound of Brian's voice as so many would when thrust suddenly into the heart of a crisis: he completely lost his sense of reason. With head pounding and blood racing, he brushed aside the curtain covering a small shower and hid behind it, then very suddenly and unreasonably left this sensible hiding spot and started climbing into a wicker towel hamper that lay near. The hamper was slightly smaller than Tinky's body mass, yet he contorted himself in ways he never thought possible to make himself fit. The old man, who stood relieving himself, thought the act far more entertaining than anything the BBC had ever broadcast and he swiveled his hips to stare in wonder and wound up soaking the floorboards under the commode.

By the time the top of the hamper closed, the basket had adopted a rather lumpy appearance and subtle moans of discomfort could be heard from within. The old man, sympathetic and feeling generous, cracked the top of the basket and tossed in a fresh roll of toilet tissue.

"Ye'll probably be needin' this!" he said, then snapped the lid down on Tinky's face.

From inside the hamper, Tinky heard the door open and Brian Corrigan's voice. "Uncle Bercan, is everythin' alright? Ye smell as though—" Here Tinky heard steps pass by his refuge toward the toilet. "Aaagh! Uncle, ye missed the bowl again! I keep askin', sit down when ye do it, will ye please? Great cripes!"

A rustling of sorts was heard as Brian presumably cleaned up the old man's mess, then Uncle Bercan said, "Yer friend is lovely!"

"Aye, he's grand, is he not? He sold me some exquisite books recently."

"He's helped me to no end. He's lying there in the hamper now, like a ship in a bottle!"

Tinky's blood chilled to a paste and he quite abruptly found religion.

"He's got business to do," said Uncle Bercan earnestly.

"Off with ye, Uncle, I've got business o' me own here!"

The door closed and Tinky heard water against water. Since it was not the sound of the hamper lid flying off and twenty-four grit sandpaper hands grabbing his face and pulling him out, he was enormously relieved.

The toilet flushed, water ran in the sink, a rustle of towel, and the top of the hamper flew up with a sudden and sharp *creak!* of wicker. Tinky's heart fell out of his body and he did a little something that required the roll of paper Uncle Bercan had thrown in.

A hand towel dropped in the basket, covering Tinky's paralyzed face, and the lid of the basket fell him back to darkness. Brian's footsteps echoed through the library outside and grew gradually silent. He hadn't noticed a small man folded up in his towel hamper. Out of routine, he probably hadn't bothered to look down at all. Tinky, safe, silently praised the underpants over his head for helping to blend him in with the towels.

Although the toes on his left foot were cramping against his right shoulder, Tinky remained still and counted to three hundred. Satisfied that he was alone in the dark, he clambered out of the hamper and painfully pulled the knots from his limbs, then utilized Uncle Bercan's gift to clean himself.

*   *   *   *

Laying in the dust over a bookshelf in the second massive library, Mac Malone was having an enlightening experience watching John Doyle peruse the shelves below. At any other time, Mac would've been thankful to have a quiet moment like this to catch up on sleep, however there was something engrossing about watching a man allowed to run free through the fields of his own passion. John traveled from shelf to shelf, pausing randomly to examine certain novels, to flip through them, to read them, touch them, smell them, to experience them in every way he could. His face was alive with excitement, adoration, youth. A chord struck deep within Mac's belly that made him empathize wholly with this face; his emotions stirred at the sight and he yearned to one day ornament his own features with that very same heartfelt expression.

"I found me uncle!" It was Brian coming in from the other library, the old man close behind. "John, this here is Uncle Bercan, up from his nap, apparently."

"Pleased to meet ye," John said below, extending his hand but receiving none in return.

"I knew a man once," Uncle Bercan blurted. "He told me he was a farmer!"

"How lovely!" said John, playing along.

Uncle Bercan then looked up to the top of the case where Mac was hiding and pointed directly at him. "Did ye see the man who lives in the ceilin'?"

Mac gasped in surprise and pulled back from the edge of the bookcase. He buried his cotton-bound face in the dust and tried to recall the Hail Mary that Tinky had been blabbing about as he climbed the stone wall earlier.

"He's wearin' *yer* underpants!" Uncle Bercan was saying.

"Hail Mary, full o' sauce," Mac whispered to himself beneath the underpants, "yer Lord is a tree. Blessed is the art o' thorny women...."

Below, the voices continued. Mac expected a ghoulish head to appear over the top of the ladder at any moment. He expected to be pulled from the bookcase and thrown to the wolves. He braced himself for the violence that was but moments away.

The voices grew distant and Mac soon heard only muted words from the next room. He stared at the top of the ladder before him, expecting the Devil to pop his head over and incinerate him with a mere twitch of the nose.

Yet nothing came.

Mac counted to one hundred. Still nothing came. He counted to another hundred. Again, nothing. When at last he reached the end of his third and final hundred, a ghastly, misshapen head popped over the top of the case and shoved a towel in his face.

Mac screamed like a startled schoolgirl.

Fortunately, Tinky had foreseen this and brought the towel with him to mute Mac's cry. "Oy!" Tinky whispered, "Quiet down that sissywhistle, ye knucklehead! D'ye want to expose us?"

Despite the fright, Mac was relieved to see Tinky. Perhaps now they could finally find the elusive *Moby Dick* and return to the comforts of town. Mac was certain to sleep well after the shenanigans of today.

He crawled over the edge of the bookcase and follow-ed Tinky down. Back on solid ground, he took his position under the ladder and resumed searching for the book. Tinky, meanwhile, grasped Uncle Bercan's elbows and stared intently into his eyes.

"Where's *Moby Dick*?" Tinky asked.

Uncle Bercan's ever-present smile swelled, for he surely knew the answer to that one. "He's in the ocean!"

"I mean the book!" Tinky whispered. "'Tis thick, green, an' expensive."

Uncle Bercan placed his hands on his hips authoritat-ively and furrowed his brows and drew the sides of his mouth down as a child might to imitate a grumpy parent. He then performed his best juvenile impression of his nephew Brian, dropping the tone of his voice dramatically. "Only expensive books in the case, Uncle Bercan, *no sandwiches*! Harrumph harrumph pppttthhhhhtt!" His flapping raspberry soaked Tinky with spittle.

Tinky smothered Uncle Bercan's mouth to silence him. Looking over his shoulder, he at last saw the case stand-ing apart from the rest of the collection, its beveled glass sparkling under the lights. Tinky thought himself an idiot for not noticing it before.

He rushed to it, both Mac and Uncle Bercan following. All three peered down and were enamored by the sight. Just as Uncle Bercan had said, it was there lying in the far left corner of the case, as green as emeralds and entirely unassuming for what it was.

It was a mouldy, half-eaten sandwich.

Next to it lay *Moby Dick*.

Tinky nearly cried. Mac tapped his shoulder and lifted his brows and pointed to it as though asking a question.

"Aye, Mac," said Tinky softly. "'Tis our treasure. We've found her!"

Tinky turned to Uncle Bercan and locked eyes with him like a hypnotist entrancing his subject. "Go back upstairs now, Mister Bercan. Time fer a nap, ye hear? Ye're gettin' tired. Sooo tired. Oh, soooooo tired." He waggled his fingers at Uncle Bercan's eyes like he'd seen in a magic show once.

The grin decorating Uncle Bercan's face grew, as did his eyes. He was thoroughly entertained. He showed no sign of leaving.

Fine, then. To work! Tinky returned his attention to the case and examined it carefully. The top pane was affixed with hinges and he took hold of the corners to test it. The lid raised with only moderate resistance and remained suspended when Tinky released his hold. He reached in with both hands and wrapped his fingers around the cumbersome volume, then lifted it out with utmost care. His imagination suspected that it might be connected to some sort of alarm contraption, yet no wires were visible and the book moved easily enough. *Simple!*, he thought, until he remembered what he and Mac had been through to find it.

It was time to go. Yet…wait…had he just seen…? He looked back in the case and noticed the rest of the collection. Here was *Huckleberry Finn*, beside it *Treasure Island*. *Anna Karenina*, *The Raven*, the entire serialized first run of *David Copperfield*, they were all here. Tinky found himself instantly and wholly enraptured.

Unable to peel his eyes from them, he passed *Moby Dick* into Mac's hands. "Take this, just fer a moment," he whispered, then reached into the case and began handling the books inside, marveling at the simple beauty of each precious volume.

Mac looked over the book in his hands. It was heavy. Bulky for a novel. The green in its cover wasn't the shade he'd imagined and he thought how easily he could've passed it over had it been lodged in the shelves with the other thousands of books.

He wondered what was inside that was worth such fuss. He opened the cover and read the title page. Immediately, his head began to ache. He saw nothing of interest, so he took the substantial block of text in his hand and used his thumb to flip through the pages. There certainly were a lot of them. As the pages flashed by, all he saw were words. No jewels. No pound notes tucked within. No treasure maps. Just words. Silly, cockamamie words.

It was a heavy book and Mac easily lost his grip as the pages flipped. His right hand maintained its hold on the cover while gravity took the rest. The spine cracked, the binding split, and all six hundred and sixty-five pages fanned out over the marble floor.

Somewhere in the room, a cricket casually rubbed its forewings together. *<cricket! cricketcricket!>*

Tinky whirled around and saw the mess. The floor was covered in yellowed parchment. Mac stood frozen, the broken cover swinging impassively from his right hand, his dull gaze revealing no emotion. His single blink was all that hinted at the minor tickle he felt in the back of his mind that suggested to him that something was, perhaps, amiss.

<cricket! cricket!>

As for Tinky, the shock, fury, and herculean disbelief that was simultaneously released into the natural energy of the world by him at that moment caused a very minor earthquake in a rural area on the outskirts of Beijing. There were no casualties.

Uncle Bercan, having witnessed the violent disintegration of something priceless, reacted accordingly: his eyes lit up like searchlights in a blitzkrieg and laughter exploded noisily from the hollows of his chest.

Tinky looked Mac squarely in the eye. "Must be going!" he said.

He wrapped his arms around Mac's midriff and forced him to run. A burning squall of adrenaline helped him push Mac through the library, into the next library, and toward the toilet at its far end. He imagined a furious Brian Corrigan nipping at their heels the entire way. They reached the bathroom in seconds and Tinky slammed the door and fumbled with the flimsy hook-and-eye lock. Damn his trembling hands! Damn that tiny eyelet! It was like trying to thread a needle during the invasion of Normandy.

Mac watched, annoyed, as Tinky clumsily labored with the lock. He rubbed at the bruise on his belly where Tinky had grabbed him so roughly.

When at last the hook caught and the door was mildly locked, Tinky twirled and leaped onto the toilet seat. He smashed the glass from a small window over the commode with his elbow, then grabbed a loose roll of paper from the toilet lid and cleared the remaining shards with it. He jumped down and took hold of Mac's arm, but Mac refused to budge.

"Ye'll have me slitherin' out that tiny window thar, won't ye?"

Tinky pumped his head in the affirmative and pulled at Mac again.

"Hang on, then," Mac said begrudgingly, and he reached for a jar of Brylcreem by the sink and began lathering his torso with it.

The door pounded and nearly splintered to shards. The gruff, mortar-like voice of Brian Corrigan bellowed dangerously from the other side as Tinky scooped the rest of the hair cream into his palm and shoved Mac toward the window. Mac stepped daintily onto the toilet lid as Tinky followed behind, frantically lathering the pomade around Mac's belly. The door cracked again from Brian's weight, but the hook and eye miraculously held. Mac positioned himself with his arms through the tiny window and, with a shove ignited by Tinky's terror-induced strength, slipped slickly and painfully through and fell heavily onto the lawn. As the door lock surrendered to Brian's weight, Tinky's legs bent and sprung and sent his small frame flying through the window.

Outside, Mac had failed to remove himself from the line of fire and Tinky landed roughly on him, sending the flatus that had been accumulating inside Mac's gut rushing noisily out. It was a perfectly black night and their eyes struggled to adjust. Tinky looked up and saw Corrigan's wild eyes sizing up the window, doing the math. He then disappeared into the house and Uncle Bercan appeared, choking himself with raucous laughter once more as he saw the men lying disheveled outside.

"Come now!" Tinky slapped Mac's shoulder and clambered to his feet, pulling Mac up. They ran around the side of the castle and were soon back to the gravel drive. The white stones glowed in the darkness and the road acted as a beacon directing them to freedom.

Soon the entire front lawn was soaked in pure, blinding light by a series of elevated floodlights. Hinges squeaked shrilly behind the retreating pair and they heard the guttural barks of what they unanimously presumed was the most savagely evil of all banshees, a horrifying sound that turned their hearts to glaciers. Tinky braved a look over his shoulder and saw a low, dark mass with gleaming fangs moving rapidly toward them, cutting the distance between them in half with every leap it made.

As if the sight of the creature weren't enough, Tinky also saw Brian Corrigan appear behind it with a massive double-barreled shotgun that flashed and bellowed in their direction. Tinky looked to the sky and sent a mental message to his dearly departed mum that he'd see her in short time. Another blast rang out and he sent the same message to his dearly departed bastard of a father.

At that horrible moment, which was perhaps the very worst moment in both Mac and Tinky's lives, fate played a hideous joke on both. First, Tinky's loose pants fell down around his ankles, slowing his run to a mere shuffle and exposing his flat rump to his pursuers. Then the knot holding the blanket around Mac's waist, already loosened by oily Brylcreem, slipped and sent it floating to the ground, exposing Mac's portly breech to his pursuers. Neighbors in the surrounding hills later swore to authorities that they'd heard guffaws of laughter emanating from the heavens around that time.

Moments after they'd both lost the confidence that comes naturally with clothing, the rapidly closing barks behind them changed in tone and seemed to come from another direction, a direction behind the hedgerows lining the rose garden they'd just passed, the garden where earlier Tinky had discarded Mac's trousers. The black banshee's barks turned to shrill yips and squeals and soon the sounds of the crying beast were well behind them. Naked, cold, and overwhelmed by the worst fear they'd ever experienced, Mac and Tinky bounded over the hill, away from the castle and the lights and the beast and the book, their mission failed yet not entirely without worth, and into the quiet and secure embrace of Ireland's rustic beauty.

*   *   *   *

With Mac's body reeling from two full days of strain and excess, it took nearly six hours to walk back to Dublin, much longer than it should have. Country roads at night are quiet, however, and they made for a peaceful hike. A car passed every great while and when they did, the men would retreat from the road and lay low in case it was coppers or, worse, Corrigan and his Beast. When one car passed almost an hour after they'd started walking, Mac swore it had been occupied by John and Brian, though he saw no sign of a Beast.

The matter of Mac's nudity was problematic and had cost them nearly twenty minutes' delay in their escape. As soon as he was certain they were no longer being pursued, Tinky had slowed and paused to rest. Mac kept running — down the gravel drive, across the main road, over a fence into a neighboring field, and straight up a towering oak. Tinky was able to pull his pants back up and hold them steady, but Mac had nothing to clothe himself with other than his dusty, Brylcreemed shirt and boots. As Tinky stood at the foot of the tree, coaxing Mac down as he would a stranded kitten, he realized they were both still adorned with disguise. He pulled the underpants from his head and slipped them over his own loose britches. Wearing them on the outside stretched their elasticity and kept his pants from falling down again. He then made a suggestion to Mac.

The one thing Mac feared most in the world was public nudity. Even with the underwear removed from his head and worn traditionally, it wasn't enough to reinstate his modesty, so he utilized the next nine minutes — precious minutes that could've been used to further distance themselves from the Corrigan residence — to fashion together a secondary covering. By the time Tinky had urgently yet tenderly wheedled him down from his high limb, Mac was costumed in a skirt of leaves and branches, twisted, toggled, and tied securely around his waist.

"If ye find yerself ready to leave, yer Eminence," Tinky said to him, "'tis high time we skedaddled *posthaste*."

They set out toward the glow of Dublin. Mac had difficulty walking in his improvised covering and was forced to bow his legs to keep the twigs and leaves from scratching his undercarriage. Each rustling step made it sound like he was traveling through thick jungle brush.

Later, as they passed through Aiken's Village, Tinky turned to Mac and confessed, "At the very least, 'twas a grand adventure!"

"Yer bollix are a grand adventure!" Mac spat.

Tinky fired right back. "Ye'll not be gettin' riled with me, boyo! *Ye're* the one who disintegrated a Melville!" He stopped and finally allowed this information to soak. His lids curled back behind his eyeballs and his hands flew atop his own head and tried to remove his scalp. *"Disintegrated!"* he screamed. *"Melville!"*

Mac grumbled something about fellation and continued walking.

Later, when the air of a cool night had calmed Tinky, he chimed in again.

"Alright, we made it out o' that castle without John's book, *but*," he emphasized, "if we accomplished nothin' else, we made sure that if John can't have it, then no man can." He nodded certainly to himself, as though sold by his own idea. "The affliction is cured."

"And," he added, "despite the outcome, ye yerself did a fine job. Why, ye haven't stopped fer a nap in hours an' ye climbed that wall like a true Himalayan. Ye was able to curb yer slothful ways an' emerge triumphant, like a knight errant!" He patted Mac's shoulder encouragingly. "I owe ye a fine meal, I do."

Mac belched. "What d'ye mean, *slothful*? I hasn't got a slothful bone in me body!" He finally dislodged a string of marinated pork gristle from between his molars and swallowed it down. "An' tanks fer the offer, but I know there's no feast in it fer me. Ye just promised it to get me to help." He blew the remaining dust from his nostrils into his fist and said, "Besides, I'm on a *diet*."

They walked in silence for a moment before Tinky smacked his dry lips and said, "What I wouldn't give fer a taste o' whiskey after this day!"

"Hrrrmmm," Mac agreed. Then, thinking on it, said, "I need to have a tinkle."

He found the nearest tree and disappeared behind it. Not twenty seconds later, he rejoined Tinky on the road and the men continued their walk.

An old familiar scent wafted over Tinky and he lifted his nose to smell the air. His curious nostrils led him straight to Mac's lips.

"Why, ye banshee-buggerin' bastard!" Tinky accused. "Ye carry shine an' fail to offer even a nip to yer ol' chum Tinky O'Shea! Where ye been hidin' it, then? C'mon, where is it?" He slapped Mac's back and chest and under his arms. Mac, as ticklish as can be, chortled like a bobbysoxer.

Tinky felt a lump and reached in the front of Mac's shirt and brought out a hot water bottle fastened to a twine necklace. He uncorked the bottle and sniffed, then looked up to Mac with scorn in his eyes.

Mac, entrapped, relented. "Yes, please, have some."

Tinky knocked back the water bottle and was soon coughing bloody murder from his lungs. The potion nearly ate through the lining of his stomach. After a solid minute of hacking and hawing, he corked the bottle and returned it to the warmth of Mac's chest.

"Aye," he said tightly, "'tis some fine elixir ye got there!" He took Mac tenderly by the scruff and led him toward the dawn of another fine Dublin day. "Ye're a grand mate, Mac, me boy. Just grand!"

CHAPTER NINE
The Demons of Tyche

How infectious a smile can be.

When he hit the lane to clear his head, John saw what he always saw on the streets of Dublin: stern, enigmatic faces of surly stone coursing past as rapids flow. Round, vibrant faces, white like pearl, pigmented with pink and orange and red and often gray, each wearing a mask of defense, as they were bred to. Ingrained is the cold expression, the aura of *tough*, worn as armor to deceive and defy.

Introduce to these faces a smile, however, a single, blatant, honest smile, and the milieu is shattered. Granite turns to clay, lips part to crescent, and crooked, broken teeth emerge to ornament their surroundings. One simple smile vanishes all trace of what lay souring before.

A young boy looked out the window of an idling city bus, his face thoughtful and stern. He locked eyes with John, who smiled and waved. The boy's burden lifted as John's smile illuminated his own face. He waved back, then turned to his mother, who saw his grin and adopted it. The driver, catching the smile in his mirror, embraced it as his own and by the time the light turned green, not a frown nor furrow remained aboard.

A gray man on the cusp of old age stood by a storefront, puffing a pipe as he begrudgingly awaited his wife. John smiled and the man was seized by it, his pipe clutched now in an upward arc rather than the pout that had just been. People walking by took possession of the smile and passed it along to those they next encountered.

Still it spread. A group of boys in muddy football kit were walking from the park when they passed John. Easy targets all and it didn't take much to change their rough-and-tumble glares to glistening grins. The gang of teenaged rowdies John next encountered was harder to crack, but as soon as one scowl crumbled, the rest fell quickly. They, in turn, came across a group of teenaged girls and broke the stony casts clouding their mugs. The girls lit up and giggled and caused a gathering of seasoned men at the chess tables to jettison their concentrated visages in favor of the smiles surrounding them.

John walked and felt much better doing so. Over the course of mere moments, he'd broken the tradition of the fortifying scowl with his own contagious beam and for one brief, radiant moment, an entire city block was cheered in the wake of his smile.

* * * *

To imply that John Doyle needed the walk to allow him a more cheerful perspective on life would be a gross misusage of the word "needed." If he hadn't had it, he very well may have exploded, and he was in no mood to clean up the mess. He'd done enough of that for one day.

When he'd lain down for sleep the previous night, his wandering mind had almost settled into rest when he heard the noise.

<plink!>   *<plink!>*   *<plink!>*

His brain filtered out the extraneous sounds of urban white noise and a light drizzle outside and honed in on the foreign sounds. They were barely audible, high in tone and short on duration, and seemed to emanate from the ceiling. John counted the time between sounds and usually made it to six before the next <*plink!*> started his clock fresh. There was a rhythm to it, a slow cadence, bringing to mind the lullaby his mum had sung to him as a toddler, as slow as the slowest dirge.

Ten minutes passed and never once did the tempo change. Sleep was out of the question at this point, so John rose and headed upstairs to investigate.

The second floor of the Chivalric Nobleman de La Mancha was very similar to the first, busy with tall, mahogany shelves bursting with books, although the shelves here were slightly fewer in number and allowed more room to wander. John switched the light on and walked to the spot that lay over his bedroom. Nothing looked out of place. He stood perfectly still and closed his eyes and listened.

<*plink!*>

It was louder here, but just. He took a few steps toward the sound, but saw nothing unusual. Again, he stopped to listen.

<*plink!*>

This time he had a firmer gauge on its location. He went around the corner into aisle seventy-eight, Government & Politics G - Z and saw it immediately: a thin, wet line trickling down the spines sitting on one bookcase. On the floor beneath was a shallow puddle the length of his forearm. Overhead, a brown, damp circle roughly three feet in diameter stained the ceiling. A drop fell from its center and landed in the puddle below, splashing a few water-soaked books on the bottom shelf.

<*plink!*>

John set to work quickly. In less than a minute all the damp books lay in stacks around the corner, away from the damaging drip. Several volumes along the bottom shelf that had been steadily splashed for who knows how long were unsalvageable and John set them aside to throw out. Luckily, only about thirty books were in peril, most of them appearing to have very minor damage. Satisfied that the books were protected well enough for the remainder of the night, he headed upstairs.

The third floor was entirely empty and had stood that way for many decades. There was little ventilation here and the odor was typically musty, but tonight there was an additional hint of fetid mildew. The overhead lights hadn't been engaged in years and when John clicked the switch only a few reacted; one even exploded in a juvenile display of defiance and showered a corner with glass.

He saw the floor in the opposite corner and could make out what lay there even from this distance. The puddle sprawled over the lacquered oak floor and when John approached, he was stunned to see it was as wide as he was tall. The circle of dun-drab plaster directly overhead was significantly larger and the drops fell slightly faster, a bit heavier, a trifle louder than they had downstairs. Most alarming was the gaping hole they fell through; it was the size of his fist.

John stood underneath, positioning himself just beyond the drip's trajectory, and looked up into the breach. He was incredulous to see into the empty fourth floor above, dark save for a soft, blue hue that lined the rim of the cavity. It was in that moment that he gazed deeper and realized the glow was coming from *above* the fourth, and topmost, floor. When he bent at the belly and leaned forward, judiciously avoiding the soft wood in and around the puddle at his feet, John gazed up through two ceilings at a perfect three-quarter moon hanging, soft and blue, between the clouds gently raining over his aged and wounded Nobleman.

*   *   *   *

"The *moon*! Christ be Jaysis!" Tinky O'Shea had been listening attentively despite his nervous fidgeting with a well-read copy of *The Odyssey*. The *thipping* sound made by Tinky's thumb running repeatedly over the text block had been irritating John since he first began regaling his tales and had grown louder and faster when John told of his wild night at Brian Corrigan's house. Tinky seemed enthralled by the story and John forgave him his nervous tic as he finished explaining about the leak in the roof.

"Certainly ye're insured, yah?" Tinky asked.

John nodded. "Aye, but me deductible is the highest I could get an' I haven't enough to cover it." Quiet, he added, "I just wonder if it's all worth the effort."

Tinky's eyes grew wide. "What's worth the effort? The shop? Cease yer blaspheme! Why, 'tis only as valuable as the beat in yer own breast. Enough o' that talk, now. Tell me, back to *Moby Dick*, what's become of it after it blew up real criminal-like?"

"I spoke with Brian this mornin', says the gent he knows in Cork has it an' is tryin' his best to restore it. We'll have to wait an' see."

Tinky appeared both pleased and upset by news of the restoration. "Well, I'm happy. Fer the book, at least."

A whistling from the back drew John's attention. "That'll be the kettle, then. I'll get the tae."

He retreated to his bedroom and removed the kettle from the hot plate (*unplug! unplug! unplug!*) and brought the steeping tea out front, pleased to see a customer waiting at the register. When he finished the sale, meager as it was, his attention turned back to Tinky, whom he spied near the door glancing over titles in Erotic Lit. *I really must move that section to a more discreet area,* he thought.

Quite out of the blue, John asked, "Tinky, answer me this. Ye've known me practically all me life. Should I write a novel?"

"A *novel*?" Tinky said, surprised. "Where is this comin' from? A novel? Why, that's the very first mention of it I ever heard." He thought on it a moment. "D'ye *want* to write a novel?"

"I rather tink I would. Someday."

"What are yer ideas, then?"

"Well...." John thought a moment. "No real ideas as yet, but 'tis a notion I've always considered. It'd be grand to have somethin' published, add a little title o' me own to these shelves."

"Aye, it'd be grand indeed. But if ye haven't ideas...." Here Tinky paused. "It brings to mind the record I made. An' ye'll not tell me ye can't recall 'cause I know ye got it here somewheres. I seen it meself lyin' about just last spring."

John went moon-eyed and his index finger shot up: *wait right here.* Before Tinky could object, John disappeared into the back room and returned carrying a tattered record sleeve. He walked straight to the phonograph and lay the disc on, carefully minding the stylus as it settled and slipped easily into the spinning shellac's groove.

The most wonderful whistle filled the shop, a perfect flux of air and sound and tone. Unaccompanied, it blew a melodic theme, textbook in its controlled passion, divine in its crisp pitch, confident in its power, before segueing into an emotional rendition of *Londonderry Air.* Long, sustained notes held firm, a minor vibrato taking effect when appropriate (but never overdone), and a pair of robust lungs backed it all like powder in a cannon. John spun the volume dial and the music commandeered the room.

Tinky closed his eyes and swayed his head in rhythm, hearing and feeling each note, his forehead a flurry of muscular movement causing his brows to lift, ruckle, and rumple like waves in a tempestuous sea. Both hands swirled with the tempo, rising and falling and circling in a ballet of grace and improvisation while his lips pursed and panto-mimed perfectly with each whistled note. John watched in awe and dared not interrupt such a clearly defined passion.

At the end of the final verse, the whistle slowed and quieted, then concluded with a soft, low, sustained F that continued to echo through the room even after John lifted the needle. Tinky, nose aimed at the heavens, slowly emerged from his trance, a delicate dizziness twirling through his head.

John asked quietly, "Ye mean *that* record?"

Tinky opened his eyes and nodded tenderly. "That's the one." He reached for the album cover. "Let's see."

John passed it over and Tinky examined the photo-graph on its worn face. There he was, just a lad out of school, gangly, misshapen, pocked with pimples, wearing his Sunday best and standing in the center of a line of kicking chorus girls tucked into one-piece bathing costumes. Young Tinky's lips were formed in a perfect O as though he were whistling the cadence for the girls' march. A title in yellow hung over them all, reading *Wondrous Whistle: Tinky O'Shea Blows For You.*

Tinky fixed a bent corner on the sleeve. "Sold twelve copies, it did. I blame the cover."

"Perhaps," John mused. "We'll never know why it failed to catch, although I'm sure the cover had somethin' to do with it."

"But ye see, 'tis what I'm speakin' of. Whistlin' was me life fer a while. I whistled mornin', noon, an' night, I'm sure ye recall." John nodded and suppressed his grin. "An' I was good. Everyone said I was headed fer greatness, that I'd be whistlin' in concert halls in short time, that I was one o' the finest whistlers to come out o' Ireland in many a year."

He handed the record back to John and dropped his tone. "An' I *loved* it, I did. Born to whistle, I was, an' I'd still be makin' records if I could only earn a decent wage. To answer yer question, then, aye. If writin' novels is somethin' that moves ye, consumes ye, holds yer heart dear — if it was what ye was born to do — then, absolutely, do it."

"I never said I was *born* to do it," John said to the ground. "I just had the idea to have a go at it."

"Well give 'er a try an' see what happens! Tell me, what's the worst that could come of it?"

"I waste a few years o' me life writin' a novel just to find out it stinks. I do believe that'd be the worst thing. An' highly plausible, too."

"Alright, sure. But at least ye tried, aye?" Tinky thought of an old adage. "Do what ye love an' ye'll be compensated well!"

He paused to consider that statement. "Unless, o' course, ye love to whistle."

Discouraged simply by talking about it, John wanted to change the subject. Tinky read this and led the conversation back to the frantic evening at Corrigan's castle. His questions seemed to have no end and were very specific. He asked, "so's ye're sure Brian never got a good look at the intruders?" and "although the parts o' *Moby Dick* were scattered to pieces, none of 'em seemed to be irreparable, yah?" and "the dog, ye say, the vicious an' black-hearted dog, d'ye truly believe he'd've *killed* those poor gents? Truly *murdered*? To *death*?"

For two hours and some many minutes, Tinky stayed and kept their chatter continuous. This was a pleasing development for John, for it proved to him that their friendship was as solid as ever, something he hadn't been certain of before this evening. He was warmed to be in the prolonged presence of his talkative friend once again and cracked the seal of a fine bottle of Irish whiskey he'd been saving to celebrate an occasion. They drank from dainty porcelain teacups so as not to draw suspicion from the clientele who came through.

Both men were lightheaded by the time Tinky bade his farewell and they paused on his way out to speak of their mutual friend, Mac Malone. They agreed that ol' Mac was quite the character, yet showed noticeable improvement from his typical selfish, pigheaded, slovenly ways.

"'Tis no mission o' mine to fix any man from his natural state," said John, "fer I'm a firm believer in 'to each his own.' However, I'm proud to see the man tryin' to be a wee more civilized."

"Agreed," said Tinky. "I saw him pickin' through a rubbish bin on the Green durin' me lunch hour just yesterday an', I swears on me mum, the man set with me fer a full five minutes to say 'how-de-do.' Well, not 'how-de-do,' per se, it was more grumblin' 'bout the pepper steak they serve down the lockup on Thursday nights, but that's more than I ever got before."

They bade their farewells with a masculine embrace — a light hug with two loud, painful wallops against the shoulder blades — and John set about closing the shop for the evening. His duties fulfilled, he prepared his supper on the hotplate in back (*unplug! unplug! unplug!*) and dined as he wrote a letter, this time to a young lady from his past now living in Kilmacow with her beau, forty-eight head of cattle, twelve goats, and two one-eyed cats. He took advantage of the scotch to wash his supper down, which helped romanticize his writing. By the time he concluded the correspondence by writing *With all my love and most endearing affection, I am, Yours, Johnny*, he was suffering another attack of the dreaded blue lonesome and thought it a good idea to mind it this time around.

Only one available companion came to mind when John thought on it. She was, perhaps, the most admired and thought-upon lass in all the county. When at last he found her, Sweet Emily Moore was walking the railing of the Ha'penny Bridge over the River Liffey, balancing her meager weight on the post between soil and sea on a dare from her friend, Constable Cooney. Doing a mighty fine act, too, she was. John had lovely words with the old Constable as they admired Sweet Emily Moore's prowess on the beam — she even executed a perfect handstand and walked on her palms over the railing as the men stood clapping below — and he eventually enchanted her into taking a walk with him to enjoy a warm, charm-struck evening. They strolled together, hand in hand, and enjoyed the better part of an hour on the lane and off in each other's company. As for how they enjoyed their time together, the scandal-seekers and gossip-mongers should look to their imaginations for nourishment, for it shall remain untold. A good man is subject to loneliness and fragility just like any man, and even the mighty Hercules craved a hug now 'n then.

*   *   *   *

In the morning, there swam through the air a sense of confidence and melancholy. John woke early despite the brevity of his sleep, feeling wonderful, rejuvenated, spry. The ever-diminishing spirit of youth pervaded him for the first time in ages and he tossed on his favorite flannel robe and put on his favorite record and sang awfully along with his favorite song. Early morning hours are unkind to any voice, particularly without tea or coffee or a fine liquor to strengthen it, but he cared not a shred and slashed his chords to bits with his energetic performance while his kettle warmed. He then read aloud a number of favorite passages from his most treasured books and, after each monologue, hopped up and down gaily on the shop's creaky floorboard and basked in the applause of his finest friend.

'Twas a grand morning, indeed, and he fell crazily in love with his own world.

He opened the shop ten minutes early to an eager queue of none. No matter, there was still work to be done. He would make his dear, his good, his sweet bookshop as presentable as can be whether it had a legion of supporters or none. He danced down the aisles to his most uptempo album and straightened any book that slouched or leaned or was not in absolute, perfect harmony with its surroundings. The cabinet doors to the Rare Books Collection swung wide and allowed their contents to breathe fresh air while the glass panes were wiped clean to the beat of a swift 2/4 tempo. An ill-conceived, impetuous cartwheel was executed down the narrow lane dividing a row of shelves and resulted in a painful collapse against the outer edge of Current Affairs A - S, but it still felt damned good regardless. John thought for the thousandth time that he should adopt a shop cat, for he had a sudden craving to tie long shoelaces around his ankles and run down the aisles with a frisky kitty prancing and batting and pawing behind. At one point in the morning he took two minutes to write a naughty poem and spent the next twenty minutes reading it aloud and re-reading it aloud and howled with laughter after each recitation.

John Doyle was mad and it was the most divine feeling he'd felt in many a morning.

After what was certainly the eighteenth performance of his randy rhyme, his riotous howl was cut short by a curt clearing of throat. John whirled around to find Peter Devlin, Esquire standing silhouetted in the front door. John knew him by the perfect beard and exquisite tweed and embroidered leather satchel. Devlin gave a pinched smile and John blushed as he lifted the needle from the record.

"Ah! A-ha!" John laughed nervously. "Mister Devlin, is it? I thought I might see ye again."

Devlin took a few steps in. As always, his eyes were more interested in the shop than they were in John. "Good mornin', Mister Doyle. Am I interruptin'?"

"Aye, as a matter o' fact, ye are indeed. I was just havin' a spot o' fun, somethin' ye probably know nothin' of, so kindly see yer fat arse out o' me shop an' leave me be," was what John wanted to say. Instead, he replied, "No! No trouble. Please, come in," as he was bred to do.

Devlin approached the cashier's desk and laid his satchel on it. "Mister Doyle, pardon me fer appearin' unannounced, but I have business in these parts today an' thought I'd stop in."

"Well, aren't I the lucky man!" This John said boldly and playfully aloud. He was answered by Devlin's most dour expression.

"Mister Doyle," said Devlin, "as my next appointment is just fifteen minutes from now, I'm afraid I must be brief." He extended his hand, which held his calling card. He flipped the card over to reveal a number written in ballpoint, a number preceded by the symbol of the Irish pound.

Although it was simply a number and John had never been good with numbers in school, he recognized this number and thought it a very good one indeed. Come to think of it, a number had never before given him such pause.

"I present to you my final offer," Devlin was saying. "Ye'll notice it is a very fair amount. Perhaps even *too* fair fer this buildin'. My clients have a particular affinity fer the neighborhood an' consequently a particular affinity fer this here property. They've given me clearance to offer an amount beyond what the property is worth, which is the number ye see now."

The card hung suspended by his well-manicured hand. "Bear in mind, however," he continued, "that this here number represents our final offer. No more numbers shall come henceforth. As ye see, this is a very fine an' honorable offer an' we look forward to hearing from ye at yer earliest convenience."

"Incidentally," he added, almost in passing, "this number will no longer exist one week from today." He placed the card on the counter in front of John.

John's playfulness still lingered despite the solemn intrusion of Peter Devlin and he was inclined to prance around the desk and grab Devlin's lapels and pull them down around his shoulders and kick him, helpless, into the street, followed by a swift drop-kick of the leather satchel with the gold initials that would hopefully, in a history-making stroke of luck and Divine intervention, land in a pool of Mac's urine outside. Instead, John locked eyes with Devlin for several uncomfortable seconds before responding in his most solemn tone.

"I'm afraid I want nothin' to do with yer offer." His steadfast eyes remained hooked around Devlin's. "An' I believe I've made it clear in the past *why*."

When eleven of the longest seconds that ever *ticked* or *tocked* through the Chivalric Nobleman passed and Peter Devlin still stood attempting his stare-down, John added, "As I'm sure yer engagements are pressin', I'll wish ye a good day, Mister Devlin."

A further smattering of seconds crept uncomfortably through before Devlin softened his eyes and said, curtly, "Good-day" and turned and walked out the door.

Alone, John realized he'd been subconsciously holding his breath during the long final seconds of Devlin's intrusion and he sucked air back into his lungs. He picked up the calling card and read the number over and again before blurting to no one in particular, "I need fresh air!" With that, he rushed outside and made his way down the lane.

He caught up with Devlin just before the broker merged into the foot traffic of Grafton Street. "Mister Devlin!" he said, grabbing the man's arm to stop him.

"Mister Doyle," Devlin said frigidly.

John looked back at the shop, then spoke to Devlin quietly. "Look, if I was to consider yer offer, would ye—" here he looked behind him again "—would ye tink about lettin' me retain two floors — just two — an' ye can have the rest to do with as ye will? Just two floors, that's all I need."

The response was immediate and to the point. "I cannot guarantee that in the least," Devlin said.

"However, what I can offer," he continued, "is a lease fer space in the new property at a reduced rate." He added, "it would be a rate which I'm sure ye'd find accommodatin.'"

John let the word bounce around his head. "Accommodatin'. Right." He looked at Devlin's sharp vest and jacket, then up at the buildings lining the lane. They were empty structures, facades from a different era that housed nothing but rodents and pigeons and costly disrepair and one meager bookshop. Standing here at the point where the quiet lane met the bustle of Grafton Street, it was difficult to see how the sleepy laneway remained so close, yet so far from it all.

He turned and headed back toward his Nobleman, thrusting his hands in his pockets. The word continued to rattle around his mind and he said it again to himself.

"Accommodatin.'"

*   *   *   *

Shortly after John's encounter with Devlin, two construction workers sent by the insurance broker arrived and asked to see the damage upstairs. John led the way to the upper floors and stripped away his makeshift coverings of tarps and towels to show each patch of rotting wood. They hurried through and, within minutes, the men in matching overalls announced they'd seen enough and were ready to commence. They trotted downstairs and returned to the fourth floor with two sledgehammers and a toolbox.

Hammers swung and smashed the weakened oak around the hole, sending chunks of wood and splinters flying. There was no grace to the men's savagery, yet the way they worked quickly and confidently, John was sure they knew their business. Despite this, he winced and reacted every time the hollow *crack!* of hammer on wood echoed around the room. He felt suddenly ill. Each swing sparked a feeling that he was observing a sort of torture, something inhumane and vile, and he found need to excuse himself quickly lest he lose either his emotions or his lunch.

They continued for almost an hour, gradually nearing the ground floor, until the clubbing stopped suddenly and they appeared and walked past John at the front desk and out the door. They tossed their sledgehammers clamorously in the back of the van and unhitched an industrial-sized rubbish skip they'd towed with them. It took twenty minutes to carry the smashed wood from the shop to the skip and never once did they appear winded or weary. At lunchtime, they told John they'd be back and drove off, leaving the skip parked in front, full of decayed wood and a strong odor of mildew. They did not return at all that day.

After his lunch and during one of the many quiet moments in business, John ventured to have a look at what they'd done to the second floor. The sight wasn't so awful here, the damage minimal compared to the upper stories. The rug covering the rotting floorboards was still there. When he stood on it, it held. He bounced up and down on his heels and tested the strength of the floor. It remained firm. Satisfied that his customers were in no danger, he left it at that and dared not look under the rug at what the workmen had done. What remains out of sight remains out of mind.

Keeping an ear open for the bell downstairs to announce company, John lingered to have a look around. Most of his working days were spent on the ground floor and he rarely ventured upstairs for anything other than a quick pass-through in the evenings when he was closing. One corner held the least-traveled aisle in the whole shop, aisle fifty-nine, containing books in several subjects that never seemed to grow or gather much interest, random subjects like Eighteenth Century Music Criticism, Alchemy, Bodies of Water, and one shelf simply labeled "Beans." The floorboards in this aisle showed not a scuff nor scratch, as though they'd never once been trod upon in almost eighty years of use.

John began examining the titles. He paused just four books in and removed an old, tattered copy of *Malaysian Influence in the Great Italian Operettas 1762 - 1812*. The cover had no jacket and was torn and soiled, thin pages ravaged by age and oxidization. Many long passages had been underlined in ballpoint and crude, hand-written notes filled the margins. To John's eye, it was an unsellable book. He kept it in his hands and continued to scan the titles.

Ten minutes into his scrutiny of aisle fifty-nine, John heard the bell rattle over the door below. He carried the six volumes he'd pulled, each utterly unsatisfactory in their condition and profitability, down the stairs in order to mind the shop. He piled them on the front counter and stared at them. The properties they shared — age, decrepitude, subjects irrelevant or of little interest to modern time — helped negate each idea he had to dispose of them. He could create a bargain bin. He could display them up front. He could give them away to anyone who spent more than five quid on a purchase.

It would never do. John knew the books didn't have a chance. He eyed the rubbish skip sitting by the front window, then looked away. He couldn't do that. He couldn't bear it.

And so the books sat unwanted in a crooked pile by the till for the rest of the afternoon, pleasing no one, informing no one, bringing joy to no one. They only succeeded in looking wretched and vagrant. Such are the outcasts.

John wished to hell the construction workers would come back and haul that skip away.

A slight surge in business toward late afternoon kept his attention rapt, particularly when a young lad trailing behind his mother dropped a carton of chocolate milk very near the floorboards covering *Don Quixote*. John jumped to action and ran with a rag to sop up the mess before it could seep between the boards and fall on the carved box housing his family's heirloom. Minutes later, the same boy unpeeled the peanut butter and jelly sandwich in his hands and wiped the bread over the glass on the Rare Books Collection case. His mum grabbed the closest object — *Malaysian Influence in the Great Italian Operettas 1762 - 1812* — and walloped the boy's behind with it, then tossed the book carelessly back on the counter and walked out with the fruit of her womb screaming behind. Neither purchase nor apology were made.

Six o'clock arrived like a slug trudging through sludge. John cleared the second floor and avoided the urge to continue searching for inadequate stock. He headed downstairs to lock the front door and paused only momentarily to collect the six volumes that had blemished the counter all afternoon. Stepping outside, he hauled them over the rim of the skip. They fell heavily and echoed dully against the base of the metal and John turned his back and returned inside, stopping only to draw the shade and bolt the door behind him.

* * * *

The issues weighing heavily on his life plagued John's sleep that night and refused him a good night's rest. When he looked over the shop the following morning, it was with an eye of transformation. If he were to downsize, how would he do it? What would stay and what would go? Which were his most profitable subjects? Could he liquidate the most valuable stock by sending his entire Rare Books Collection to auction all at once? If he did, what would that leave him with? A cruel, taunting jerk of a headache cut into his forehead and soon took away his peripheral vision, forming quickly into a migraine. He sat with a glass of water and a headache powder and let it slowly dissolve on his tongue. As he did, he felt blood vessels in his nose break and begin to flow. The trifecta of sleep deprivation, migraine, and nosebleed told him this would not be a day to celebrate.

By noon, he'd ventured upstairs several times and collected fourteen more books. Looking through, he wondered how they hadn't turned to dust already; most were very old and had probably been bought or traded when his Grandfather still owned the shop. All of them suffered from disrepair and none had any chance of collecting a profit. As the workmen still hadn't returned to collect their skip, the books were thrown in with the rotted wood.

Two o'clock arrived with Brian Corrigan close behind, paying an unannounced visit to present a gift of an early edition of Joyce's *The Dubliners* ("not fer the shop," he explained, "but yer own collection."). John was relieved to see a friend and responded to the gift with a masculine embrace and a heartfelt word of thanks.

"What's the latest on *Moby Dick*?" he inquired.

Brian wandered to the Rare Books cabinet and gave it a once-over. "Me man in Cork says it was beyond his skill level an' had me post it to his mentor in London. Says he's the best. No word on when it'll be finished."

"Our poor Melville. I'll never be more horrified than I was at the sight o' those pages scattered about the floor. An' to see ye tearin' out with the dog an' the gun...'twas all a bit surreal. Any lead on the culprits?"

Brian turned his attention back to John. "I suspect 'twas two o' them drunkards been out carin' fer the landscape. When they come back the next day, I sent 'em all packin' with help from the dog an' the gun. I got a bit o' pleasure watchin' 'em runnin' down the road, throwin' their tools in the air with arms a-flailin'."

"The gall o' some men," John said, shaking his head. "If it *was* them, I feel confident sayin' they'll bother ye no more."

Brian chuckled in agreement. "What's say? Got time fer a quick jaunt to the pub?"

"'Fraid not, lad. I must remain with the ol' ball-an'-chain here. Not sure where me substitute cashier is at the moment. Out runnin' through town with coppers at his heels, most likely. Might I take a raincheck?"

"'Course ye can, matey. Another day." Brian lowered his lids conspiratorially and looked around like a secret agent in a melodrama. "But fer now, ye'll have somethin' to show me, aye?"

John was puzzled and cocked his head slightly. "Hmmm?"

"*Quixote*, man! Ye said ye'd show it to me one day. I awoke this mornin' hopin' this was the day." Excitement pinched his voice and his anxious grin stretched wide.

"Oh, right! Sure, sure. Let me wait just a moment to clear the place out. I'll not be boastin' it with strangers about."

Only two customers walked the aisles, each having been there for quite a while already. While the men waited for them to finish their shopping, they spoke of the stories in *Dubliners*. John's favorites were *After the Race* and *A Little Cloud* and *The Dead*. Brian agreed about *The Dead*, but thought *Two Gallants* far superior to the others. This is why John admired Brian so...they could argue the merits of a fine piece of literature and understand the language that each spoke. He relished the thought that he'd found in Brian a contemporary counterpart, an equal in curiosity and fancy. Tinky O'Shea was a fine friend, sure, but John felt a tighter connection, a trust, with Brian Corrigan. The more time they spent together, the more John liked him.

When at last the two straggling customers paid for their troves and left, John knelt at the loose floorboards and pulled them up. He covered his hands with a pair of cotton gloves and handed a second pair to Brian, then pulled the carved box from the paper bag protecting it and placed the boards delicately back. Brian helped him to his feet, nearly salivating with anticipation, and John led him to the counter where he theatrically placed the box down and wiped the dust away with the meaty side of his gloved fist, purposely and comedically taking his time with the rub down.

Brian laughed and shouted, "Alright, alright, enough pussyfootin'! Let's see!"

Just as Brian had been proud to show off his collection, John was eager to boast over his own. He couldn't stifle the grin that caused his cheeks to swell like a pinched balloon. After a further moment of taunting, he lifted the carved box top to reveal the namesake of the Chivalric Nobleman de La Mancha Bookshop. Brian stared at it with eyes aglow, as though he were his much younger self leering lustfully through the display glass at Caitlin O'Hanegan's Confectionery.

After a quiet moment of looking at the book nestled in its custom-fit case, Brian reached out to touch it. Catching himself, he looked up. "May I?"

John nodded with an understanding, grandfatherly smile.

With *Don Quixote* in his hands, the world slowed and became keenly delicate as it does when holding a newborn. Brian carefully examined its exterior, noting only slight wear in the cover and a minor yellowing of the page's edge. His thumb cracked the text ever so gently and he opened the book at a forty-five degree angle to a random page. Seventeenth-century publishers had printed on notoriously acidic stock, yet there was little sign of the chemical foxing or mildewing common to this type of paper. Subtle spots and blemishes were visible and there was an aged and yellowed tone to the paper, but for a book printed in 1605, it could well be considered immaculate. It was shockingly clean and well-cared for, as though a devoted army of knightly wards had kept guard over it since its birth. Perhaps this was not far from truth.

Brian carefully closed the book, minding not to crease the pages, then opened the front cover and tenderly turned to the title page. *Ingenioso... Saavedra... Lvcem Post Tenebras*

Spero...it was all there. *1605*. 1605! Just the thought of it sent another chilled wave along his spine.

Sentiment welled in Brian's eye as he looked the book over and John took heed, ready to lash out and catch any falling moisture as he had when Tinky first held *Moby Dick*. Brian was able to curb his emotion in time and prevented the tear from swelling and he eventually closed the cover and looked at John with flushed cheeks and a calm, cherub-like softness gracing his features. He attempted to speak, but was unsure of what to say. Since he shared with John a similar passion, he knew words were unnecessary.

Brian took hold of the book in one hand and reached the other into his coat pocket, withdrawing an object the size of an apple. His swimming eyes never left John's as he lay the item on the counter between them.

John looked down and stared at it for a moment. "What is that?"

Brian's voice was uncharacteristically soft. "What's it appear to be?"

"It appears to be a roll."

"Aye."

"Appears to be a roll o' bills, thar."

"Aye."

"Appears to be a heavy one at that."

"Mmmm."

Brian's grin grew wider, his eyes locked firmly with John's. He cradled *Quixote* to his chest as he would the shoulders of a lover.

John looked at the roll once again. It was held together with a thick elastic band, stretched fully to white. He'd seen similar rolls at the cinema emerging from pockets of duplicitous gangsters or presented to heroes collecting their noble rewards. Never had he imagined he'd see one in person. Never had he considered they might actually *exist*. He even questioned its authenticity until his nose told him it was real; he could smell the bank notes without even bending near.

His eyes again met Brian's. "What's in it?" he asked.

"Ever'thin' that this here book is worth. Plus some."

John took the roll in his hands and felt its weight, its texture. He lifted it to his nose and inhaled the familiar scent closely, reminding him of the paper in a well-read book. He rolled the cylinder over his fingertips, feeling it, sensing it, around and around, over and over. It possessed a very certain beauty despite its tatty appearance. A feeling of liberation dawned within him and he discovered then a better, a more realistic sense of wealth. It was, surprisingly, far less over-whelming than he'd imagined. It was, he thought, merely a state of being.

Still, the freedom he felt at that moment was real. He enjoyed the sensation. He enjoyed it very much. In fact, he wanted more.

The tinkling of the bell over the door broke the silence and snapped the men from their hypnoses. As a gentleman entered and wandered toward the Fiction aisles, both John and Brian became tangibly aware of the small yet substantial drum in John's hands.

John looked it over one last time before handing it back. "Return that to yer pocket before one of us gets into trouble," he said amiably.

CHAPTER TEN
The Loot of All Evil

Ah, morning!

If you're into that sort of thing.

Usually, Mac wasn't. He typically made it a point to be deep in slumber by the time the light of dawn hit the skyline, but there were times like this when he forced himself to remain awake a few extra minutes to witness the colors of the sky morph from blue and gray into a series of vibrant pastels, simply to be reminded of what a sight it was, what a *feeling*. The sensations stirred by a sunrise like this typically reflect invincibility, prowess, energy and strength and life. The term "dawn of a new day" is very appropriately linked to notions of rebirth and reinvention, both of which Mac could feel tingling at the base of his subconscious of late.

Morning dew was still forming on the grass lining the Grand Canal as grey wagtails arrived to break the silence with their clipped, soprano calls. A flock of mallards landed for their daily bath and soon the swans would arrive to do the same, after which they would all gather near the benches to await the elderly men and women with pockets full of stale bread and day-old scones.

At least, that was the plan. On this particular morning, the terrific *slap-slap-slapping* of Mac's oversized loafers as they flapped and flopped against the towpath was enough to startle the fowl from their serenity, causing them to take flight in a mad dash for the door. It was as though an intoxicated hunting party had suddenly appeared, blindly firing artillery in every direction. For an instant the sky was black with motion and then was just as suddenly clear again.

On the ground below, Mac felt grand. He hadn't been out for a calisthenic jog in ages, if ever. Crisp air filled his lungs and shocked them deliciously. His legs, rutted in the groove of a fine, fast tempo, carried his mass a little easier than normal and he was sure he'd lost a few pounds in the past week. His heart thumped a steady pace, his mind was clear, and his pores opened to expel the toxins within. Even his flesh felt good.

Of all the lessons he'd learned in his life, Mac was reminded this morning of the one he'd learned the most: a body sure can move when motivated.

The path along the canal was the perfect spot for an enjoyable run and Mac made a point to remember it for future use. Only a smattering of early risers were out at this hour and the flat, elm-lined trail was relatively clear. Occasionally he encountered a fellow jogger or a protruding root or a stack of hot pooch patties that he'd dart around or leap over, but he welcomed the challenge since it made him feel all the more Olympian. Ahead, he saw a lass pushing a pram in his direction, her young daughter at her side, and as he ran past he reached out to ruffle the child's mop top hair.

"Top o' the mornin'!" he exclaimed as he flashed them an enormously rare glimpse of his smile. Their necks craned as he slap-slap-slapped past, the young girl giggling delightedly as her mother scooped her into her protective arms and stood horrified by what had just occurred.

Mac dared a peek behind him and was pleasantly surprised. He'd been able to sustain his three yard lead over Constable Peter Bonner, who was still in hot pursuit. Mac, oblivious to the thundercracks coming from his own shoes, wished that young Bonner would abandon the blowing of his policeman's whistle since it very abrasively interrupted the peace of such a fine, quiet morning, but the lad was obviously eager to follow every procedure outlined in the Garda training manual. Bonner seemed to be doing just fine in his new role as Constable (no longer Probationer); he'd found Mac pinching the damp boxer shorts from a stranger's clothesline and immediately gave chase. Mac initially damned the copper's knack for being in the right place at the right time (or *wrong* time, if you were to ask Mac), but he couldn't fault the man for being so good at his job.

Besides, it had all led to this glorious jog along the canal. Nothing wrong with that, Mac supposed, providing he maintained his lead.

*   *   *   *

Hours later, Mac stepped into the Chivalric Nobleman de La Mancha to visit his friend John Doyle and inquire whether he needed any help for the working day. This was, of course, after he'd shaken his tail of the very determined and entirely pesky Garda Bonner back by the waterway.

Mac had successfully gained the upper hand over Bonner after leading his pursuer to Fitzwilliam Square, in the heart of the posh business district. The square was surrounded by Georgian manors and their vibrantly colorful doors, home to solicitors and diamond merchants and the type of man who wore a cutthroat expression and eagerly looked forward to encountering a mirror. Fitzwilliam Square was a recreational park as large as a city block, yet was gated and locked and strictly available only to paying members. Mac was familiar with the secrets of gaining access, however, which gave him the advantage over Bonner in their game of Coppers 'n Robbers. He ran the southeastern length of the iron fence, then rounded the corner and utilized a secret method of entry known only to him and a handful of others.

Laying still in the brush inside, he panted quietly as Bonner rushed by outside. Mac waited for the copper's whistle to fade in the distance before climbing from the shrubs. Free now from authority and safe from any additional company, he regained a steady pulse and refilled his lungs, then lowered his trousers and took his usual position over the greens to make an unabashedly bold statement against the tyranny of the members-only culture. *Let 'em stuff their pipes with THAT,* he thought as he re-buckled his belt.

Now it was early afternoon and Mac was standing by the till of the Chivalric Nobleman, still energized from his morning exercise and insisting that John put him to work.

"I wish I could, mate," John was saying, "but I just cannot at the moment. Truly, I wish I could."

"Ye deserve an afternoon off an' ye should take it," Mac said insistently. "Never ye fear fer this here shop, I'll keep a good eye on 'er an'll make sure no harm comes, includin' that caused by stray dogs or felled jars o' peanut butter."

John gave a strained smile and his eyes betrayed his anxiety. "Mac, I appreciate ye stoppin' by," he explained, "but I haven't got it in me budget. I know I promised ye work, but I need to go back on me word. It was irresponsible o' me to expect I could keep ye on a payroll an' I do apologize, although ye certainly helped me out those few times."

"An' a few times more to come! John Doyle won't be riddin' hisself o' Mac Malone anytime soon, no sir! Thar's no need to worry 'bout bein' able to afford me, neither, fer I'll be workin' complimentary-like — with no hidden fees nor taxes nor surcharges — from here on out."

John's eyes were softened by sentiment. Mac began to fidget under such a pregnant gaze; it was an expression he rarely received and it made him uncomfortable enough to look away and read the titles on the nearest shelf, which in turn caused his head to pulse painfully. He only returned his focus to his friend after he felt a hand on his shoulder.

"In good conscience, me friend, I can't," John said. "I just cannot."

Mac grabbed John by the shoulders and forced him onto the stool behind the counter. John seemed surprised to be so suddenly manhandled, but sat obediently as Mac waved his stubby index fingers through the air, indicating that he'd be right back. He disappeared into John's living quarters and soon returned with a near-empty bottle of whiskey from the shops' secret stash, along with two Old Fashioned glasses. John was astounded by Mac's brazen act of retrieving John's own liquor from his own home, but he accepted the act of familiarity by allowing Mac to pour them both a hearty glass, finishing off the bottle.

Without offering a toast, Mac downed a mouthful and said, "Right! Now what's all this about?"

John sipped from his glass, then placed it away from view under the counter. "'Tis nothin' to concern yerself with, Mac. Truth is, I've absolutely no right to complain about finance when people I know have so little."

"*Horsefeathers!*" Mac cried. "That's all simply a namby-pamby means o' sayin' ye'd rather not discuss it with *me*. Finances, eh? John," he commanded. "*Talk*."

He watched as John took another healthy slug from his glass. He watched as John pricked up his ears and gave a look around the shop for any spies or listeners-in. Then he listened as John surreptitiously confided in him his most troubling secrets.

They sat for nearly three quarters of an hour, John talking, Mac listening, pausing just once to tend to a single paying customer. John held nothing back, detailing his dreams and realities, his conflicts and dilemmas, as one might to a dear and trusted friend. He'd never genuinely talked about his woes with anyone before, not only because he rarely had any meaningful afflictions to discuss before late, but because he always felt that, in the general spirit of creating a bright and cheerful environment in which to live, one simply did not act as one's own scandalmonger.

When he came to the end of his tale and had no more to say, John appeared rather shell-shocked from having told his story so intimately; he looked weary and perhaps a touch surprised at himself for opening up in such a trusting and revealing manner, complaining in detail of financial problems to someone who, by all appearances, had *nothing*. The heat of embarrassment flushed John's cheeks as he remembered his audience's own quagmire of disadvantages and he finished his monologue the same way he'd begun, by stuffing himself with a double helping of humble pie and wishing he were alone, removed from the humiliations caused by both vanity and humanity.

Only after Mac offered to lend him money did John seem the most astounded, the most crestfallen, and his cheeks were again overtaken by heat and shame.

"Tanks, but no, Mac," he said. "I'll be alright."

Mac could scarcely believe it. For the very first time in his middle-aged life, he'd offered his most precious possession, his life's savings, his cash on hand, to a man, a good and worthy man... *and was refused*. It was certainly not the outcome he'd expected. Perhaps John didn't believe he was capable of parting with his cherished nest egg. That must be it, of course. He must prove his sincerity!

Mac gruffly pushed John out of his seated position and strenuously lifted his left foot and balanced it atop the stool. He *oofed* and *ughed* and inched his limberless torso toward the foot and it took his sausage-like fingers several attempts to unfasten the five knots in the frayed lace of his shoe. When it was finally done, he pulled the loafer off to reveal a black sock that had at one point in its life resembled something much more — what's the word? — something much more *white*. Guardedly, he glanced around the room for any thieves lying in wait, then peeled the sock down over his ankle and pulled the rest of it from the filth and hair on his flesh. Holding it protectively with both hands, Mac dangled the stocking in the air and looked upon it as one might look upon a favorite son graduating from The School For the Exceptionally Gifted and Good-Looking. A lumpy mass protruded from within, its weight stretching the sock's fibers down to their limit.

"Take it!" Mac said with a proud, cocky grin as he thrust the sock toward John.

A laugh blew from John's nose and cleared his sinus into the air. Embarrassed, he wiped his lip with a kerchief and stifled his amusement. "I won't be takin' yer sock, Mac, nor can I take yer money. I would'na do that to ye."

Frustration steamed from Mac's scalp. "'Tis yer *pride* speakin', the most dastardly of all dastardly sins! Well, that's all fribble an' flummadiddle, I tell ye! Complete rot!" He again thrust the sock forward. "Won't ye please take some o' these here bills that've failed to burn holes through me pockets? Er, socks!"

A jingle from over the door alerted the men to the entrance of a patron. John reached out and cupped Mac's hands in his, hiding the sock and its contents in his soft grip. It was several moments before he spoke again, and when he did he carried the tone of a man in unflappable earnest.

"Me problems belong to just one man, Mac. 'Tis *his* responsibility — an' only his — to deal with 'em. Whatever issues I have at the moment are mere pennies to yer millions an' I have no right to speak of 'em."

Mac exhaled brusquely. He wore the face of a dejected child. As he sat on the stool and twisted his torso laboriously to re-don his sock, he grumbled, "Too polite. Too independent. Too damn *proud* is what ye are. Killin' yer own self with kindness!"

John sidled up and held him steady as Mac nearly lost his balance putting his loafer back on.

"Possibly. Do ye know that yers is the second hearty offerin' o' currency I've turned down this week?"

A dramatic double-take was perfectly executed by Mac upon hearing this. "Then ye're all o' those things I just described an' a foolish one at that!"

"Perhaps. Yers, however, is the more generous o' the two. The other gentleman wanted somethin' very dear in return." He chuckled to himself. "Funny. It would seem the man with everythin' wants, while the man with nothin' gives. Such is the nature o' men, I suppose."

They guzzled the final inch of their whiskey and Mac excused himself with a handshake and a heartfelt squeeze of the shoulder, obligated to dealing with pressing matters of his agenda. These matters had been swelling within him while John spoke, had been born and grown to maturity as John outlined his burdens, and became further pressing when Mac's offer was refused. How he was to deal with these matters, Mac hadn't the foggiest.

Exiting the shop, he passed the skip that continued to take up space outside, as inconspicuous as an African bush elephant. It was now more than half full with discarded books. Mac stared at it with his most critical and his most evil eye and he understood better the intensity of John's dilemma.

Fueled by the notion that something *must* be done but not quite grasping a sense of what, Mac filled the tails of his overcoat with the afternoon breeze and set forth at a frenzied pace to find his answers, which, at this hour, would presumably still be hovering somewhere between the General Post Office and Vice Admiral Nelson's Pillar.

*   *   *   *

O'Connell Street bustled. The thoroughfare bustled with taxis, double-decked buses, cars, and cyclists, hundreds of cyclists. At the taxi stand, the front car pulled out with a fare and a line of drivers behind put their newspapers down, climbed out, and pushed their cabs one car length forward in an effort to save a few coppers-worth of fuel. The footpath bustled with thousands of pedestrians, the middle-aged sauntering leisurely while the elderly hunched over canes, inching along as the youth flowed past like stream water coursing over rock, all the while, amidst them all, a solitary drunk lurched, stumbled, and scraped a serpentine path until he could no longer fight his way around so many in such a discombobulated manner and resigned himself to hold up the nearest lamppost until the crowd thinned.

Caps and hats were held down while the acrid winds blew north over the Whiffy Liffey. Cigarettes and cigars were omnipresent. Children played "hit the can." Peddlers selling cheap jewelry, fruit, flowers, toys, and souvenirs sat on over-turned produce baskets by their stands at every corner. Most delightfully of all, eager young women and men waited to meet their lovers under the double-faced clock hanging over Clery's Department Store, the popular rendezvous for romance.

Mac plowed through them all like a bowling ball, a man determined, altering his course for no one. Most pedestrians were fortunate enough to see him coming, their senses alerting them to danger by the glint of the sun off the single lens in his women's oversized zebra-striped sunglasses or by the loud grunts, growls, and grumbles he made, brought on by a cramp slicing through his abdomen. During his journey, he managed to knock over a vendor's ramshackle stand, sending hundreds of leprechaun charms and Guinness bottle openers and "Kiss Me, I'm Irish" belt buckles jangling to the curb. He hurdled over a little girl, who froze and stared at him as if he were a raging Triceratops, then promptly broadsided a kissing couple under Clery's clock, sending them sprawling to the ground in a single mass of flailing arms and legs and lips. Never once did Mac slow his pace.

As predicted, Lousy the Soothsayer held court under the Pillar, standing on a milk crate and pontificating to a rather large audience, this time dressed in a sari of solid canary yellow with matching headscarf. Her strong yet soothing orator's voice cut through the ambient sounds of traffic and hubbub and delivered its message unto her temporary flock clearly, the tone of her voice causing all within earshot to crave a cuddle in the arms of the matronly gentlewoman.

"...And when she returned from the rock, she bore with her the collected alms of the poor masses," Lousy said, stepping from her milk crate and slowly walking the crowd's inner circle with arms outstretched, "buried there so many moons prior for just such a predicament as they now suffered. However, when she stood before them with treasure in her arms and asked them to come forth to claim what was rightfully theirs, to cure their accursed malady with their own fortunes, well, my children, not a soul stirred, nor an eye batted, nor a foot strode forward. For, you see, the poor had observed firsthand the wickedness of these treasures, had tasted the inflictions ailing the gentility via an osmosis of experience, and no woman endeavored to accept the return of her very own property—"

At this point, Lousy was abruptly silenced by the appearance of Mac Malone, who halted his run mere inches from her, huffing and hawing and snorting. He stood so near to her that the sweat ran off his nose and landed on her bare feet.

"Hiya, Mac!" she said happily. If she was annoyed by the interruption of her parable, she failed to show it. On the contrary, she weaved her long fingers through the wet hair on the side of Mac's head and tenderly brushed and shaped it until it was elegant. "How's tricks?"

"Tricks is somethin' awful, Lousy! I need ye!" Mac took hold of her forearms and pushed her back toward the Pillar, away from her crowd. Lousy skipped backwards with him, her Ginger Rogers to his Groucho Marx, until they were far enough away from her audience to achieve relative privacy. The temporary flock began to disperse, baffled by her sudden departure.

Lousy looked endearingly into Mac's eyes and said, "Speaketh now, child."

"I'm hoppin' mad an' fail to know why, Lousy!" Mac said it in frustration. He paused, staring into space, then very suddenly and very literally began hopping up and down in place as though trying to stomp through the pavement into Japan.

Lousy took his arms and eased him out of his tantrum with a series of *shushes* and *there, theres*. When he settled again, she patted his back in a slow rhythm until Mac belched. She then massaged his earlobes. "Sing me your song, dear one," she said with the tone of an imperturbable kindergarten teacher.

"A man I know — or a female, however which way it pleases ye — is havin' a rough go of it lately an' 'tis all due to *finance*."

"Your timing is impeccable, Mac, for today's lesson encompasses that very subject. Perhaps you were able to hear a portion when you arrived?"

"If ye're talkin' about all them fancy-type words ye spew in front o' the crowds, I heard 'em but did not care to listen."

"Fine, that's fine," said Lousy. "Continue."

"He's a general respekable-like kinda fellow, with a good head an' a carin' heart an' fine intentions an' bla-blee-bla-bla-bloo. All o' that an' more, I tell ye. Deserves the world like so many of us, but hasn't got much to show fer it, like most of us. He's got a sufferin' mind an' a sufferin' business, no tanks to hisself." Mac paused to think through his thoughts. "*Money* is his problem, Lousy, so's I offered him all o' mine an' ye know what he done? Can ye tink o' what he done? He done the *untinkable*. He *refused!*"

For a small moment, Lousy seemed uncharacteristically perplexed. "You offered all of your money? Everything that lies within your socks?"

Mac's eyes bulged from their sockets and damn near popped out. His voice hit prepubescent octaves when he shouted, "How d'ye know 'bout me socks!?!"

Lousy's perplexity vanished and her face was endearing once again. "Oh, sweet Mac, every woman and child I've encountered seems to know about your socks. It is certainly no big secret how you keep your cash vaulted underfoot, and how the soles of thine feet are permanently indented by the impressions of folded bills. But tell me true," she said in earnest, "you didn't really offer him the lot of it?"

"I most certainly did. Each an' every guinea!"

Very suddenly, Lousy appeared ashy. Her hands began to tremble and her lids receded behind their sockets. She aggressively took Mac's head in her hands and pulled his face to hers, smushing his mouth open, her eyes frantically searching deeply into his own.

Unable to properly move his jaws under the pressure of her grip, Mac asked, "Ish dr shuntin ron?"

"Illness! Disease! Virus!" Lousy cried. "It must be in you! You are a sick, sick man, Mac Malone! We must get you to a doctor!"

"I'n furficly fine, Laushy. I'n nau shick."

She unhanded Mac, slightly calmed. "If you're not sick, Mac, then how would you explain trying to gift your beloved money to another?"

Rubbing his jowls, Mac replied, "Out o' the sheer an' glowin' goodness coursin' through me heart! Come now, 'tis not as though I'm greedy or nothin'!"

"No, greedy is much too insignificant a word for what you represent." Lousy said this not facetiously, but matter-of-factly.

"Ung? What ye mean by that?"

"I mean only that you are not just a greedy man, Mac, but are leagues beyond that description. Your type of greed is spelled in all capitals, with fudge and whipped cream and nuts and a cherry. To call you greedy would, frankly, be like calling Adolf Hitler *troublesome*."

"Balls!" Mac cried defiantly. "I haven't a greedy corpuscle in all the gallons o' me blood! Not a smidge nor speck, I tell ye!"

Lousy paused and eyed him patiently. "One day. There was one day in years past when a wager you placed through me paid off sixty-two to one. You were so happy, you invited thirty of us — friends — to join you at the pub and offered to pay for drinks *and* dinner. We had a grand old time and ran up quite a bill, and when it came time to cash out, you climbed out of a third-story toilet window and left us to scrub dishes for six weeks."

"Yer memory deceives ye, Lousy!" Mac said defensively.

"Do you recall the instance when Dribble O'Doole's daughter needed life-saving surgery? We passed the cap at the weekly feast and had over two hundred quid in it when it came around to you. You put the cap on your head and tried to walk away."

"Never happened!" Mac protested.

"There was an evening when I came to you in desperation. Over the course of a single day, my mother died, my spouse left me for a younger woman, and I spent my very last pound on a sturdy shipping box to shelter me, which was promptly destroyed by a wayward IRA grenade. I was suicidal. For perhaps the first time in my life I needed help and I sought you out. I found you counting your money and asked if I might borrow a half crown until the following week. You stuffed wads of cash back in your socks and said you hadn't a single red copper to your name."

"I am not, nor has I ever been, a greedy man, Lousy! I swears it on all the graves o' me dearly departeds!"

"Mac," Lousy said in her mild and even tone, "may I borrow a quid?"

"Get yer *own* quid!" he shouted back.

Lousy chuckled. "Oh, Mac," she said. "How easy life would be if it were as subjective as you believe it to be."

"Enough o' this vicious attack on me integrity! Lousy, tell me true!" Here Mac dropped his tone and leaned in close. "These events ye describe…did they really happen?"

Lousy's eyes smiled as they nodded the affirmative.

"*Mein Gott!*" Mac bellowed, utilizing a term he'd learned from Archie Farchie. "Ye're tellin' me that money has cursed me soul?"

Lousy's twinkling eyes closed and continued nodding. "Your friend's problem, Mac—"

"Money, blast it all!"

"Is also—"

"—is also me own problem?" he asked.

Her head kept bobbing up and down, answering yes. She smiled.

"Dastardly money!" Mac cursed. "The loot of all evil!"

"Root. But, yes. That."

It was then that Mac remembered something John told him at the weekly feast. What was it? Something along the lines of "a true friend will point out your greatest flaws and encourage you to conquer them." Mac's hands took one of Lousy's and held it tightly. "Tell me, then. *Please*, Lousy! What's I must do to free me shackled soul from its salacious grip?"

"You have already done a good thing—"

"—in offerin' it to me friend in need," Mac finished. "Right."

"But now you must—"

"—conquer me own flaw. Got it."

Now, Lousy the Soothsayer had experienced much with Mac Malone over the years. They'd lived on the same streets together, feasted together, gambled together, become unintentionally enlightened on wild mushrooms together, they'd even built an igloo out of snow and cuddled for warmth on a frigid winter's night together. She'd certainly helped him out with many a personal problem before. The point is that Lousy thought she knew Mac well, which is why it astonished her so to find him one step ahead of her now when consulting for advice.

She continued, watching him closely. "What you must do, then, is—"

"—rid me own self from that which plagues us both!"

The endearing smile returned, the smile that shown just as brightly and as warmly as the stars on a cloudless country evening. "Yes, Mac, you must—"

"—take drastic action to make certain the problem is put to rest!"

"Mmm-hmmm." Still the smile polished everything surrounding it. "Only then, Mac—"

"—shall I be truly free."

The Soothsayer was particularly famous for her hugs — she gave them often and indiscriminately — and at that moment she bestowed upon Mac one of the finest, longest, loveliest, most maternal embraces she'd ever delivered. Its power was so effective that Mac swiftly shed his conscience of all strife, slumped the weight from his body, and dangled like a rag doll in her arms. Had there been an adult-sized womb available, he would have assumed a fetal position and crawled inside.

One final, parting thought struck Lousy and she spoke it slowly and softly. "But remember, Mac, your act must be —"

Here she stopped, expecting him to finish her statement as before. He did not. Instead, he leaned back from her arms and cocked his head at her like a bewildered hound.

The smile of smiles beamed as brightly as the sun and not a wrinkle did it prove. She finished her statement.

"—*virtuous.*"

*   *   *   *

Mac was seven steps away from Lousy the Soothsayer, seven steps into his newfound journey, when he collided with Kooky Cullen and rolled with him, entangled, for a good twenty yards. Pedestrians were sent flying — a frail and elderly babushkaed woman and her frail and elderly babushkaed daughter, six German tourists, and Professor Farrell's entire Figure Drawing class, who were bored with sketching nude models and had ventured out of the classroom to sketch the generally-clothed public. Little blood was drawn, but casualties were great.

When Mac stood and began running determinedly again to his target destination, he was once more toppled to the ground, this time by Kooky Cullen's anchoring grasp on the cuff of his trousers. Kooky held on desperately, an eager grin decorating his near-toothless mouth.

"Hold steady, thar, Mac!" he pleaded, his grip tightening on the fabric of the man's pant leg. "Where's ye off to?"

His only response was to be kicked at viciously by his quarry.

"No, really, Mac! Where's ye off to? Would ye minds comp'ny?"

His answer was several fierce blows against his temples. The aging man's head bounced back and forth like a balloon in the hands of a frisky child, yet he laughed with each wallop. Had Kooky been entirely sober, the damage would've been great. As it was, his laughter continued and the hopeful smile remained as though chiseled by a sculptor.

"Just allow us to tag along!"

"Take the gas pipe!" Mac answered with an un-neighborly tone.

"Please, Mac! It'll be me an' you, just like auld tymes!" As an afterthought, he added, "I'll buy us both a pint when we reaches the end of our adventure!"

Mac ceased his brutal counterattack and thought for a moment. "*FINE!*" he barked. "But I'll not be slowed further by the likes o' you! If ye can't keep up, ye can bugger off an' straddle the tracks o' the Belfast Express fer all I care!"

Kooky's grin widened to reveal even less teeth. He scrambled to his feet and helped Mac up. "Where yous go, I's go! Say, where's we off to anyhows?"

His question received no answer, for as soon as Mac was on his feet, he was off. Kooky sprung forward in pursuit, his stiff legs propelling him in their awkward goose-stepping run, moving faster than ever just to keep up.

*　　　　*　　　　*　　　　*

Down O'Connell they ran, Kooky falling behind simply because he chose to dodge pedestrians rather than bound *through* them as Mac did. The thickening lunchtime crowd made it difficult to progress, but determination is a shroud over a rational mind and Mac was indeed a man determined. He couldn't spare time to weave around people in the interests of public safety as Kooky could. Besides, if Mac retained just one piece of knowledge from his formal education, it was that the shortest distance between two points is a straight line, caution be damned.

Never one to pass up an opportunity for music, Kooky drew a tin whistle from his pocket and played *The Flight of the Bumblebee* as he shooflied hither and thither about the crowd behind Mac. The music served its purpose well and those pedestrians before him heard the shrill and frantic melody and were saved from almost certain collision.

When at last the pair had carved their way through the hawkers and browsers and rabble, they arrived before the great O'Connell Street Bridge, a substantial breeze blowing off the River Liffey. Heedless of traffic signals, Mac led Kooky across the busy intersection at the junction of Eden and Ormond Quay and was honked at by many angry and impatient drivers who were forced to stop abruptly.

"Get out o' the way!" they shouted.

"If we must play by the rules, then so must you!" they cried.

"Hurry yer britches, ye monkey's arse!" they hallooed.

Mac paid them no mind and hopped up to the curb that circled the glorious O'Connell Bridge. The heart of Dublin, O'Connell Bridge was the widest and certainly the most traveled of all bridges crossing the Liffey. Activity was constant here; the locals tried to traverse it with their usual quick pace but were slowed by lingering tourists struggling to position themselves near the balustrade to get an un-obstructed view of the river. The motorway was dense with traffic, mostly buses, cabs, and the ever-present bicycles weaving in and out of bus lanes. The bridge was so congested that nothing ever seemed to move beyond the pace of an intoxicated tortoise.

It was this slow pace that allowed Kooky to finally catch up with his mate, who was attempting valiantly to slice his way through the gawkers and make his way to the bridge rail.

"Make way, louse and swine, make way!" Mac roared as he tried to karate-chop a path through the riffraff. The shutterbugs and their subjects had struggled to secure a photogenic spot along the bridge's edge, however, and none were eager to vacate without taking the time to fully ap-preciate its beauty. Mac hit a wall of humanity and could not break through.

Enter Kooky Cullen. The old man instinctively knew what to do.

"But we've only been drinkin' a few hours!" he fibbed, raising his voice for all to hear. "Are ye sure ye needs to vomit *here*? *Now*???"

Within seconds, a wide swath cleared between Mac and the balustrade and he found himself with at least twelve square feet of space to do with as he pleased. He looked at Kooky, impressed, then took his place against the wide concrete rail and gazed anxiously at the river below.

Kooky took his place next to Mac and rested his folded arms over the barrier. "So, then. What's brought the likes o' you's an' me to this spot, specifically?"

"'Tis a personal matter," was all Mac offered, quietly and retrospectively.

"Okey-doke," said Kooky genially.

"*FINE!*" Mac spat. "As long as ye continues to pester me 'bout motivations an' reasons why, I'll never be able to carry on! So here 'tis, *Master Grand Inquisitor*! 'Tis been decreed that I must rid me soul of all its greed an' unhealth-like desire here, now, fer good or ill. Yer own self is here to bear witness, I s'pose, so bear it an' take deep mental note o' what goes on in this most profound moment. Ye're about to witness...a *rebirth!*"

With that, Mac began the painful task of removing his shoes. Kooky watched him bend his torso stiffly and lift his foot as much as it would raise. Noting Mac's complete absence of agility, Kooky knew this was going to take a while.

"Could we maybe speed the rebirth up a bit? I'm gettin' tirsty from all that runnin'!"

Glaring eyes answered him. "Ye could lend us a hand if ye're in such a blasted hurry!"

Kooky's face lit up at the suggestion and he kneeled on the ground, slapping the top of his raised thigh. Mac placed his foot as instructed and Kooky unlaced the shoe and gingerly slipped it from Mac's foot.

"Now the sock!" Mac said. "But do it gently, fer what lies within is precious!"

"I knows all about yer socks, Mac. I promise to handles 'em as I would the bars o' gold in Fort Knox!"

"HOW IN THE HIGH AN' HOLY—!" Mac was unable to finish his curse, he was in such a state of flummox. How did everyone and their Uncle Herbert seem to know about his bloody socks??? He fumed to himself as Kooky carefully rolled the top half of the sock over the heel and pulled the mass from his toes.

"'Tis a tankless job, I tell ye!" Kooky said, repulsed by the health of Mac's sock. "If we ever gets to that pub, Mac, the second round is on you, an' the third an' fourth as well!" He handed the black mass up and refused to breathe again until it was safely stowed in the pocket of Mac's coat.

The right foot replaced the left on Kooky's thigh and they went through the procedure again. Soon Mac held his horrid and heavy hosiery in his hands, feeling their weight and staring transfixed at them, his eyes full of doubt. He became suddenly quiet, seemingly introspective.

"The cotton in me mouth, pallie," Kooky prompted meekly. "The pub!"

Mac sighed dramatically and broke his stare. "Help me up," was all he said.

Kooky stood and took Mac's offered hand, then bent his knee slightly to allow Mac a step up. It took some doing, but within moments Mac stood tall atop the balustrade, leaning against a streetlamp for balance. The wind had settled, at least for the moment.

He reached into his socks and withdrew great fistfuls of cash. The discarded socks floated to the river and were swept away with the current. Mac's eyes never left the wads of paper he held in his now-trembling hands. They trembled not from fear or uncertainty, but from excitement and the energy of redemption.

Kooky looked up at the money in awe. "Me God an' his sweet baby Jaysus...there must be *thousands*—"

Yes, Mac thought. Many of those. A lifetime's worth.

Without breaking his stare, Mac raised his voice to the Gods. "Mighty Liffey, giver an' taker o' life, accept this, mine gift, these notes which once held such significance, an' grant me a life free from their binds! A life free from the greed o' common men! A life well-lived!"

His fists unclenched. His fingers spread. His heart skipped, then swelled.

The winds attacked the falling bills and the air was quickly littered with swirling pound notes — quid, crowns, tenners, twenties, fifties, even hundreds — that flew gracefully into the current below. A collective gasp sounded from the pedestrians who'd stopped to watch along the bridge. Many hands reached out and tried to snatch the bills from their fate, yet few found success. One gentleman of distinction, an elected official out for a lunchtime stroll, even leapt into the river after the discarded paper, but only managed to grab a fiver before the current swept him away to Dublin Bay.

Mac turned on the parapet to address his audience. "'Tis a far, far better thing I do than I has ever done before!" he cried. "'Tis a far, far better—"

It was then that his bare, sweaty feet lost their grip on the concrete and he slipped most unexpectedly and most violently from it, landing hard on the man standing below, who happened to be his acquaintance, Kooky Cullen. Both men screamed painfully, Kooky perhaps a wee louder since he bore the full brunt of Mac's weight and wound up very much incapacitated under Mac's mass.

Several concerned citizens helped Mac, who grabbed his oversized loafers on his way up. Back on his feet, he looked proudly at his surroundings, at the city of Dublin, his very own Dublin, while the good samaritans rushed to aid his companion. Another breath of fire filled his newborn lungs and he kept the air drawn a moment, savoring its life-giving essence.

"Come, Kooky!" he said, exhaling, failing to notice that Kooky still lay disabled from his injuries and probably would for some time. "Let us find the nearest pub an' raise a glass to honor the moral renaissance o' yers truly! I'll beg ye to lend me a few shillings, however, fer I seem to be a bit short at the moment...."

Mac hiked up his trousers and stuck out his chest proudly, then led his own way across the street, eager to detail his humble story to the friends and strangers who awaited his introduction within the warmth and intoxication of Ireland's finest comfort.

CHAPTER ELEVEN
Pomp and Circumstance

The wheelbarrow suffered a slight bend in its axle and as John maneuvered it carefully between the Nobleman's shelves, he was embarrassed by the *squeaking* and *thumping* and general carrying-on reverberating from under its concave belly. So much for not drawing attention. He was as inconspicuous as a man pushing a baby grand with square wheels through the post-op ward. Still, it was as good a time as any to being doing this, with only two ladies shopping on the second floor, presumably out of earshot.

The weight of the beast was beginning to draw on his back, so John promised himself just one more shelf before taking it outside to unload. He was becoming proficient at passing judgement and the wheelbarrow was topping off more quickly than ever. To be nonjudgemental in his scrutiny had initially been terribly difficult, but as the project progressed, he found himself becoming increasingly rational in his faculty to pick and choose which ones stayed and which went on the pile. He felt revitalized by his ability to finally think clearly again.

Finishing his examination of the first shelf in Fiction X - Z, John took the handles of his load and wheeled it loudly to the front. It always took a bit of finagling to get the brute through the door, but he found, perhaps strangely, that the heavier the load, the easier it was to clear the hump in the threshold. He pushed it outside along the front windows and brought it to rest beside the skip that now lay further away from the entrance than the last. This skip was larger and certainly more presentable than the one belonging to the construction crew. When they'd at last finished the flooring and removed their container (making sure to register complaints about the additional, unauthorized, and unnecessary weight before they left, as expected), John rented a replacement that could handle the job and still be out of the way and much less of an eyesore in front of his business. It was the greatest investment he'd made in a while.

When the task of throwing the old books from barrow to bin was nearly complete, he heard his name spoken and turned to find Mac standing in the lane, holding a crumpled paper bag. "Mac!" he said, pleased to see his friend. "Just the man I need. Come, help me finish this an' we'll go inside fer a sandwich."

It took Mac a moment to respond. "I cannot help ye with that, John."

John bent and touched his toes, then stood and stretched his back left, then right. "I know what ye mean, kiddo. 'Tis rough on the back." He jockeyed the wheelbarrow neatly beside the skip, out of the way. "Let's disregard the work an' head straight fer the sandwiches, then. Come in!"

He led the amble into the shop and pulled up a stool for Mac, but they both wound up leaning against the counter instead. "What can I get fer ye? Cheese toastie with tomato? A ham sandwich, perhaps?"

"I broke me fast not long ago, but you go 'head." Mac was uncharacteristically solemn today.

"Tae, then? Or perhaps somethin' with more gruff to it?"

"No, John. I'm not tirsty, neither."

"Well, that's fine," John said. "If ye change yer mind...."

"I wanted to come by an' tell ye," Mac said. He seemed to be having difficulty finding words this afternoon. "How much I.

"Tink about what ye done fer me.

"Lately, that is.

"An' I'm fond o' the way.

"Ye been treatin' me an' such.

"Lately, o' course.

"Ye treated me real good-like.

"Givin' me a job an' all.

"An'.

"Well.

"Bein' a friend an' all.

"All o' that.

"An'.

"I learned.

"A lot.

"So.

"Sure.

"I tink.

"I tink I."

He floundered again and looked up to his brows, trying to recall the word.

"Tanks.

"I.

"Tanks, John."

He stood awkwardly, emotions exposed, and crossed and uncrossed his arms several times. His eyes never made contact with John's. A few attempts were made to speak further, but only silence emanated. Eventually he ceased trying to open his mouth, indicating he was through talking.

John felt humbled by his speech. He knew how difficult it was for a fellow of Mac's nature to offer just one of those words, much less all of them. Not wanting to embarrass the man by making a show of it, he smiled appreciatively and put his hand out. Mac stared at the hand, not seeming to comprehend the gesture, then remembered and put his own hand forth. The handshake lasted but a moment, yet John considered himself fortunate to receive it.

The crumpled bag Mac held rustled in his nervous grip and he remembered it. "Oh. An' this," he said, offering it to his friend.

John took the bag and unrolled it, reached in and pulled out a wide book, worn and dirty and slightly torn, bound with spiraled wire. The plain, off-white cover bore only the blue seal of the Ordnance Survey Office. He flipped through the pages; each sheet was fully illustrated with a map, an overhead rendering of what appeared to be city streets and buildings, whole neighborhoods on each page, around eighty pages in all.

"A land registry book," John declared, trying to mask his bewilderment.

"Uh-huh," Mac said, nodding. "A book. I found it yesterday an' was keepin' it fer ye. I know how ye love the books an' all." His anxious eyes settled on John, trying to gauge his reaction.

At last John understood. "Oh. No, no, 'tis grand. Truly." He looked up and smiled broadly. "I adore it. 'Tis perfect. It'll make a very fitting addition to me collection. Tank ye, Mac."

Having survived the demoralizing part of his visit, Mac snapped out of his bashful trance. "When's yer next business meetin', then? I fancy comin' in to work."

This gave John pause. He wanted to reciprocate Mac's kind gesture, certainly, and his friend Sean Brannon, owner of the Rosie Grace Café, was due to arrive soon for a visit. It'd be nice to take a few hours off to socialize. Besides, he'd have some spending cash soon enough, so why not?

"As a matter o' fact, Mac, are ye free this very afternoon? I could stand to take the final hours o' the day to rest me weary back an' entertain a visitin' friend."

"Today, uh?" Mac thought long and hard about the offer. "Well, figurin' 'tis Garda Bonner's day off an' I would'na be in jeopardy o' bein' caught here, what with the binds o' genuine responsibility an' nowhere's to run, I'll say there's a good chance I could come in today, aye."

"An' even if Bonner *did* enter the premises, say to make a purchase in his civvies, ye wouldn't flee yer post?"

It took a while for Mac to respond, his eyes moving to and fro, up and down, going through a variety of scenarios in his mind. Finally, he settled on an answer. "No," he said. "I'll stand me ground come hell or high tide."

"Ye're a good man fer doin' so, Mac. Tanks fer helpin' out. Here," he said, noticing the two ladies making their way down the stairs, "will ye man the till an' ring up the ladies fer me while I see to some business in back?"

"Off ye go!" Mac shooed, and he assumed his station by the till.

John paused on his way past the ladies. "Mrs. Byrne, Mrs. Fagan," he greeted. "Find anything to pique yer interest?"

"Yes, plenty, tank ye, Mr. Doyle!" Mrs. Byrne answered.

"I'll leave ye in the comp'ny o' me good man Mr. Malone here, then. Go see him once ye've finished yer perusal an' he'll ring ye up. Tanks fer stoppin' by, ladies!" They all offered friendly farewells and John shuffled back to his living quarters. After changing his shirt, he proceeded to dig through a dresser drawer. He found the small envelope under a pile of sweaters and took from it one of several keys that jangled within, then returned to the front. The ladies had gone and Mac sat behind the counter, looking bored.

"How'd it go?" John asked.

"How'd what go?"

"The sale."

"What sale?"

"Mrs. Fagan an' Mrs. Byrne. They were just here. I heard the door bells chirpin' when they left."

"Oh, them's. Right. Uh…" He looked to the ceiling to search his memory. "Nine books between 'em an' ye're two pounds twelve wealthier than ye was when ye departed."

"Very good, Mac, tanks. Nice work. Now, since I'll be out the rest o' the evenin', that means ye'll have a new task to add to yer duties. Ye'll have to close up fer the night at six o'clock sharp. Do ye accept that responsibility?"

Again, Mac's eyes searched to and fro, up and down, before he came to a decision. "Aye."

The key appeared in John's fingers. "I'll hand this over, then. 'Tis a spare fer the lock on the front door. At six o'clock, check upstairs an' all down here to make sure no one's left browsin'. When all customers are out, simply pull the shades an' lock the door. An' flip the sign on the door from open to closed. Easy-peasy."

"Sure, I seen it done in the filums! I always wanted to flip the sign from open to closed." Mac looked excited at the prospect.

"An' Mac, I want ye to keep that key. Fer good. Keep it in a safe spot, right?"

"Right. Easy-peasy, as ye say. I'll keep it in me sock."

"Excellent choice," John said encouragingly. He looked down to the floorboards in front of the counter and had a thought. "There's one more very important matter ye should know of."

They were interrupted by the rattle and jangle over the door and Sean Brannon walked in, looking clever in herringbone vest and matching jacket. John had never seen him without rolled shirtsleeves and a trickle of sweat on his bulbous head and was pleased at the thought of a night off to look presentable and be sociable. He made a mental note to dress in his best tweed to match.

"Sean! Lookin' as sharp as a cheddar on the choppin' board! Welcome!" They pumped hands and slapped shoulders and grinned with a sense of brotherhood. "Might I introduce a good chum, Mac Malone. Mac, this here's Sean Brannon."

"How d'ye do?" Sean greeted.

"Deee-lighted." Mac said it grumblingly and unconvincingly, yet John was certain it was as cheerful a tone as he'd ever used when greeting a new acquaintance.

"Say, Sean," John said, "Mac has kindly offered to watch the shop, so we're free to venture out. Bewley's is just 'round the corner, would ye care to sit over tae?"

"Tae is grand in the mornin', John, but I prefer somethin' with a wee more heft to it past noon," Sean countered. "How d'ye feel 'bout O'Donoghue's?"

The grin spread over John's face like spilled syrup. "I'm reminded that we two are men o' the same mind. You just express it better than I. O'Donoghue's it is! Say, would ye mind if I called to invite another friend along?"

"'Course not. It can't be a party without numbers."

"But first let me show ye 'round the place, give ye the grand tour." He took Sean in tow and walked him through the aisles of the Chivalric Nobleman. After they'd seen all of the first two floors, Sean asked to have a few minutes to shop, so John returned downstairs to wait. He found Mac again looking bored at the front, but was pleased to see him awake rather than sprawled unconscious over the counter.

"I wish ye could join us at the pub, Mac. We'll have to make it another time, to be sure."

Mac yawned. "O'Donoghue's, that's where they got all that music playin'. Not fer me, no sir. That music stuff infests me soul with the heebie-jeebies, makes me skellington rattle like the palsy!"

"Perhaps that's not such a bad thing," John said. "Ye should give it another try sometime." The floorboards had squeaked as he walked over, reminding him of a topic to broach. "Come here 'til I show ye somethin'."

Stopping first to find two pairs of cotton gloves, he led Mac to where the loose floorboards lay. They knelt together and John pulled the boards up and reached into the cavity. *Don Quixote* was soon unwrapped and unboxed and lay in Mac's gloved hands. He looked upon it with sheer disinterest.

John explained in great earnest, his voice quiet yet commanding. "If ye're ever in here an' somethin' bad happens, some emergency that might threaten the shop, this is the only thing to carry with ye on yer way out the door to safety. This here is the one thing. The *only* thing. Understand?"

"But. 'Tis a book," was Mac's insolent reply.

"Aye, a book," John said. "A very important book. This particular book is worth more money than all the others combined. So keep it on top o' yer mind whenever ye're here, if ye please."

"Right," Mac nodded. "In times o' crisis, grab the book an' scram."

"Precisely." John squeezed Mac's shoulder. "Good man." He returned *Quixote* to its nook and replaced the floorboards. "Ye can always tell where it is due to the squeak in these here boards. D'ye hear it?" He stood and stepped over the two boards and they answered his weight with their cry. "That there is the voice o' the Chivalric Nobleman. She'll always be here to keep ye entertained in times o' restlessness."

Mac rather enjoyed the thought of that and took his place over the loose boards, springing up and down on his heels and making the shop sing. *Creakcreakcreak!* it sang. *Creakcreakcreakcreakcreakcreak!*

You'd never know it by the placid look on his face, but Mac was having a hell of a time.

"Mac—"

Creakcreakcreakcreakcreakcreakcreakcreakcreak!

"Say, Mac—"

Creakcreakcreakcreakcreakcreakcreakcreakcreakcreakcreak!
Suddenly he stopped. "Well I guess that's enough o' that, then," he said, and stepped away from his entertainment.

After suggesting that Mac might want to take a stroll around the shop to better acquaint himself with its layout, John took to the telephone to ring Brian Corrigan and invite him out for a pint. It was agreed that they would meet at the pub within the hour. Sean eventually appeared with an armful of books and John gave him an honorable discount, assuming his friend was only purchasing them to be supportive since he'd mentioned once that he wasn't much of a reader. John double-bagged the sale and afterward disappeared briefly to his living quarters to don his best jacket and cap. When he stepped back into the shop, Mac had returned from his exploratory circuit and taken his place on the stool.

"Righto, Mac, time to head out!" John said as he motioned Sean to the door. "No need to stick around once ye close up, but ye're welcome to, as always. If anyone comes wantin' to sell or trade, tell 'em we're only sellin' at the moment. I'll catch up with ye later to hear how the rest o' the day went. Until then!" He waved and they were off.

*   *   *   *

By six o'clock, O'Donoghue's was packed. They'd been there for over three hours already, having arrived early enough to claim the best table in the corner, and had gulped and gobbled their way through four rounds and a supper. The table was littered with empty pint glasses and the remnants of one chicken and bacon boxty, a ham and cheese toastie, and a plate of fried white fish with a side of mushy peas. Another round had been ordered more than a half hour prior, but no one tending bar in Ireland is likely to put a rush on any request for drink, for the pace of the person pouring drinks is directly correlated to the pace of the person drinking them, and all good things come to those who pace themselves.

In the corner opposite, a group of musicians sat intimately in a circle, playing and singing and tapping their feet in time. There were almost as many people playing instruments as there were patrons in the bar. All the traditional instrumentation was represented: guitar, banjo, tin whistle, Uilleann pipe, fiddle, harp, melodeon, flute, concertina, and bodhran, some of which there were more than one, and the small table in the center of their circle was littered with strings and reeds and one modest bowl for cash tips. People took turns singing and each voice was drastically different. The soft, the loud, the vibrant, the elegant, the robust, the delicate, the proud, they sang their songs of love and humor and tragedy and vice. Some were seasoned pros and some trembled with stage fright, yet they were all of them good. Their singing was infectious and at times one voice grew to a roomful of voices as the crowd sang along and threw their arms out to embrace the shoulders of their neighbor. As time wore on and more pints were delivered, the voices became bolder and the performances less inhibited. The only action that could possibly stop a person from making this music was the delivery of their drink; only then did the individual rest their instrument and rise to collect their glass, clearly illustrating their priorities.

Sean was finishing his tirade to John and Brian. "If it's a tussle with a group o' men, that's fine, I'll join in anytime. If it's a fight between females, I'll refrain from participatin', tank ye very much. They fight *dirty!*"

They all laughed and Brian slapped his hand against the table and cried, "hear, hear!" The barmaid appeared through the crowd and delivered three more pints. "What's this about females, then?" she demanded.

Sean confessed, "I was describin' to me mates the differences between a row with males versus a row with females."

"Oh, ye'll not be wantin' to mess with the females, boys," she shouted over the din. "We won't stop 'til ye lie broken an' bleedin'! Ye want equality, ye can sail right t'England, 'cause we rule this isle!" The boys gave a hearty roar as she left their soiled dishes on the table and disappeared into a swarm of bodies.

John leaned in and asked, "Has any o' ye prepared fer this storm that's supposed to be makin' landfall tomorrow? I heard 'tis to be vicious, one o' the worst we've seen in ages!"

Sean piped in, "The last time they predicted somethin' as awful as that, it turned out to be a mere spit in the bucket. I'm consequently wary this time 'round. Me money says it'll be nothin' we can't handle."

Brian added, "Me home's been standin' fer nearly seven hundred years, I'm sure she can handle another rainfall!"

The musicians were deep into a rendition of *The Wild Rover* and the three men halted their conversation to join the room in singing its chorus,

> *And it's no, nay, never,*
> *No, nay, never no more!*
> *Will I plaaaaay the wild rover*
> *No never, no more!*

Two of John's friends were sitting in the crowded musician's circle, Emma on tin whistle and Jack beating the rhythm on his bodhran. Emma caught John's eye from across the room and flashed him a comradely smile, then motioned for him to come up. Jack saw her beckon and also encouraged John to join them with a come-hither nod. John scoffed and shook his head, waving his hand to decline their offer. He wasn't nearly inebriated enough to attempt what they were inviting and gestured as such by pointing at his watch, then to the glass before him, then pantomiming a look of drunken stupor. Emma laughed and nodded her understanding as Jack shook his head and rolled his eyes in mock disappointment.

Sean raised his voice over the music and said, "'Tis grand to see so many out enjoyin' each other's company tonight! The economy bein' what it is, me place hasn't seen a crowd in some time. I need to apply fer me liquor licence — in times o' trouble, the only thing that seems to sell is intoxication!"

Brian chimed in, "Although I'm certain fornication is thrivin' as well, an' I'm not talkin' 'bout the type we get free from the government!"

"'Tis deadly, man!" John said. "I'm havin' the same experience meself. No one wants to buy books anymore, they're only interested in tradin' or sellin'! 'Tis fast cash people want an' the second-hand shops are bearin' the brunt of it. I had to put a hold on buyin' an' tradin' until sales pick up."

Brian's glass was nearly empty and he scanned the room for the barmaid as he spoke. "Seems to me the second-hands would be thrivin', what with no one wantin' to pay full price fer somethin' new when they could get it almost as good from previous owners."

"Ye'd tink, an' yet business is dry." John shook his head. "Location has a lot to do with it. Ye've both seen the shop, it might as well be built on the bottom o' Dublin Bay."

"Insanity, it is!" Sean said, passionate. "To be right smack dab in the middle o' the best shoppin' district in town, yet just far enough from the lane to go unnoticed. Have ye thought about relocatin'?" he offered. "It might be worth investigatin'."

"Or scalin' down yer stock? Keep what's likely to sell?" Brian still hadn't found his barmaid. "I assume cookbooks an' travel guides an' DIY handbooks still sell alright, eh?"

"How 'bout advertisin'?" Sean asked, his mind in brainstorming mode.

"I'm ahead o' ye there," John said. "I placed adverts in five o' the top collector's magazines an' trade journals highlightin' the finest in me stock. Not a single inquiry yet, an' that with some prime books listed at *undervalued* prices." He shook his head. "Not a nibble."

John lifted his stout and took a gulp. The glass remained at his mouth and he took another healthy chug. He then opened his throat to it all, a full half pint, and slammed the empty glass down harder than intended. "I fail to be motivated anymore. I'm tired o' the grind. I was never meant to be a man o' business, anyhow. I may just be gettin' too old fer it, but I've lost any interest I ever had. I'm tired o' livin' bill to bill, o' never seein' me accounts rise, I'm tired o' watchin' the shelves expand until I got nowhere to breathe. I'm tired o' bein' a nice guy. An' I'm tired o' livin' like a vagabond in me own home. I got nowheres to go. All I got is a failed business an' one tiny room in the corner. John Doyle, the hermit o' Dublin! No family, no money, nobody 'round, just me an' a bunch o' worthless books in a worthless buildin'. After fifteen years as a bookseller, I got nothin' to show fer it but a *worthless fuckin' life.*"

The song ended and the room exploded with applause and laughter, punctuating John's outburst with an undeserved humor. John seemed to break from his trance and looked up at his friends, who both sat silently, looking a bit startled.

"Well, that was...*unexpected,*" he said after the brouhaha had settled, a bit startled himself. His cheeks became heated with embarrassment. "I hope ye gents'll pardon me, I hadn't intended to, uh, go on like that."

Sean smiled reassuringly. "No trouble at all, mate. 'Tis what we're here fer."

His attention ambushed from the pursuit of more drink by John's exclamation, Brian spoke boldly over the raucous pub. "'Tis time ye made a change, then! Get out o' that shop an' free yerself to do whatever it is ye wish. If it's draggin ye down, then, by Christ, unshackle yerself!"

"Not an easy thing to do, I'll have ye know," John said, shaking his head. "'Tis complicated. Still, I've had ideas—"

"Walk away! Jus' walk away from it," Brian continued. "Begin anew! Start fresh! Relieve yer mind o' this burden!"

It was Sean's turn to lean in. "Perhaps 'tis not as simple as Brian sees it, but 'tis certainly not impossible. Hell, I did it. Me cousin done it, too, just a few years back. Quit her job outright to give a go at bein' an actress, she did! I was proud when she done it, too."

"How's she fared?" John asked.

Sean gave a chuckle and pursed his lips. "Not well, I'm afraid. 'Tis a hard profession to try a hand at. Cutthroat with all the competition." He lowered his head, ablush. "Perhaps not an appropriate analogy to make."

Brian shook his head reproachfully. "Actors an' writers, two professions o' the eternally destitute! The only difference between the two is that writers possess the ability to *tink*. Some of 'em, at least." He finally caught the eye of their barmaid and motioned for another round. He continued, "Neither is able to earn a living wage unless luck is on their side, an' there's precious few who possess that!"

A mindful smile crossed John's lips. "Speakin' these words to a man who's considerin' a stab at bein' a writer, I'll have ye know!"

Brian said nothing, merely sat like a child caught with a pinched lollipop until, finally, he let out a great guffaw and slapped the table once more. "Damn me cursin' tongue! An' pardon me bein' insensitive. I hope ye know I fully support ye in any course ye travel."

"I know indeed, an' no harm done. How was ye to know? Anyhow, 'tis all just a notion at this point. I dug up a few essays an' stories I'd written in school an' can't say any of 'em were any good."

"How do ye know 'til ye try it?" Sean was being optimistically encouraging. "Ye wrote those stories a long time ago. People change, John. We're supposed to. Isn't that the meanin' o' life? Evolution? Give 'er a go an' see where it takes ye!"

"Good point, Sean, an' well taken." John pushed his stool back from the table and slapped his knees. "But fer this moment, I've had enough o' talkin' 'bout meself. God, 'tis enough to drive a man to drink!"

"That's the spirit!" Brian shouted.

John laughed and continued, "If ye'll pardon me, I need to hit the loo. When I come back, no more heavy talk, eh? A man joins his mates at the pub to get *away* from his problems! Reach out an' twist me nose if I bring yer spirits down again." He started off, then turned back. "An' see to it we've each of us got another pint by the time I return!"

His friends nodded their agreement and John weaved his way toward the gent's in back, stopping several times to greet and chat with other friends and acquaintances. This pub was one of his favorites due to many factors, mostly because he was familiar here. He used to spend more time at O'Donoghue's, but the frequency of his visits aligned directly with the potency of his aging metabolism. On many occasions he'd even been asked to join the musicians for a song, depending on who was playing on any given night. Some of his finest memories were of drinking and singing here with his chums and making a fine, king-hell time of an evening. He longed for that again.

While in the toilet, he was reminded of an incident that happened to him there many years prior. While standing, urinating into the porcelain hole in the floor, he was overcome by a flash flood of giggles that grew until his cheeks hurt from smiling so hard and the man relieving himself next to him had to ask if anything was wrong, which made him laugh all the more.

As promised, a fresh pint awaited him when he returned and he sat down and claimed the purity of the flawless head that floated on top. He wiped the foam from his lip and addressed his friends. "Bein' in the toilet here reminds me of a time, 'bout ten years past." He took another swig and continued, "I'm here at O'Donoghue's with me mates, standin' right over there by that partition at the end o' the bar, an' I start feelin' the pressure o' what must'a been 'bout eight or nine pints pressin' on me bladder. The feelin' is growin' an' growin' an' I just stay there laughin' with me mates until I can stand it no more. So I make me way back to the gent's just as quick as can be, cuttin' through the masses before I explode an' make a mess o' the place, right? I get back there an' unbutton me fly an' proceed to let it all out into that little hole in the ground an', God as me witness, 'tis the best feelin' a man's ever had throughout history. 'Tis *amazin'*, this feelin', an' I stand there an' enjoy it fer its shrill an' utter *magnificence*. It goes on an' on, as though I'd been drinkin' since the day o' me birth without a moment o' relief. On an' on an' on it goes! But after a while o' standing there, I notice that somethin's not quite right, there's a sensation that somethin's — what is it? — somethin's *missin'* from the traditional experience o' makin' water. Then I notice, 'tis the *sound*. It didn't *sound* right, it didn't resemble the sound o' yer everyday, normal, healthy urination. Come to tink of it, it didn't make a sound a'tall! Yet I feel the liquid leavin' me body nonetheless! Then, then I sense the *heat*, like a vast, warm hug all 'round me hips. The warmth is spreadin', an' *fast*. 'Tis creepin' all down me leg, gettin' warmer all the time. So I look down an' what do I find? Ye can prob'ly guess it by now. I hadn't released the bugger fully from the confines o' me trousers! Hadn't even made it past the buttons on me fly! I was four sheets, I was, an' never bothered to check! Who does? Anyway, the ol' boy is still layin' safe an' sound inside me pants an' I'm starin' at a wet spot that's gettin' bigger an' bigger — hell, ye could name the thing Lake Doyle by now — an' I just watch it come on like the Easter parade. Just starin' at it like a drunken eejit, I was! Well, I finally found me senses an' pulled the bugger free an' out he comes, just a-sprayin' an' a-splashin' all over the place like a fire hose gone rogue! I got him aimed at the right place an' it didn't take long to finish the job since most of it'd been done already, but by then the front o' me pants looked like a map of Africa! An' I was wearin' *khakis* that night, there'd be absolutely no hidin' it!"

They were all howling. The people packed close around them had overheard the story and added the sounds of their laughter to the festivities. Their corner of the room was overpowering the music with Homeric fits of boozy laughter. "An' that's not the end of it!" John shouted. "The worst part of all was when I come out an' had to face a pub full o' mates an' act as though nothin's wrong!" He stood and pantomimed standing stiffly at the bar, staring ahead like Buster Keaton as he brought an imaginary glass up to his mouth repeatedly. "It was *horrifyin'*!"

The song came to an end and the room responded with spirited cheers, knuckles and pipes and empty pint glasses pounding encouragingly against tabletops. From the musician's corner, Emma stood up, having noticed the ruckus surrounding John, and shouted, "John Doyle! Come give us a song!" Applause and calls of encouragement followed, and John placed his glass down. "Oh, why the hell not, I'm loose enough by now!" He made his way to the front and conferred with the musician's circle. They agreed on a song and John spun to face his audience, then pulled up a short stool and stood on it for show, as he used to do.

Inside, he was trembling with trepidation, but no one suspected it by the look of him. He gave the impression of being a true showman. The alcohol helped, certainly, but so did John's need to break loose and have a little fun.

He shouted behind him playfully, "let's play this one in Q-sharp!" After a deep breath, he began to speak-sing the first verse slowly, without accompaniment:

Young Paddy O'Shea
Walked the Wellington Quay
Hand-in-hand with his beautiful lover
They had their first lover's spat
And she laid him out flat
So he stumbled to the pub to recover!

On this final line, the musicians joined in with an up-tempo melody and they were into the full swing of the song:

He threw back a pint or six
And was soon in quite a fix
For he picked a fight with massive Liam Goggin
The row was barely more than farce
For Liam handed him his arse
And scrubbed the floor with Paddy's cringin' noggin!

When your life has got you down
And no sunshine can be found
And you're pickin' fights because you're tightly wound
Wipe the blood from off your face
Give your foe a warm embrace
Shake a hand and buy the house a round!

At this point, half the voices in the room rose to join him on the chorus:

Buy the house a round, boy-o
Buy the house a round
Shake a hand and buy the house a round!

They all cheered the relevance of the lyrics and John continued:

The Sheriff Street Gang came
To drink and fight and drink again
But before they could, ol' Paddy interrupted
He proceeded to attack
With one hand behind his back
But he wound up with his nose and pride corrupted!

Young Paddy was on the ground
When Mrs. Brazzle came around
Of the regulars, she was the eldest lass
He said, "I'll fight you with eyes closed!"
Reached out and tore her pantyhose
And old Brazzle swung her cane and whipped his ass!

When your life has got you down
And you're writhing on the ground
And you're pickin' fights because you're tightly wound
Wipe the blood from off your face
Give your foe a warm embrace
Shake a hand and buy the house a round!

More voices came to sing the chorus with him this time, and many a hand raised their glass and swung it in time overhead.

Buy the house a round, boy-o
Buy the house a round
Shake a hand and buy the house a round!

Now John crouched lower on his stool and dropped his tone for the final verse. The room became quiet with him.

When the night had reached its end
Paddy took his newfound friends
To his lover's house to heal from all the violence
Liam, Brazzle, and the Gang

Stood arm-in-arm with him and sang
'Til his girl came down and beat them all to silence!

He raised his voice once more for the finale:

When your life has turned around
While your lover's sleeping sound
Just be quiet or she'll serve your bollix ground
Wipe the blood from off your face
Give your gal a warm embrace
Shake a hand and buy the house a round!

And now, for this, the final chorus, the framed photographs on the wall rattled from the sheer volume of every voice singing in unison:

Buy the house a round, boy-o
Buy the house a round
Shake a hand…
and…
buy…
the…
house…
a…
ROUND…!

The clapping of hands and stomping of feet and general raucousness raised the atmosphere in the room to one of family. John turned and offered Jack a trembling hand to shake while he gave Emma an endearing wink of thanks. He wound his way through the crowd to reunite with his friends and encountered many adoring slaps on his back along the route.

Brian and Sean welcomed his return with shouts and applause of their own. "The extroverted introvert here!" Sean bellowed. "Look at ye, ye held this room right square in the flesh o' yer palm! A hermit?" He scoffed. "Ye couldn't be a hermit if ye tried!"

John sat and took a considerable pull from his Guinness. "Gents, I'm glad ye're here with me tonight, fer I've just now come to a few conclusions an' have some big news to share!" Whatever stout remained in the glass went down his throat in a single, final gulp. "I've decided to enroll in courses at the business school, focusin' on real estate an' finance. 'Tis time I open meself up to change an' no better time to do it!"

"Good fer you, John! That's the way to go!" Sean raised his glass to toast him. "But what's to become o' the bookshop?"

An intoxicated grin stole past John's lips. "I've been made an entirely respectable offer just this week an' have decided to accept." He felt giddy delivering such news; it nearly stuck in his throat. "So if any o' ye's happen to hear of a country cottage fer sale, I'm officially in the market."

Brian took John's shoulder and pulled him close. "Congratulations, man! 'Tis a big step to be takin'! What's to become o' yer stock, then?"

"I suppose I'll put it all up fer auction."

Brian lowered his chin and gave his friend a questioning look. "An' *Don Quixote*?"

John's eyes glistened with excitement and inebriation and he slapped Brian's knee familiarly. "Funny ye should mention that book, Brian, fer I was about to bring up the very subject with ye…."

CHAPTER TWELVE
Fear of the Devil

Evening relinquished to night and the goddess Luna shot moonbeams over the land from her bow, then dove for cover as they ricocheted back from impenetrable storm clouds. A sense of foreboding unnerved the community as the sky turned black and the weatherman left suddenly for Barbados. Schoolteachers had sent their students home early, hardware merchants stayed late to sell plywood for window boarding, city engineers worked diligently to prepare for emergency, and bankers escaped to country estates while their underlings were made to stay into the wee hours and do math.

The streets of the Temple Bar district were predominantly barren when Mac Malone wandered through in search of a supper. Hunger scorched his belly and made him dizzy, images of steak and wine and candied bacon prancing through his frenzied mind. He was certain his current state of starvation would lead to a blackout or, worse, death. He swooned at the thought. Never mind the fact that he'd eaten a sizable lunch only three hours prior.

As anyone who's ever been on a diet knows, there comes a point of relapse, a moment when all sense flies out the window and the craving for pizza and cheeseburgers and lard-fried butter and molasses pound cake overwhelms. Mac had risen from his nap swimming in these dangerous waters;

he'd dreamt he was the ruler of a small country just east of Freedonia and his royal cook had served him a feast fit for a man of his title, complete with pizzas and cheeseburgers and lard-fried butter and molasses pound cakes. He'd woken feeling the sharp pangs of hunger, topped off by a vicious case of the mulligrubs. His foul mood somehow made his hunger infinitely worse.

After an hour passed and his dreams of roast beef and honey-glazed ham and chateaubriand with sauce Béarnaise still remained intangible, Mac fell, spent, against the lamppost in front of O'Rourke's Tavern and swung sluggishly from it. His mouth hung open and dribbled saliva down his whiskered chin, his lids floated just above the pupils of his vigorless eyes. The few pedestrians who passed quickened their step, imagining he might be an inmate escaped from the Belfast Lunatic Asylum come home for vengeance.

He'd been leaning listlessly against the lamp for mere moments when his own name pierced his ears. "Mac Malone!" cut through his head like a buccaneer's cutlass, sobering him to his surroundings. Standing not two paces away was a crusty little man dressed in a wear-weary tartan peacoat buttoned loosely over a thin, imitation Scottish kilt.

"Wilder Molyneux, as I live an' breathe!" Mac cried, unable to disguise his disgust. "I thought ye'd ceased livin' an' breathin' years ago!"

Wilder was ablaze with excitement at seeing his old chum. "Alive an' nearly well, as ye can see, Mac!" he said in his bastardized accent of French and Irish. "Just returned from a lengthy tour visitin' family in Paris, I have, an' I can now report there's no finer folk on this here planet than the ones we got in ol' Dublintown! I've come back to live rough with me best mates, an' to hell with me family tree, the inhospitable swine!"

Mac pointed at his ear. "Can't hear a word over the growlin' in me stomach! If I was interested in the least, I'd ask ye to repeat, but as I'm not...." He turned and started off toward Westmoreland Street.

Wilder's words stopped him. "Hungry, then, are ye? Why, 'tis a supper I hold in this here bag, an' plenty enough fer two!"

Mac whirled around and noticed the greasy bag in Wilder's hand. A light breeze wafted enticing scents in his direction and he sniffed at them like a bloodhound. Each whiff intensified his interest and caused his belly to grumble in one long, uninterrupted spasm.

"It smells like—" Here he lifted his nose again to the air. "—like *beans*. An'— an'—," still sniffing, "—good cripes! *Jalapeño peppers!*"

Wilder's eyes electrified at Mac's power of conjecture. "Saints be praised! Yer sense o' perception could be earnin' hundreds at the county fair! 'Tis indeed what lays within, only the finest straight from the back door o' La Traviata Mexicali! Will ye join me?"

Mac detested the food slopped from the back door of La Traviata Mexicali, but his hunger got the best of him. "Have ye steaks?" he asked greedily.

"Nay, but I do have shreds o' chicken gizzard!"

"Potatoes?" asked Mac with a slurp of his lips.

"'Fraid not, though the rice 'n beans is held together with a tantalizin' paste!"

"Cakes an' burnt creme with wild raspberries?" Mac's craving came to a boil.

"None o' that, but I have got the most appealin'-lookin' fried dough with a pinch o' cinnamon sugar!"

"*FINE!*" Mac cried in surrender. "I'll share yer supper! Had I more time, I'd find a better meal with better comp'ny, but, bein' the lateness o' the hour, I'm forced to oblige. Perhaps if we dig up some ale, I might become squiffy enough not to mind as much."

Wilder was ecstatic. "If we do find this nectar, we'll toast the patron saint o' friendship, whoever he may be, fer bringin' us together over the meal we's about to receive!" He spat in his palm and Mac spat in his and they shook on it, then ventured together to find a quiet nook in which to dine, away from the winds beginning to blow in from the west.

*　　　　*　　　　*　　　　*

The human body is a wonder, to be sure, and it comes as no surprise that certain factors of its engineering remain a mystery to both science and psychology. Take, for example, the appendix. It hangs from the large intestine like an idle squatter and tricks us into believing it's a part of the crew working the digestive system, yet its function is unknown to modern physiology. Similarly, the study of dreams is rampant with hypotheses yet lacks the certainty of proof. Many have guessed at the meaning of arithmetic exams in dreams, or why some folks venture into the Dreamland workplace having forgotten to toss on their trousers, but none have discovered any hard evidence to explain the enigma of the human mind at rest. One thing we can be certain of in regard to the relationship between psychology and biology is that particular foods can have nefarious effects on the dreams of the living.

And so it was that undercooked chicken innards and refried beans and pungent peppers from foreign lands thrust Mac Malone into an unsettling sleep rampant with horrors of the imagination.

In his slumbering mind, he sat on the porch of his uncle's cottage, built on Lake Sillan in County Cavan, a place he hadn't been to since he was a boy. The solitude was exactly as he remembered, made all the more calming by long grass swaying in a passive breeze and a team of ducks slowly bobbing together atop an otherwise motionless lake. Mac seemed to be the only soul around for miles and he reveled in his aloneness as he sipped tea and gazed out at Paradise.

Laying on a hand-carved table by his side was a bag of jumbo marshmallows. Mac tore the seal eagerly and popped two into his watering mouth. They dissolved slowly and his buds pleaded for more.

"Damn you, mallows o' marsh, fer yer wicked temptation!" he cried. He tossed three more in and rejoiced in their goodness, squishing them through his teeth like when he was a child and almost expelling them slobberingly from the juvenile laughter he failed to control. One laugh escaped through his nose and lodged a marshmallow in his nasal passage, but he snorted it down and was able to enjoy it a second time.

As is often the case in dreams, the scenery changed very suddenly and very drastically: the afternoon sun fell like a bucket of lead and a slivery moon hurtled like a boomerang to take its place. Mac was left under a thick blanket of darkness and his eyes failed to adjust. He stood and felt his way to the cabin door, moving slowly in his blind state.

Inside, his searching hand found the light switch and pushed it on. The cabin was immediately coated in a warm luster and Mac sat in his uncle's reclining chair and ruffled open the newspaper waiting there. A perfect, blazing fire self-ignited in the fireplace and Mac kicked off his shoes to warm his toes.

Rustling and racket outside caused him to lower the paper and peer out the bay window. The darkness of night was impenetrable and the window looked like it had been painted with ink. The noises ceased just as suddenly as they began and Mac turned his attention back to the news.

A moment later, horrible scratching sounds erupted from the window and Mac dropped the paper to find countless demonic faces grinning evilly at him through the blackness. They floated in the opaque atmosphere, sharp horns jutting from their temples, pearly fangs dripping blood down their long chins. Claws like crescent blades flew toward the glass and noisily *ticked* and *tapped* a prickly cadence, chilling Mac's blood. He sat frozen at the sight.

Heavy, thudding footsteps shook the porch planks and alongside the ghoulish faces appeared a tall devil, its flesh the color of spilt blood, its chest dense in muscle. It had a long face with skin pulled taut over a sharply-defined skull with thick, oil-black hair slicked back over its scalp. A grin as demonic as the fires in Hades arced across its face and Mac realized that this was the one true Devil of devils.

The Devil entered the cabin and Mac expected the creature to break through the floorboards with each thunderous step. A long, lashing tail flicked about distractedly like that of an irritated dog. The couch in the center of the room bent and creaked as the massive beast sat on it across from Mac and penetrated the man's soul with its hateful eyes. When the Devil spoke, its voice was grave and full and scratched Mac's ears like broken glass.

It said, "I know you."

Every muscle in Mac's body clenched tightly, preventing movement.

It said, "You are ——." It spoke the name of Michael Malone. "Your father was ——. He was a thief and a swindler and fathered many bastard children."

Mac's apoplectic mind pleaded with his legs to bolt, but they refused to carry him.

It said, "I know your fear. It is strong within you. I am pleased to see you acquiesce to it."

Mac was defenseless as rats appeared from under his chair to gnaw on the meat of his unresponsive limbs.

It said, "You see? Your knees are soiled from kneeling before this fear."

Mac looked down and saw his knees caked in mud and filth. The surrounding flesh began to ripple and swell and fanged earthworms ate through and wriggled forth over his legs.

It said, "Do not think it degrading to surrender so resolutely to your fear. It feeds you, and you it. It protects you from valor and that which might harm you."

Mac's hand lay numb on the chair's arm. He watched helplessly as the nails grew long and the fingers curled back and the hand disintegrated to dust.

It said, "You must never mistrust your fear, for it shall forever guide you and keep you safe. It shall forever keep you compliant."

The Devil of devils stood and grew, limbs stretching like taffy, becoming taller, heavier, fatter until its head bowed under the ceiling and its thorny back spread between the beams. It leaned forward, its head mere inches from Mac's, and cleft its mouth open wide. A grotesque stench ravaged Mac's senses and he could see fire dancing from the Devil's throat.

The monster inhaled, drinking every breath of oxygen from the room, and the fire surged from its lungs. Mac struggled to breathe but could not.

The creature's mouth opened wider and a great tide of flame billowed toward Mac. In an instant every inch of him would ignite and burn, yet he sat horrified, paralyzed by fear, unable to protect himself from the onslaught.

As the flames touched his body, his voice restored and screamed the song of the damned.

"Jesus Joseph an' Peter!" The familiar, malodorous breath of Wilder Molyneux blew into Mac's nostrils. "Mac, ye unholy wretch, be still yer kickin' legs!"

Mac awoke screaming and shot upright, connecting his head sharply with Wilder's. They lay writhing in pain together in a narrow alley lined with empty pub kegs, the grease-soaked bag that once held their supper reminding them of the evening's events. Mac was relieved to discover himself in familiar territory, far from demons and devils.

"I was dreamin' somethin' fierce!" he cried, rubbing his bruised forehead.

"An' yer arse was belchin' somethin' awful!" Wilder added.

Mac scrambled to his feet, revitalized. The dream lay fresh in his mind and he wrapped his brain around it all. As he did, his sails filled with frenzy and his eyes floated in madness.

Wilder looked apprehensive. "Goin' somewhere?" he asked politely.

Mac said nothing, just turned and ran.

Wilder, having just stared into the eyes of a man afflicted, felt helpless. All he could do was throw his head to the clouds and cry out.

"Be careful out among the world tonight, Mac Malone!" He pointed to the treachery blowing in overhead. *"There's a Hell a-comin'!"*

*   *   *   *

Mac bolted through the sleeping, shuttered streets of Dublin, past storefronts and tenement houses and fellow nighthawks defying the storm, over cobblestone streets and broken footpaths and flocks of feral cats feasting on the city's refuse. The vibrant doors of Victorian townhouses blazed by in a blurred palette of blueblackwhiteyellowredgreenorangepurple, a flurry of colorful succulence streaking the corneas. The wind caught the brim of Mac's cap, seizing it from his head and sending it twirling away. His overworked digestive system exhausted a liberal burst of hydrogen and methane and increased his velocity accordingly.

In good distance, cobblestones turned to paved streets and eventually to sprawling greens and uneven ground. Mac unexpectedly found himself surrounded by trees and hedges and was forced to fend for his right at passage, bobbing and weaving his way through a dark thicket of overbearing branches like a jungle explorer. Boughs hung low and stabbed his scalp, poked his cheeks, scratched his ears. He raised an arm to shield his eyes, but was forced to cease his journey to deal with an irritating twig that ladled his nostril and refused to let go.

Angry, frustrated, and now sporting a severed twig dangling from his schnozzle, Mac broke through the thicket and found himself in familiar territory, the northern end of St. Stephen's Green, the centralized park of the city. An explosive sneeze sent the twig whizzing into the earth like a lawn dart and Mac continued his run only to be stopped again several paces in, this time by a soft mass that squished under the weight of his foot, followed by a terrible bellow.

WHAAAAAUUUUUGGGGHHHHH!

The noise was horrific, like the horn of a motorcar screaming under torture, and the earth at Mac's feet began to move and roll, parting before him like the Red Sea. The soft mass laying underfoot was sizable enough to spin his ankle and he started to pitch forward, losing his equilibrium, and it was then he saw the pond sprawling just inches from his toes. As he fell, his last resort reflex ordered him to bend and fall to his knees, to do it *NOW* before momentum plunged him up to his neck in cold water and pond scum, and he pulled his legs up as he toppled toward the rock formation circling the pond and landed crushingly on his kneecaps, the sharp *crack!* of bone on stone reverberating over the face of the water almost as loudly as his pain-fueled wail. His subsequent agonized murmurs were drowned out by the flurry of honks and howls that bleated from the retreating earth, which, now that his eyes were able to focus, he saw to be a group of ducks fleeing his undignified intrusion.

One duck remained, however, the fat fowl Mac had stepped on and caused to honk so horribly, and it began an unrelenting, vindictive attack on the heels of its assailant, snapping and smacking and pinching with its bill, forcing Mac to his feet to dance a defensive jig.

"Back, ye scurrilous quack!" Mac shouted as he step-danced away, but the duck limped after him and continued its assault, nipping at the human's Achilles until eventually it tired of the chase and waddled off to find its mates.

With his bushwhacker defeated, Mac sat on a boulder to soothe his shattered kneepans and ponder the mysteries of his own subconscious. Such a horrible dream, but what did it mean? What was the Devil telling him? He implied that Mac was servant to his fear, but what fear? The villain mentioned no specifics and Mac could think of nothing to warrant the Devil's accusations. He was afraid of no man, no animal, no scenario, no circumstance. He admitted to himself proudly that he was afraid of nothing. Throughout his life, he'd met every conflict with the bluster and confidence of a knight errant and had purposely avoided any situation that might have proven otherwise.

Still, something was tickling the outskirts of his subliminal self, but he couldn't quite put a name to it.

The wind blew harder now and a raindrop fell on the tender area under his eyelid. He blinked it away and felt another drop on his hand. Within moments, his overcoat was speckled by falling rain. He stood and rubbed his knees, then wandered in search of shelter.

The Swiss shelter, a high-ceilinged retreat housing a roundabout of benches, stood just south of the pond and by the time Mac scurried underneath its rooftop, the rain was falling with much greater force. The wind and moisture put a chill in the air and Mac turned his collar up against it. He sat on the edge of a bench and watched the rain pour around him. It was a beautiful sight, scattered lampposts backlighting the falling drops to silhouette, wind blowing through and creating patterns in motion. But the sound, the sound was what Mac loved most about rainfall. No matter the force with which they fell, gentle or heavy, the sound of raindrops always soothed his soul. The only other true aural pleasure he knew was a cat's purr and he wished now that he'd snatched a feral cat along his route so he could sit and listen to the rain with one ear and the kitty's affection with the other, a smorgasbord of soothing sounds *in stereo.*

A rustling of leaves caught his attention and he spun on the bench to see a crooked figure emerge from a patch of oaks. The figure stood in the shadows and Mac had trouble making out its physical features, but by the way the legs bowed and the back arced in an arthritic hump, he figured it must be Mad Connor O'Keeffe. Mac hadn't seen Mad Connor in ages, not since the elder had moved permanently from his home adjacent the rubbish skips at Kingsbridge Station several years ago. The figure headed west, limping anxiously through the rain, and disappeared behind a wall of shrubbery.

Shadows shimmied over the flowerbeds in the Victorian floral display and soon two bodies appeared. They nimbly and playfully pranced together, shedding their clothing as they skipped, and followed Mad Connor's westerly direction. Although it was difficult to tell through the flurry of rain, one of them had the size and shape of Lucky Lonergan, a gambling fool and old school chum of Mac's. The other gave the impression of being Missy Glynn, a lass who had a tendency to fall desperately in love with nearly every man she met. As soon as the couple had completely stripped themselves of clothing, Mac knew it was indeed young Missy Glynn.

The Green began to writhe with shadows and bodies and motion. People rushed in from all around, crawling through hedges, making their way through trees and bushes and shrubs, walking, limping, running, skipping, one couple even playing hopscotch over the tulips. They came from nowhere and they came from everywhere: Lucy McGoosey, Archie Farchy, Lousy the Soothsayer, Critter Danforth, Dribble O'Doole, Sweet Emily Moore, Crier Maloney, Shackled Jack O'Hara, Georgie O'Brien, a trove of Dublin's haggard and ragged trekking from all points to converge among the Green. Mac knew all or most of them — it was difficult to identify certain individuals through the inclement weather — and he counted more than thirty silhouettes making their way east.

Intrigued, Mac abandoned his shelter to follow. Cutting through the trees behind the Swiss shelter, he ran along the playground fence toward the arboretum until he saw them. When he did, he halted and stared curiously at the vision before him.

A mass of people gathered over the field of the arboretum, hugging and slapping backs and laughing together in the rain. By now they were all quite wet, some fully clothed while others stood in various states of undress while others still, like Missy Glynn and Lucky Lonergan, frolicked together with neither a pocket nor patch to cover their *puris naturalibus*. It was a fantastic sight to behold.

Along the footpath to his left, Mac saw Old Mother Fodder pushing Old Father Fodder in his wheelbarrow toward the revelry and he called out to them. "Oy! Fodders! Come here to me!" He motioned them over and Old Mother Fodder obliged, parking her husband on the lawn beside Mac.

"What's all this, then?" Mac asked, pulling his coat over his head to replace the lost cap.

Old Father Fodder seemed to be unconscious in the barrow, but Old Mother Fodder answered in a hushed tone. "Ye've not heard? 'Tis the annual public bath, called fer tonight by the Crier. He says the storm'll provide the perfek water works needed." She looked across the path at the merriment, eager to join in. "Come in, won't ye? There'll be no party without ye, Mac!" With that, she wheeled the barrow across the footpath to the field, leaving Mac alone to make his decision.

Bodies appeared from all directions and soon there were over a hundred forms gathered in the rain, some dancing, some wrestling playfully, some singing as though confined in their own private washtubs. They scrubbed their fronts, their backs, their overs and unders, and everyone volunteered to scrub the hard-to-reaches of others. Soon a bar of soap appeared and was passed from hand to hand.

Sean Little Sean caught Mac's eye and approached. He was a man of slight stature, standing just under five feet, as thin as a bundle of bamboo. Mac grumbled to himself as the fellow neared, for they had a long history of mutual disregard for each other.

"Mac Malone, ye old dog, is that ye standin' all by yer lonesome?" asked Sean Little Sean through a face of dripping water.

"'Course 'tis I, ye dwarf o' body an' brain! Who else would be standin' here lookin' like I?"

Sean Little Sean chuckled to himself, then beckoned with his arm and said, "Well come in an' have yerself a splatter! Or are ye still workin' on that alley tan?" He pointed to Mac's neck and the ever-darkening tone of his flesh, a result of many months of sanitary neglect.

"I shan't have a thing to do with ye!" scowled Mac, crossing his arms and looking defiantly away.

"Ah, 'tis just like ye, it is!" This came from Lucky Lonergan, who hovered nearby with Missy Glynn jumping gaily on his arm. "Just like ye an' the Rotten Rotter's Club!" Lucky lifted his head to the heavens and roared his slow, resonant laugh at the memory.

The Rotten Rotters! Damn the man's recollection! Mac twirled and walked away, wrapping his coat-cap around his chin to further protect himself from the elements. Curse the Rotten Rotters and their dastardly, self-righteous order!

*   *   *   *

Many years prior, around the time when young Mac's voice began sounding like a rusty hinge, he first heard mention of the Rotten Rotters Club through his close friend (back when one had close friends), Scarge Delaney. Scarge informed him of the club's history, how it had been founded centuries earlier by a small group of potato farmers who were discontent with their unscrupulous treatment by the local market barons. The farmers of County Dublin had formed a secret society intent on disrupting the general productivity of the town markets and each week they stormed the market-places, faces disguised behind dirty burlap potato sacks, creating pandemonium by overturning carts and dragging produce through the mud. They ambushed scores of reserve vegetable shipments from England and Scotland, raided and burned the offices and residences of the market barons, and invented stories about a pathogenic water mould that was causing the potato crop to wither and die. Certainly, the farmers suffered a loss in profit during these years of rebellion, but ultimately their efforts turned the tide of inequality and, as a term of their eventual truce, the market barons assisted them in establishing the very first trade union to be formed under the flag of the British Commonwealth, christened the Irish Alliance of Fruit and Vegetable Farmers (I.A.F.V.F), Local 100. William B. O'Sullivan, Esq., owner of the largest vegetable market in Dublin, described the recently-organized rebels as "dirty rotten rotters" in the press and the objects of his disdain were quick to adopt the nickname as their own, wearing it both proudly and defiantly.

That, at least, was the history as told to Mac by Scarge Delaney. The organization had since evolved into a group of pubescent boys who skipped school to shoot craps and get sozzled with their mates.

Regardless of its history, Mac was dazzled by the idea of joining the ranks of the Rotten Rotters at the restless age of twelve. He learned that the only obstacles between status as a mere boy and that of a Rotter were acceptance and initiation. The four senior members of the club (or, rather, the *only* four members) had approved three probationers for possible admission and Mac stood proudly along with Scarge Delaney and Lucky Lonergan that fateful autumn day at the busy corner of Suffolk and Grafton Streets to await his selection, initiation, and official hazing.

Wee Robby McDonagh, whose nickname had remained despite his summer growth spurt of five inches, stepped forward from the row of senior Rotters to address his pledges. "Lads!" said he. "We o' the Royal Order o' Rotten Rotters 'ave agreed to allow ye three scamps into our fraternity *provided*—" here he wagged a conditional finger in the air "—*provided* ye complete the mission we offer now." He paused to let his snicker recede and to calm the knowing giggles from the other senior members behind him.

He continued, "Ye shall, ever one o' ye, be officially by us named as members in good standin' o' the Rotten Rotters Club *if*—" and here he paused for effect, "—an' only if ye remove every stitch o' warmth from yer body right here an' trot through the courtyards o' Trinity College fer *no less than* fifteen minutes without bein' caught by higher authorities. If ye make it back to this here corner after the fifteen, as free an' bare as ye will be when ye depart, then ye'll rightly be given the honor o' callin' yerselves Rotters. Plus the initiation fee o' two farthings to be spent on supplies an' crap. *Gen'amen!*" Wee Robby concluded with a yielding bow. "The choice is yers!"

There came a pause after Wee Robby's instruction during which the three potential initiates looked each other over, attempting to gauge the opinions of their fellows while desperately trying to conceal the terror behind their eyes. Their minds frantically wrapped around the idea and juggled notions of worth and consequence. After several moments of silent consideration while the senior members stood with arms crossed and groins thrust daringly forward, it was Lucky Lonergan who made the first move. He threw his peacoat on the ground and followed with his shoes, socks, trousers, shirt, and undergarments. He then disappeared into the luncheon crowd, as pared as a peeled potato, heading in the direction of the Trinity gates that lay one seemingly interminable block north.

Wee Robby McDonagh whirled around and looked down the street to the clock hanging over O'Neill's Pub. "Twelve twenty-two!" he cried, and Eamonn Doolan extracted a pencil and pad from his pocket to make note.

Every piece of Mac shivered with fear as he whipped his head to Scarge Delaney and watched his friend follow Lucky's example. In seconds, Scarge stood bare before a pile of his own clothes. Leaving his pal Mac with a supportive whack on the shoulder, he padded into the crowd, clothed only in goose pimples, and was gone.

Wee Robby twirled again to the clock and shouted, "Twenty-three minutes past!" Eamonn Doolan scribbled on his pad and all eyes of the senior staff came to focus judgmentally on Mac.

The concept of public nudity shook the foundation of fear in Mac's heart, for he'd inherited the cruelty and shame that best described the Malone physique. His paternal Granddad had only been intimate with his wife the one time, abandoning the practice for good after being made to stand in the spotlight of her dignity-shucking laughter on the night of their wedding. The result of their intimacy was Mac's Pappy, Mick Malone, who later suffered chuckles and finger-pointing by his peers in the locker room. Even Mac's fair mum was subject to ridicule by her neighbors after tales swept through local launderettes and afternoon teas detailing her husband's manhood. Mac himself had felt embarrassment even as a toddler in the bathtub and he failed to understand why until schoolyard expectations learned him in the matters of what was socially acceptable versus what was basic anatomical comedy.

Still, twelve is an age when one is expected to define and prove oneself and Mac's conceit would not allow him to consider failure on this busy street corner, despite the cost. In the boldest move yet of his still-young life, he raised his hand

and began creeping the buttons on his coat from their eyelets. When the coat hung loose, he peeled it softly from his shoulders, progressing as though each movement brought great strain to his muscles. His would-be fellow club mates watched as Mac folded the coat and bent to place it tenderly atop Scarge's clothes, never achieving a speed greater than the tempo of a funeral march.

By O'Neill's clock, it took Mac more than six minutes to undress to his worn, eggshell skivvies and, after folding each sock and placing them with painstaking symmetry atop his other garments, he stood stiffly, thumbs caressing the edge of the elastic band holding his drawers up, spine arced forward like that of a defensive animal, eyes vigilant and wild.

The Rotten Rotters stared anxiously back.

They faced each other, unmoving, for what seemed like ages.

The lunchtime crowd passed indifferently by as tourists took great trouble to frame the nearly-naked boy out of their photographs.

The clock at O'Neill's chimed once.

"Half twelve!" screeched Bobby Molloy, by far the oldest and most vile member of the Rotters. Shattering the standoff, he pounced forward and, in a motion that modern martial arts masters would marvel at, tripped Mac to the ground and ripped the worn cotton of his drawers easily from his waist.

Eamonn Doolan snorted and made note of the time.

Mac was seized by a terror he'd neither known nor imagined, a barrage of invisible thorns prickling his flesh and brain while his blood seemed to stop flowing despite the Gatling tempo of his heart. His scalp dried to cracked leather and his mucus evaporated; his toes went numb and icy chills swept over the unfamiliar lump that was his body. His birthright, already inhibited by heredity and cold, receded further into shelter.

He shot into the air like a firecracker and ran. He ran with a purpose that most boys — or men, for that matter — never know. His unprotected feet pounded over the streets with senseless passion, never bothering to acknowledge the stones and twigs and broken glass that scarred them. On and on he ran, past the gates of Trinity, through the major thoroughfares of Dublin, blind to the people who stopped to stare and laugh, until he finally reached the safety of his own tenement. Even then he had to streak humiliatingly by Mrs. McCarthy, who stood blocking the stairwell entrance chatting with none other than Mrs. Mick Malone, and he blew past them and flew up four flights of stairs and crashed through the door of his flat and leaped past his blue, wide-eyed mutt and finally came to rest in the sweet embrace that was the sanctuary of his own bedroom, slamming the door behind him.

Whatever emotional frailties Mac may have succumbed to at that point, it is not our place to know.

The ironic element of the whole situation was that it took Mac longer than fifteen minutes to run home; the two new members of the Rotten Rotters had been dressed and drinking with their newfound mates by the time Mac reached his flat. In the treachery that was his life, however, it mattered not, for the Rotters never intended to allow Mac a place in their club anyway. As it happens, none of them fancied him much and only allowed him the chance as a joke amongst themselves. Lost, too, was Mac's friendship with young Scarge Delaney.

Such is life.

*　　　　*　　　　*　　　　*

This recollection of his own ill-fated history caused Mac's eye to begin twitching as he walked indignantly away from Sean Little Sean and Missy Glynn and the aged Lucky Lonergan underneath the pouring rain in St. Stephen's Green. He wanted nothing to do with the likes of them and their hateful, mocking memories. His mind churned with ideas of how best to scorn them in return as he headed back to the refuge of the Swiss shelter. He pushed through the trees, shaking loose the rainwater from their leaves, and by the time he was back under the roof, he was soaked through.

It was quieter here. No longer were forms and figures seen wandering through the Green, for they'd all joined the bath by now. Bucking wind helped drown out the sounds of merriment and festivity. Mac sat on a bench and shivered and pondered again the challenge set forth by the Devil in his dream.

Fear.

Right. Fear.

Hmmmm...fear.

What fear?

Snakes? No. Spiders? Nope. Heights? Never.

He simply had *nothing* to conquer; his life hadn't an ounce of fear in it.

"Oy!" came a voice from behind, and Mac screamed like a sissy.

He spun around to find Sweet Emily Moore standing under the shelter with him. She held a collapsed yellow umbrella in one hand and her dress was perfectly dry. "What ye doin' way over here, Mac?" she asked in an accusing tone. "The party's over there!"

Mac turned away. "I'll be havin' nothin' to do with that! An' ye'll not barge in here with a mind set on draggin' me in fer a scrub, no sir! I'll be droppin' me shorts fer no one!"

Sweet Emily Moore thrust her hands on her hips. "Aww, Mac, what are ye so afraid of?"

"I'm afraid o' noth—"

He stopped.

His brow furrowed.

His eyes started dancing about, up, down, to, fro, as they will when his brain was forced to action.

"Christ knows ye could use a bath!" Sweet Emily Moore scolded.

Mac couldn't hear her, his mind was far too overworked. Dreams, demons, devils, dares…hadn't he been challenged to free himself of his weakness, to liberate his soul from its inhibition? Hadn't the Devil himself appeared to commend him on his cowardice and mock his vulnerability? A quest for salvation had fatefully led him here, he realized, and was now presenting him with both means and measure to confront that which gave him the greatest anxiety. The food, the dream, the run, the rain, it was a perfect chain of events and he suddenly hated it for what it all meant. Yet he had to go through with it, had to face this down no matter the consequence. His awakening conscience told him he must.

His senses returned and he heard Sweet Emily Moore saying, "Come now, Mac, let's go in together." She was holding her hand out to him.

He stood and faced her silently. He looked at her outstretched hand, then at the downpour falling outside the shelter. Finally, he reached out and accepted her touch.

"Aye," was all he said as he squeezed her hand.

Sweet Emily Moore spun and pulled him toward the bath, but Mac did not move. When she looked back, he was unbuttoning his shirt. He took his hand back and peeled the soggy coat from his arms and lay it delicately on the bench, then stripped his torso of the shirt and placed it beside the coat. Next came his matte vinyl shoes and argyles, which he lay under the bench. He peeled his undershirt from his shoulders and popped it over his head and blushed in the presence of the lady. Still he continued. His belt was loosened, the slacks fell to his ankles, and he lay them flat with his other garments.

Sweet Emily Moore noticed his manner, his pace, his trembling hands. She saw the embarrassment in his eyes and knew she was witnessing something profound. "Ye'll not be needin' to bare down to yer skellington, now, Mac. The option is yers whether ye want to arrive in the buff or not."

A silent stare conveyed his message and she understood it well. "Fine, then, suit yerself," she said, and she began to remove her dress.

Mac watched her as she'd watched him, only it took Sweet Emily Moore far less time to remove her attire. When they stood together nearly ready to depart, she completely naked and he wearing only his patchy nappies, he took a moment to breathe and steady himself, his thumbs absently fondling the elastic band of his underpants as they had when he was a lad in the presence of Rotters. Then, with humility and resolution, mind afire, ears shrieking with terror, he closed his eyes and dropped his drawers.

Wind blew through parts of him that had never felt wind before. The moisture on his body dried quickly and the hairs covering him stood at attention in the cold. He refused to open his eyes to the sight of the mockery that lay in wait.

Yet laughter failed to scorch his ears. There was no snickering or giggling or chortling to be heard. The only sounds were that of the falling rain and the candid tone of Sweet Emily Moore's voice.

"Come on, then. Off we go!"

He opened his eyes and found no eyes staring, no fingers pointing, no bodies rolling on the ground with laughter. He saw only his friend, who again held her hand out to beckon. "Here we are!" she called as she unceremoniously grabbed him by the hand and pulled him behind her, beyond the shelter, through the trees, past the playground and straight across the footpath to the waiting party.

Upon entering the field of everyone's vision, Mac's eyes again shut tightly and prepared for the worst. He stood with Sweet Emily Moore blindly for a moment amidst the frolicking of his friends, enemies, and acquaintances, feeling more naked than he ever had in his life, more so even than his run through Dublin in the buff so many years ago, and his imagination painted vibrant pictures of scorn and ridicule and deception and indignity. His mind's eye saw the people before him to be the vile and wretched humans they were.

When at last he'd experienced enough of their supposed derision in the face of his blatant nudity, he opened his eyes. What he found was nary a trace of scandal, gossip, nor disgrace. On the contrary, he discovered in their stead a state of indifference in its very simplest form.

"Hiya, Mac!" Lousy the Soothsayer shouted from across the field. "Good to see you with us!"

"Mac!" called Lucy McGoosey, "how grand ye came out to join the fun!"

"Guten abend, Mac!" cried Archie Farchy as he tossed a bar of soap to him. Mac caught the slippery disc and held it firmly to his chest, the only apparel to be found. He felt strangely comforted by it and squeezed it as though it were his childhood woobie.

Sweet Emily Moore raised her foot and kicked his hind quarters. "Ye see? Not so bad, is it?"

It wasn't bad, no. In fact, it was quite liberating. Mac let go of Sweet Emily Moore's hand and stood alone, straightening his hunched back, standing tall, no longer feeling scrutinized, the sensation of being on exhibition falling quickly away. He stood before the world a man exposed and was accepted by it unconditionally.

With eyes aware again of the world around him, he saw people, his friends, making merry amidst a terrible storm. They sloshed effervescently over the sodden earth, screaming with delight, and laughed and hugged and scrubbed and loved. He was warmed by the sight and, at this moment, neither wind nor rain nor embarrassment could send a chill to his bone.

A tremendous puddle was forming in the center of the field, in a clearing between the oak and sycamore and laurel. Mac eyed it thoughtfully, feeling a sudden craving to express his newfound confidence and show the world that he'd accepted and embraced his current state of reveal. He imagined, too, that perhaps — just perhaps — his friends would want to share this profound moment of discovery with him and celebrate his spirit.

With the agility of an elderly gimp who's just learned to walk again, Mac skipped and tripped and leaped across the lawn and, when he was just two paces from the edge of the puddle, crouched and sprung his great weight several feet into the air, landing gracelessly near the center of the tiny lake, sending a plume of water into the air with the force of a fire hose. Part of the spray caught him directly in his undercroft and he let fly a muffled wail as his nethers were assaulted by a frigid jet of rainwater. Regaining his composure quickly, he struck the pose of a conquering Spartan, one knee bent slightly, hands on hips, muscles flexed, chin held high, and stood in the middle of the still water as one might imagine a returning hero. A final thought came to mind and he raised two defiant fingers of one hand to the sky and cursed the Devil and all his fearsome demons. A smattering of applause hailed him and Mac hoped that the future sculptor of his memorial statue was present to witness his posture for reference.

The bath resumed, cakes of soap dissolved to slivers, and the cold began to swell the people's clean, round faces. A monstrous crack of thunder rolled over the great city and disturbed its very constitution, sending a chill through each spine. Soon people began to gather belongings and say their farewells, for the time had come to seek shelter. They all stopped to bid Mac a pleasant evening and a cheery-bye and he greeted each with an air of triumph. Lousy the Soothsayer parted with a warm embrace and Sweet Emily Moore stood across the lawn and left him with a simple, knowing wink.

When he returned to the Swiss shelter to gather his clothing, he found them colder yet less saturated than when he'd left. He screamed bloody murder putting them back on, the chill almost unbearable, but began to warm by the time they hung heavily once more over his form. He went out into the elements again, not bothering to turn his collar up this time since he was already sufficiently damp, and crossed a path of lime trees to exit through the northern gate.

Along the street outside the Green sat a row of taxicabs, a queue of three on a night that normally would see eight or ten. Drivers sat snugly inside, dreaming of fares despite the reality of the storm, and buried their noses in woolen scarves while reading novels or washing the inside of their windscreens with newspaper or contemplating an early end to the shift. Each of them looked up hopefully as the man strolled by outside, but he made no motion to enter a cab, merely walked proudly past, erectly postured, wearing an attitude of impenetrable pride. The man tipped his imaginary cap to each car and continued sauntering forth.

At the end of the taxi stand, Mac stopped to thrust his nose in the air, to feel the rain pouring over his flesh, to invite its beauty and power to meld with his own. He wanted to enjoy this feeling of accomplishment just a little longer before seeking out a place to rest his head for the night. In the face of a storm growing fiercer by the minute, he congratulated himself yet again on his success of this day.

As he looked up at the bleakness hanging low and dark over the city, he noticed a blur of motion that fell in line with the clouds blowing rapidly by. It was smoke, thick and black, as black as coal, and it rose from the ground somewhere deep within the fringes of Grafton Street.

CHAPTER THIRTEEN
Grievances

As five o'clock neared, John stood at the shop window and craned his neck to see the sky past the surrounding buildings. It was no use, though, his neighbors were built far too close and much too high to see over their rooftops, so he stepped outside on a mission of reconnaissance. It was just as gloomy and ominous outdoors, if not darker and colder, and a wisp of wind ruffled his hair from its natural hold. Looking skyward, John saw clouds sailing low and fast, headed east. He'd heard talk of the coming storm for days and knew they were in for a royal thrashing tonight. For perhaps the first time, he was glad to have the shop nestled so tightly within the narrow laneway, for the brick and mortar structures crowding around would surely prevent the winds from knocking out his windows. The first of the rains were due soon, so John stepped back into the protection of the Chivalric Nobleman de La Mancha and felt safe once more.

A short while later, as John killed the final few minutes of business in an empty shop inspecting the books in Fiction S (Cont.) with ambiguous care, he heard the loose window panes in the front door rattle and the coloratura soprano of the overhead bell jangle not once but four times in succession, announcing his friend as they always had. John smiled rigidly to himself and inhaled deeply, then counted to ten and made for the front to greet his chum.

He found Tinky O'Shea with his head cocked right, examining the rare books case. When John rounded the corner, Tinky jumped and huffed a muted, startled gasp. Identifying the intruder, he bent over and laughed, relieved.

"Johnny boy! Administerin' heart attacks is no way to treat yer regulars!" He leaned on John's shoulder, simulating hyperventilation, still laughing.

"Me apologies, mate," John said solemnly, "I'd no intention to."

Tinky ceased laughing but kept the smile, saying, "Ye know I'm playin', John." He slapped John's shoulder and handed him a sealed bottle. "Will ye kindly take this before I down it all on me own?" Removing a pair of cheaters from his pocket, he raised the bottle in John's hand and leaned in to examine the label. "'Twas a gift from old Domnall Dunne on the occasion o' me birthday last. Aged eighteen years, it is. Ye can spend what ye like fer the twenty-one, to me, eighteen'll always be the perfect age fer whiskey. An' women." He looked up at John over the top of his glasses and winked playfully. "Will ye help me break the seal?"

"If ye insist I must," John said, returning the wink. He found the nick in the seal, but Tinky stopped him before he pulled. "Not just yet, Johnny boy! I'd like to have a look 'round first, perhaps gather some titles fer me weekend readin' pile." He looked around the room. "Place looks clean," he noticed.

John set the bottle down. "Aye, I've been tidyin' up a bit."

"I see that." Tinky returned to the rare books cabinet and leaned his head horizontally to read the spines. "Have ye seen him this week?" he asked.

"No Melville this week," John said, "although I haven't been takin' in much new stock lately. Tryin' to be rid o' what's here first."

"Right." Tinky withdrew a small paper bag from his pocket. "Say, I was in Bewley's this afternoon visitin' the

Widow Mullan an' she gave me this." He handed the bag to John. "More pastries to pad yer waist. I fear if I admit me allergy to wheat, she'll not be inclined to give gifts an' make eyes with me no more. I believe there's a chicken an' brie toastie inside as well."

The bag was warmly received and stashed under the counter to enjoy later. "Ye know me belly'll always be here to support ye," John said. "An' I tank ye fer tonight's supper."

As Tinky made his way to peruse the fiction aisles, John occupied himself by absently re-reading the front page of the morning's *Irish Times*. Words made it past his eyes but progressed no further for the melancholy plaguing his spirit. The decisions he'd made over the past few days had been so thoroughly liberating, had revived his spirit to such a soaring degree, that he no longer felt reticent about executing them. The liberation had continued the previous evening with libations and liveliness, with songs and drink and camaraderie, with candid sharing of thoughts with good friends — good, understanding, supportive, nonjudgemental friends — until he was certain that what he was doing was right.

Yet now he was thrust suddenly into a morose sense of foreboding with the arrival of Tinky O'Shea. Tinky, his oldest friend, whom he'd known since they were both just bucks. Tinky, the fellow with whom he'd shared his lunches, play-times, and exam answers throughout their years in school. Tinky, the boy, the man whose honor John had defended many times with words, fists, and the spilling of his own blood. Tinky, who'd presented John with gifts upon each greeting, nursed his friend through heartbreak and sorrow, sat with him until the early morning hours soothing a bruised ego after Kelly Brady left him for a rugby forward. Who stayed with him and got him drunk and cried with him the night of his mum's death. Tinky, with his flawed character and annoy-ing habits and genuine care. Tinky, the loyal provider. John was discouraged that this man had come to pay a visit today, now, during the very moments when he was finally feeling good about himself. The fact that the one person who knew him better than anyone had come to pay a social call terrified him and he wished to hell that his friend would go away and leave him be.

Returning with a short stack of paperbacks, Tinky placed them near the till and removed a thin money clip from his pocket. Atop the pile, he placed a single monetary note. "I trust this'll cover these here books, plus some o' the debts on me credit tabulation?"

"It covers everythin', Tinky. In fact, there'll be some change due ye. But take this back, kiddo, an' buy yerself somethin' worthwhile. Yer credit'll always be in good health with me." John tried to give the bill back, but Tinky held his hand out in refusal.

"Take it while ye can, Johnny boy! 'Tis not every week I'm as fortunate with the races. Now, help me recall where we last stood with this fine whiskey." The bottle appeared oversized in his dainty hands as he picked at the seal with his thumbnail.

"Are ye certain ye'd like to have a taste o' this now?" John asked hopefully. "The storm is comin' fast an' likely won't ease up fer some time."

The stopper gave a dull report as it escaped the bottle's mouth. "Rain'll not be botherin' me, John. An' if I need to cab it home, so be it. Let's start with a wee nip an' see where it takes us, eh?"

"Fine, that's fine." John excused himself to gather two glasses from the back, praying to the Lords of Kinship that their talk would be entirely bland and profoundly, unedifyingly superficial.

*　　　　*　　　　*　　　　*

And it was. For hours, they sat at the front counter and nearly finished the bottle, laughing and remembering and telling stories, all the while becoming increasingly tight with drink. The rain had begun to fall, they could hear it pattering against the windows, and it came down harder with each story told. At this point, however, they'd both reached a whiskey high strong enough to make them care not a lick about falling water or blowing winds or threatening storms. For the moment, they were basking in each other's company and John released his trepidation in order to allow himself another enjoyable evening away from the stresses of life. He settled back and listened, the slight smile laying still upon his lips.

Tinky jabbered in his usual fashion, telling pointless yet amusing stories, mostly tales from the office about the imbecilic Jacko who ran the department. John was engaged despite the lack of plot and point simply because Tinky was a talented storyteller — he relayed each anecdote as though it were a grand-high adventure, affecting voices for each character and pantomiming their actions and speaking in such an animated manner that no listener could deny having a fine time. At one point, in a lull between narratives, Tinky, balancing precariously on the cusp of drunkenness, abruptly began whistling *The Dawning of the Day*. John had always been partial to the song and Tinky's performance was spellbinding. His body sat motionless on the stool but his head bobbed and bounced, swirled and swooped as the music left his puckered lips and filled the room. It may seem silly, being a whistle and all, but John thought it the most beautiful sound he'd heard in ages. When Tinky finished and emerged from his self-induced trance, John applauded enthusiastically, then filled their glasses with the last of their sweet nectar and toasted the gift of music.

Now, an abundance of alcohol will always affect different situations in varying ways, but it will never change the underlying mood of the party. Whatever is brought to the table in the minds of the drinkers will only be enhanced by liquor; if the drunk finds people gathered in celebration, then the evening will end on a celebratory note, just as a drunk finding people with grudges to bear will most certainly not end well. A good drunk will *enhance* the mood of the drinkers, rarely will it *alter* their moods. It could be said that alcohol is the most effective of all truth serums, really, for the way it dulls the senses and lowers the guard and injects courage into the inebriated. And so it was that, despite the current merriment of the drinkers, the stewing tension in the Chivalric Nobleman de La Mancha Bookshop was forced to the front by a single bottle of 70-proof Limited Reserve.

"Rains be Jaysis, but would ye listen to that ruckus outside?" Tinky pointed his nose to the front windows and they listened to the pouring rain and the mild rattling of wind-blown windowpanes. "I certainly hope the skip out front has proper drainage, otherwise ye'll be dealin' with quite a mess in the mornin'. Garbage floatin' over the sides, pulp all down the lane." What was left of his final drink fell down his throat and caused him to belch hotly. "We wouldn't want that, now."

"Hmm," John hummed vaguely. He most definitely did not want to chat about the rubbish skip out front.

"Yer shelves are lookin' sparse these days," Tinky noticed, feigning temperate ignorance. "Are ye in the midst o' some sort o' massive spring cleanin', then?"

John bowed his head and pursed his lips. Trying to remain patient, he looked at Tinky and said, "Tinky, ye saw the skip. Ye saw what was in it."

"And...?"

"An' I'm sure ye can come to yer own conclusions."

John sat back and chewed the inside of his cheek as Tinky leaned forward, saying, "'Tis just that I've never once known ye to toss a book in the rubbish. Of all people. Ye've always been to books what me Gram was to stray pups, never givin' one up unless it was to a good an' carin' home. 'Tis not like you, no sir, not at all."

After John passed a moment of reluctant silence, Tinky continued, "What's happenin' here, Johnny boy? Ye can tell me. 'Tis I, or do ye ferget yer oldest mate? Look, ye're not as fine an actor as ye tink. 'Tis apparent there's some sort o' strife plaguin' yer spirit, so would ye *please* tell me 'bout it." It was spoken less as a question and more a demand.

Bound by the laws governing friendship, John knew that concession was his only choice and he huffed a heavy sigh to relieve the stress constricting his chest. In a low voice, he said, "I have a meetin' first thing in the mornin'. With a developer. A real estate man. He's made me a fine offer. An' I'll be signin' over the deed to this buildin'."

"To relocate," Tinky volunteered. "I assume."

"No." John said it firmly. "I've decided against that."

A silent stare burned from Tinky's eyes. To escape it, John began talking more freely. "I was never meant to be a businessman. This is somethin' I was not born to do, I believe that's obvious. I'm now firmly established in middle-age an' have not a shillin' to show fer it. 'Tis high time I tried a different trade." He wagged his finger at Tinky in warning. "An' ye can't argue *any* o' that."

"No. No, I don't suppose I can. Ye recommend books to customers, then give 'em away, askin' to be paid only if they enjoys it. I've seen ye do it many times. An' ye've told me yerself ye'd rather keep these here books as yer own personal library than sell 'em to other people's homes. No, John, ye're right, as a seller o' books, ye *stink*."

He continued, "But books is what ye love an' ye've rightly made it yer business. Whether ye're talented at the business end is irrelevant. What would ye do if ye weren't surrounded by books all day? What's yer plan, to join the accountancy? Run fer political office? Plumb the pipes o' the workin' class? Business can be learned, John. But to give up yer heart, to lay down what it is ye love an' walk away, it just fails to ring true an' I'll not be understandin' a bit of it."

"I need a change, Tinky. A drastic change. I've become far too restless. I'm in need—" John hiccoughed on the thought, reluctant to continue, yet proceeded regardless, "—I'm in need o' money as well."

"Money? To do what?"

The question caught John off guard. He assumed the answer would be obvious. "To live as I please. What else would it be fer?"

"So that's why ye're givin' up the shop? Bank accounts?"

"'Course not, that's only part of it."

"Let me ask what is it ye want, then, John? If ye had the perfect life, what would it be?"

"I don't know." Being put on the spot caused John to run his hand distractedly through his hair. "Can *you* truly answer that? I want to be free. I want to be happy. An' pay no mind to what they say, money *can* buy these things. I've seen it meself. So. I'll start by liquidatin' everythin' that's made me a failure thus far. The shop, the books, anythin' o' worth. I'll start fresh. 'Tis the obvious choice."

"What'll ye do with the books?"

"Any book that has no worth goes in the skip. All else goes to auction."

"No worth? Great Christ, ye're speakin' o' books as though they was commodities in a brokerage!" Tinky's next question boiled with accusation. "Do these plans include *Don Quixote*?"

"You leave *Quixote* out of it," John said sternly.

Still Tinky persisted. "Does yer plan at liquidation include *Don Quixote*?"

John looked directly and defiantly in Tinky's eyes. "Brian Corrigan an' meself have settled on a price fer *Quixote*."

If a boulder had rolled through the shop and tumbled over Tinky O'Shea, he couldn't have appeared more dumb-founded. Of all the words he'd heard in his life, these were the least expected, the most concussive, and he reacted accordingly. Trembling with emotion, he raised his index finger and pointed it threateningly at John. "Do not." He said it reprovingly through clenched teeth, as an aggrieved father before his contemptuous son, then repeated it to prove his fury, igniting the simple words with his passion. *"Do not!"*

John stood and turned his back to Tinky. "Oh, come off it, man," he said scornfully. "'Tis just a book!"

"I would argue that it's not yer book to profit from! This belongs to yer *family*, not just you! Have ye no respect fer them, fer Grampy Doyle, fer yer forefathers?"

The accusation of familial sacrilege infuriated John and he turned to face him again. "It is my property an' I'll do with it as I please! An' family? What family? Ye're lookin' at him, the end o' the Doyle line. There isn't a soul on this earth that'll miss it once it's gone. When I tink o' what I could do with the money it'll bring.... Besides, I'd rather it go to a good home than lie under the floor with rats crawlin' over every night."

It was Tinky's turn to stand in defiance. "The fact that ye believe there's a better home on the planet than the one it's in now is *ridiculous!* Do ye hear yerself talkin', John? I cannot, I cannot believe it! An' what's all the talk o' money? What the hell good will it do ye? What'll ye do when it's *gone*, eh? I'll tell ye what ye'll do, ye'll wish ye had *Quixote* back!"

"The money shan't go to waste. With the sale o' the shop an' the stock an' the book, I'll be doin' alright. I can find an affordable flat an' live simply, I'm accustomed to that already. I shan't be unemployed, either, I intend to learn real estate an' finance. I'll invest the money proper an' worry no more 'bout runnin' a business."

Tinky could only shake his head in wonder. "I'm hearin' Brian Corrigan's voice comin' out o' yer own mouth! That's what corrupted ye, or am I wrong? Yer days spent with yer pal Corrigan, eh? Seein' his home, his castle, his life, the property sprawlin' fer miles an' miles. Am I right? Seein' his vast book collection built floor to ceilin', it put ye in a trance, made ye hungry fer it, did it not?"

"How do ye know 'bout Brian's house?" John was distracted by Tinky's perplexing knowledge of all things Corrigan.

"Never mind how I know. Perhaps I seen it meself, with me own eyes. An' perhaps it sickened me to no end, not just the sight of it, but the idea of it all." Tinky again went into his mode of attack. "But it affected ye, or am I wrong? An' suddenly ye want what he has, ye want to live carefree an' lazy, ye want to abandon yer responsibilities an' wake up in the afternoons an' watch yer programs on the telly and go from pillar to post with no sense or meanin' to any of it."

"What ye say is nonsense, Tinky. I'll never have what Brian has." Here John paused to gather his thoughts, for debate was a sport he'd rarely practiced. His belief was a hard sell, he knew, a philosophy lacking in cold, hard facts to argue, but he tried his best to explain with a mind numbed by whiskey. "There's no reason why we should never have a taste of it. You, me, the other guy, too, all of us, an' I'm just sayin' a *taste*. 'Tis out there to be earned, an' why not me? Why not *you*? Brian was handed his fortune an' never once had to work fer it, I'm aware, but to know that the key to happiness lies at the foot of every man, I've come to realize how silly it is not to grab it. With hard work an' commitment, I can have it, I can earn a good wage an' learn to make wise investments an' before ye know it I'll have the situation turned around! I can travel an' keep a home in the country an' take the time to write a bad novel if I please. It won't matter, I'll be free to do as I wish, because by then I'll have accounts large enough to allow it."

"Would ye listen to yerself?" Tinky said, failing to grasp the spirit of John's argument. He was pacing now with nervous energy. "Ye're like ol' Mickey Fitzpatrick, puttin' half his pay on the numbers each week an' tellin' one an' all 'bout how it'll be someday an' never once strikin' the pot! Ye're goin' on about makin' a fortune as some sort o' real estate baron or tycoon tradin' in potato futures! Posh!"

"Now hold on—" John interjected, but Tinky continued.

"Ye sound like a lad in secondary school, tryin' to figure out who ye are an' what to do with yer life. Well, ye're way past that, boyo! Ye knew who ye were twenty years ago an' have been livin' true to that — with a very firm head on yer shoulders, I might add — every day o' yer life. *Until now.*" He stopped pacing for a moment. "What in hell's happened to make ye lose yer mind? Sounds like a crisis o' middle age if ye ask me."

John glared at him incredulously. "Well 'tis a fine thing to know I have yer wholehearted support in me endeavors."

The drink in Tinky caused him to animatedly and absurdly shake his head in the negative. "No, sir! I'll not be supportin' *this*. I'll be planted firmly by yer side when ye make choices that are good an' right an' noble — as I have before an' always — but *not this!*"

As an afterthought, he added, "Tell me why ye tink Brian has it so good. What do ye see that I cannot? Do ye tink money makes the man happy? Can ye truly say he's fulfilled with his life? 'Cause I'll not be seein' it, meself. If anythin', Corrigan is dulled by it all, he's bored with his own place in the world. Uninspired an' unmotivated, he is! The man seems not to be talented in any particular field!"

"How can ye say this, ye hardly know him!" John argued, but Tinky didn't stop.

"Is that what ye're searchin' fer, a life so easy an' simple? Ye want to give up yer work ethic an' initiative in order to hasten a death o' pure *boredom*?"

"I'm not Corrigan an' ye know it, so enough with the comparisons," John said, trying to restrain his anger.

"Then ye're blind to the big picture, ye are. Ye just don't see it, do ye?"

John shot right back, "*Ye're* the one who can't see the whole of it! If ye'd even stop to tink of it a moment, ye'd see that what I'm doin' makes perfect sense!"

The debate was making Tinky's head pulse and their talk was quickly becoming passionate, dangerous even, so he decidedly calmed his tone and changed tactics. "I understand ye feel ye're stuck in a rut. Believe me, John, I've been there. 'Tis the grind o' daily routine that puts us there. Life becomes regular an' repetitive an' we can only take it fer so long without havin' some sort o' change. After a while it drives us batty! An' once ye're in that rut, when it's all repetition an' dreary banality day after day, it takes everythin' just to get yerself out of it. By the time ye reach that point, no small change'll relieve ye, 'tis got to be *drastic*. An' alterin' yer life drastically was never an easy thing."

Finally, the man was speaking truth and John interjected his agreement. "'Tis imperative, it is! Change is essential if we're to continue growin'. We are human, Tinky. Restless beasts. Sediment unstirred lies dormant an' it'll not be in our nature as humans to lie dormant fer so long."

"Aye, ye speak truth, John. 'Tis evolution, is what it is. We grow by makin' the adjustments throughout our lives, all along the journey we change direction here an' there while always keepin' mindful of our ultimate goal. An' everythin' ye're tellin' me tonight tells me ye've lost yer vision fer that goal. Ye're not just ammendin' yer course with this decision, John, ye're veerin' completely off the track!"

How quickly Tinky returns to the offensive! A man can only defend himself for so long before his anger boils over, and John was perilously close. It took what patience he had left to respond. "I have a mate who did it. In the middle o' life, at that, an' he was entirely successful. Saw what a dreary mess his life had become, saw how counter-intuitive his job was — an' his marriage — so he turned his back on the whole soul-suckin' situation an' began fresh. Opened a restaurant, he did, an' is havin' the time of his life operatin' the place with his own family in his employ. Me point is that sometimes the change has got to be earth-shatterin'! An' that's where I'm at!"

"That's *fine*, John! I'll not be speakin' out against a change, if that's what ye need. I'm tryin' to tell ye 'tis got to be fer all the right reasons an' ye've got to have a plan! There's no use in improvisin', 'tis far too important fer that!"

"I do have a plan, if ye would just open yer stubborn ears fer a moment!" Spittle was flying from John's lips. "I'll go back to school, I'm enrolled in courses already. Play the eager student an' absorb all the knowledge I can. I'll be focused, man — as I've explained — learnin' not just one new trade, but multiples! 'Tis not like I'll be puttin' all me eggs in a single basket like I have been, I decided on this route in order to keep it specifically diverse, to have options!"

"I hear ye, John, I do. But as yer friend 'tis me job to tell ye I tink it's all wrong! Ye need to take the time to consider *all* the angles — somethin' ye've obviously failed to do — to make sure the change ye seek will cause neither harm nor regret. If ye're goin' to do it, then do it, but bear this knowledge, John: ye have but one chance to do it *right*."

"Time fer consideration is somethin' I haven't got, Tinky. The offer fer the shop expires tomorrow. Do ye understand? Tomorrow! 'Tis a grand amount o' money bein' offered, over an' above what she's worth, an' I had to come to a decision. I am out o' time. I'm not sayin' me plan can't be altered as I go along. But I had to come up with *somethin'*."

"So ye'll proceed by turnin' a blind eye to yer passion, is that it? 'Cause that's everythin' I'm hearin' from ye."

"What ye fail to hear is that I've *lost* me passion, Tinky! Me heart's not in it anymore. I need to get on with life before 'tis too late. Hell, 'tis already too late!"

"So each mornin' ye'll rise an' don a suit, go to the office to trade in stocks or plots o' land or whatever the hell that school teaches ye? Buy low, sell high, foreclose on the poor farmer to make way fer the newly rich, is that it? That'll be yer new day-in an' day-out? Ye're out o' yer skull, John!" Tinky stomped to the center of the room and threw his arms out. "*This room is yer passion!* Everythin' in it! Ye're surrounded by it!" He ran to the counter and slapped its surface. "This!" His fists rapped on the glass of the rare books cabinet. "An' this!" He picked up his stack of waiting paperbacks. "An' these! It all stands plain as toast before the very eyes that've gone blind to it!" The books shook in his grasp. "These are yer loves, yer children! 'Tis inherited, it is, ingrained, 'tis in yer blood! Tell me, have ye ever had a single bad day here in the shop? Never mind business an' money an' holes in the roof, I'm askin' about this room right here. Have ye ever felt a truly horrific day here, with the books in yer care?"

John was silent.

"I'd bet against it!" He again shook the books in his hands. "This is what ye love, John, an' ye can't give it all up simply because time has been cruel to the location! So the place is fallin' apart an' the traffic is dwindlin'? Then move! Ye're not an effective businessman? Educate yerself! Bored with the routine? Make it fresh again! Find the fun once more! But never lose sight o' what ye're truly passionate about!"

"I've no idea why ye continue to argue when 'tis too late fer that. I'll not be swayed an' I shan't turn back. From here on—"

"Too late?" Tinky countered. "Fer Chrissakes, why—"

"*Me mind is made up!*" For the first time in its history, the walls of the Chivalric Nobleman echoed the sound of its owner's words shouted in fury. "I'll not be goin' backward no more!"

"Do ye honestly believe—"

"'Tis over! Done! Consider it signed an' notarized, so ye can keep yer thoughts to yerself beginnin' *right now*! I've had enough o' bein' preached at by the high an' mighty!"

"I'd not be doin' it if ye didn't need it!"

John motioned to the door. "I wonder if ye'd make yer exit an' leave me head to ache in peace."

"I will not, not until we have this settled—"

"Ah, fer Chrissakes, Tinky, ye've no right — absolutely no right — to tell me what to do! Will ye not pat me on the back an' tell ye're proud, try to be encouragin' rather than lashin' out like ye was me worst enemy? Will ye not do that fer me?"

"*Worst enemy?*" Rage scorched the flesh of Tinky's cheeks. "To hell with ye, John Doyle! Right straight to hell with ye! If ye tink I've not earned the right to care, earned it through all the years o'—"

"*GET! OUT!*" The words were piercing.

Tinky stepped toward the door, but didn't get far. He turned back, shouting and shaking his finger. "Ye need to rely on friends to tell when ye're doin' right an' when ye're makin' an ass o' yerself, an' I'm here to say there's not a single positive outlook to this whole situation! Ye're not bein' honest to who ye are, John! This goes against—"

John rushed him, catching Tinky mid-rant and shoving him toward the door, sending him flying against the doorframe with force enough to jingle the overhead bell and crack a pane. The shock of the violence echoed through both men and John instantly felt remorse. He hadn't meant to push so hard.

Tinky kicked out, trying to keep his assailant at bay. "Touch me again an' I'll kill ye! Keep away from me!"

With a heavy conscience and good intentions, John reached out to Tinky, but his hands were slapped away. Tinky threw the door open and the cold and commotion of the storm filled the room. The little man's body was only halfway out the door, yet his clothes were sopping wet in seconds. "To hell with evolution! Ye want to betray yerself, be me guest!" He ran into the laneway but turned and shouted over the thunderous rain, "Fer the way ye've treated me, 'tis a wonder I stuck around so long!" He staggered away through a river of water and was almost instantly made invisible by the blur of crashing rain.

At the door, John stood ruffled and disturbed in the suddenness of the aftermath, rain blowing in and saturating his shirt. The cold shocked him to action and he slammed and bolted the door against the weather. Pacing the floor, going through it all in his intoxicated mind, he tried to make sense of the deterioration of an evening that at one point had been so enjoyable. As he stepped over the floorboards guarding *Don Quixote*, the Chivalric Nobleman gave an innocent squeak.

"*Oh, shut up!*" John snapped, stomping his heel hard enough against the floor to make the loose boards bounce.

After walking about in anxious circles, he collapsed on his stool, dizzy, the room zooming around him like racers at the speedway. He felt he needed a drink despite his drunkenness. Rumbling in his belly reminded him that he hadn't consumed anything but a half bottle since — when? Since lunch, surely.

Remembering the gift from Bewley's, he found the bag of pastries and an uneaten chicken and brie toastie lying under the counter. As he stumbled his way to the back room, his mind ran through the argument and made every assumption of how it could've progressed other than the way it had. He plugged in the hotplate to warm the toastie and voraciously gnawed on a black currant tea cake as his emotions stretched in all directions. It was unfair to say that Tinky had no right to speak to him as he had, yet John remained unswayed. He was doing what was right under the circumstances and felt no remorse for that. In fact, he looked forward to trying something new.

A well-read paperback of *Don Quixote* lay by his bed; he was reading it again for perhaps the tenth or twelfth time. The bed lay unmade still and accepted his body like a welcoming lover, embracing him in flannel and warming his chill in seconds. Picking up his place in *Quixote*, he read but retained nothing, his mind still churning over the argument while attempting to prevent the room from twirling too rapidly. Three paragraphs into the new chapter, John's anger and frustration got the best of him and he threw the book across the room, sending it to ricochet against the wall and onto the small desk by the door. His head hit the pillow like a flying fist and, with a final wave of despondence, he passed out.

On the desk, *Don Quixote* lay ruffled and torn where it had landed next to John's to-read pile and the pastry bag. The hotplate that had broken its fall was still warming and the splayed pages resting against its surface began to flutter and curl in its heat. Outside, a monstrous crack of thunder rolled over the great city and disturbed its very constitution.

CHAPTER FOURTEEN
The Dawning of the Day

If clairvoyants, mystics, and dreamers are to be trusted, then there exists within us an additional sense beyond that of the five already identified by science, a sense that proves an intuitive connection between humans. It suggests to us every once in a great while that something profound either is happening or will happen to someone we hold dear. This occurred to Katy Donal, who insisted her friend not take her usual morning train into town, the same train that would derail just hours later. It happened to Peter Devlin, whose wife told him they were going to have a child when he already knew it to be true in his heart. It happened to Tinky O'Shea when he described to his sister a vivid dream he'd had about her, only to hear she'd had the same dream that very night.

Mac knew.

He knew and he ran. He ran with a hell burning in him. As far back as any of his friends could recall, they'd known Mac to run. Whether he was sprinting in search of a someone or racing to a particular destination or being pursued by Garda, he'd logged more miles through the city on foot than anyone. And tonight, despite the treacherousness of the slick pavement, despite the weight of his wet clothes, despite the flurry of rain and wind and cold that tried to hinder him, he ran more resolutely than ever.

He knew.

His sense had picked up on the location of the rising smoke. It was close, much too close. He was familiar with the city, every cleft and fold of it, every side street and narrow laneway, more familiar than cops or cabbies, and he knew. Intuition and supposition be damned, he *knew*. As he ran down Grafton Street, past the locked storefronts and flooded gutters, through the darkness and emptiness and loneliness of what had been bustling and alive just hours before, he saw the smoke coming nearer, the sight and smell and sense of it and now the sound, the crackle of flame cutting through the pounding rain to tickle his ears, a sound barely whispered yet growing ever closer as his feet soared over the flooded cobblestones and carried him to it.

He knew.

In the distance he heard a clamor of bells and wails and, under it all, deep within the canals of his ear, his mum's voice, a sound he hadn't heard or been able to remember in many years. Yet it was there, soft, present, unmistakeable. The words were gibberish, nonsensical, yet he could tell by the pitch and cadence they were encouraging words, soothing him amidst his apprehension and fear and sense — no, his knowledge — that something was hideously, frighteningly wrong.

The corner was nearing, he recognized, not because he could see it through the shroud of rainfall but because his memory of this land told him so. He'd rounded the corner and been down the lane many times and he began to slow his pace in order to take the bend without sailing past or crashing to the ground. The mouth of the laneway appeared through the sheet of water deforming his vision and he arced his path wide and veered into the street. Momentum carried him and never once did his step tremble or fall from the deluge. This is the gift, the seemingly supernatural power of the truly determined.

Suddenly it was before him, darker than the scene in his imagination, and he slowed to a stop. He expected to find this familiar place, surrounded by the black of a tumultuous night, lit up as if a Hollywood premiere were taking place right here in this cramped alley with fluid, burning spots of ten-thousand-watt Klieg lights flurrying over the walls. What he found in its stead was the indifference of a moonless night, with only the faint glow from a single bulb in a streetlamp across the street to illuminate the darkly horrific scene.

Dense, black smoke poured in rolling tufts from the open door of the Chivalric Nobleman de La Mancha Bookshop, rising against the onslaught of rain to join the storm clouds above. Smoke breathed from every open port, from the cracked window on the third floor and the ventilation shaft on the roof. Mac registered a delicate glow from inside, flickering like a picture show but giving barely enough light to see by. He felt waves of heat cycle past, heat that attacked his lungs and diluted the breathable air.

What alarmed him most was the shape that lay before the smoking structure, rocking against the opposite wall like a boulder spit from a volcano. It vibrated from peak to base with the recurrent wave of a triple-time cadence, as yolk will when split over a hot skillet. Only when the form rose from its crouched position did Mac know it was his friend, John Doyle, seemingly safe from peril and flame. Although John stood in silhouette, Mac was able to read the despair rippling from him like waves of mirage in heat.

Mac crept along the northern wall of the alley toward John, hugging the brickwork to keep as far from the heat as possible. When he was near enough to touch, he halted and stood by his friend, watching the smoke and finally seeing the flames kick their jig deep within the shop. The first thought to fill his mind was the same that simultaneously flooded his friend's mind, a simple and obvious warning that had lingered in John's psyche since he'd taken over as proprietor of the

Chivalric Nobleman so many years ago, repeating torturously over and again:

paper burns paper burns paper burns paper burns paper burns

And indeed it did, before Mac's own dampening eyes. The glow became increasingly bright, smoke flowing darker and thicker until it became nearly impossible to see past. Surges of orange and yellow filtered through in intermittent strobes and he could see the intensity of flames decorating the shelves on the far wall, crawling over book after book after book after book, starving, consuming every word that lined its path and fed it, allowing the beast to continue moving forward, side over side, rolling into itself and then expanding further, nourishing, growing always, bloating and coursing and taking the life from everything it touched. The volumes, the ideas, words, thoughts, languages, emotions, lyrics, history, humor, the very compassion and humanity that existed within each book all combined with oxygen — the giver of life turned deadly — to feed the fire and fuel its cancerous spread.

John leaned against the wall to keep from toppling over as he watched the living nightmare radiate before him. Mac saw his helpless expression, shock and terror and bewilderment contorting his normally gentle features, saw in his stance the paralysis preventing him from fleeing. John seemed not to register Mac's presence, though they stood within inches of each other, so entranced was he by the surrounding horror.

Only when John turned his eyes from the slaughter did he seem to acknowledge Mac's presence, and then only dreamily. Although his hand reached out to clasp Mac's arm, he continued looking about, making note of his surroundings despite his inability to firmly comprehend. Finding it was just the three of them huddled together, himself, his friend, and his shop, he turned to face Mac again and it was then that Mac lay witness to the emotion screaming deep from within John's eyes, past the double reflection of bucking flames ingesting home and heart and memory. Through these mirrored flames Mac saw fear and helplessness and the heart-wrenching hue of remorse.

Yet the flavor of John's eyes began to change, began to morph into something softer, perhaps wiser. Behind the regret and the guilt, a genesis of mind was awakening, developing visibly, a realization of self, of situation, a spark of sensibility that caught the flame in his eyes and ignited. The fire heaved and matured quickly, steadily, and Mac stood in awe, the sole witness to its evolution. Shining from within its center was the light of truth, of purpose, a beam of clarity slicing through the darkness, blinding the shame and contrition that had stood so unwaveringly just moments before. The flames seethed from John's eyes, gaining mass and momentum, a fireball of realization swelling until it engulfed the sheen of regret and melted away the numbing shock so desperately protecting him.

In an instant, the warmth, wisdom, and honesty that had always burned so brilliantly from John's eyes had returned. Mac recognized his friend once more and John comprehended Mac's presence, signaling his familiarity by kneading Mac's upper arm softly where he clenched it. His fingers gripped and loosened, gripped and loosened, enchanting Mac with their affection and kinship, and Mac, in turn, took John's forearm in hand and stroked it tenderly with his thumb as his mum had done to him when he was a child, assuring him that all was well, that he was safe, that everything would be alright.

From that moment and throughout Mac's remaining years, one particular detail of this exchange would haunt his dreams consistently, namely, the barely perceptible motion of John's head, a small yet significant nod that Mac understood to signify a choice made. Although the gesture was quiet, it deafened Mac and turned his blood cold.

John gave Mac's arm a final, firm squeeze and returned his attention to the home disintegrating before him. His breath came faster and heavier and his eyes sparked with the comprehension of duty. The shop let out a shrill creak, the entire structure shifting and groaning under the onslaught, and its scream carried through the air and chilled the very foundation of its city. John reacted to the noise as though he'd been violently struck.

He exhaled a small whimper.

He breathed a heavy sigh.

He ran into the burning Nobleman and disappeared behind a wall of smoke.

Mac stared, heaving, shocked to disbelief. The decisiveness of so bold an act left him reeling and he had to look at the empty space beside him to confirm it had really happened. He expected his instinct to bellow instructions at him, explain what to do and where to go and how to rescue his friend, but there was no guiding voice, no sense of future or fate to assure his safety. He began pacing like an anxious dog, wondering what to do, what to do, *my god and jesus christ oh christ what should I do*? There was no sign of John behind the smoke that was growing more dense by the moment. The shimmer of flame peeked through and proved itself to be expanding and evolving; it now lashed over the bookshelves visible through the second floor windows and crawled its way up. The heat grew more intense and standing so close to it was becoming unbearable. The rain continued and did nothing to curb the temperature nor suppress the fire.

Frantic, Mac looked up and down the lane for help. The clang of bells and screams of sirens he'd heard ages or minutes or moments ago were closer, yet he saw neither cars nor trucks nor lights flashing. What he did see was a cluster of people standing at the edge of the lane, beyond the danger, observing, their clothes heavy with water. Mac registered a familiarity with several but was too preoccupied to identify them. He paced another step and another while the urgency of the situation prevented him from thinking clearly. John had not emerged from the shop. How long had he been inside? Seconds? Minutes? Hours? There was no way to tell from the screaming in his head.

A constant wall of heat assaulted every bit of exposed flesh and Mac ceased pacing to raise his arm and shield his head. Several of the shop windows began to shatter due to the ascending temperature and flames leapt out to pursue the escaping smoke. Mac's heart sank into the pit of his belly. He was helpless to save his friend from the talons of such a beast. He possessed no answers. All he could think of was what John might have done had the roles been reversed.

And with that simple thought, his course was made clear, suddenly and unexpectedly. The answer floated before him, as definable as his own life. He knew what John would do.

Hesitation no longer held him in trance. He knew. It was as easy as taking a breath. He opened his mouth wide and filled his lungs and belly with air. When he thought they were full, he inhaled another gulp. He held it all in and thought he would burst.

He draped his rain-soaked coat over his head, then crouched low and drew his limbs tightly into his torso, making himself as small as possible. Bowing his head, he barreled headfirst past the flaming doorframe and into the shop.

Inside, visibility did not exist. His eyes were met by burning, stinging smoke that made him cry, but heat licked the tears away before they could fall. He decided to keep his eyes clamped shut since they were of no use to him here.

Mac utilized his hearing in lieu of sight. The cruel cackle of flame surrounded him, as did the muted rush of —

what? — oxygen burning? Smoke barreling past? He couldn't know. He kept his nose pointed south at all times and traveled only in a straight line so as not to lose his sense of direction. If he became lost here, he'd be finished. Something heavy — shelves or a wall or a piece of the ceiling — crashed nearby and he backed up along his line to escape it. Still he did not dare a breath.

Bent low to where the air was less smoky, he reached out, feeling for anything organic, anything human, kicking his feet in all directions with the same purpose. He felt nothing but scorching debris and hard, spiritless wood. His cracked voice cried out, careful not to expel all of his preciously stored oxygen, enunciating a single name long and clear, the name of John Doyle, but his ears received no answer.

To find John, he searched within himself once more. Where would John go? What purpose had overcome his sensibility to force him back inside? Was he in the rear bedroom, lashing at flames with bedsheets in attempt to save his home? Was he searching for shelves as yet untouched by flame to rescue books? Was he here for a particular—

Struggling to remember the way, Mac kept his nose south and took three steps forward and two steps right. Running his hands along the floor at his feet, he continued stepping right, one, two, three more baby steps until he nearly stumbled and fell over a flaccid object. Mac opened his eyes for an instant but could still see nothing. His hands skittered over the softness and knew at once that it was human. It was even damp still, despite the heat.

In a flash, he found John's midriff and lifted, his spirit dampened to find it a dead, inanimate weight. His arm cinched around John's belly and pulled tightly, expelling the air from John's lungs as his other hand found John's head and squeezed his cheeks. Mac put his mouth over John's and gave him almost all of what was left in his lungs, then clamped the mouth closed again. With adrenal strength, he swung John's body over his back and took three baby steps to his left, then two big steps past, placing him near his axis of entry, then started walking his line to the door.

Just two steps in something tripped him, a large and sharp obstacle that hadn't blocked the path before, and sent Mac crumbling to the ground and John rolling clumsily away. The heat accosting Mac multiplied tenfold and a wave of pin-pricks assaulted the flesh on his back and he knew his coat was on fire. Scrambling to his feet, he threw the coat as far as he could, then just as steadfastly continued his mission. The fall, however, had discombobulated his sense of direction and he no longer stood facing south on his line of axis. Worse, he'd blown out what little oxygen was left in his lungs and had inadvertently drawn a breath of hot poison, sending him into a spasm of coughs and sputters. Instinct took over and, while his lungs lay seizing within his chest, Mac's desperately foraging hands found John on the floor nearby and took a limb — he wasn't sure if it was an arm or a leg — and pulled in a direction he guessed lay the door.

The gamble was informed only by sounds flooding his ears. By now the wail of sirens was piercing. He followed their direction. Pounding rain plunged from the heavens outside and he followed the direction of its roar. Something fell nearby, within just a few feet, and he recognized the familiar jangle of the bell over the door as it melted from its mount and clattered to the floor.

Caution had no place here anymore; the men were desperate for air, with John in the critical phase. Mac lunged toward the sounds, pulling John closely behind, and in just a few steps his left side from shoulder to knee collided with something tall and firm, sending a wave of sharp pain through him, and he heard the clash and rattle of loose windowpanes in the door. Still he continued toward the noise and now it was all much louder, as though cotton had been removed from his ears. Keeping his eyes closed still, he exhaled the smoke convulsing his lungs and dared a small breath. The air was hot and humid and clean. A fit of coughing overwhelmed him.

He tried another, deeper breath in the brief interval between chokes and knew he was outside. The weight of rain fell on his back once more and oxygen, although tainted with traces of smoke and ash, filled his lungs and was delicious. A charred flavor stained his tongue and he spit what saliva was left in his mouth.

Other hands grabbed him and he felt a dry, comforting weight over his shoulders. A strong and unfamiliar arm coiled around his torso and led him forcefully away from the shop. Abruptly, a vast sensation of loneliness struck him and folded his stomach over and he clenched his hands tightly and felt nothing in their grip. He must have let go of John at some point and a wave of anxiety flowed through him, as though he'd lost his talisman. His eyes fluttered open and stung instantly, but tears rinsed them away. He fought against the person clutching him and was suddenly free and he ran back toward the heat and saw John Doyle being carried by a pair of men wearing the slick black coats of the fire brigade, the familiar oversized helmets bobbing heavily on their heads. They jogged toward him with John in their arms and Mac could see that his eyes were still closed, head rolled to one side, his flesh and clothing darkened with soot, and clutched tightly against his chest with both arms was the ancient book that John had shown him once under the floor, the Spanish book with the funny name, *Don Quixote de La Mancha*.

Mac trotted with them, leading the way to safety around the corner at Grafton Street, past three trucks idling loudly with lights flashing, past a cluster of firefighters swiftly unspooling their hoses, past the gawking crowd gathering to watch the burn regardless of the storm. When they'd achieved a safe distance from the blaze, the firefighters lay John tenderly on the footpath, away from the rush of water flowing over the street toward the drainage grates. Mac scooped the book from John's arms and was relieved to see his friend's chest rise slightly, almost imperceptibly. Continuing his duty, Mac hunched his torso over the book to prevent the rain from scarring it further and scanned the area for a sheath, something to protect the book with, then realized that the heavy, comforting warmth on his shoulders was a woolen blanket from the fire brigade. He stripped it from his torso and bound the book within, wrapping it tightly until there were no more layers to be folded, preserving John's book in a thick mass of wool that weather could not easily penetrate.

Another pair of strong hands took him by the shoulders and he saw a fireman towering over him, forcing him to take a seat on the ground, and Mac lashed out and knocked the man's hands away and shouted, "Not me, man! 'Tis him that needs yer help!" He pointed to John on the ground. "That's me friend, John Doyle. Leave me be an' help him! Please!" As he said it, he was aware of more tears riding the lines around his eyes, only this time they had no smoke to clear from his vision, no duty to perform. They poured naturally and recklessly and savagely and could not be controlled.

Hovering over John as the medics took to task, Mac realized he could do no more for him and stepped back to allow the lifesavers room to save. Nowhere was his destination, although he had to remain close. His legs carried him to a wide and empty space across the street, where he dropped his weight heavily on the curb and embraced his legs to his chest. The pinpricks along his back returned, a sharper and deeper pain this time, and he shifted uncomfortably. With his arms wrapped around his knees, he finally noticed his shirtsleeves; they were torn and black and hung in tatters. He looked down at his chest and saw only a charred rag hanging loosely over his shoulders. The shirt must have burned when his coat caught fire in the shop. So, too, must have the flesh on his back.

A better vantage point could not be had, for here he could see the fire raging down the lane, illuminating the surrounding walls with a glow of strobing red light. Teams of firefighters wrestled with their bucking hoses and aimed massive jets of water at the great hands of flame leaping from windows on all four stories of the shop.   More sirens approached from the north.   Any firemen not tending the flames were gathered around John, two of them resting on their knees over him, one massaging his chest, the other blowing into his mouth.   It was a slow and tedious and nerve-jangling process to resuscitate a life.

The small crowd of observers huddled together along the perimeter of the scene.   They stood tall and not one seemed to notice the terrible storm battering them.   Mac looked and saw them, truly saw them for who they were, and the idea dawned over him that he was familiar with every face. They were people like him, the vagabonds, the ones who had no home and yet stood before the fire as though it were their own home falling to the ground.   They were Archie Farchy and Dribble O'Doole and Crier Maloney.   They were Murky McKay and Missy Glynn and Kooky Cullen.   They were Lousy the Soothsayer, they were Sweet Emily Moore.

They stood together before the fire and watched.   But they weren't watching the fierce and dramatic spectacle of the blaze.   They, all of them, were watching Mac.

A great silence hung over them.   They stood rigidly, as though at attention.   As though in awe of something great.

Mac instinctively turned back to the men concentrat-ing their efforts on John.   It had been a long time now, or so it seemed.   Still they worked.   Still the man massaged.   Still the man breathed.   Still the others watched.

The muscles in Mac's chest began to tremble.   It spread to the muscles in his arms and his neck and jaw.   It ran down his back and into his legs.   The shaking was uncontrollable.   His tears fell just as heavily as the rain.

In a moment he'd found enough control of his body to raise his head again.   He stared at the men surrounding John. They were all standing now, no one knelt with him.   Their heads were bent, every pair of eyes on the figure at their feet. One man placed a hand on the shoulder of the man beside him, a gesture of tenderness and kindness.   And remorse.   The firefighter standing by John's head took a blanket from under his arm and unfurled it. Another man at John's feet caught a corner, and together they lowered the blanket until it rested over John.

It covered all of him.

Mac's head fell into his own arms. He'd never felt anguish before.

A comforting weight again draped his shoulders. The blanket was dense and worked effectively at battling the wind and rain and cold. Sweet Emily Moore ran her fingers through Mac's hair, smoothing it, then brushed the loose water from the top of his bald dome. She sat beside him, the hem of her dress falling into the river flowing under their legs. Her arm wrapped firmly around his shoulders and she pulled him to her. Mac fell easily in. His head found the comfort of her breast and rested in its warmth.

Firefighters drew on all their strength and knowledge and experience to battle the unquenchable fire. More men in trucks arrived to watch them do it.

The storm raged just as passionately as the fire and helped to cool the area. It also helped fan the flames with gusting winds.

The crowd of Mac's friends continued to stand together at a respectful distance, giving Mac room to be alone while making certain he was not alone.

Mac sat, embraced, and hugged the woolen package protecting John's book tightly to his chest. The whole of his body was full of a sadness he'd never experienced, yet harmonizing with it from its very core was a sense of wonder, a feeling of change that was both intimidating and frightening. A mystic scent of growth electrified the air, as it does at the start of springtime when buds blossom and colors emerge and nature matures to a fresh season.

It was the scent of evolution.

For the rest of the night, Mac cried as he never had before.

Epilogue

Over the span of centuries, one trait that has helped define the Irish people has been their resilient spirit. When faced with disaster, the prevailing reaction is to accept the dire fact and move on, always forward. Progression is imperative. Subject an Irishman or woman to misfortune and you'll witness a transcendence, usually with a shrug and a smile and a pint held high in honor of any fallen kinsmen. The Irish know better than anyone that for every act of violence, there must be an opposite and equal — or greater — act of beauty.

The storm lasted three days, dousing and blowing and thrashing everything from Dublin to Galway, and when the clouds finally broke, there lay devastation for miles. In the country, structural damage was everywhere; cottages crumbled where trees had fallen through and old barns lay blown to the ground. Low stone walls marking property boundaries now snaked through fields in scattered piles. In the city, the scene was just as gruesome. Entire roofs of buildings lay scattered over city blocks. Thoroughfares flooded and refused to let traffic through. Almost a whole city block lay black and smoldering. Yet, once the tally came in, it was discovered that the storm had resulted in only one fatality, and even that was later ruled the tragic outcome of a careless accident.

On the first calm day to follow the storm, when the sun shone weakly yet unwaveringly through retreating clouds, several perceived miracles were reported within the community of down-and-outers in Dublin. Rickety shelters believed to have been flattened were found repaired or rebuilt. Hovels that had been abandoned due to flooding were discovered siphoned and dry. Makeshift containers of scavenged food were found at the feet of those needing it most: the elderly, the infirm, the children too young to know. Like the Loch Ness Monster or Sasquatch, no one ever got a good look at who was responsible for these deeds, but in several instances a figure was seen by witnesses, described by one as being "squat and hairy and loathsome in body, but moving in swift, graceful motions, appearing something like the bastard child of the Loch Ness Monster and Sasquatch." A single out-of-focus snapshot of the man was later produced, but quickly disregarded as hoax.

The calm was not to last, however. Reports circulated of yet another storm on the horizon and all of Dublin rallied to better prepare themselves this time around. Crier Maloney spread word on the streets that an emergency meeting of the vagabonds would be held within the hour at the usual meeting spot. Soon hundreds of people crowded Foster Place, brainstorming amongst themselves on how best to handle another thrashing. Once order was brought by the oratorical voice of the Crier, the brainstorming broadened and practically everyone threw suggestions into the fray. Like any democracy, not everyone agreed with the proposals of how best to deal with the coming threat and the meeting quickly spiraled into chaos, fueled by speculation and fear.

Surprisingly, it was Mac Malone who finally stepped to the center and raised his teeth to the sky and bellowed a shrill, penetrating wail that had the immediate effect of silencing every bally that hooed. All eyes turned to the source of the shriek and when they saw it came from Mac, they kept their mouths shut and ears open, for tale had spread through the grapevine detailing Mac's selfless heroism at the bookshop and a deep feeling of respect now followed wherever he traveled. With order again restored, Mac very simply and rather quietly outlined the events that needed to take place in order to assure everyone's safety. Every ear strained to hear the plan and one man who sang drunkenly in the corner was swiftly muted by a mouldy sock that somehow found its way aggressively into his mouth.

Mac's words were not opinions; they were straightforward facts of what had to happen quickly if they were to survive another storm. To everyone gathered, they made complete and drastic sense. When Mac was finished delivering the plan, he closed his mouth and stepped back into the crowd. The Crier took the floor again and began assigning duties and soon everyone had a task to perform in what would become known as the Malone Mobilization Plan, or MMP, since it's difficult to incite anyone to action without an official abbreviation of some sort.

The plan utilized the very space they were in, Foster Place, because it was contained on three of four sides by structures several stories tall and would be nearly impenetrable to wind. All that was needed was a roof to cover them all, several hundred people, and the Collection Brigade set about finding strong, lightweight materials — tarps and canvas and old clothing and such — while the Sewing Committee set about quilting the fabrics together in layers. The Erection Committee was having a hell of a time trying to figure out how to make the giant contraption stay airborne until Missy Glynn stepped forward with a diagram detailing a series of beams and columns that she claimed would help considerably. The construction of the shelter was in full bustling motion less than thirty minutes after it was first suggested. Such is the commitment of a headstrong people.

Several hours into their work, when it was apparent what they were doing, a detail of streetwalking coppers arrived to break up their preparations and ordered every man, woman, and child to desist and leave the premises at once. Ranks and files were formed on both sides and sleeves rolled and fists clenched and teeth gnashed and the threat of a great battle loomed over the courtyard. It was only when Copper Cooney sauntered leisurely down the lane and requested that his uniformed peers accompany him up the street to aid Mrs. McKenna's pussycat out of a hedge that the authoritative presence dispersed, leaving the street dwellers to carry on in peace. As the officers reached the end of the lane and rounded the corner, Copper Cooney's voice could be heard saying, "Alright, lads, if I only teach ye one thing in life, let it be this...."

Twenty-three hours passed before the next storm arrived, and when it did, it appeared to be just as dramatic as the previous. Yet by the time the first winds howled through, the street dwellers felt sufficiently prepared. Their makeshift roof hung low over Foster Place by a series of ropes and pulleys, low enough to keep it safe from the threat of winds, and wooden planks reinforced it from the ground, giving added support as well as lending a tent-like shape to keep the rainfall from pooling and breaking through. Many people suffered from exhaustion, having worked twenty-three hours straight to bring the shelter to life. When a great feast of leftovers had been collected from back doors and waste bins, it proved to be the first meal in almost a full day that most people had been offered. Perhaps strangely, the arrival of the storm was welcomed by all, for it granted them their first true rest from the labor involved in preparing for it.

Mac hadn't eaten in over a day, yet his work was so consuming and his mind so distracted that he was never aware of being hungry. He finished sewing a leak in the tarp just after the rains began and settled down in a corner to take his first rest. He was exhausted as only a delirious man can be. Only after a sack of corned beef and carrots was delivered to him did his belly truly roar and his appetite make its presence known. He sat against a wall and took a hearty bite of the corned beef and was convinced it was the most delicious food he'd ever tasted.

Across from him sat a family of four, a mum and dad and two boys, all unfamiliar to him. Between them they had a single plate of food and were divvying it up in small portions. Mac watched the father break a small potato into quarters. A stick of bacon was pulled into eight bite-sized pieces. A can filled with cold soup was passed among them and they each took a single sip.

Mac looked at his own food, then placed his hand on the fat of his belly and squeezed. He squeezed again and felt the padding, watched it fill his grip. He was a fat man. He hadn't been aware of this. He squeezed again and thought he'd never felt anything as soft as himself.

Shuffling over on hands and knees, he placed his corned beef and carrots beside the family's meal, then returned to his wall and closed his eyes to rest.

He was almost asleep when he felt a kick against his foot. Opening his eyes, he found the two boys standing over him. The taller of the two spoke first.

"Oy! Our pap wanted us to tank ye fer the grub." He jerked his thumb toward his chest. "I'm called Luke. This here, me brudder, he's Josh." He poked his thumb into his brothers belly, sending the boy into a ticklish fit of laughter.

Luke continued, "Pap says ye used to be a real tosser." He said it as though he'd just tasted something nasty.

"But now ye're alrigh'," Josh said, as earnest as only a child can be.

"Anyway, here." Luke leaned in and shoved something into Mac's shirt pocket. "'Tis a cigar. Josh found it a while back. We was gonna smoke it together the next time we got in a scrap, like a peace-pipe sort o' thing, but thought ye might like it better."

With that, they abruptly ended the conversation and ran back to sit with their parents. Mac put his hand over his pocket and felt the cigar. He caught the father's gaze and saw it shine, even in the darkening light. The father touched his hand to his heart and Mac nodded in return. He then lay his head against the cold stone wall and fell into a bottomless sleep.

That evening, as the sound of falling rain soothed the community to slumber, everyone under the great tent lay his or her head down with a similar thought. "That man, Malone," they thought, "he sure took charge to keep us dry. His was a good plan. His is a good soul. We wish him well." Although they failed to praise him to his face, they praised him in their own minds, and that is nearly just as good.

*　　　　*　　　　*　　　　*

The second passing proved ultimately to be a gentler rain with more delicate winds and quieter thunder. After a day lapsed and the clouds again cleft apart like a stage curtain to present the sun, little damage was found. In the city, only the Lemon Sweets Company reported any loss worth noting — a minor rooftop leak had tragically soiled the packaging of an entire shipment of gumdrops and left thousands to suffer without their weekly fix of candied gelatin. In the country, only Farmer Branigan reported a loss, that of his prized cow, Maggie, who was lost, presumably, to the minor flood that had washed through the barn. This report was later amended when Maggie was found alive, slightly bruised, just a few miles down the road, laying snuggled with Farmer O'Shaughnessy's prized bull. All parties involved appeared satisfied by the time Maggie was led back to her stall.

Back in Dublin, life continued despite nature's interruption. Crews worked overtime to clean the streets of debris and floodwater. Fallen trees were cut and cleared. People returned to work and children played in the muddy fields of Phoenix Park. News circulated quickly around town of a wake to be held that evening at O'Donoghue's Bar to celebrate the life of John Doyle, proprietor of the Chivalric Nobleman de La Mancha Bookshop.

Sweet Emily Moore found Mac among a small group who remained in Foster Place to disassemble the mighty shelter. She took his hand and led him away from the work and sat him down on the curb behind a line of waiting taxis. She draped her arm over his shoulders, carefully avoiding the bandages covering the burns on his back. From under her skirt she pulled a rolled bundle and handed it to him.

Mac unfurled the roll and found it was a leather satchel, thick and durable, with a buckled flap and a zipper over the pouch and a long strap that could be worn over his shoulder. The flap itself was decorated in paints depicting a scene of nature: snow-topped hills and rain clouds and lightning bolts on the left that became rolling fields of green and grazing cattle and a sunny, cloudless sky as the eye moved further right, all done with such artistry that it stirred Mac's soul.

"Ye know," she said. "Fer the book."

Mac kissed her cheek sweetly and rose to his feet. "Wait here," he said, and was gone.

In a matter of minutes he returned, satchel slung across his chest, pouch laying perfectly against his hip, bulging slightly. He sat beside Sweet Emily Moore and lifted the flap and unzipped the pouch. Inside, she could see the top of *Don Quixote*. It seemed to fit perfectly.

"'Tis a beauty unparalleled," he said. "She'll be with me the rest o' me days."

Sweet Emily Moore smiled and blushed, something she hadn't done in many years. The pair sat together in silence and watched the cars go by.

Finally, she spoke. "Ye've been quiet lately."

Mac thought about this for a long moment. He thought of something to say in response, but decided to keep quiet. There would be another time for words.

Traffic flowed before them. Pedestrians walked by at their typical hurried pace. Life continued.

*   *   *   *

By six o'clock that evening the crowd in O'Donoghue's had grown so large that it spilled into the street. It's a funny thing that we rarely know exactly how many friends we have until we're no longer around to appreciate them. John had lived the relatively quiet life of the introvert, always preferring an evening at home with a book over the social scene, yet whenever he'd been dragged to the pub by his mates, he always had a good time and, better still, consistently wound up breathing great life into the party. His wake was no different. The spirit of John Doyle hovered over the entire room as friends and acquaintances and even some who barely knew him at all gathered to celebrate his life. No matter how marginally or profoundly, John had made his mark on the lives of these people and to see so many gathered in honor of such a good man caused every heart in the place to weep for the loss the world now suffered.

The circle of musicians was as crowded as ever and the music was constant and heartfelt. Throughout the evening, there were times when every voice lifted to sing in unison, each pair of lungs in competition with the rest to project the loudest, and the man on the moon, having cursed the pesky Irish for centuries, incredulously stared into the face of yet another sleepless night.

Mac arrived late. He'd been roaming the streets for most of the day, unsuccessfully trying to lift the heavy weight from his heart. Death had consumed him for days and he couldn't shake it. Worse, he was beginning to emerge from shock and could no longer rely on it to help him get through basic tasks like breathing and eating and walking. Despite his noble actions of the past few days, he felt utterly alone and dispirited.

He hadn't squeezed into O'Donoghue's more than a few steps when Tinky O'Shea embraced him and shoved a pint into his hand. Tinky was one of the organizers of the wake and had been there for many hours already. He was sufficiently scuttered by now, his mouth set into a wide grin, his eyes bloodshot and wet and older.

"Mac!" he slurred, "Ol' Mac, me pal! We had a grand adventure, I an' you, we did indeed! All fer the sake o' John Doyle, rest his soul! Aye, we did it fer ol' John. You an' me together. Joined forces, we did! All fer our mate John. But we could have done more, boy-o! We sure could have done more. Here!" He smashed his glass into Mac's and cracked them both. "Let's toast our departed chum...to John!" He raised the bottom of his glass to the ceiling and downed what was in it. Mac had a sip of his, then handed the rest to Tinky. For Mac, it was a dangerous time to drink and he resisted the temptation to lose himself in alcohol.

It wasn't until minutes later that the words really burrowed under his skin and took residence. *Could have done more...we sure could have done more.*

A man was now speaking with Tinky, a man Mac recognized as Brian Corrigan, the fellow who owned the castle and library in the country, the man who'd chased them in the dark with an evil dog and an equally evil shotgun. Mac heard him ask Tinky about the fate of John's book, *Don Quixote*. Tinky, appearing even shorter and thinner and frailer in Brian's bulky presence, stood swaying drunkenly, then smiled up at the big man. In an instant Brian lay on the floor, bloody and beaten, the mighty brought down by an unexpected attack from the weak, who continued to stomp and clobber until a group of twelve strong fellows were able to rip Tinky away. As they carried him off, Mac saw a strange look of satisfaction on his friend's face, as sober and proud as the look Tinky carried when they'd walked home together from their grand adventure at the castle. The musicians came to the final notes of *Carrickfergus* and were greeted by whoops and cheers from the crowd. All the players took a break except two; Emma, John's friend who'd called him up to sing only a few nights prior, stood with her tin whistle in hand and played the opening notes of *Danny Boy* while her brother Jack picked up a fiddle to support her melody. Apprehension struck the crowd when they first heard the tune, for the song had fallen into the realm of cliché over the years and was often over-played and over-sung and over-sentimentalized. But it was a good song and an appropriate one at that and Emma and Jack played it without the traditional vibrato and bravado that so often romanticized it. They performed each note with a base simplicity and allowed the music to speak for itself. Tinky O'Shea was moved to join them and he raised his whistle and followed their lead, always mindful to keep the song stripped to its roots, never to embellish. Very soon the entire room was silenced by the music's grace and eventually one strong voice raised to sing a verse. More lifted to join him on the second and by the third verse, no throat was silent.

Mac made his way out and past the overflow crowd lingering by the door. The sun was set and a spring chill cooled the air, a remnant of the storm. Mac turned the collar of his new second-hand mackintosh up to warm his neck, adjusted the strap on his satchel, and headed north.

When he hit the River Liffey, he veered left and walked along the quay. Although cool, it was a storybook evening, the winds hanging low and quiet, the universe glistening prominently overhead, unimpeded and sharply-defined. The storm had brought a great clarity to the city, had, in a sense, refreshed it, as nature is wont to do. The crisp air felt good in Mac's lungs and he savored each breath.

As it was still early in the week, the night was quiet, and Mac nearly passed O'Connell Bridge without realizing where he was. The hustle and bustle of O'Connell Street had been replaced with the tranquil hum of a city at rest. The bridge was nearly void of pedestrians and Mac made an impulsive right turn and stopped in the center and looked east over the river, leaning his elbows on the balustrade and becoming transfixed by the reflection of a fully-waxed moon shining from the surface of the Liffey. He stuffed his hands under his arms to keep them warm and felt a lump in his shirt pocket, reminded of the gift bestowed by the lads Josh and Luke. He pulled the cigar out and, with it, the wooden match he'd found and thought this moment as good a time as any to enjoy it.

He had only the one match and was therefore very cautious after scratching it against the bridge stone. Flame leapt from the tip and grew fat as sulfur fed it. Mac's hand protected the match from the breeze and touched fire to tobacco, tip to tip, drawing in several puffs until the cigar was properly lit. He threw the match into the river and blew softly against the end of the corona, watching it closely. A farthing-sized disc of orange, perfectly round, glowed from the tip and Mac knew the burn would be even and steady.

It was a fine, medium-bodied cigar that tasted of cedar and spice and freshly-fallen leaves and he enjoyed it all the more for its history. It simply wouldn't have been as good a smoke had he purchased it or found it on the street himself. He raised the cylinder to the sky as he would a glass of whiskey and toasted the health and prosperity of those who'd gifted it.

Mac drew and exhaled and drew again, then craned his neck and sent the smoke billowing into the air. He watched it swirl over his head in a dense mass of brown and grey, backlit and highlighted by the street lamps lining the quay as though it were the central character in a stage play. The smoke rose over the water, twirling and traipsing in a fluid waltz, ever growing yet remaining somehow as solid as when it first escaped his lips. A subtle breeze carried the cloud over him and allowed it to dance, floating as freely as a murmuration of starlings with wings flapping in unison, turning, climbing, falling together, always together, as a ruffled bed sheet does while riding the air. Another gust escorted it further out and the smoke evolved into something new, thinning yet continuing its unpredictable rhythm, now fighting to remain whole while corrupted by this trifling wind. It rolled and folded into and out of itself. In mere moments, it dissipated and was gone.

Mac watched the dance, read it, with newfound understanding. It was elegant, balletic, and had been unleashed from his own self only to evolve into nothingness. The image of this short-lived burst of grace burned indelibly into his mind and he would think of it often in days and even years to come, remembering whenever the unanswerable questions returned and begged for resolution. He realized then that there was no answer when he asked, "why?," that everything in his life, everything he knew, was but a brief surge of beauty. In this moment Mac finally understood his melancholia. An unexpected comfort settled over him and he suddenly felt as light and as free as a starling.

A throat cleared behind him and a man's voice spoke. "If ye'll pardon me, sir, I believe we've met somewhere before."

Mac turned to find a well-dressed gentleman standing near, a wrapped umbrella in hand with a bowler hat resting slightly askew on his head. Mac had no recognition of the fellow and said as much.

"I'll not be tinkin' we've met, but I could be mistaken."

"The name is Heaney, Shea Heaney. Were ye ever at Belgrove Junior Boys school?"

Mac thought about it. "Nay, never Belgrove. I come from the other side o' town, closer to St. Joseph's."

"Ever work in radio? We get a lot o' people comin' through."

Mac's eyes looked north and south, side to side, deep in thought. "Nay, never radio. Are ye a dweller?"

"Beg pardon?"

"A dweller. A down-an'-outer. Livin' rough."

Mr. Heaney scoffed. "No, never that. Not yet, at least."

"Well, I been around," Mac said. "Perhaps even more so than the next fella."

Heaney's eyes abruptly widened to the size of chestnuts. "That voice!" he cried. "'Tis you!"

"Me? Me who?" Mac was taken aback and confused, made defensive by Heaney's accusatory tone.

Heaney stepped uncomfortably close and wagged his finger in Mac's face. "Ye're the one who left me to drown in the river!" His features were turning a shade of red that could best be described as swarthy brick.

Mac still had no recollection. What river? Heaney? He knew no such fellow. He took one step back and stood tall. "I've no memory o' the event, Mr. Heaney, however I'll offer me hand an' ask that ye take it, if only out o' friendship an' to accept the apology fer whatever it is I done that I sadly cannot recall."

Shea Heaney was taken aback. He hadn't expected such a response from the ogre who'd practically drowned him with his urine one night along this very stretch of water. He wasn't sure how to react to the hand being offered.

"Please take it an' know that I done a lot o' silly things in me past. But I'm tryin' like hell to do better."

The sincerity in Mac's tone had an affect on Heaney and he reluctantly shook Mac's outstretched paw. Mac hugged the hand to his chest, startling Heaney with his familiarity.

"I wonder if ye'd accompany me up the road a piece. There's a grand little pub called McDaid's not too far from here. I'd be honored to sit with ye over a pint an' hear yer story."

Heaney looked entirely unsure of himself, uncertain of what to do or how to respond. Mac answered for him, taking his hand and pulling him along behind.

"Come with me, then, Mr. Heaney, an' we'll sit an' get to know each other." As he pulled the man along behind him, he added, "Do ye happen to speak Spanish, Mr. Heaney?"

"As a matter of fact, I've summered often in Madrid."

"That's grand, just grand. Perhaps after we chat a while, ye could read to me from a little book I gots here in me bag...."

The swelling moon hung high over the city and splashed a light over the beauty of it all.

Made in the USA
San Bernardino, CA
14 June 2020

73330097R00212